Praise for THE1

"I'M PLEASED TO REPORT THAT THE NEW MCLUHAN HAS NOW ARRIVED, IN THE PERSON OF JASON OHLER..."

"In 1988, I had the pleasure of interviewing Hugh Innis, the son of Marshall McLuhan's mentor, Harold Innis. Said Hugh: 'We desperately need another McLuhan to give us some ideas about where the new media are going. Nobody is providing his kind of stinging, probing overview. Without a McLuhan to see the big picture, we're traveling blindly into the future.' I'm pleased to report that the new McLuhan has now arrived in the person of Jason Ohler. Read THEN WHAT? and see where we're headed."

Robert J. Sawyer
Nebula Award-winning author of CALCULATING GOD

"BRILLIANT...TRUTHFUL...DELIGHTFUL..."

"THEN WHAT? is brilliant, truthful and filled with hidden and not-too-hidden wisdom. It is delightful to read.

Beth Vishnevsky
Poet and columnist for The Greenwich Village Gazette

"JUST THE RIGHT MIXTURE OF HUMOR AND SERIOUS INSIGHT...PROFOUND, INTELLIGENT, POWERFUL..."

"If you are at all concerned about the way that new media are shaping our lives, and how to cope in an increasingly technologically dependent world of rapid social change but would also like to have some fun while doing it, you'll need to read THEN WHAT? A FUNQUIRY INTO THE NATURE OF TECHNOLOGY, HUMAN TRANSFORMATION AND MARSHALL MCLUHAN. Uniquely constructed with just the right mixture of humor and serious insight, the book presents us with profound intelligence, powerful observations and deeply held opinions about living and learning in the Information Age."

From the Foreword by Ian Jukes
Author, NETSAVVY and WINDOWS ON THE FUTURE

"I AM VERY SELECTIVE...THIS IS A BOOK I WILL READ SEVERAL TIMES..."

"THEN WHAT? is a seminal work in the field. I have read Clifford Stoll's THE CUCKOO'S EGG and Seymour Papert's THE CHILDREN'S MACHINE several times (so far); this book is in that league. Ohler artfully draws us into his world where provocative ideas, innovative concepts in education and self-assessment are delightfully painted by his engaging style. Ohler is a visionary who reduces complex issues to an understandable level through his writing skill and personal experiences. I am very selective—this is a book I will read several times."

Dr. Rob Reilly
MIT Media Lab

"INVALUABLE AND INSIGHTFUL..."

"THEN WHAT? is both a delightful romp through and serious treatise on a lot of important subjects in today's technologically dependent world. Ohler's conclusions on education are invaluable and insightful. This book ought to be read by anyone who works in the fields of technology or education."

Michael A. Burstein
Winner of the John W. Campbell Award for Best New Writer (1997)
Secretary of Science Fiction and Fantasy Writers of America (1998-2000)

"ONE OF THE FEW TECHNOLOGY CRITICS WHO HAS BOTH A SENSE OF HUMOR AND THE ABILITY TO TELL A STORY..."

"If you are concerned about the ways technologies have shaped our lives but still want to have some fun thinking about solutions, tune in to Jason Ohler—one of the few technology critics who has both a sense of humor and the ability to tell a story."

Howard Rheingold
Author, TOOLS FOR THOUGHT, VIRTUAL REALITY and VIRTUAL COMMUNITY

"THIS BOOK IS FOR EVERYONE...AN INSTANT CLASSIC..."

"An instant classic for the eclectic reader who loves science fiction, time travel, new age, serious speculation and Marshall McLuhan. Run to your computers and get a copy of Jason Ohler's, THEN WHAT? A FUNQUIRY INTO THE NATURE OF TECHNOLOGY, HUMAN TRANSFORMATION AND MARSHALL MCLUHAN. This book is for everyone. Told in a witty voice, you'll be amazed at what's in store for the world. Congratulations Mr. Ohler. You have an entertaining voice and exciting future ahead."

Diana Kirk
Author of 2000 EPPIE winner A CADUCEUS IS FOR KILLING

"JASON OHLER DOES MCLUHAN ONE BETTER IN THEN WHAT?..."

"Clothed in originality, intelligence and a fierce regard for learning in the Information Age, a cast of wacky characters takes us on a grand adventure into the future with just the right degree of wit and serious insight. Ohler has a prodigious talent for making technology understandable by anyone. THEN WHAT? is a book to ponder, to have fun with, but most of all to learn from. If you have yet to discover the unique voice of Jason Ohler, you have a special delight awaiting you."

Geri Borcz
EPPIE 2000 Award winning author of DEVIL'S KNIGHT

"REMINISCENT OF HARRY POTTER... FOR ADULTS WHO WANT TO UNDERSTAND...THE DIGITAL AGE AND HAVE A GREAT TIME DOING IT..."

"Ohler has written a book reminiscent of the world of "Harry Potter"...a book for adults who want to understand the issues of the Digital Age and have a great time doing it."

"Ohler takes us on a fun, allegorical romp beyond technology to a place where the only reasonable response to our societal obsession with microprocessor speed and wider bandwidth is *"then what?"* A more cynical author might have said, "so what," but Ohler pushes beyond the simplistic negativity of popular media to suggest that the problem with technology is really the behavior of the people who use it. Technology is just an amplifier. Ohler casts the educator as the unlikely cultural warrior committed to right action in the Information Age and creates a vision for educational technology that will inspire America."

"It's kind of a HITCHHIKERS GUIDE TO THE GALAXY meets Marshall McLuhan with some Merlin and Arthur on the side, a host of quirky characters and a good measure of astute observation on human behavior in the Information Age. It's a must-read for teachers and a great read for the rest of us. When they make the movie it will be a cartoon with big-name actors doing the voices. Can't wait."

Christopher Dray
Executive Director, Yukon Arts Centre Corporation

"MARVELOUS DIDACTIC SAGA..."

"Ohler's marvelous didactic saga of education reads in one sitting and reminds us that technology is as useful as we know how to use it."

"In the search for the virtual world equivalent of Proustian "temps perdu," Ohler's novel, THEN WHAT?, tells us of a fast-forward generation representative William Tell, who looks like Harry Potter, acts like an extremely benevolent Kevin Mitnick and learns of a new dimension like Carroll's Alice...Tell's tale deals with the struggle to leave a monotonous world of computer data and reenter the real world of learning and communication...Ohler's marvelous didactic saga...reminds us that technology is as useful as we know how to use it."

Vladislava Gordic, Ph.D. (American Literature)
Columnist for the Yugoslav daily "Danas"

"THOUGHT-PROVOKING...WITH DELIGHTFUL HUMOR...MCLUHANESQUE..."

"Food, clothing, shelter...and THEN WHAT? Jason Ohler leads you on a thought-provoking journey tempered with delightful humor that explores the who, what, when and where of McLuhanesque possibilities. Are we empowered by our technologies or enslaved by them? How do we define ourselves in a rapidly changing environment? How do we interact with the world around us, and what responsibilities do we have both as learners and as educators to our global community, to ourselves and to future generations? And, after all the mountains have been climbed, books written and read, degrees awarded and values systems analyzed...THEN WHAT?"

BJ Berquist
Associate Educator, TAPPED IN

"PERFECT BLEND OF FICTION & NON-FICTION... (PACKED WITH) UNCOMMON INSIGHTS..."

"In a perfect mix of fiction and non-fiction, we find an up-to-date, even slightly futuristic, view of modern Internet technology, as seen through the eyes of the main character, a network engineer at a large corporation. The book becomes an intelligent deprogramming manual for the modern unfulfilled and unbalanced technology-drenched lifestyle. Ohler has managed to pack uncommon insights in a remarkably present-day scenario, especially illuminating various issues of education."

Robert Pearson
Creator, ParaMind Brainstorming Software and Creative Virtue Press

---

"A GREAT BOOK...A BREATH OF FRESH AIR..."

"THEN WHAT? is a great book. It is an experience that exists somewhere between high-tech sorcery with words and a breath of fresh air from the other side of the looking glass. The timing is perfect for Jason's book and it deserves all the success that I am sure will come its way."

Margo Nanny
Interactive Learning Design

"A MUST-READ GUIDE FOR EVERYONE..."

"Somewhere between Boethius's CONSOLATION OF PHILOSOPHY, THE MATRIX and Monty Python, Ohler creates a must-read guide for everyone seeking to understand today's students and the techno-organic world that has spawned them."

Darin Sennett
Director, E-Media, Powell's Books

"WHAT AN ENTERTAINING AND EDUCATIONAL RIDE! ONCE YOU PICK THIS...BOOK UP, IT IS SIMPLY IMPOSSIBLE TO PUT DOWN."

"What an entertaining and educational ride!"

"Jason Ohler takes us through the looking glass into a world in which the present intersects with the future, technology is both exciting and terrifying, and the only thing that is important is creating an educational system that is innovative, responsive and humane. It is a world in which technological invention is seen for what it is: a manifestation of all our hopes and fears, tragedies and triumphs, myopia and vision. In this world teachers are the most important people in society as they help those overwhelmed by the speed and glitz of innovation realize what is truly important in life: understanding how to live a technological lifestyle with compassion and wisdom."

"Ohler is philosophical, explaining everything from the spiritual basis for machinery to the importance of Marshall McLuhan in terms everyone can understand. But Ohler is also practical, revealing in his last chapter a blueprint for schools of the future that could be a reality right now if we '...only had the nerve.'"

"In the land of THEN WHAT? Jason Ohler clearly understands that life and education will not be about the technology, but about relationships, partnerships and learning community. Reading this book is to look into the future through the open eyes of a true teacher. This is a thoroughly enjoyable, readable book for anyone who wants to understand life and learning in the Digital Age. Once you pick this insightful book up, it is simply impossible to put down."

Mark Standley
Co-author of GLOBAL PROJECT-BASED LEARNING WITH TECHNOLOGY and TECHNOLOGY STANDARDS: A LEADER'S MANUAL

"THIS ENTHRALLING STORY ADDS...SPIRITUAL DIMENSION TO LIFE WITH TECHNOLOGY..."

"Jason Ohler has a delightful and witty writing style. If you loved his last book, TAMING THE BEAST, then you will be captured by THEN WHAT? This enthralling story adds another mysterious, even spiritual dimension to life with technology. I recommend it highly."

Dr. Netiva Caftori, Director Inter/National Board
Computer Professionals for Social Responsibility

"ENTERTAINING AND ENLIGHTENING ON MANY FRONTS, FROM THE TECHNICAL TO THE CULTURAL TO THE PERSONAL..."

"I thoroughly enjoyed reading THEN WHAT? and found it entertaining and enlightening on many fronts, from the technical to the cultural to the personal. It was a little spooky how this book gave voice to many thoughts that I have almost had, but not had the context before to really express. A wonderful feeling of relief comes when someone names a demon that has been riding like a nagging splinter in your sweater, poking you occasionally but eluding your grasp. Jason has named a dozen such demons that our culture has been struggling to acknowledge as it tries to understand the real potential of the 'Information Age.'"

Matthew Blais
Software consultant, writer, musician, SpiritWeb contributor

"THOUGHT PROVOKING... ENTERTAINING... (A) MUST-READ ..."

"THEN WHAT? represents a thought-provoking journey into the potential realities of our technological future. Master of the metaphor, Jason Ohler is at his pedagogical best weaving his messages through the adventures of his memorable cast of zany characters. A must-read for anyone interested in shaping our future technology agenda and having some fun while engaging in the quest."

Dr. Michael Adams
Director of Distance Education, College of Education
California State University, Sacramento

"I STRONGLY RECOMMEND THIS BOOK FOR ANYONE WHO LOVES STORIES AND WANTS TO UNDERSTAND THE AGE THEY ARE LIVING IN…"

"Jason Ohler's THEN WHAT? plucks you from the light-speed changes occurring in our tech-driven society and gently places you on a boat slowly drifting down the river of culture. The sharply defined and humorous characters point out not only what we gain, but also what we lose when our technology fantasies turn all too real. By the time you finish reading THEN WHAT? your world will be a bit different. I strongly recommend this book for anyone who loves stories and wants to understand the age they are living in…"

Brett Dillingham
Director, Storybox Storytelling Theatre
Author, RAVEN DAY

"THIS ENTERTAINING BOOK WILL INTRODUCE A BROADER AUDIENCE TO (JASON'S) IMPORTANT IDEAS…"

"Dr. Jason Ohler has spent over 20 years helping educators learn how to use technology appropriately to increase learning. This entertaining book will introduce a broader audience to his important ideas. I continually use a quote from his book to motivate in-service teachers, inform parents and inspire students:

'There is no more important position in society than that of teacher, especially in this culture, especially now. The future is rushing up to meet us with unbelievable force and our survival, as well as the quality of our survival, depends on the quality of our teachers.'"

Cristine Crooks
Director, Educational Consultants Alaska,
K-12 teacher and administrator for 30 years

"(AN ELEGANT) HIGH-TECH FABLE (THAT) REVEALS...POWERFUL TRUTH..."

"Jason Ohler's high-tech fable elegantly reveals a powerful truth: Intelligence is not the same thing as wisdom, and who we were yesterday doesn't determine who we can be today...or tomorrow."

Leslie Guttman
Journalist, author of MESSAGE PENDING

"PROFOUND...PRAGMATIC...FUN. IT DESERVES A WIDE AUDIENCE."

"Ohler's goal is to use technology to make ongoing education less of an activity and more of a lifestyle that you can't escape—and don't want to because you learn how to attack real-life problems in your community...The book maps out that journey...He dramatizes the power of involving students in their own learning, personalizing the experience and treating every student as an indispensable part of teams that address projects to improve the community...The route is at once profound and pragmatic, democratic and educationally challenging, ethically ambitiou but not self-righteous. It *is* fun...It deserves a wide audience."

Robert Landauer
Senior Editor, The Oregonian

"I RECOMMEND IT TO ANYONE CONCERNED ABOUT THE FUTURE OF EDUCATION AND TECHNOLOGY..."

"I thoroughly enjoyed reading THEN WHAT? As usual, Dr. Ohler has made me think, and he's done it with a delightful sense of humor and a crafty turn of phrase. I recommend it to anyone who is concerned about the future of education and technology in our lives — which should include everyone."

Carole Novak
Manager, TECHNOS Press
Editor, TECHNOS: Quarterly for Education & Technology
Agency for Instructional Technology

"A WONDERFUL AND IMPORTANT BOOK..."

"Ohler has written a wonderful an important book that helps interpret the meaning behind the use of technology and our relationship to it. I would make THEN WHAT? required reading for people seeking meaning behind technology in our society."

Dr. Kathleen Allen
Senior Fellow, James MacGregor Burns Academy of Leadership

"GREAT...AND COMES AT THE RIGHT TIME..."

"THEN WHAT? is a great book. Ohler's insight into teachers, and how technology can ruin a perfectly good education if not used judiciously, reminds us that computers – particularly those used in the classroom – are only as good as the people using them. For years, people have considered technology the end-all of classroom instruction, when it is – at best – a means. The best teachers are those who consider students first and develop a vision to educate them. The worst are those who consider technology first, as a 'clever' replacement for solid classroom instruction.

Ohler's book comes at the right time in our development when we are realizing that the technology revolution is overrated and humbling."

"Ohler is a skilled wordsmith with an amazing ability to articulate collective conscience. His use of metaphor in Then What? proliferates his message more clearly than any stodgy tome would. I recommend this book to anyone who wants to understand the true meaning of living and learning in the Digital Age."

Karena O'Riordan
Britannica.com Education

Other Books by Jason Ohler

TAMING THE BEAST:
CHOICE AND CONTROL IN THE ELECTRONIC JUNGLE
TECHNOS PRESS, 1999

FUTURE COURSES:
A COMPENDIUM OF THOUGHT
ABOUT EDUCATION, TECHNOLOGY AND THE FUTURE
TECHNOS PRESS, 2001

Learn more at www.jasonohler.com

Candice — thanks
for being a reader!

Then What?

A FUNQUIRY

INTO THE NATURE OF
TECHNOLOGY, HUMAN TRANSFORMATION
AND MARSHALL McLUHAN

[signature]
9/2003

Published by Brinton Books (books@brintonbooks.com), (Juneau, Alaska), a subsidiary of Azadian Media, in association with XC Publishing (Laurel Oaks, California). Contact XCPublishing to obtain a copy of the book electronically: www.xcpublishing.com.

This novel is a work of fiction. Names, characters, places and events are either products of the author's imagination or adaptations from reality that are used fictitiously. Any resemblance to reality—other than the direct, intentional references to real people made in the book—are purely coincidental.

Art work by Jere Smith, Seattle, Washington.
Cover design, artistic inspiration & consultation by John Fehringer, Ferhinger Studios (www.fehringer.com)

Printed in the United States of America.

ISBN: 0-9711824-0-X
LCCN: 2001117923

Learn more about the author through www.jasonohler.com; email him at jason@jasonohler.com.

Dedication

To teaching, the oldest profession; **to teachers,** who miraculously balance curiosity, chaos and caring.

To mom and dad, the best teachers I have ever had, who taught me right from wrong, but who also taught me it was more important to forgive those who were wrong than it was to be right; who taught me "above all, don't be mean," and that kindness was the music that soothed the savage beast; who taught me to ask "Why?" as well as "Why not?" and, ultimately, "Then What?"; who taught me that every moment of life was a precious and Divine gift, potentially joyful or regrettable, a choice which I needed to make every moment of every day, both consciously and unconsciously; who taught me that the greatest blasphemy of all was to take the great gift of life for granted and fail to celebrate it to the fullest; who taught me that the greatest sadness of all was to realize all of this too late.

To brothers Rick and Michael, who taught me brotherhood in the truest sense, and with whom I shared a wonderful childhood and continue to share a special adulthood.

To my wife and family, who continually teach me that life is short but it is wide, and who breathe life, love and purpose through me every day.

Acknowledgements

Everyone I have ever met has been a teacher of mine in some way, from the noise-less strangers on the morning subway commute who spoke volumes in their silence, to the stentorian Marshall McLuhan who held forth in modern poetry class about everything including, occasionally, modern poetry. Teachers are everywhere; real students are harder to find.

There are those whose ideas have surfaced in THEN WHAT? who deserve specific mention. I would like to thank Brett Dillingham for my anthropological awakening and for my ability to see sapes all around me; Jim Dator for his concept of cross-generational dialogues in stable societies; Dick Meeker for teaching me to suspect incompetence before I suspected conspiracy, and from whom that quote is taken directly; Mike Ciri for TLAs; Don Shalvey for his concept of the Paradigm du jour; Margaret Riel, for "What's Unique, What's Universal" as an online activity; Tim Wilson for Silicon Valley + Hollywood = SillyWood; Dr. Harry Dillingham, for his insight about a gentleman needing to carry a pocket knife and a handkerchief; McLuhan for stretching my mind to the breaking point only to have me realize that it had more flex than I thought; Miss Phelps for helping me understand that teaching is largely a matter of heart; Mander, Wheatley, Tanner, Wolfe, Burke, Levinson, Winn, Postman, Comstock, Tapscott, Waterman, Rothfeder, Negroponte, Dertouzos, Turkle, Papert, Winner, Davies, Dyson, Weizenbaum, Rheingold and the many other writers I have read and should have read who have applied their mental muscles to wrestling with the issues that arise when humans amplify themselves with tools.

I would like to thank Ian Jukes for being an inspiration, wise friend and great mentor.

I would like to thank John Fehringer for teaching me the real meaning of "art the fourth R," for showing saint-like patience with my learning curve and my questions, and for being a true friend all these years.

I would like to thank Scott Christian and Michael Sfraga for making the impossible possible and for being great friends and friends of greatness.

I would like to thank Xina Marie Uhl and Cheryl Dyson (of XC Publishing), Mardell Raney and Carole Novak of TECHNOS Press for their belief in my work; Bob Landauer of the Oregonian for his wise counsel; Dr. Bill Demmert for his vision and multicultural insight; Dr. Mike Adams for his inspiration and vision; Dr. Anita Dosaj for her wisdom; Darin Sennett of Powell's Books for teaching me the way of the e-book; Kelly Kennedy for her excellent editing; Dr. Arthur Petersen for being an excellent keeper and teacher of the written language; and Len Peterson for being an excellent keeper and teacher of the technology.

A special thanks to Brett, Clay and Mark for the many lessons learned from their inspired friendship.

I would like to thank Blair and all the others at Bales Post Office in Cedar Mills, Oregon, for being such excellent couriers and friends.

I would like to thank Miss Phelps (first- and second-grade teacher), Mrs. Brown (third-grade teacher), Wayne McNaughton (high school English), Gerry Hilfiker (science and human relationships), John Hassleback (high school music), Loy Londberg (workmanship), Father Belyea (theology), Father Madden (literature), Dr. Priestley (religion), Dan Malick (management and planning), Marybeth Darrow (educational technology), Dr. Bill Richards (communications), Dr. Frank Darnell (cultural studies), Bill Willard of Fitness Plus in Juneau, Alaska (fitness, mind-body connectivity) and the other fine teachers I have had throughout my life.

I would like to thank Shakespeare, Kafka, Dostoyevsky, Camus, Joyce, Salinger, T.S. Eliot, Campbell, Beethoven, Brahms, Mozart, Bach, Bernstein, Shostakovich, Roddenberry, Asimov, Arthur C. Clarke, e.e. cummings, Vonnegut, Kesey, Gibson and many other writers, composers and artists who taught me the importance of using tension-resolution while simultaneously creating breadth and depth in the course of telling a story.

I would like to thank the communication theorists who helped to connect linear and transactional communication to the human experience; and Mother Teresa, the Dalai Lama and the works of Walt Disney for providing optimistic tools for calibrating the human condition.

I would like to thank John Pugh, Robbie Stell, Scott Christian, Jim Johnsen, Michael Sfraga, President Mark Hamilton and others at the University of Alaska who believe in putting education first; my colleagues at the Center for Teacher

Education who believe it as well; all those who have worked with me and taught for the Educational Technology program from whom I have learned so much, particularly Susan Warner, Michael Ciri and Brett Dillingham for their help facilitating my many mental upgrades; also Michael Byer, Mary Wegner, Cathy Carney, Cathy Carson, Peter Anderegg, Tom McKenna, Geoffrey Wyatt, Sue Kocyba and others whom I am sure leaky RAM prevents me from remembering; Margaret Grogan and Mary Bowen, whose support is intelligent, friendly and always a gift.

I would like to thank the kid on the playground in fourth grade—I believe his name was Francis—who loved reading me stories more than playing dodge ball.

Above all, I would like to thank my students, both those who have graced my classrooms as well as the many I know only as thoughts and ideas attached to email addresses and web sites. You have been, and continue to be, some of the greatest teachers in my life. Thank you for completing the circle.

Whatever you believe, that's who you are…

Contents

FOREWORD by Ian Jukes

PROLOGUE
Human Evolution: From Spear-it Spirit to Net Values
The only adventures worth undertaking are those requiring fear to overcome.

CHAPTER 1   Credo's Doorway   **1**
Beware of strangers who know you.

CHAPTER 2   A Real Education Begins   **5**
Beware of pain that you get used to.

CHAPTER 3   Avatars and Who We Ares   **13**
Ignorance may be no excuse, but you don't know what you don't know.

CHAPTER 4   Mr. Big and the Ledge of Objectivity   **19**
What happens when you give a bad guitar player a bigger amplifier?

CHAPTER 5   Theory Meets Reality   **23**
Seeing is believing, unless you no longer believe what you see,
*in which case what **do** you believe?*

CHAPTER 6   Kim (Maybe it's a she, maybe a him...) 31
The most elusive substance in the universe is nothing.

CHAPTER 7   It's About Time   **35**
You can always make more money, but you can't make more time.

CHAPTER 8   The Value of Mystery   **43**
There will always be a gap between our technology and our imagination.

CHAPTER 9   The World of Ed Tech   **45**
Before you suspect conspiracy, don't rule out incompetence.

CHAPTER 10   Teaching Rulz   **55**
*The science of teaching is knowing a number of instructional
methodologies, while the art of teaching is knowing when to use which.*

CHAPTER 11   A Measure of Success   **59**
*When the instrument of measurement dictates what is important, the
measurement becomes the message.*

CHAPTER 12   Untangling the World Wide Web   **65**
*The first step in getting an education is not knowing something
you want to learn.*

CHAPTER 13   The Problem with Our Gods   **73**
Whatever you believe, that's who you are.

**CHAPTER 14
Learning that the Business of Business is Learning**   **89**
Plan for change, rather than change your plan.

**CHAPTER 15
How Life Acts and Smells Like an Onion**   **109**
So many dimensions, so little time.

CHAPTER 16   Where Machines Come From   **117**
*Catch 33: The illusion of progress. For every two steps forward,
there is at least one back, eventually three.*

CHAPTER 17   Filters   **127**
*Choosing your information filter is as important as choosing
your neighborhood.*

CHAPTER 18   Agents of Change   **139**
In the past, we went to school. In the future, school will come to us.

**CHAPTER 19
There's No Such Thing As the Technology Itself**   **151**
With enough practice, we can take back the future.

CHAPTER 20   Appreciating Art   **169**
Artists are meteorologists with an attitude.

CHAPTER 21 Appreciating Art Literacy **181**
Perhaps our past is no present for the future.

CHAPTER 22 Why Technology Needs People **201**
Catch 77: You have to, just because you can.

CHAPTER 23 Communicating With Kim **211**
What is the meaning of meaning?

CHAPTER 24 Email Bonding **221**
What does the phrase "the seasons of man" mean to a woman living at the equator?

CHAPTER 25
There are two types of people:
Type A, Type B and those who can't count **227**
Anthropology 101 in a sentence: Everyone is inherently insecure; the rest are details.

CHAPTER 26 Love, Life & Statistical Probabilities **231**
What's love got to do with it? About 33% of everything, give or take a 5% margin of error.

CHAPTER 27 What's Important **239**
Talk is cheap. Inaction is expensive. Doing pays for itself.

CHAPTER 28 The Big Day **245**
Now has a way of creeping up on you.

CHAPTER 29 Rebirth **251**
How come you never see the headline, "Psychic Wins Lottery?"

EPILOGUE There's No Page Like Home Page **255**
Everything clicks.

Then What?

A Funquiry

Into the Nature of Technology, Human Transformation and Marshall McLuhan

Foreword

Ian Jukes, 2001

"If I hadn't believed it, I'd never have seen it."

Buckminster Fuller

Almost 15 years ago, in the midst of a hectic work schedule full of mounting and missed deadlines and completely out-of-the-blue, I received a phone call from a stranger. Clearly I had other far more important matters on my mind, but out of a sense of professional politeness, I impatiently listened as Jason Ohler introduced himself to me.

More than two hours later, the phone still glued to my ear, I was utterly transfixed and transformed by the powerful and insightful observations that Jason was making about the near and distant future of technology, learning and life. Jason asked a series of deep and personal questions that challenged every assumption about our world—questions that compelled me to step back from the tyranny of everyday life and reconsider the who, what, when, where, why and how of our existence. Fifteen years on, the same questions have become more important than ever because many of them remain unanswered.

If you are at all concerned about the way that new media are shaping our lives and how to cope in an increasingly technologically dependent world of rapid social change—but would also like to have some fun while doing it—you'll need to read THEN WHAT? A FUNQUIRY INTO THE NATURE OF TECHNOLOGY, HUMAN TRANSFORMATION AND MARSHALL MCLUHAN. Uniquely constructed with just the right mixture of humor and serious insight, the book presents us with profound intelligence, powerful observations and deeply held opinions about living and learning in the Information Age.

Above all, questions drive this humorous, powerful tale: Do we control our technologies or do they control us? What does it mean to be human in our frenetically changing world? What are our social and cultural responsibilities as both learners and educators in our increasingly global community? And, after all is said and done and after every mystery in our world has been solved and every challenge overcome, *THEN WHAT?*

Jason explores these questions by following the comic adventures of a technological savant, William Tell, and his new Digerati—a group of strange and unforgettable characters—who are struggling to leave the monotonous world of computer data and rediscover the world of learning and communication. In doing so, we are taken on a journey into our future where the only reasonable response to our obsession with techno-drool, techno-lust, bandwidth and processor speed is *THEN WHAT?*

As Jason moves us beyond the threshold of diminishing astonishment about the growing power of our machines, he helps us to understand that the real issues of technology are related to the mindsets and behaviors of the people who use it. He reminds us that technology is just an amplifier of the good, the bad and the ugly of this world, and that it is only as powerful as we know how to use it. To this end, he presents the educator as the change force in American society: a cultural evangelist, committed to right action in the Information Age.

This sets the stage for his last chapter in which Jason presents a magnificent blueprint for the schools of the future—schools that could exist right now if only we truly believed. In the land of "What Could Be," Jason clearly understands that the future will not be about the technology but about the relationships, partnerships and learning communities it cultivates.

Make no mistake. Masked in humor and wit is an essential book that contains simple yet powerful ideas. Jason has provided a detailed map to take us from where education is to where it needs to be. It is a compelling map that shows us how we can truly transform an aging and increasingly irrelevant institution called "schooling" into something that will have real meaning and relevance to the lives of this and future generations. Therefore the challenge is up to you: How will you use this map? What will you see and how will you respond when you gaze at the terrain that stands in front of us? More important, what concrete actions will you take as a result of reading THEN WHAT? As you journey across the terrain called school, heed the words of Helen Keller...

"... the only thing worse than not being able to see, is being able to see and having no vision." Helen Keller, 1932

Ian Jukes
Kelowna, British Columbia
May, 2001

In order to be a good teacher,
you've got to be a good student...

Fugguduh

The cultured technologist prefers the expletive "fugguduh" to the many coarser alternatives in wide use in other professions. The word is pronounced *FUHG*-uh-duh. I recommend you try saying it aloud a few times before continuing.

Prologue
Human Evolution: From Spear-it Spirit to Net Values
The only adventures worth undertaking are those requiring fear to overcome.

In the spirit of full product disclosure, and in an effort to adapt to the modern reader's busy schedule, I offer this summary of my book in a paragraph. Consequently, if you don't have $20 to buy my book or the time necessary to read it—or are simply trying to decide whether my book is worth your investment—then read this prologue as a condensed version of my thoughts about living, learning and having fun in the Digital Age. I only ask that after you are done, please place the book back nicely on the shelf without bending any pages so that others who have the time, money and inclination to invest in my book will be allowed to buy a fresh copy.

In a paragraph—a rather *long* paragraph, admittedly—the book says this...

Education in the Information Age does not require that U.S. schools neglect or discard large numbers of children, whether willingly or carelessly, who don't appear to be "making the grade" by traditional standards. We have the technology, proven teaching methods and the heart to create educational experiences that can bring all students into the present and carry them to productive futures of personal fulfillment and community advantage. To do that we must take back the future from those who feel threatened or victimized by our technological progress. All we lack is a concrete vision. The short list of essential components of this vision follows:

- using wisdom to guide our increasing intelligence
- setting schooling in the larger "real-life" context of community and industry to shape it in ways that make sense to adults and young people alike
- requiring our students to contribute to the neighborhoods that nurture them
- raising the role of "teacher" to an elevated status in which classroom leaders deservedly are respected equally for their knowledge and their practical wisdom
- preparing and compensating teachers for their role in society

- loving the mystery; knowing that not knowing all the answers provides us an opportunity to explore our imaginations, believe in magic and push ourselves to overcome our fears
- celebrating the differences between humans and machines
- seeing all of our new technologies as story-telling amplifiers that allow us to create social narrative in new, often-confusing yet enlightening ways
- engaging in the active stewardship of our technologies so that we can direct them—at least as much as they will let us...
- learning the language of art—which has become the fourth R or next literacy in the age of multimedia—so that we can communicate effectively in the global village and reflect on the machines that overwhelm us
- accepting that getting lost is part of any journey no matter how well we plan, and that planning for change is preferable to changing our plan
- believing that our attitude about learning will control our aptitude because knowledge will be so fast-changing that only those who actually enjoy learning will thrive
- accepting that the linear, "either/or" problem-solving approaches of the past no longer work in the continuum-based, "both/and" world of the Digital Age
- understanding fully that who we are in an age of highly amplified and far-reaching tools—ethically, cognitively, socially, spiritually, emotionally, interpersonally—is a matter of human survival and liberation, not simply cultural preference or predisposition
- reading McLuhan—as unreadable as his work tends to be—so that we can better understand our ancestry as global citizens
- practicing the art of having fun because it is the only way to keep the child within from becoming horribly adult-like
- viewing the world through the lens of absurdity because doing so is often the only way to visualize the sanity we seek
- accepting each other's limitations as a prerequisite to emotional networking, and practicing compassion as we do so
- believing that we are what we believe—spirit made flesh, and not the other way around
- believing that technologies are just ideas with clothes on—just mirrors that tell us who we are

- accepting that "Then What?" is an ageless question, both historically and personally
- and, most importantly, knowing that the degree of kindness and compassion we show others during our lives is all anyone will remember about any of us at our memorial service

This is the book's message. All the rest in the pages that follow consists of case-building and commentary.

If you feel you already understand all that this message implies, then feel free to pass up my book in favor of something else—perhaps a good music CD, or maybe a contribution to your local school. But if some of the points in the summary intrigue you, or if you simply would like to hear me tell the tale of living in the remarkable age in which you find yourself, then by all means read on. It is a journey that I promise you will never forget.

CHAPTER 1 Credo's Doorway

Beware of strangers who know you.

Coffee and anxiety, the lifeblood of commerce, pumped through my body and urged me forward. Yet I couldn't move.

Like every other morning, I was hurrying to work, unconsciously negotiating a path among the multitudes descending upon the financial district in early morning. As usual, the world outside my mind was an irrelevant blur as my thoughts focused on the intricate weave of computer networks I had developed to transform Banter and Associates Diversified Investors' global empire into one vast spider of a company. I was in the middle of a long, frantic slug of a supergrande, triple-shot latte with whipped cream, sprinkles and a touch of macadamia-nut flavoring, when an old man's gravelly words from nowhere pierced my concentration:

"Then what?"

That was all. Just two words surrounded by the large, hollow silence of an odd moment appearing in the middle of an otherwise ordinary day. Normally I would have dismissed it as an intriguing overture from a street scrounger and just kept moving. But the voice was familiar, reconnecting me with a past I had forgotten since I left school at 15 and entered the frenzied asylum of high technology overtime. That was the year someone from Banter and Associates Diversified Investors discovered me at a computer fair and proposed to rescue me from the tedium of school by offering to take advantage of my talents. With the reluctant endorsement of my mother, I had left school exiting through the cafeteria hollering, "See ya later, spirit crushers!" and immersed myself in the relentless challenge of the marketplace that school never provided. I became instantly addicted to the feeling of adrenaline spiking through my body as I sprinted to keep two steps ahead of the jaws of technical obsolescence constantly nipping at my heels. Every software upgrade, product enhancement and unreasonable demand made by an uncompromising manager who wanted me to make the network do something miraculous kept me blissfully overwhelmed. And I got to wear jeans, t-shirts, a pocket protector and propeller beanie just for goofs. Life just couldn't have gotten any better.

My progression through the ranks had happened quickly and mostly by accident. Within a year, a fluke of reorganization made me a member of the elite Network Control Unit in charge of BADI's entire North American division. A reporter for Business Life Magazine found out about it and wrote a feature article about me called "Teaching Yourself to Succeed." In it, he described me as "a testimonial to the death of formal education and the supremacy of the cult of personal initiative; one who enthusiastically retrains himself in a world of work ever roiling with change." By that point my propeller beanie was gone and my pocket protector had moved to my inside jacket pocket.

The following year I had been pushed into a void at Network Control created by a senior programmer's heart attack. Then someone got married and took another job, someone else had a midlife crisis and moved to Nepal in search of himself, a few others scattered to places unknown for reasons unrevealed, and there I was, the only logical choice for temporary director of BADI's entire international network while management looked for a permanent replacement. But six months later life at BADI had picked up so much momentum, and the network had continued to hum along so smoothly, that the search to fill my position was quietly suspended. Now, three years later, at 22-years-old, I had become everything I thought I wanted to become a decade ahead of schedule. My jeans and t-shirts were nowhere in sight, replaced by tight, black non-designer clothes that wrapped my tall, unnaturally thin body like an extra layer of dry skin.

"Then what?" came the voice again, like sandpaper slowly being dragged across a piece of rough wood.

Like every other morning, I had been drawing the schematic of BADI's computer network in my mind as I raced to work, girding myself psychologically to serve another day as networking god for a corporation whose survival depended upon my magic. As usual, the goal at the end of my morning power walk from the subway had been to arrive at work with a clear vision of BADI's neural pathways and international tentacles, to spot potential aneurysms and strangulation points and to anticipate the bitter struggle managers would wage for a piece of my crowded day. Normally I was flattered by their desperation to have me add a touch of wizardry to their pet projects. But today, for some uncomfortable reason, it bothered me, like an itch too far below the surface of the skin to reach. Normally I was quite happy to be rewarded with ever-faster machines so that I could kick myself up more excruciating, late-night, social-life-rending learning curves in the name of productivity. But this morning the idea seemed grotesque.

Focus, I told myself.

Normally my focus was exquisite and precise, allowing me to intertwine a number of threads of thought algorithmically, like a geometric tapestry. But two words from an invisible old man had turned my brain into a child's finger-painting of the mind, in which ideas and chatter just smeared together. Somehow those two words had pried open a storehouse of resentment that had been silently accumulating in the background of my life, like reinvested dividends in a blind trust. Suddenly so much was so simple. I wasn't happy anymore. Worse—*I was angry*.

Several times I had been unfairly denied a position in BADI's training division, despite the fact that I was qualified, inspired, deserving and frantic to take it on. I loved to teach. More to the point, I loved to help other people learn. I didn't understand why, exactly, and it would take me years to fully understand it. But at the very least teaching felt like a way to regain the fun I'd lost when I'd surrendered my adolescence prematurely to the world of work. I was a good teacher, and despite the fact that everyone knew it, the "suits" wanted to keep me down on the data farm, cranking out network tentacles for clients to attach themselves to. It was my fault for being so good at my work, I guessed. But I had turned some corner in my mind. Doing a gazillion-dollar deal in a single Trans-Atlantic bit burst had lost its luster, while watching people bask in the glow of learning had become sensually gratifying. The real highs of the day were witnessing support staff in the hell of software minutiae screech the "ah hah" of self-discovery, throw their heads back with a conquering smile, and relish their newfound understanding of a computer idiosyncrasy which had theretofore made them positively cranky and temporarily insane.

"Then what?" the voice asked me again.

I loved spending time with support staff; they actually enjoyed learning. The "suits," on the other hand, just blustered away on their keyboards until they got stuck and then hollered for me to come fix something (that had only appeared to be broken because they'd never read the help sheets, *which* I had spent my weekends creating, *which* I had prepared just for them to make their lives easier and more productive, *which* I had delivered on their desks with a smile and the promise of help if they would just familiarize themselves with the list of simple commands, and *which, which, which, fugguduh, fugguduh, fugguduh! RTFM,* I wanted to yell at them—*Read The Frigging Manual!*—a catchall condemnation of those wannabe computer power users who were too busy, lazy or tantrum-dependent to help themselves).

I was suit-bashing again, a habit I had developed when my request for transfer to the training division had been denied. While it felt like much-needed therapy, I had to focus on the day's upcoming events or else risk arriving at work dangerously unprepared. While I tried to concentrate for the nth time on my mental model of BADI's Euro-Asian network in preparation for a leveraged buyout that was rumored to be happening any day now, I couldn't keep from musing that I was a lot like a god in the worst sense—there to blame when the going got tough, easily forgotten when life was good, but always expected to work miracles. As I struggled to draw the details of the satellite connections between London and Hamburg and Singapore in my mind, it occurred to me that no one had ever stopped into network headquarters on a good day just to tell me everything was working just fine. Life just didn't seem to work that way.

A wave of desperation suddenly swept through me. The prospect of another day at BADI was closing in on me like an endless prison sentence. Today would be the day I would tell management to either give me the training position or I was out of there. Period.

"Then what?" the old man coaxed insistently.

Enough was enough. The network schematic in my mind's eye dissolved. The incessant grind of brain chatter ceased. I began to fidget as I squinted, trying to discern my interrupter's face in the pitch-black cavelike indentation in the side of the building.

"Then what?" came the words, gently, insistently. "Or, if you prefer, *What then?*"

"Say what?" I cried, clutching my latte in a death grip.

"No," the voice calmly corrected me. "The question under consideration is '*Then what?*' Ready?"

CHAPTER 2 A Real Education Begins
Beware of pain that you get used to.

"What the freak are you talking about?" I cried. "Ready for what?"

The anger came too easily, lurking just beneath the surface and waiting to attach itself to something. I glanced at my gold watch with the shiny metal flexible wristband that pinched my skin. I had intended to replace it with one more comfortable made of leather, but had just grown used to the pain instead. The square green numbers said 6:31. Wall Street, the distant mother ship, didn't open for a while, but Banter and Associates Diversified Investors needed me well before then to take the upgraded network out for a test spin to make sure we were prepared to execute the leveraged buyout with accuracy and style.

On the docket today was a typical schedule of global buying and selling. BADI was in the brains-per-minute business. Move information, not stuff. Easier. More leverage. More turnover. More opportunity to dip the middleman's ladle into the stream of commerce. It was my job to connect the dots in the great pointillistic business plan with satellite connections, telephone lines and wireless pathways that could pass through solid objects, making BADI's scheme to bring mouse balls to the masses a reality.

Mouse balls. I began to focus on mouse balls and the trip they were going to take around the world.

BADI was going to buy mouse balls from Indonesia and sell them to a mouse manufacturer in Singapore, who would then assemble the mice and sell them back to BADI, who would then sell the assembled mice to a Taiwanese computer maker, who would package the mice with fully assembled desktop computer units, which they would sell in lots of 1,000 to BADI, who would then market them to European retailers. BADI didn't actually buy the mouse balls; they invested in the company that bought them. Actually, they had invested so much in the company that they practically owned it. Owned it, but did not run it. They didn't want to run it. Too much heavy lifting. Too much real work.

Normally I felt as if I lived on an invisible high-speed conveyor belt with no off-button. Yet today I was stalled, talking to someone I couldn't see. I was disoriented, flustered and about to leave when a shaft of sunlight bounced off something in the darkened doorway and hit me in the eye. As I reared back, an old man stepped forward, a gold-capped tooth sparkling as he grinned warmly, his warm brown eyes inviting me to come closer. He was medium height, medium size, medium build—just plain medium, as though he were daring me to scrutinize him.

I had become so adept at avoiding the legions of street scroungers who swarmed the financial district in search of spare change that in seven years of walking to work I had never looked one in the eye. But there I was, transfixed by the visage of a beggarly old man smiling at me. Furrows carved by the wind and the rain of countless seasons on the street crisscrossed his unshaven face, creating a map that went everywhere at once. His body slouched, wrapped in a dark coat with a high collar and rips above both pockets exposing white lining that dangled like dead skin. His shoes didn't match. One was a brand new red sneaker, the other an expensive penny loafer that looked as if it had been sitting in a snow bank all winter.

"You can't learn anything when you're afraid," the old man said to me. Those words would underpin everything else he would tell me in the days ahead. "That's rule number one about real education. When you're afraid, all you can do is react. It's a great way to find out who you really are beneath the fancy clothes. But it's no way to learn."

"My clothes aren't fancy and I'm not afraid," I muttered, lying on both counts. My tight shirt and pants suddenly seemed to merge with my skin, leaving me feeling naked. I did a little dance to try to cover myself which must have looked completely idiotic. I tried to relax.

"Then I guess you're just a little nervous. I'm part dog, see, and, well, dogs smell fear. It's our job."

I retreated, pulling up my sleeve to check my watch.

"It's 6:33 AM," the old man said. "A wise man always knows what time it is…or doesn't care. It's the same thing, when you think about it."

"How profound," I threw at him. It was, in fact, exactly 6:33.

"And don't bother feeling sorry for me," the old man continued. "I'm doing very well compared to the people who picked the coffee beans that went into your designer cup of coffee this morning. Forgive me; I'm a sentimentalist. I grew up when coffee came in one flavor. You kids drink it with all that garbage in it. It throws me every time I see a cup of coffee with suds. Your coffee looks like it needs a haircut."

"Foam," I told him impatiently. "It's foam, not suds. It's a European thing. Now look, sir, whatever, whoever—"

I was unable to finish my thought, borrowing an unnatural feeling of disdain from my other self, the one who would soon be assaulted by suits hell-bent on world domination. I guzzled the last bit of my latte, announced "download" as I pitched the empty Styrofoam coffee cup into a nearby trash can and reached into to my suit coat to pull out my wallet.

"And put your wallet away," the old man said. "Thanks for thinking of me, but it was just your guilt chakra talking. That doesn't count."

"There's no need to be proud," I told him. "I've had hard times too."

"Really? Name one," the old man demanded.

I stared at my wallet as the moment elongated uncomfortably, waiting for the old man to rescue me.

"Have you ever gone without eating for a day?" he asked.

I set my briefcase on the sidewalk and extracted a few dollars from my wallet. "No, and you shouldn't either. Here, you need this more than I do."

"How would you know what I need?" he asked, shaking his head in disgust as he watched me flap a few dollar bills in front of his face. "You *are* America, you know that? You assume everyone wants to be just like you. You can't believe anyone would want less than what you think you have. Well, you have to go, William. Work calls."

"Do I know you?" I exclaimed.

"I read your name tag."

"What are you talking about?" I asked, patting myself all over, searching for a nametag from a forgotten conference hiding in the folds of my jacket.

I was so inept at managing the details of personal appearance that each morning I submitted to inspection by a receptionist who looked for signs of shaving cream, breakfast or excessive hair gel. Ever since I'd pitched the new BADI network strategy to the upper suits with a sticky note stuck to my back saying, "Fix the frigging printer!" I hadn't trusted myself completely in public. I never did find out who did that to me, but I suspected it was someone from Floor 3, suit heaven, where the real players at BADI moved and shook the world.

I will never forget that printer. Stupid thing. It kept jamming and I kept telling management to throw it out and get a new one. But despite the fact that they had enough money to buy a gazillion new printers, they chose instead to humiliate me into repairing it by hinting that perhaps I wasn't the hotshot tech god I thought I was. Sadly, their strategy worked; I spent many unpaid hours pouring over obtuse, inhumane documentation until I found the clue that rescued an aging printer from certain obsolescence. Even though the suits were frantic to have their toys in working order at all times, they loved it when I was wrong. It made them feel good about themselves to know that I wasn't as smart as they hoped I was. My public embarrassment was their way of reasserting themselves—power over knowledge, the talkies triumphing over the techies. The problem with the printer had been an outdated printer driver—just a stupid little piece of software that allowed the computer to talk to the printer that I hadn't thought to check. Stupid printer driver. Stupid printer. Stupid suits.

As I tried to concentrate on speaking to the old man, I instinctively checked my zipper, stuck a finger in each ear and wiped my face with my hands. All clear.

"So how do you know me?" I asked. "Did I see you at a conference or something?"

The old man started to laugh, and I could feel my cheeks glow with embarrassment as I realized how absurd the notion was.

"Sure, William," the old man said. "I was at the booth next to yours at that computer convention in Vegas last year selling virtual brownies. Didn't you see me? Look, your homework for tonight is to answer this question: What comes after food, clothing and shelter?"

"Homework?!" I gasped. The word instantly brought back years of bad memories.

"That's right," he replied.

"HOMEWORK!?"

"Correctamundo," he said a bit indignantly. "If you like, you can all it 'an extended-learning problem-solving opportunity'—an ELPSO. Or, if you prefer, an ECTBWOWAH: an exercise in critical thinking bridging the worlds of work and home.' Choose your euphemism acronym. Makes no never mind to me what you call it. It's all just work that's got to be done. By the way, a word of advice:

You can learn a lot about people by studying the euphemisms they use. Euphemisms are like drugs. They enable the overwhelmed to rationalize what they are doing with their lives or, more to the point, what they're *not* doing with their lives."

"Whatever. I don't do the school thing," I insisted proudly as I crammed the dollar bills the old man had refused back into my wallet. "I made my own way a long time ago. I got an education from life. I left school when I was 15 and never looked back. Business Life Magazine actually published an article about me called 'Teaching Yourself to Succeed.'"

"Glory be, not a whole magazine article!" he chided. "There were only a million of those published yesterday. And who said anything about school? We're talking about learning. Don't confuse the two. Do you know who said, *'School interferes with your education?'*"

"No," I replied, feeling a bit lost.

"Marshall McLuhan. Do you know who he was?"

My cheeks started to glow again. McLuhan was one of those people I knew I should know about, even if only a few sentences deep, but I didn't—a deficit made all the more poignant by the fact that a street scrounger was apparently going to tell me all about him. "Sort of," I sputtered. "I mean, I've heard the name, certainly."

"Certainly," he said, not trying to hide his disappointment. "Of course you've heard the name. We've all heard the name. That's what McLuhan called *being well-known for being well-known.* William, William! It's a good thing you came to me. We've got a lot of ground to cover before the big day."

"What do you mean, 'came to you?' What big day?"

The old man ignored me, a standard operating procedure I never did get used to.

"McLuhan was your great-grandfather, whether you like it or not," the old man said. "See, the way Marshall saw it, thanks to TV there was more information outside the classroom than inside, making school an impediment to learning. I guess school was keeping kids from all those cartoons and sitcoms where the real education was. I sort of knew McLuhan. I was one of those students who were too afraid of him to actually sign up for one of his courses. So I sneaked into his classes and just listened to him pontificate. Now, there was a man in love with himself. He was, to put it in the vernacular, a real jerk. A really smart jerk, but still a jerk. I remember him screaming in class one day that women lacked the sexual presence to become priests. He didn't believe anything half-heartedly, no matter how outrageous it was. That was before the time when women would have told him to kiss-off in public. He wouldn't get away with that today."

I just stared at the old man with a dazed attention: curious, attracted, resistant and unable to move. I would wonder later how someone with no visible means of support knew someone as famous as Marshall McLuhan.

"But," he continued, "McLuhan was one of those loudmouths you loved to disagree with, which I did quite often. I told him that I thought the issue with TV didn't have so much to do with the amount of information as it did with who was in charge of it. There was always a lot of information outside the classroom, but the adults controlled it all. The adults, however, couldn't control TV. For instance, my dad didn't want me going into town to see the ghettos. So, before TV, I didn't. After TV I didn't have to. The ghettos came to me. Are your grandparents still alive?"

"My grandpa is," I replied.

"Well, then, he can tell you," the old man said. "Their primary mission in life was to make sure that nothing changed. Their job was to stoke the cultural inertia machine to make sure that it kept running in place. Funny thing about running in place—at the end of the day you're still tired as heck even though you haven't gone anywhere. Our grandparents were usurped by a box of electrons undermining everything they said. God that must have hurt. You know how culture is preserved? Like this: A boy goes to his father and says, *Dad, I got a problem.* Dad says, *Son, I understand, because when I was your age I went to my father and said, 'Dad, I got a problem,' and my father told me, 'Son I understand, because when I was your age I went to my father and said, 'Dad, I got a problem...'* and so on. Understand?

"Now what happens? Son has a problem, goes into a chat room on the Net and finds a virtual buddy who tells him things that would make his grandfather sit up in his grave. Or maybe he calls the psychic hotline. Or maybe he escapes to TV land and gets another perspective from Oprah, or one of the sex channels, or MTV or ESPN. Maybe Dad gets involved, maybe he doesn't. Maybe Dad's around, maybe he isn't. Maybe Dad's got a clue, maybe he doesn't."

"You know about the Net?" I asked excitedly. "You?"

"I predicted it," he said flatly.

"Fugguduh!" I laughed, the last five minutes suddenly feeling like a setup for a punch line. "You predicted the Net? That's a good one. Boy, you really had me going, mister."

"Believe what you want," the old man said as his gold tooth twinkled in the sunshine. "But just remember: Whatever you believe, that's who you are."

A pause stretched between us, the moments passing more painfully for me than for him as we studied each other. Suddenly the old man was smiling coyly.

"Hey," he said buoyantly. "Do you know the difference between a venture capitalist and a gargoyle?"

"No," I replied cautiously.

"Me either!" The old man howled, disappearing as he fell back into the shadows of the doorway. It was a howl, usually at my expense, that I would hear many times and which I would never get used to.

"Oh, very funny," I scoffed. I suddenly felt as though I was observing myself as a character in a play whose motivation was transparent and predictable. "Did you make that up yourself? I suppose that was a dig at me. Well, I'm not a venture capitalist. All I do is make the networks run. All I do is make sure that people can talk to each other. All I do is keep people from getting real confused and pissed off. Do you have a problem with that?"

I waited for a reply, but the invisible world within the doorway was silent. The sounds of the street behind me began to fill my head—cars screeched, taxis honked, police sirens wailed, people buzzed about like angry hornets. Another scrounger was already on me, asking for change. I could smell bagels somewhere in the distance, taste the last few drops of coffee that lingered in my mouth and feel my shirt collar tighten around my neck. I became aware of the fact that people were looking at me strangely as they stepped around me on the sidewalk.

I inched timidly toward the doorway. "...Hello?"

I got the nerve to stick my head all the way inside. A cool gust of air sent a shiver down my spine. The old man was gone.

CHAPTER 3 Avatars and Who We Ares
Ignorance may be no excuse, but you don't know what you don't know.

Usually my life was my work and usually the parts of my life meshed like bits of code.

Usually.

But the encounter with the old man was so far outside the program that it nagged at me, daring me to make sense of it. The harder I tried to ignore the old man's words, the faster they spun in the back of my mind until one of the suits accused me of the worst of all possible sins: distraction.

I understood their concern. In a crisis-driven world ruled by leveraged minutia in which failing to grasp the slightest technical detail at a crucial moment could make the difference between triumph and defeat, distraction simply could not be tolerated. Once, when trying to explain what I did for a living to my grandpa, I had compared running BADI's network to driving in bumper-to-bumper, six-lane, over-the-speed-limit traffic, in which everyone was afraid to slow down, take their eyes off the road, or become the least bit distracted for even a split second. He had commented that it didn't sound any more demanding than running the ore crusher he had operated at the mine for 23 years—just a bit more detailed.

The end of the day came and I couldn't wait to see the old man again. I literally sprinted from work to his doorway and called out.

"Hello? You there? Anybody home?"

I could hear someone moving around in the shadows, so I leaned in a little closer.

"Hello? Mister?" I announced. "Is that you? Say, I did my 'homework' during lunch. Food, clothing, shelter and... weapons!" Silence. I waited.

The old man sat up and leaned forward far enough so that I could see his face. "And where did you come up with that?"

"I snuck in some pretty serious chat room activity on the Net during lunch," I said, ballooning with a kind of excitement that had been missing from my life for some time. "Actually, I posted the question as soon as I got to work, and then hopped into the fray on my lunch break. By the way, great question...um..."

"My name is Credo. C-R-E-D-O. The 'E' is hard. It rhymes with *neato libido.*"

"Credo. Got it! Great question! Jeez Louise, there was this guy from Magadan in western Russia—"

"Eastern Russia," Credo corrected me. "Never mind."

"Anyway, he really got into it with this woman from somewhere in Nebraska. She said love came after food, clothing and shelter—something about a guy named Maslow—but he and I said weapons. We were all using avatars. Avatars are so cool. They are these things that—"

"Virtual representational identities. Cyber masks. More like cyber suits. Be who you want, avoid who you are."

"You know about avatars?" I asked in disbelief.

"I predicted them."

"Oh, fugguduh!" I howled as I clapped my hands together. "That's a good one! You predicted avatars, huh? You're too much!"

"I didn't write the code for them, but I told all the big shots they were coming. The big shots used to listen to me, you know. Oh yes. And I told them to get ready for them. Avatars were easy to predict, actually. Technology after 5 PM is basically entertainment and the purpose of entertainment is to help people avoid looking at what they are doing with their lives. Add an interactive element to TV, and you get email-in-drag—avatars. It's just a grown-up kind of Halloween."

I folded my arms smugly. "Look, Credo, you don't have to make up all this garbage. I already like you. I'm just impressed that you read as much as you obviously do to know about all this stuff."

Credo ignored me and continued. "The big shots didn't get the fact that most of all those millions of people out there who used email actually liked the fact that no one could see them. When video mail came along, most chose to turn off the audio/video part. Email was their chance to be someone different, to avoid who they were, to reinvent themselves. This is the after-5 PM crowd, mind you. During the day you had to represent the boss man, and usually the boss man wanted you to show your face on a conference call. But after work, people turned the audio/video part off. They'd rather use an avatar, or just text on a screen, than show people who they really were. Did you know it was me who came up with the idea of a shaving filter for video?"

"A shaving filter?" I asked, intrigued but skeptical.

"That's right. Let's say you're working out of your house and you have to go virtual for a meeting, but you've been out all night and look like hell. Use the shaving filter. It makes you look like you just shaved. You have options to raise your eyelids a bit, comb your hair and even put a tie on. Voice filters are coming that make you sound interested even when you're not."

"Oh yeah?" I snorted. "And who's got this?"

"A little startup out in the Sillywood."

"Where?"

"Sillywood," Credo said. "It's where Hollywood and Silicon Valley meet. The name of the company is Fallacom. I think it's short for Fallacious Communications. Check into it if you want. It might be a good investment."

"Thanks for the tip."

"So, where were we?" Credo resumed. "I know I get sidetracked pretty easily. Ah yes—avatars. Most of the big shots thought I was crazy when I told them they were coming. That was back in the old days, when if you asked the average software developer what he was working on, he would have rattled off something that only an engineer could understand. Me, I knew better. All this glitz was just to allow people to connect with each other. In a word: community. It's as if we woke up one day and realized we had put all this technology in-between people and there was no way to get rid of it, even if we wanted to. Technology was no longer a choice. Zillions of people needed it for a zillion reasons: for their support system, for jobs, for their health, for comfort, for fun, to feel civilized, to give their kids stuff they never had, to stay alive, or just because they were too scared to let go of it because they're sapes, and sapes don't like change—all except the panhandlers here, who'll take all the spare change you got...get it?!"

I got it, but it wasn't funny. I smiled politely and waited for an opening to ask a question, a patience I would learn to hone to a fine edge under his tutelage.

"So then," Credo continued, "the name of the game became: As long as we can't get rid of the technology, how can we use it to get back home—back to community?"

Finally he came up for air and I dove into the conversation. "It's all very interesting. But what are sapes?" I asked.

"Sapes. Homo Sapiens. We're all the same basic model of barely intelligent protoplasm, and don't ever forget it. The only thing more consistent than the weight of water, from continent to continent, is human nature."

"So, community comes after food, clothing and shelter?" I asked hopefully.

"Not exactly, but that's close," replied Credo. "Weapons was a good guess, too. How did you come up with that?"

"Well," I began timidly, "I figured that once you had the food, clothing and shelter that you need, then you would have to make sure you can keep them. To do that takes weapons."

Credo nodded slightly. "I see. And the lady from Nebraska countered with love. Why?"

"She said that once you have your physical needs met, you begin to meet your emotional needs."

"And you didn't like that?" Credo asked.

"It wasn't that I didn't like it. My point was that you hadn't met all your physical needs until you could protect what you had. Then maybe you could concentrate on other things, like love."

"So, what is your objection to love?" Credo asked.

"I didn't say I objected to love." I was a little perturbed at the inquisition, his sanctimonious tone of voice and what seemed to be a deliberate misreading of my words. "I like love just fine. I just think that—"

"You like all the whiz bang, don't you?" Credo interrupted.

The question caught me totally off guard, as if he had just violated an unspoken rule of engagement. "What do you mean?"

"You know," Credo continued. "All the high-tech stuff. You're hooked on it. Interactive telecasts from Mars, fake people from Russia, transcontinental Trivial Pursuit games...."

"Sure I like it. Up to a point."

"What point?" Credo asked.

I could feel a long-unused part of my brain warming up, as though it had been idle and just waiting for me to put it in gear. It was the part that controlled reflection and introspection, activities that there just didn't seem to be time for anymore as the steady state of techno-logical evolution picked up more and more velocity. Maybe it was my fantasy, but I thought life had been different at one point in time. My simplistic understanding of history gleaned from PBS specials and overheard conversations was that history used to be kind, giving us a few millennia of downtime between the Agricultural and Industrial ages, then a few centuries of respite before the Information Age took over. Whatever life used to be, we were now living in a constant transition zone in which things changed while they were changing, in which an acceleration of thought and invention had made reflection more important but more impossible than ever. We were literally out-of-control, but too busy to notice.

I liked the challenge Credo was presenting me, but I felt at a disadvantage. After all, Credo had all day to think about these things. I had a job.

"Well," I began academically, "for instance, I hate the genetic engineering stuff. It's way over-the-line."

Credo moved all the way out of the doorway and stood up. It was hard for me not to fixate on the fact that he wasn't wearing socks.

"Einstein didn't wear socks either," Credo said. "And at least my clothes fit. I don't understand how you can walk around in pants that cut off your circulation."

As I started to object, Credo cut in full force. "So you hate genetic engineering, huh? And you probably hate mining, too, despite the gold on your briefcase, the silver in your ring, the copper inside your computer. And you hate drilling for oil in the Alaskan wilderness, despite your GORTEX tent, your fiberglass skis and the plastic top that keeps one of those fancy cups of coffee of yours from spilling all over your polyester jacket."

"Huh?" I said unconsciously.

"This is pretty basic stuff, William. You have technology on the brain. I think you need to take another shot at your homework. It's due tomorrow."

"Well, thanks for all your help!" I said angrily.

"I can't give the answer away!" Credo protested. "That would be cheating, don't you think? Just because you don't believe in school doesn't mean you can start cheating. Think of life as one long exam in which you can't cheat, and the only passing grade is to die without regret."

I looked him in the eye, swinging—as I often would—between feeling privileged and foolish to be in his presence. "Why the freak am I talking to you?"

Credo shrugged. "Because people your age bore you? Because I remind you of your grandfather? Because you see your own future in this gnarly face of mine? Because I predicted the Internet? Because you're ready to morph? Take your pick."

"Morph into what?" I asked.

"Into yourself," he replied.

"And what the hell does that mean?"

"It means follow your bliss," he said calmly. "It means get a job you love and never go to work again. It means if you really like to teach, you should be a teacher."

"I gotta go," I said, genuinely spooked. I retreated as I glanced at my watch.

"Look," Credo said, "before you go, you need to go see a friend of mine. He can help you sort out the technology thing. It will only take a minute. His name is Mr. Big."

Ah hah! Finally! Here was the punch line. Suddenly all the bits of code came together and, although I felt pretty stupid, I finally knew what was going on. Or so I thought. "Oh, I see! Time to see Mr. Big, is it? And just what does Mr. Big do, sell drugs? Sorry, not my style."

"Mr. Big's a bit odd, but he's no druggie," Credo assured me. "You really should see him. It will help us communicate better."

"I'm not sure that how well we communicate is a priority for me right now," I said, watching the numbers on my watch change from 5:00 to 5:01. "I'm sorry, but I don't have time to meet your friend. I've got to catch the 5:12, otherwise my evening gets all messed up."

"It's already messed up." Credo laughed.

"That's for sure! Sorry. Gotta go!"

"It won't take but a minute," Credo said. "In fact, it won't take any time at all."

Credo snapped his fingers.

CHAPTER 4 Mr. Big and the Ledge of Objectivity
What happens when you give a bad guitar player a bigger amplifier?

As Credo snapped his fingers, my mind suddenly went blank. In my next conscious moment I was sitting in a lawn chair on the edge of a cliff looking out over a shallow canyon that was packed with millions of people buzzing about in an open-air market. From my spectator's perch, the white noise of so many overlapping conversations and the colorful dance of too many people trying to navigate an overcrowded space reminded me of video footage I had seen of a day in the life of Calcutta. However, the video hadn't prepared me for the smell, the feeling of hot perspiration clogging my skin and the invasion of thought caused by so many people converging on one place at the same time. Even at a distance I felt claustrophobic, like an invisible vise was slowly ratcheting, compressing me to my essence against my will. I began to panic and decided to focus on my immediate environment in an effort to keep calm. My right hand began its coffee twitch but was already clutching a glass of lemonade sporting a paper parasol. My left hand was resting on the arm of the lawn chair. I was wearing Bermuda shorts, sandals, sun glasses, and a straw hat that I couldn't keep from touching. There was an unusual feeling of space between my clothes and skin.

"Cool lid, eh?" came a raspy, jovial voice next to me.

I turned and there sat Mr. Big with a broad smile, a barrel chest, an unkempt beard and bushy eyebrows. He was dressed like me except that he was wearing a white cowboy hat. He seemed unusually tall, but otherwise looked fairly ordinary, even familiar.

"I got your hat in Panama," he continued. "Do you like it? I can tell you do. It's yours whenever you're here."

"And where is *here*?" I asked nervously.

"You're in school," he answered with a smile. "Consider it a field trip."

"Very impressive technology," I announced. Years later, I would realize that my mind had been in a box most of my life. Some things happened, others didn't and anything else that was too weird to explain had to be high-tech sorcery. "But if you are trying to lure me into a start-up company, this is not the way to do it. You are way over-the-line with your recruitment tactics."

"I'm not trying to lure you into anything," said Mr. Big, "except maybe to get you to re-think where the line ought to be. That's what any good school ought to do."

"Where am I?" I snapped. "And who are all those people down there?"

"Calm down," he told me, still smiling, still hopeful, though about what I wasn't sure. "They can't see us. They're on the other side of the looking glass, so to speak. And you wouldn't be here unless you wanted to be."

"Well, I don't want to be. I have to catch the 5:12. I don't suppose I can get a cab around here."

Mr. Big rumbled with laughter. "Credo was right about you."

"Right about what?"

"Right about you," Mr. Big said.

"I don't know what you're talking about, but this is kidnapping. I could sue the pants off you for this!"

"I guess that's the American way," shrugged Mr. Big. "Why talk when you can litigate? It's good for the economy. Look, before you do anything rash, let me show you how things work here. Pull back on the right arm of your chair, like this."

Mr. Big pulled back on the arm and his chair lifted off the ground. He shifted the arm to the right and the chair moved up and to the right a few feet. "See? Just like those Dick Tracy cars."

"What cars?" I asked, shielding my eyes from the sun as I watched Mr. Big glide through the air.

"I hear you don't know who McLuhan is. I see you don't know who Dick Tracy is, either. Never mind. We'll get to all that in good time. For now, just treat the arm of your chair like a joystick. Come on, boy, grab the throttle. We've got places to go."

There was no way I was going anywhere. I could tell I was spoiling his party, but I needed some answers.

"How the hell did you know about the McLuhan thing? Where's Credo? Is he here?"

"Here? *Here's* a relative term, don't you think?" Mr. Big called down to me.

"Look, I want to know how you know Credo and how you know about me! And I want to know now!"

As Mr. Big set his lawn chair back on the ground, he stared into my eyes with a condescending compassion that reminded me of

Credo. "Networking, my boy, networking. When you get right down to it, everything is networking. You, of all people, ought to know that. Now, give your lawn chair a whirl. You'll just love it! Just pull back on the arm and see what happens."

I set my glass in the cup holder and reluctantly pulled back on the arm of my chair. Suddenly I was 20-feet in the air with a flock of crows incoming at 3 o'clock. They came out of the sun, screaming and pecking at my head.

"Oops," Mr. Big shouted up to me, "I forgot to tell you. Only think good thoughts when you take the chair out for a spin. Here, let me help you. Take your hand off the arm."

I let go of the arm and grabbed my seat to keep from falling. As I drifted toward the ground I could see the masses of people moving among the shops and market tables in the canyon. No one seemed to notice me.

"How did you get control of my chair?" I demanded to know.

"It's like the cars they used in driver's ed. in high school. I can take over if I need to. Anyway, don't go flying around unless you're in a good mood. The chair is an amplifier. All technology is an amplifier. And what happens when you give a bad guitar player a bigger amplifier? Ouch! Now, how about today's lesson?"

CHAPTER 5 Theory Meets Reality
Seeing is believing, unless you no longer believe what you see, in which case what do you believe?

Mr. Big maneuvered his chair in front of mine, raised his glass, and proposed a toast to me. After a prolonged hesitation, I joined him, quietly demanding to know what I was doing here, wherever here was. The entire time I was with him he never stopped grinning.

"We'll get to that. By the way, I love your name, *William Tell.* I'll bet you got a lot of crap as a kid!" Mr. Big guffawed.

"How did ya' guess?" I asked sarcastically.

"Anyone ever try to put an apple on your head?"

"Fugguduh, now that's original!"

Suddenly my chair lifted off the ground and was wobbling uncontrollably. A slug of lemonade flew out of my glass and on to my shorts. When I demanded to know what was going on, Mr. Big apologized, saying that it was his fault, that the joke about my name had put me in a bad frame of mind and gave my chair an attitude. I told him he was a jerk several times. He apologized as he tried to keep from laughing and recommended we get on with today's lesson.

"You hate school, so let's begin with some practical advice," he said. "Let me tell you how to tick off a bunch of academics. It's real easy. But it's best to wait until they post your grade.

"Find an average group of academics standing around in an average hallway in an average university. Then walk up to them and interject a statement into their conversation about how awful television is. Maybe say something like it robs people of their ability to imagine; it gives corporations control of the population by projecting a single image of reality into the minds of millions of people at the same time; it obliterates cultures by blanketing them with misleading and irrelevant images of who they ought to be; it limits interpretations of reality to those advertisers are willing to pay for; you know, that kind of stuff. You might help them along with a couple of references, maybe Marie Winn's THE PLUG-IN DRUG, or Comstock's TELEVISION AND HUMAN BEHAVIOR, or Postman's AMUSING OURSELVES TO DEATH or Mander's FOUR ARGUMENTS FOR THE ELIMINATION OF TELEVISION. There's a ton of stuff out there—everyone loves to hate television. So, just use whatever it takes.

"Then step back and let 'em have at it. The academics will work themselves into a frenzy about how evil television is, quoting Kierkegaard and Dewey, Kant and Descartes, existentialists and fundamentalists, anyone who might impress their dean, or any members of the promotion committee who might be listening. When they're frothing at the mouth, and you figure they're about ready to implode from self-importance, quietly ask them, "So, any *Seinfeld* fans among us?" Without thinking, a few of them will holler, "Yeah!" That'll catch the rest of them off-guard. Usually someone will quote something from one of their favorite shows and everyone will laugh. Then you got 'em. Most of the time it will take them a few seconds to figure out what's going on. My advice to you at that point is—*run like hell!* Get out of there fast! Academics hate to be caught liking television.

"See what I'm saying? When it comes to technology, we are all two people. We hate TV, but we love *Seinfeld*. We hate deforestation but we love our mahogany tables. We hate electronic eavesdropping but we love it when the cops use it to nab an ax murderer. Technology. We love to hate it; we hate to love it. It splits us right down the middle, creates two people out of each one us and then pits one against the other. Stinks, doesn't it?"

I nodded absently.

"We're all two people," Mr. Big continued. "The philosopher and the philosophee. Each of us is the philosopher standing on the ledge of objectivity, looking out over time, space and humanity and seeing technology in terms of the big picture. From that vantage point we can afford to be as philosophical as we like. By the way, that's where we are now, on the ledge of objectivity."

I squeezed the arm of my chair, nudging myself forward to the edge of the canyon so I could get a good glimpse of the hive of humanity that swarmed below me. I realized that I was unable to discern specific features on anyone's face.

"From here," Mr. Big continued, "you can't see anyone in particular too clearly. From here the focus isn't people; it's humanity. From here, we make judgments like *genetic engineering is wrong because it weakens our ability to adjust to environmental change, and it tinkers with some of the basic relationships between humans, nature and spiritual essence*...right?"

"Yes," I said, catching my breath. "Yes. Right. Exactly."

"I mean, no matter how helpful genetic engineering might be to someone down there, wrong's wrong, right?"

"Yes. Exactly," I said definitively.

"I mean, we have to draw the line somewhere, don't we?"

"Right again," I assured him.

"The problem is," Mr. Big said with uncharacteristic seriousness, "that while each one of us is a philosopher, each one of us is also one of those people down there, complete with a history, family, friends and a ton of irrational human desires. From a down-there perspective we forget all our theoretical problems and focus on what makes us feel good right here, right now. If you want one thing you can take to the bank, it's this: I don't care how fancy the technology gets, sapes are sapes and sapes will do whatever it takes to keep them and their families alive and happy and screw philosophy. Let me show you." I heard his fingers snap, and my mind went blank.

Suddenly I was in the canyon among the millions, fighting the crowds as I walked toward the doctor's office on the other side of the street. I was back in my street clothes, my tight, black non-designer look at odds with the colorful, airy clothes of everyone else. My Panama hat was gone, and as the sun beat down on my head, the goo in my hair heated up enough to start streaking down my face. I looked up, trying to catch a glimpse of Mr. Big, but the ledge had disappeared into the haze of sunlight. As I crossed the unusually wide street I looked deeply into the faces of the people I encountered, as though I was trying to extract something from each one of them. I stood outside the doctor's office for a moment and watched people in the process of every-day life trying to make it from dawn 'til dusk. They were all different. They were all the same. Sapes.

I sat down inside a lime-green waiting room, knowing somehow that it was where I was supposed to be. Hollow music meandered in the background as the faint odor of formaldehyde circulated in the room. A receptionist with a beehive hairdo and blue fingernails called out my name with deadpan intonation and then told me to go straight to examination room three where the doctor was waiting for me. As I walked toward the door, I involuntarily checked my ears for shaving cream and wiped the hair-goo drizzle off my face with my sleeve. My right hand was flexing for the mid-morning latte with macadamia-nut flavoring that wasn't there.

The doctor was a short Caucasian man with bloodshot eyes and a serious look on his face. He laid a clipboard with a blank form on it in his lap. "Mr. Tell, your son is going to have asthma. I haven't told your wife yet."

"Look," I said, clearing my throat hastily, "I'm not sure what's going on, but I don't have a son or a wife...do I?"

The doctor blew his nose loudly into an off-white handkerchief. "Denial is common, but not helpful," he said. "It's best to deal with these things head on. But I have good news! Because your wife is so recently pregnant, some simple genetic therapy could fix things so your son can lead a long and healthy life. Now, I know you don't like all the genetic stuff. I know you think it's way over-the-line. So, if you want your kid to grow up with asthma, as a matter of principle, I'll understand."

"No!" I blurted. "For god's sake, no! Do whatever you've got to, I don't care whose kid it is!"

"All right, all right," the doctor said as he filled in a few lines of the form. "Good choice. A humane choice. And a smart one, financially speaking. Some kid just sued his old man for not giving him the gene therapy he needed to keep him from having sinus problems all his life. The kid won. The insurance companies supported the kid because they would have spent far less money just fixing the problem in the beginning rather than treating the symptoms for a lifetime and wanted to set the precedent. Family is family and all that stuff, but you still can't be too careful.

"Say, while I'm at it," the doctor continued, "I can do a little more therapy and give him some athletic skills he might not have otherwise."

"Like what?" I inquired.

"Well," the doctor said, "I can't be too sure, but the genetic profile suggests he probably won't be able to run very fast. Would you like me to go ahead and fix that?"

"Is it legal?" I asked.

The doctor chuckled. "Yes, it's legal. It's practically expected these days. It could be a lawsuit somewhere down the road if you don't take care of it now. Imagine—your kid develops a yen for soccer but never makes the first string because dad was too stingy with the genetic engineering."

"I see your point," I said, terrified.

"Typically, your health insurance covers about half of it."

I paused. "Well, sure, go ahead. I guess."

"Okay, got it," the doctor said as he continued filling out the form. He blew his nose again. "Pardon the cold. I've had it since last winter."

Suddenly I was feeling exposed, faint and close to vomiting.

"You don't look so good," the doctor said matter-of-factly. "Put your head between your legs...or is it elevate your feet?" He started to chuckle under his breath. "God, I can never remember which it is—and I'm a doctor! It all depends on what you are feeling. What are you feeling?"

I tried to explain that what we were talking about hit me sideways, like food poisoning of the body and soul. I just couldn't continue to sashay through a conversation about playing with my son's body chemistry as if he were a Tinker Toy. What we were doing just wasn't, well, *right*, and was potentially, well, *hideous*...wasn't it? Wasn't it the kind of thing you might actually go to hell for? The fact that I didn't believe there was a hell, that none of this was real, and that I didn't even have a son didn't seem to help me at all. I told the doctor that, to put it in scientific terms, I felt what we were discussing gave me the creeps and grossed me out all at the same time.

"Oh, I understand," the doctor said. "Most people feel like this the first time they come face-to-face with this in any real way. It might help to remember there was a time when the idea of slicing open a live human being to perform a life-saving operation was just plain repugnant, odious—the work of the devil! Then a funny thing happened. People began to realize what it offered their dying mother or child or wife, and then they couldn't get it fast enough. Suddenly, something that had been an unthinkable abomination in the sight of man, society and God became just one of those hard realities you had to face up to if you wanted a better life for your kids. There's nothing new here, Mr. Tell. Intellectual change is much easier than emotional change and in the immortal words of someone I can never remember, *People are drops of reason in oceans of emotions.*"

The doctor sneezed a few more times while I continued wondering whether my head should be between my legs.

"Let's talk about something more pleasant," he continued. "What about music? That usually cheers a person up."

"What about it?" I asked.

"Do you like it?"

"Of course I like it," I said. "Why?"

"Well, it looks like your kid won't be too musical. I can fix that too if you want. "

"What if I *didn't* like music, " I asked. "Could you make sure my kid didn't have any musical talent? "

"More or less," the doctor said without emotion. "We could make it a lot less likely that he would have musical talent. Interesting idea, by the way. I could think of some fundamentalist groups that might go for that. But I wouldn't do it if I were you. You could open yourself up to a lawsuit. For example, your kid could come back as an adult and sue you for not being able to dance. Anyway, I am sure you were just speaking hypothetically. So, let's keep going here. It looks like your son is going to be a little short. That's an easy one to take care of and I am sure you don't want to burden him with short- ness for an entire lifetime. And do you want him to look just like you or would you like me to fix his nose?"

"What's wrong with my freakin' nose?!"

"Well, Mr. Tell, it's a little big, don't you think?"

"NO!" I screamed.

Suddenly I was standing at Credo's doorway feeling a bit queasy. "I think I'm going to throw up," I said quietly.

"Just close your eyes and rest your brain for a minute," Credo reassured me. "You'll be fine."

I closed my eyes until the images in my head stopped colliding and then slowly opened them to check my watch. 5:01. My meeting with Mr. Big had taken no time at all.

"Where's my lawn chair?" I asked.

"They're pretty nifty, aren't they? Mr. Big needs to keep those for guests."

I paused, afraid to say anything. Finally I asked, "Was all that real?"

"Maybe. But you know what maybe means: maybe not."

"Don't you ever give a straight answer?" I pleaded.

"Let me ask you something," Credo said, ignoring me entirely. "Suppose someone applied for a job in your networking department and you had a gene scan of the person. Would you look at it?"

"No," I replied. "That's over-the-line."

"Suppose your employer already had the information and said you had to look at it."

"Then I'd look at it," I conceded. "But it doesn't mean I would do anything with it."

"And suppose you saw that the person had a gene potentially linked to alcoholism or violent behavior," Credo pushed.

"If they weren't violent or alcoholic, I'd consider hiring them," I said confidently.

"And suppose you had to choose between two equally qualified people, one who had the gene and the other who didn't. Whom would you hire?" Credo asked.

I was silent and suddenly feeling very heavy.

"The weight you are feeling is caused by the burden of information," Credo explained. "We know far more than we would like to. We know far more than we are capable of dealing with. Knowledge is power, and our power is outpacing our wisdom at an exponential rate. *Ignorance is bliss* is not just a saying. It was a way of life that kept people sane and communities together for eons—until recently."

He had spat his words at me, testing my resilience as if probing the depths of my psychic armor. In his reaction to me I could see my own reflection—a calm, distraught young man whose thoughts whirled like an out-of-control vacuum cleaner. I must have seemed horribly fragile and transparent to him because suddenly he changed his tone to something a little less aggressive.

"Remember," he smiled, "whenever you are confused, you can always flip a coin. Just don't tell your boss."

In a lame attempt to regain some momentum and, I fantasized, generate some credibility, I insisted on an answer to my earlier question about whether the events I experienced with Mr. Big had been real. He jokingly told me that to give me a straight answer I had to give him a straight question. As he began to laugh he assured me that he was dead serious.

"Look," I said with the calmness of a muffled explosion, "I was there. I saw it! All these people, the flying chair, Mr. Big. Was it virtual? Is that it? Is it new technology, Defense Department stuff? Are you trying to get me to go to work for you?"

"Do you think something is real just because you can see it?" Credo asked.

I stared at him, searching for something to say.

"Look, William, the important point to understand here is that your eyes, your entire body, are just another piece of technology with built-in limitations that you get so used to that you forget they're there. Your eyes don't tell you what's *out there*. That's just a super-stition we all buy into to keep us from panicking. Your eyes just let you see the very small part of reality that they were built to detect. Sapes. God Almighty, they're self-centered. It's rule number one for them. They can't help it. It's their job! Understanding that puts a new spin on why 2-year-olds are so impossible. If they weren't, they would never survive. You know the first word a kid understands? *Mine*."

"I thought it was *mama*," I ventured.

"That's a myth. It might be the first word they say, but it is not the first word they understand. *Mine* is the first word that takes hold in their psyche. The concept of 'mine' helps them wire themselves for survival. If it weren't for the impossibility of 2-year-olds who thought the entire world belonged to them, the Earth would be populated with just plants and the animals. Have you spent much time with kids?"

I shook my head *no*.

"Hmmm, well, that's coming. But don't worry. No one is pregnant—yet."

"What?" I exclaimed. I waited anxiously for him to explain himself, but he pushed on like a freight train with a mission.

"Anyway, our eyes see only a very small part of the light spec-trum, not to mention all those things that can't even be detected visually. Trust me on this—what's out there would not fit in your head. It's best you can't see it. But hey, I could give you a kind of 'super eyes' for a minute and let you have a peek at a broader light spectrum if you'd like. But I have to warn you: If you think you feel sick now, this would be sure to make you toss your lunch."

Suddenly I checked my watch: 5:04.

"Gotta go!" I yelled, running off in the direction of the subway.

"Hey!" Credo yelled out after me. "Tomorrow bring me some doughnuts, would you? Plain fry cakes. No sugar, no filling, none of that garbage. Just plain, okay?"

CHAPTER 6 Kim (maybe it's a she, maybe it's a him)
The most elusive substance in the universe is nothing.

I love to sleep. Like everything else in life, I do it aggressively. I power sleep. When my head hits the pillow I am instantly, deeply unconscious. The next morning I remember nothing.

But that night I lay awake in bed for hours, cuddled in the flannel Star Trek pajamas my mother had made me for Christmas. As I stared off into nothingness I could feel my metal watchband digging into my wrist, reminding me of the slow passage of time. The last time I looked, it was 2:35 AM, long after Leno and Letterman, O'Brien and Kilborn, countless infomercials for exercise gear, psychic readings, and intimate phone encounters with busty cat-like women who wanted to lay claim to the dissatisfied souls of men. I didn't even climb onto the Net. I just lay there, rerunning the last episode of my life in an endless loop, distilling, synthesizing, collating, trying to extract cause and effect from the events of the day. Now and then I would focus on the mess of computer manuals, empty pizza boxes and general mayhem of my room, all of which was an embarrassing testimony to a distant former self. In fact, the distance between who I was yesterday and what I had become in the last few days could only be measured in light-years.

Thinking about Credo made my brain feel distended as it filled with thoughts that circled themselves, like ideas being chased on the Web; click, go here, click, go there, go back, go forward; no planning, no flow chart, and no distinct needs to direct my activity. Instead, there was just a vague hope that something would eventually make sense and justify my time. I couldn't even blame my inability to sleep on coffee. That day I had consumed no more than my average daily recommended requirement: 3 double lattes in the morning, two espressos at lunch, and as much office coffee as I could stomach during the rest of the afternoon. All that coffee kept me thin, I told myself.

Suddenly, my computer screen blinked once, twice. From my bed I pointed the remote control—my "God wand" as I liked to call it—at my computer and clicked once, twice. An incoming e-message. Person-to-person—that is, a message from a person's email account rather than a chat room. A prurient hope rose within me as I clicked twice more to accept. Once again I was going to celebrate the body-disconnected by attaching a wild fantasy to a stranger I would never meet. I walked over to my computer, moved a pile of dirty clothes and settled in.

"Let's just use text," was the first sentence that came across my screen.

"Why?" I typed back to whoever it was.

"Philosophical grounds," came the reply.

"What philosophical grounds?" I asked.

"A belief in the inherent goodness of fantasy and the inherent prejudice of visual contact."

"What?" I asked.

"A belief in the inherent value of the delayed, reflective nature of the written word and the inherent negligence of immediate, real-time communication," was the response.

"I'm not feeling all that serious tonight," I typed in. "All I want to do is chat, which I find to be a much more pleasurable experience if I can see the person I am talking to."

A few clicks later I was watching a woman's pastel face fill my screen. It had come quickly, outlined in jagged edges. A smooth image would have taken more data to construct, more time, more waiting, and I wanted to see her image *now*.

"Hi, Mr. Unseriousness," she said.

Her voice was throaty, smooth, intoxicating. It was processed by some new technology that was so good that it made me notice it and then instantly not care about the fact that it was there; it was impossible not to become captive. And yet, as I slid hopelessly into the conversation and felt her voice flow around me like the warm water of a hot tub at the end of painful day of work, something nagged at me. I squinted into the screen and suddenly realized what it was. I couldn't tell if Kim was a man or a woman. Then I realized that it would be impossible to tell even in person these days, let alone on a computer screen. And with a conveniently androgynous name like Kim, how could I know anything about her gender...his gender...its gender.

But I let it all go for now. The soothing water of her voice swirled around my brain, beckoning.

"Don't you remember our conversation today?" Kim asked, a little disappointed.

"Yes," I finally said. "Yes, I remember. Food, clothing, shelter, and...love."

"Or weapons, depending on your point of view," she said, the corners of her mouth curling up in a splotchy smile, the square pixels of the screen contrasting with the roundness of her face. "I thought you would like to talk some more. What do you say? I say let's do."

It was too intoxicating. The camera mounted on top of my computer monitor followed me as I got up and paced around my room. "You're the woman from Nebraska?"

"The same one," she assured me. "So, it was love vs. weapons. Where shall we begin? Whose turn was it?"

My head began to hurt again and I asked her if we could change topics.

"To what?" she asked.

After thinking for a moment, I told her I wanted to talk about nothing. She would have dismissed it as a joke except for the fact that I was obviously so serious that only pride kept me from pleading. I told her that I realized that "nothing" was unquantifiable, statistically implausible and certainly lacked commercial potential. But all the same, I placed an irrational value on it and asked her to join me.

"Nothing?" Kim asked.

"Nothing," I replied.

She asked me for further definition and I replied...*nothing*. You know, nothing with weight. Nothing with merit. Nothing with conflict or depth. She prodded me for more specifics. I told her, for starters, that it meant not mentioning life, death, work or love, but who knew just where nothing might lead...

She was giddy, laughing in little squeaks that just deepened the intoxication. "Well, that's a new one," she said. "Certainly. Let's do."

We reveled in mutual oblivion, crafting a wonderland from the supposedly inconsequential details of life. I never knew it was possible to say so much about so little, that so much time could pass without disagreement on any point, that banal pleasantness could be so satisfying. We both loved coffee, so we talked about that. To her, coffee and chocolate comprised the staples of the often overlooked "brown food group," an observation I was compelled to agree with. I had spent a summer as a groundskeeper for a golf course, so I gave her a blow-by-blow list of the elements and practices of maintaining a good lawn, which she genuinely seemed to appreciate. She used to be a cook and emailed me three recipes for what she called "boy food,"

mostly casseroles consisting of ingredients like hamburger, Tater Tots
and canned spaghetti. There was an art to cooking, she insisted, as
there was to maintaining a good lawn. It began with cultivating the
right attitude and letting it seep into your fingertips, bridging intent
with action like a seamless network connection. I agreed, the ethereal
beauty of the thought leaving me a little short of breath.

Twice during the conversation my mother was a voice on the
other side of my bedroom door, which she never opened, asking,
*Who are you talking to? Don't you have to get up soon? Are you all
right? Do you need an aspirin?* Both times I had to yield a little bit
more information to Kim about why I was living at home rather than
on my own, a subject she and I sidestepped quickly to re-enter our
illusory neutral zone. I really didn't have an explanation for it anyway, except that in the absence of a social life, what was the difference between living at home or in your own apartment? Many years
later I would realize that deciding to continue to accept my mother's
unconditional love *was* my social life. Contrary to what I believed at
the time, living at home had not been a default lifestyle I'd stumbled
into out of apathy. It had been an unconscious but deliberate choice I
had made about what was important to me.

The conversation with Kim drifted in circles like clouds aimlessly
passing the time of day. When we were finally too tired to continue,
we signed off, neither addressing nor avoiding plans to speak again.
Her last words to me were, "I just love your pajamas." Seconds after
we disconnected, I already missed her.

Reality returned with a thud. It was after 3 AM and I would have
to get up in two hours. I couldn't run a network with a sleep deficit!
But the fact was, I was afraid to sleep. Even though I hadn't remembered a dream in many years, I was afraid of what I would encounter
in my subconscious that night. When I was finally completely honest
with myself, I admitted I was afraid that Credo or Mr. Big might visit
me in my dreams. The thought that they might show up together as a
team terrified me. As soon as I acknowledged my fear, I fell into a
deep sleep.

It turned out that my fears had been justified. I awoke the next
morning and could recall vividly part of what I was sure had been a
long, animated, rambunctious dream. Credo had come to me and
said, "Don't forget the doughnuts."

CHAPTER 7 It's About Time
You can always make more money, but you can't make more time.

An anthropologist observing my participation in the subway ride to work the next morning would have concluded that my life continued on in a ritualistic, predictable and ordinary fashion. Through my eyes, however, life appeared so different that I felt dishonest and guilty for not saying something to all the familiar strangers I had nodded to every morning as I took a seat in the rear car. After all, they expected me to be who I had always been, although they had no idea who that was. I felt I should stand up, clear my throat ceremoniously, ask for everyone's attention and announce the following:

"Good morning. I just wanted to let all of you know that I am totally unlike the person you never knew as recently as 24 hours ago, and that it is all an old man's fault for stopping time and introducing me to a used-lawn-chair salesman who took me to the ledge of objectivity so that I could understand the practical realities of genetic engineering. On top of this, life for me this particular morning is a sleep-deprived, low-rolling fog, and moving among all of you feels like skating on an over-crowded ice rink—the slightest bumps are amplified to such a degree that I can't help but take them personally. So, in case any of you are considering breaching the barrier of silence that has allowed each of us to self-absorb on our way to work each morning and actually strike up a conversation with me of some substance, I beg you not to. This morning would not be a good time to do that. Thank you, and have a good day."

I shook my head, but that just made the fog thicken. My body felt rickety in anticipation of caffeine and the sleep that seemed too distant to think about. I stared into the window across the aisle and noticed immediately that my black clothes accentuated the bags under my eyes. I turned and looked into the nose-smudged subway window next to me. My eyes were red and swollen; my face was ghosted and hollow. "Never again will I run a network on too little sleep," I vowed. Never.

By the time I reached Credo's doorway I had downed a triple latte (with whipped cream, sprinkles and flavoring) that I'd bought from a pushcart coffee vendor; and picked up a sack of doughnuts from Chino's bakery, a turn-of-the-century, hole-in-the-wall shop that somehow had withstood the ravages of urban development that surrounded it. My hands were a bundle of coffee nerves as I gave him the paper bag.

"Steady William," he said, a touch of honest concern in his voice. "You look like something the proverbial cat dragged in."

"You're not one to talk," I countered. Credo looked exactly as he had the day before, except that he was wearing one sock on his left foot.

"I wasn't looking at your clothes," Credo said. "But, like I told you, I am concerned they're so tight that they're cutting off your blood circulation. Plus, doesn't wearing all that black give you sort of an attitude about life?"

"Food, clothing, shelter and *sleep*," I blurted out. "That's my answer—*sleep*. I need my sleep. If I don't get my sleep, I'm useless. Life's not fun if I'm useless. And I like to have fun. So, here are your doughnuts. It's been real, I haven't a clue what this all means, and I'll see you in the very distant future."

I tried to turn to leave but I couldn't help fixating on Credo's sock-less foot. After a long pause Credo said, "It's what I do."

"Did Einstein wear one sock, too?" I asked.

"No," Credo replied. "This is my fashion statement. I am predicting it will be in vogue one day."

"Of course. And when you advise the fashion industry, they'll probably ignore you, just like all those other dumb people in the technology world who don't know a profit prophet when they hear one."

"We have to talk," he said as if I hadn't spoken. "This is serious."

"No way," I protested. "Not cool. No more! Besides, I don't have time. I have to get to work."

"Oh for god's sake," Credo snorted. "Would you cease with the time crap? Didn't you learn anything yesterday?" I saw Credo motion to snap his fingers, and I yelled at him to stop. Too late.

When my focus returned, I was still standing in front of the doorway, eye-to-eye with Credo. Except for an immense quiet I could not comprehend, life seemed unchanged. Then Credo motioned for me to turn around. Rush hour stood still. The cars, the people, the pigeons were caught mid-stride and frozen in place like statues, forming a tableau of early morning in the financial district.

"Would you like a doughnut?" Credo asked.

"What's going on?" I demanded to know.

Credo reached into the bag and pulled out a doughnut. "Ahh, the good kind. None of that jelly garbage in the middle—and still warm. Thanks. I owe ya.'" He stuffed his mouth with a big bite before he began to speak.

"A simple explanation is that time has slowed way down," Credo said. "You can actually dispense with time entirely if you want, but then, as the saying correctly goes, everything happens all at once and what a mess! Imagine an infinitely large kindergarten on a finite playground during an infinitely long recess on a horrifically rainy day without any adult supervision right after the white sugar from the morning snack has worn off, and you sort of get the idea of what it's like. You need lots of training before you can handle true timelessness."

"No thanks!" I exclaimed. "I like time."

"No you don't," Credo corrected me. "You see time as your enemy. That's why we're gathered here today. And also to give you a chance to catch your breath before you go to work. Most people find time travel relaxing. You can take a nap here for a few hours and pop back into the flow just," snapping his fingers, "like that."

"Don't snap your fingers!" I pleaded. "Please."

"Still afraid, eh? Don't you want to learn about all this cool stuff?"

"No! Yes! No!" I responded in rapid succession. "I mean, I'm not ready, or I don't deserve you, or I like my ignorance, or whatever, but no, not now." Credo looked at me blankly. I paused for a few moments to survey the panorama of stillness that filled the street. "This is not normal," I whispered.

Credo began to laugh. "And talking to people dressed up in cybersuits is? Would you like to hop backward in time and tell your great grandfather that one day we're all going to have 500 channels of moving pictures from across the ocean filled with transvestites and Sumo wrestlers?"

"No!"

"Normal!" Credo bellowed. "*Normal!* That's one of those words like 'appropriate' that ought to come with a user's guide. Anyway, we have to talk. This is serious."

I relaxed my body. "Why not? I'd say I have a few minutes to kill."

Credo was instantly in hysterics. "A few minutes to kill! I have to tell Mr. Big that one! Keep your sense of humor. You'll need it on the Big Day."

"What is this 'big day' you keep talking about?" I demanded to know.

Credo took a huge bite of doughnut and shook his head. "Can't talk about that right now. It's not the right time." *He can stop time but he doesn't know he's not supposed to talk with his mouth full,* I thought to myself. *What kind of sorcerer doesn't know not to talk with his mouth full? No manners at all.* "What is it time to talk about?" I asked.

"Time."

"Time?" I asked.

"Time," Credo replied. "Time is everything. Everyone is an artist with their time, whether they know it or not. Time is the medium that everyone uses to create their lives. Let's call it painting with a wide brush. So, there are things you should know about it.

"You see time as a force. It's more accurate to see it as an environment. How we dance within time says more about us than just about anything else we do. You see time as an enemy. A playful enemy, but an enemy to be defeated, like the bad guy in a computer game. The definition of a tragic figure is someone who is afraid of time, who always feels as though there just aren't enough minutes in the day, who is always worried that life is too short. Like *you.*

"I just wanted you to know that you didn't have to worry about any of that. We're still working on getting you past your fears so you can get on with a real education. The truth is that you just can't learn very well when you're worried. It's a physiological thing. Every atom that's engaged in being worried isn't available for learning. Learning requires a mind that is not predisposed. Fear and worry predispose a mind almost entirely.

"So, the lesson is that there's plenty of time. In fact there is an inexhaustible supply of time. It's the only truly renewable resource in the galaxy. Renewable, heck, it's indestructible! So, don't worry about time. The question is: If you had all the time in the world, what would you do with it? That's the real question."

I asked if that was another way of asking me what the first thing I'd ask my clone to do if I had one. He told me yes, in a way, but what that usually meant is: What would I be doing right now if I weren't afraid to? However, he conceded, it was a good departure point and asked what my clone's first assignment would be.

"To take cooking lessons," I said. In my mind's eye I was seeing all those empty pizza boxes in my room again. They seemed to follow me around everywhere in my mind. They just gotta' go, I counseled myself. They were the old me. The new me was going to be gourmet; non-designer, but gourmet.

Credo nodded in approval. "Good, good. Do you want to do that now?" he asked, gesturing to snap his fingers. I noticed that whenever he moved abruptly his coat exuded a small puff of dust.

"No! Please. I can only take so much. This," I said turning around and surveying my situation, "is plenty for one day."

I was quiet for a moment. The silence that surrounded me seemed to roar like an ocean. "It's like something out of Star Trek."

"Where do you think Roddenberry got the idea?" Credo asked.

"From you, I suppose?" I asked.

"Yes," Credo assured me. "And I never made a dime from it."

"Oh fugguduh! Is there anything you didn't invent?"

"I don't *invent*," Credo sternly corrected me. "I *predict*. I'm a consultant, not an engineer. I didn't tell Roddenberry what to do, I just told him what I knew he would do sooner or later anyway. He, like all my other clients, then had the choice of being proactive or reactive about their lives. And no, there's not much I haven't predicted, but there are plenty of things I've predicted that I don't like."

"Like what?"

"QBC—you know, the home buying channel. God, I hate it! Day in, day out, nice people selling nice things for nice prices to millions of people. Conceptually it's not such a bad idea, but the junk they foist on the world! Of course, I'm a minimalist, so what else would I think? I have an aunt, on the other hand, whose proudest possession is her set of matching Mount Rushmore bookends. I know marketing is supposed to prey on people's vulnerability, but QBC is so god-awful blatant about it. No sense of shame. It gives telemarketing a bad name. You know why the folks at QBC are so successful? Because they know that what they're really selling is community, not trinkets."

Credo looked at me slightly embarrassed. "Sorry," he said. "I digress a lot. Back to your relationship with time."

I stopped him and told him as politely as possible that I had had enough for one day and that I really didn't want to be here right now. I told him that as unenlightened as it sounded, I wanted to get back to my dimension so I could do something trivial like go to work. He told me he smelled fear again and then warned me that the only things worth doing in life were those that required some sort of fear to overcome. When I didn't react, he asked if he could leave me with a final thought about how I had adapted to the environment of time. My mind was unusually empty and receptive, and I didn't protest.

"As a networker, you live from upgrade to upgrade," Credo said. "You live in the future, in a place where things are always just about to be better. Because software is never perfect, you are not allowed to like things as they are. The present is never expected to be good enough, and because of that, it is never really available to you. This is an interesting twist on the theme of 'time, the enemy.' It's not that you don't have enough time; it's that no matter how much you have you never have enough. The fact is, as you have seen, you have all the time in the universe."

"Okay, now," I blurted out, "I'm sorry, but as long as I'm going to stand here and listen to you, I need to disagree with a lot of what you are saying."

"With what in particular?" Credo asked.

"We don't have all the time in the world. In fact, we have freakin' little time."

"I'll bet you think time is money," Credo said.

"No, I don't," I told him matter-of-factly. "Time is not money because you can always make more money, but you can't make more time."

"Nice one," Credo cooed.

"In my opinion," I continued, "time is very limited and very precious. We should all see our lives like a night in Vegas and the minutes of our lives like poker chips. We can only spend them once so we better do it wisely."

"Well done," Credo said. "And it is because of that kind of nascent wisdom that I see in you the raw material for this journey."

"What journey?" I asked.

"Do you like irony?" he asked.

"I guess." I shrugged impatiently. *"What journey?"*

"God, I love irony!" Credo shrieked in delight. "Irony in full bloom is something quite beautiful to behold. Do you want to know what's ironic? Everything you said about the limitations of time is absolutely true."

"How can it be? You just got done telling me that I have all the time in the universe!"

"Which is also absolutely true!" Credo assured me. "That's the irony of it all—you have to believe what I tell you but live as though you're right and I'm wrong."

"Fugguduh!" I exclaimed. "That's not possible."

"It's absolutely essential. You need to stop thinking of life as a set of either-or equations and start seeing it as a both-and multi-dimensional continuum."

"Say what?"

"Either/or thinking makes you clever," Credo said. "Both/and thinking makes you wise. Life is a lot more like the Web than you think."

I started to protest, but Credo put up his hand to stop me. As he paused I studied a woman whose gray suit looked as if it were chiseled from stone. She was clutching her briefcase so tightly that her knuckles were white. She was mid-step, one foot a few inches above a puddle of vomit. The look of grim determination that gripped her face had worn grooves in her forehead that looked like furrows in a vacant field waiting for seed.

"Reality is much more complex than you suspect," Credo said, finally breaking the silence. "I get a headache sometimes trying to explain this stuff. Bear with me."

CHAPTER 8 The Value of Mystery
There will always be a gap between our technology and our imagination.

Credo stood up straight and taut, appearing for the first time to assume an air of dignity.

"Where would we be without irony?" he bellowed. "It's the mother's milk of the universe. Imagine a boss who actually gave you credit for the idea he stole from you. Imagine a religion that actually practiced what it preached. Imagine lovers who were rational. We all say we want these things, but if they actually came to pass there wouldn't be the requisite tension in life that good, creative thought needs to flourish. In the unspoken words of every artist who ever lived, *Give me irony or give me death*; or at least, *Give me irony or give me a regular day job that pays halfway decently.*

"There will always be a gap between our technology and our imagination," Credo continued. "How we deal with that gap defines who we are. That's the way this dimension works. I know it makes you mad that you can imagine things you can't have, or wish things that can't come true, or think things that are so far beyond your reach they feel impossible. I know that to you it seems almost cruel that life would be set up that way—and granted, there do seem to be some pretty serious design flaws in nature. I mean, why is it that everything we like to eat is bad for us? Are we supposed to be fat and insipid? And don't tell me we aren't made that way! Put a stalk of celery and a Snickers in front of a kid who has never seen either and see which one he takes. God, how I used to love to eat cheese. I can't eat it anymore. It makes me feel like someone jammed a ton of cotton in my head and then beat on it with a stick. Anyway, sorry for the digression.

"You have two choices, William. You can get mad at life because you are able to ask questions which have no answers, or you can see life as a wondrous and mysterious playground in which not knowing is half the fun. My suggestion: Embrace the mystery! There is darn little you can ever really know. In the absence of knowledge you have to see everything that motivates you as part of a belief system. Whether you believe the universe makes sense, or whether you don't; whether you believe in one good God, one mean God, no God, or a whole bureaucracy of little gods it is all an act of faith. Atheism is as much an act of faith as animal worship. Remember—*whatever you believe, that's who you are.*

"The tension between what we want to know and what we can know gives birth to ideas," Credo continued. "And the tension between what we want to do and what we can do is the source of all the creative power in the universe. We see something in our mind's eye, and then we embark on what seems like a torturous journey from concept to product. Our imaginations create the tension and the stress that come from knowing that the world of possibility is always larger than reality. We go around creating all these itches that just have to be scratched. Tension-resolution. Tension-resolution. We love it. We hate it. We can't live without it. We can't help it—we're sapes! If I had to define art in a phrase I'd say it is the result of the endless cycle of tension-resolution. And we are all artists with our time."

"So, food, clothing, shelter and belief systems?"

"Not exactly," Credo replied.

"And mystery?" I queried half-heartedly.

"Hmmm, no."

"And art?" I ventured.

"Close, but no cigar," Credo replied. "But hey, don't do this for the cigar. You shouldn't smoke, anyway. Boy, do you want to see Madison Avenue in high gear? They sold cigars to non-smokers with the finesse of politicians promising an end to crime. I haven't seen anything like it since the Europeans bought Manhattan for a box of trinkets. Anyway, don't do this for the cigar. Do it because you like the process of winning the cigar. Besides, I happen to know that you wouldn't be the least bit happy if you knew everything you think you want to know. You'd be bored out of your mind. You thrive on challenge, William. And good for you."

"It sounds like you've been talking to my mother," I said dryly.

Credo looked at me seriously. "Is your mother single, by chance, and looking for company?"

"YOU ARE NOT GOING NEAR MY MOTHER!"

The buzz of the street was suddenly swarming around me at normal speed. Overdressed people with pinched faces moved quickly around each other like same-pole magnets in a dance of mutual repulsion. According to my watch, not a moment had passed. I pointed my mind in the direction of work and was off.

CHAPTER 9 The World of Ed Tech

Before you suspect conspiracy, don't rule out incompetence.

Sleep or no sleep, there was a grouchiness that had become part of my job. It was an edgy, over-caffeinated feeling that came with babysitting technology that never worked quite as well as the manual promised or as management expected, and that seemed to be constantly playing hide-and-seek with an exhausted technical staff who was never in the mood for games. I had come to look forward to the feeling, cater to it and become allies with it, not because I wanted to but because doing so felt empowering, devotional, inevitable. Over the years I had come to believe that it helped me fight the slippery, invisible adversaries who had come to rule my life; the bugs in the system who, by life's design, were guaranteed to prevail simply because I was destined to look for them and not the other way around. I'd learned to use the feeling, allowing it to sculpt an efficient persona that kept co-workers at bay when I needed a buffer while allowing me to appear magnanimous whenever I decided to be approachable. All this changed, however, when I trained people. The feeling melted away completely like a mask that I had never intended anyone to take seriously. What was left was happy, personable and engaged.

Today I was beyond grouchy, past testy and well into the domain of downright surly. I was particularly prickly about the fact that my vow to myself to demand to be moved to the training division had somehow simply dissipated in the middle of a relentless day. I tramped across the street toward Credo's doorway, avoiding the miniature tar pits bubbling up from the pavement in the late afternoon sun. As I leaned against the wall next to Credo, I felt cold, serpentine and barely sapient, as though the only thing that separated me from my evolutionary ancestors was a razor-thin veneer of rehearsed culture.

"What does that mean?" Credo asked, watching my right hand flex, as if trying to grab on to something invisible.

"My hand is on automatic, looking for my coffee mug," I explained. "It means I could really go for a stiff cup of joe right now."

"My guess is that the last thing you need right now is more coffee. Bad day?"

"Fugguduh!" I exclaimed. The rest spilled out in one long, blistering exhale with my cheeks turning bright red and my arms

flapping like the wings of an angry bird. "One of the suits thought he
would help me out last night by coming in and adding some new
computers to the network. In so doing he managed to duplicate IP
addresses, which means that everyone who tried to use the Net was
told that their address didn't exist, which wasn't true, but the computer told them that because the error messages computers give are so
incredibly stupid that's what they say instead of something meaningful, like—*I'm sorry. You cannot access the Internet this morning
because some idiot suit came in last night trying to impress his 10-
year-old and screwed up everything so royally that the corporation
lost a few million that will get blamed on Networking Control.* Now
there's an error message that would actually be helpful. Anyway, the
rest is tech talk I won't bore you with."

"I speak the language. IP address conflicts? Unspecified domain
name server? Talk to me."

"Both," I said, more than a little surprised by his fluency with
tech talk. "Look, I appreciate your concern, and I'm impressed you
understand these things as well as you do. But I'm not having a
problem with you. It's them freakin' uppity VIPs! What I would give
sometimes for them to know just a little bit about what I do, or at least
to quit ganging up on me and just let me do what they pay me to do! I
suppose if you want to be dumb as a post, that's your right, but don't
subject me to it! We have laws about second-hand smoke. For
freakin' sake, we ought to have them about second-hand stupidity!"

"VIPs?" Credo asked.

"VIPs: Very Ignorant People, Veritable Idiots on Parade, Vermin
Insulting Protoplasm, Vile Insipid Pukemongers. It's code for the
traders and the raiders and everyone who makes the real money at
BADI. On a good day I refer to them as managers. On a typically
crappy day I call them 'suits.' And on a really bad day they are VIPs.
And fugguduh, today was a really bad day! They don't understand
nuthin' and they like it that way. If they had any inkling about how
the Internet works, if they had the slightest idea of what they put me
through in an average day, they'd have to be more understanding of
the problems I deal with. So they purposely conspire to know as little
as possible to justify their edge. You should hear 'em when they can't
get on the Web. Fugguduh! What a bunch of miserable, undeserving,
affluent babies!"

I paused, exhaled and then slowly swelled with embarrassment until I felt like a balloon ready to pop.

"I sound like one of them, don't I?" I finally said, breaking the silence with a whisper. "I'm no better than one of them, am I?"

"That's the tragedy of having enemies. Sooner or later you become just like them. Having enemies is like living in a video game. Enemies have one motivation in the world—to get you. Having enemies takes a complex life and turns it into formula TV just to make things more manageable. That's why most people prefer a life with enemies—it is simply easier to understand than a life without them. But it's a cop-out and no way to pursue a real education. My advice? It's best to be the water that flows around the rock rather than the water that tries to move the rock. Practice psychic Aikido. As they come at you, just step aside. They will fall under their own weight. And focus on who *you* are. The mirror is your friend. You might begin by calling them something less evil. How about just calling them *sapes*?"

It was too much good information all at once. Besides, I was still too busy cultivating my embarrassment to fully appreciate what Credo was saying. "I hate what they have turned me into," I said.

"Now, now, William. Best to figure out what is wrong with yourself first—it gives you a tactical advantage. Look in the mirror first, and then at the enemy advancing toward you. Besides, I think you are missing the bigger point here. Remember this always: *Before you suspect conspiracy, don't rule out incompetence.* It sounds to me as if you are dealing with massive incompetence. You need to meet a friend of mine."

"Oh, here we go again," I said with deep resignation. "More flying lawn chairs? Actually, taking a spin in a lawn chair sounds pretty good right about now."

"Not Mr. Big!" Credo cried. "You need to meet another friend of mine, Ed Tech. Ed knows all about teaching technology. It is truly an art form. And Ed's an artist. But you know something? You need a change of clothing before you go: dark, tight clothes produce dark, tight thoughts, know what I mean? *As we are outside, so we are inside*—or is it the other way around?"

I tried not to trip over the fact that a man dressed in rags was telling me how to improve my wardrobe as I pushed forward.

"Credo, I admit my clothes are a bit moody. But I'm really not up for a change or to meet anyone new right now. I'm sure Ed is a great guy, but-"

"Who said Ed was a guy, cave man?" The last thing I heard before my mind went blank was Credo saying, "Don't worry. This won't take any time at all."

When my mind cleared, I realized I was sitting in an old-fashioned classroom with hard wooden desks and high ceilings. I was dressed in colorful, loose fit clothing, and my body felt exquisitely comfortable, like it was breathing spaciously for the first time in years. I saw before me a tall, lean woman in her late fifties with emerald-green eyes and red hair tucked into a no-nonsense bun. She was dressed perfectly in a blue suit and black stockings and pumps. She held a notebook in one hand and a remote control in the other. Behind her was a large rectangular object with a black border and a dull, luminescent glow that reminded me vaguely of a projection screen. She set the remote control on her desk and extended her hand to me in a way that felt familiar and comforting.

As I touched her hand, I realized that on some visceral, transcendent level the woman was Miss Phelps, my first- and second-grade teacher—not because she looked anything like Miss Phelps, but because she *felt* like Miss Phelps, the way a stranger in a dream can assume the essence of someone familiar.

As I felt the spirit of Miss Phelps envelop me, a cavalcade of sensations brought me to the edge of tears. I could feel the excitement of rushing to school, knowing that I would spend another day in Miss Phelps' classroom listening to her animated reading voice and making pirate hats from thick green construction paper. I could see Miss Phelps' eyes twinkling in the morning light and feel the brush of her blue-and-white-checkered gingham dress against my skin as she gave me a hug when I entered her classroom. I could feel the joy when she visited my parents just to tell them how much she enjoyed my enthusiasm for dinosaurs, spelling and identifying bird songs. I could feel her intolerance of meanness. I could see it as a gray cloud that hovered over the classroom whenever she scolded a child for being rude or nasty to a classmate. She would not hesitate to send someone to the principal's office or schedule a meeting with parents if she suspected for one moment that one child had been deliberately hurtful to another.

Long after second grade was over, Miss Phelps continued to invite me to her house for grilled hot dogs and homemade potato salad and to lend me hardcover books from her private library. Whenever I visited my home-town I would go to see her just to walk through her library, fill my nostrils with the musty odor of old books, run my hands over them like someone reading Braille and listen to her explain the intimate lives of her favorite authors as though she had counseled each one through their personal tragedies. As I gazed at the woman before me, I felt eternally 6-years-old and caught in the spell of a teacher who celebrated me as one who loved to learn whatever the world had to teach me. For a brief moment I felt vibrant and miraculous again as my cynicism left me and naiveté, its mutually exclusive counterpart, replenished me like air whooshing into a vacuum. It felt good to trust again.

"I'm Edwina," she said, shaking my hand vigorously. "Edwina Tech. Welcome. Do you know why I have enjoyed my life so much as a technology teacher?"

"No," I said in a small voice, shaking my head.

"Because I don't feel threatened. Do you know why I don't feel threatened, William?"

I shook my head again.

"Because of the three rules of living and learning with technology. Do you know what they are?"

I didn't bother to shake my head.

"Rule Number One: Don't be afraid of anyone who knows more than you do, especially if they are young enough to be your grandchild. Here, let's take a good look at Rule Number One. We are going to revisit a past experience of yours that could have taught you a great deal more than it did, had you allowed it to. The lesson here is *letting go and opening up*. It is *commanding authority rather than demanding authority*. It is *knowing how and when to be a student*. Let's revisit an experience of yours that was trying to teach you this. Unfortunately, you weren't being a very good student at the time. Do you remember this?"

Edwina snapped her fingers. In an instant I was standing at a podium in a large hall tapping nervously on the computer next to me. Sweat was seeping between my shirt and skin as I faced a sea of stone faces impatiently waiting for an image of the BADI Internet home page to appear on the blank 12-by-8 foot screen behind me.

Suddenly the details of the experience were very vivid. I remembered—it was BADI's Family Day. The hall was stuffed with employees and their families, and it was my turn to do the dog-and-pony show to entertain the troops. The suits didn't care what I did, just as long as their kids went home with a head of full of gee-whiz glitz and their spouses were convinced that they actually worked for a living. I figured I would take the audience out on the Net for a little joy ride, but the overhead projection unit wasn't cooperating. The image on my computer screen looked fine and the overhead unit appeared to be functioning normally, but somehow the signal between the two was lost, no doubt siphoned off into the mythical land that my technician friends and I referred to as *the big byte bucket in the sky.*

I stood at the microphone trying to remember a joke when I realized I didn't know any jokes. I remembered thinking that all of the rich-and-successful suits in my office knew a lot of jokes and wondered whether there was a relationship between the two.

"Just a moment, folks," I said, stalling, waiting for a miracle, swimming in sweat.

"Mr. Tell," squeaked a tiny voice in the front row. I looked down to see a little girl in pigtails and thick glasses trying to get my attention.

"Miss," I whispered, "I hate to be rude but I am really busy right now, so if you could…"

"Mr. Tell," she interrupted, "if you hold down the control key, and then press shift and escape, the overhead program will recycle and it will come up just fine. That's if you have enough RAM. Do you at least have 128 megabytes?"

I told her I thought I did. She told me she always had a list of the technical specifications handy whenever she did a demonstration. How admirable, I managed to tell her without showing any anger.

Then she asked me if I had upgraded to Overhead System 10.1. I told her I thought so. She explained that without the new upgrade the overhead gets confused at the system fork between communication ports, re-routing the signal back into the program in an endless loop. I thanked her quietly and went back to work.

A tug of war strained in my solar plexus with glacial, megaton force. It was not bad enough that I was dying on stage in front of everyone who was important to my career; to make matters worse, a little girl was telling me how to run my computer—and she might

actually know more than I did! I could not give up that much control
to a little girl, especially in public! It was all too much. I was the paid
expert. I was the adult. I would never do this to Miss Phelps, so I
was not going to let this little girl do it to me. Period. It was for the
girl's own good.

"Don't you know where the control, shift and escape keys are,
Mr. Tell?" the little girl asked. "Here, I can show you."

"No!" I nearly screamed. "I mean, 'Yes, I know where they
are.'"

"Then why don't you press them?" she asked insistently.

I looked at the sea of stone faces. The children were starting to
squirm while the adults began to chatter. A few people in the back
left, muttering their disappointment loudly enough for me to hear. I
looked over at the little girl, back at the stone faces, and then up at the
empty projection screen. I pressed control-shift-escape. The computer
screen blinked off and on, and a moment later an image of BADI's
home page was crystal-clear and large enough to see from thirty-
yards-away.

"Ooo," the crowd cooed.

"Uhm, thank you, uhm," I mumbled. "What's your name?" I
asked the girl.

"Daisy Edwards," she replied.

"Let's give a round of applause to Daisy Edwards, ladies and
gentlemen," I managed to say despite feeling utterly conquered.

I was back in Edwina Tech's classroom, shaking my head and
thinking that I couldn't take all this time bouncing. Edwina looked at
me with concern and apologized, noting that I appeared to have jet
lag. She announced that I had had enough time travel for a while, but
that was fine because there was plenty to do right here.

Here? I thought to myself. *And where would that be?*

"Isn't the use of examples helpful in illustrating a point?" Edwina
asked. "Remember that when you teach. I just love working with the
little ones! I have learned as much from a savvy 10-year-old as I have
from any university professor. If you are a teacher who wants to use
technology in your classroom, then you need to let go of all the
control you are used to having. You will have to because you will
find that you don't know more than your students anymore! So, what
do you do with your pupils? Deputize them! You can still be sheriff,
but give them responsibilities. Have them help other students. Make

them a part of your community of learners. They love it! You, in turn, become the guide on the side rather than the sage on the stage. You get to shape them more through your wisdom than your knowledge. You get to help develop their character as well as their skills. It's fun and you learn a lot, too! William, remember this always: *The best learners make the best teachers.* You will note I said 'learners,' not 'students.' You understand the difference, don't you?"

"Yes, ma'am," I replied.

"The upshot is this," Edwina said. "If you are a teacher and find you no longer like learning, then please do the children of the world a favor and leave the teaching profession. Now then, let's move on to Rule Number Two.

"Rule Number Two: Practice Zen and the art of living with technology. In a phrase that boils down to *don't get attached.* Whatever is on your desk today will be gone tomorrow. While it is here, let it talk to you. Learn what it has to say. Push its buttons, read the messages it provides and, if absolutely necessary, read a manual now and then. But then say good-bye to your technology, thank it for what you have learned, and do your best to transfer what it has taught you to the new technology that inevitably waits for you just around the corner. Information comes and goes so quickly these days that you need the right attitude toward learning to stay on top of things. You need to feel comfortable learning on a continual basis. Attitude has become aptitude. Do you understand?"

I nodded my head. "And Rule Number Three?"

"What do you think? *Have fun!!* If you aren't having fun most of the time then something is wrong. Make sense? Good! I can tell we are going to have a wonderful day, you and I! There is nothing like learning something new to reacquaint yourself with the essence of life. So, where shall we begin? Credo told me about your problems at work, so let's start there."

"He did?" I said angrily. "That mangy old street urchin. Isn't there any privacy around here? Virtual or not, he's got no right telling everyone about my personal life!"

Edwina started tapping her foot impatiently. "Now William, while passion is quite acceptable in my classroom, name-calling is not. I understand you had a hard time in school because your peers made fun of your name—children can be very mean sometimes. But we need to learn how to redirect that negativity into something more positive."

"I am very positive," I told her defiantly. "I'm positive a bunch of suits ruined my network and blamed me for it!"

"As Credo suggested, you are dealing with people who have a knowledge deficit. This can be corrected. You just need a few skills to help bring them along. Today's lesson will deal with some of the basic rules of effective teaching. They are, in many ways, no different than the basic rules of learning. Teaching and learning are two ends of the same continuum. Which end you emphasize just depends on your role in any given situation and on where you sit on the continuum. The best educators are those who understand that there are always going to be students who know more than they know and less than they know. The best educators are those who are able to assume whatever role is appropriate without experiencing cognitive dissonance."

"You mean ego meltdown," I said.

"If you prefer," she said. "But your administrators still need your help."

"But the suits are lousy students," I said. "Kids are one thing. But the ossified mind of an adult with a control issue and an inflated sense of self-importance is something entirely different."

"Let's assume that your administrators are having a particularly good day and have come to you and said, 'William, we really want to understand the basics of the Web, especially as it relates to adding new computers to our network and the problems we experienced this week.'"

"God bless you, Ms. Tech, but that is about as likely as one of them saying, 'William, I'd like to give you a million dollar bonus this month just to make you happy. And while you're at it, marry my daughter and take my Porsche off my hands, would you?' You're a dreamer, Ms. Tech."

"Thank you," she said.

I looked away, embarrassed for reasons I could not explain, revisiting a feeling that I had first experienced long ago before I had any mastery of language, when dreams directed reality and not the other way around.

"William Tell, you weren't always this negative. Indulge me," she said, smiling, bringing me back from the edge of a personal abyss of dissatisfaction that had become too familiar.

"Sorry," I said. "Please continue."

"Thank you. First, are we agreed that most people use the terms *the Internet* and *the Net* synonymously?"

"Yes. I don't have a problem with that."

"Neither do I. And would you also agree that they use the terms 'the Internet' and 'the Web' interchangeably?"

"Yes, I would," I replied, "and I do have a problem with *that*. It's more accurate to say that the Web is a subset of the Internet. The Internet consists of all the computers in the world that are connected to each other, while the Web consists of just those computers or parts of computers that you reach using a browser, such as Netscape or Explorer. But I suppose for the average person we're splitting hairs. Most people don't know that and it wouldn't change their lives if they did."

"Agreed," Edwina said. "It's best to begin with people's common misunderstanding and correct it later. So, the goal is to explain the Web in basic terms so that your administrators can understand what happened at the office today. But first, let's go over some of the rules of good teaching."

CHAPTER 10 Teaching Rulz

The science of teaching is knowing a number of instructional methodologies, while the art of teaching is knowing when to use which.

I found myself at a wooden desk, the clean white pages of my spiral notebook gleaming in the sunlight, a black pen in my right hand, poised and ready to take notes. The discomfort of the hard, polished seat forced my attention outward, helping me to concentrate on what Edwina Tech was saying.

"Rule Number One: Begin at your students' beginning, not yours. A good example is the one we just discussed—not trifling about the difference between the Net and the Web. It is better to address any problems that arise from their difference later on during a more teachable moment and in a context that makes more sense to the learner."

As she spoke, the rule appeared on the screen behind her in large colorful letters following her voice like a perfect dance partner. However, her explanation of the rule did not appear.

"How did you do that?" I gasped, my voice rising sharply as I stood up.

"It is controlled by my voice."

"Yes, but why doesn't it print everything you say?"

"It's sensitive to my tone of voice," Edwina replied. "That way I can limit what appears. The sound bite, the bullet, the key phrase that I hope will help stimulate students' recall at a later time, goes on the screen. The detailed explanation you leave to your students to represent for themselves in ways that make sense to them, whether it is by taking notes, drawing pictures, creating outlines or even making recordings. My approach allows the teacher to strike a balance between creating a common set of goals, which is necessary for group cohesion, while allowing each student to individualize what they learn. My approach also strikes a balance between the need for students to be both active listeners *and* active learners. I give them a starting point, but they must fill in the blanks. There is no magic formula to achieve these balances. You simply have to pay as much attention to your students as you want them to pay to you. This machine is based on the principle of balance. I developed it last year."

"But I predicted it!" bellowed Credo. His voice sounded hollow and metallic, as though he were talking through the wrong end of a megaphone. I looked around but couldn't see him anywhere.

"If you are going to watch," Edwina admonished Credo, "then behave. You are such a child, sometimes."

"Oh, great!" I said. "And he's one of my teachers?"

Edwina stared at me the way Miss Phelps would to command respect, her chin dropping toward her chest, her entire body perfectly still, a stern look holding my attention in a vise grip.

"You need a child right now," Edwina said. "It is the best thing for you. Credo's a bit insecure, but otherwise a very good mentor. Somewhere inside you lurks a child ready to be tamed to do an adult's work. You lost it—or rather, temporarily mislaid it—when you went to work at such a young age. Credo and all the rest of us are going to help you find it. Understanding the basic rules of teaching is an important step for you. All of this will help you immensely when the Big Day comes."

"What big day?" I exclaimed. "What big day?! Will someone please tell me what this big day is all about? I mean should I be storing canned vegetables and magazines in my basement? Should I build a bomb shelter in the back yard? Will I need lead clothing? Is there a particular religion I should join? Somebody help me out here!"

"Not now," Edwina told me, shaking her head. "It's not time."

"Well for god's sake, when is it freakin' time?"

A stillness settled upon us that made me feel like I had wounded Miss Phelps. A shiver ran through my body. Goose bumps rose and poured over my arms. I felt lost, embarrassed and deeply resentful of my own impatience.

"William," Edwina began softly, "imagine Miss Phelps trying to teach you fractions before she taught you arithmetic. I am trying to help you. Please let me. It's just as important to be a good student as it is to be a good teacher. A good teacher waits for the teachable moment. We will tell you everything you need to know when the right moment arrives. But for now, back to work. Now please sit down."

Her gentle voice made me feel like a pliable student again. I sat down and looked up at the voice-activated screen.

"What do you call it?" I asked her, pointing to the screen.

"An Inflector," Edwina said. "Besides discerning voice inflection, it also adjusts the size of the print to fit the size of the room, ensuring that people far away can see it. The color of the print and the screen background also adjust to the room, based on the environment the screen senses. Everything is optimized for maximum learning."

"It's amazing!" I couldn't help saying. "Who is making them? Are you selling them? What are the investment opportunities?"

"William Tell, this has nothing to do with money. Not here. Not in this dimension. What would Miss Phelps say? Now, let's return to Rule Number One, which is?"

"Begin at your student's beginning, not yours," I recited dutifully.

"Wonderful, William! When you are teaching something new, particularly to adults who quite often feel embarrassed and helpless by what they don't know, you need to begin where they are. Come to them; don't make them come to you. The goal is for them to join you in understanding what you understand, not for you to impress them with what you know. Look at it this way: You are having a knowledge party and you would like them to come. Everyone brings something to the knowledge party. Everyone knows something that a community of learners could benefit from. Sometimes all some people bring is a lack of knowledge, but that's okay too."

I told her that described most of management at BADI. They were the kind of people who didn't bring anything to the office potluck but expected everyone else to.

"Be kind, William. Someday it will be you who brings a knowledge deficit to the knowledge party. Feed them now, and they will feed you later. Just make sure you bring an openness to learning; doing so is always a valuable contribution. Let's continue.

"Rule Number Two: Know your audience. This is a variation of Rule One. Pre-testing is the best method, but you can't always do that. So, take your best guess. The only thing worse than not teaching someone something they need to know is wasting someone's time by teaching them something they already know. To help me focus, I like to think in terms of talking to someone I know who represents a typical member of the audience. I usually find it best to imagine that I am trying to explain things to my mother."

"Gotcha," I said enthusiastically as I committed a flurry of writing to my notebook.

"Rule Number Three: Use a metaphor that your audience can relate to. To paraphrase Robert Frost, a metaphor involves explaining this in terms of that. This is exactly what you want to do—explain something new in terms of something familiar. Compare and contrast the subjects of your metaphor, and explain how they are the same and how they are different. For example, an attic is a hard drive—the bigger they get, the less likely you are to throw anything out."

I looked up at her and continued her metaphor. "Therefore it is essential that you keep them both clear of clutter and well catalogued."

"Excellent!" Edwina said. "Keep going."

"Your computer maintains a list of files on your hard drive," I continued. "This is called a directory and serves the purpose of keeping a list of the contents of your attic. Every now and then it is a good idea to go through the list and see what you don't need. However, unlike the things in your attic, you won't find anything you can sell at a garage sale."

"Excellent. You are a natural, William! Comparing and contrasting the new with the familiar allows your students to have one foot on a solid knowledge foundation while they venture into unknown territory. I will tell you something that I learned long ago, William. Watch the metaphors that people use: They reveal who they are without their knowing it."

"Yes, ma'am," I said.

"Rule Number Four: Tell a story. Use images to paint a picture in their minds. People don't often remember a lecture. But they *do* remember a story. Make your audience the hero of the story. Remember that you are not only helping them correct a learning deficit, you are helping them overcome their fear of change.

"Rule Number Five: Involve your students in their own learning. You know the Chinese proverb: 'Tell me and I forget, show me and I remember, involve me and I understand.' It's so true! So, get your students involved. Get them to personalize their experience. Let them walk away with something that is meaningful to them, whether it is a list of web sites, a handout that make sense to them, or one good idea. Make them masters of their own experience."

CHAPTER 11 A Measure of Success

When the instrument of measurement dictates what is important, the measurement becomes the message.

"Now on a practical level," Edwina continued, "here are a few pointers.

"Rule Number Six: Honor the media. If you are going to use media, use them well. Have you ever read bad writing or seen a video clip that was edited badly or watched a movie that used the wrong music? What happens? You stumble on the presentation, which keeps you from getting to the content. The medium should be transparent. You should be able to pass through it as if it weren't there. Pay particular attention to words and how you use them. Separate words, whether words you write or speak, into two parts: the sound bite and the explanation, as I explained earlier. I know that sound bites are getting a lot of bad press these days, but they can be remembered easily and can be used to recall more detailed kinds of information that otherwise escapes the conscious mind. That is why I developed 'The Inflector.' It allows me to separate the main points I wish to make from their accompanying explanation."

Edwina stopped, as though coming to an abrupt halt in her thinking, and stared at me. "Do you know what really makes me mad?"

I looked up fearfully. "What, Ms. Tech?"

"The damn school system is stuck on the 3 Rs."

I gasped. Miss Phelps would have never said 'damn.'

"Well, there are 4 Rs now," Edwina continued. "Reading, 'riting, 'rithmetic and aRt. For god's sake, isn't it obvious? In a multimedia world we are asking students to create web pages instead of term papers, yet where are they getting the skills to paint, draw, make movies, write songs and to do everything you need to do to honor the media? Art isn't just for sensitive types who never expect to eat well or live anywhere but on the fringes of society. It's for everyone!"

Ms. Tech was shaking a little. "Forgive me. We'll talk more about this later. For now we must move on to the most important rule of all, Rule Number Seven: Appeal to as many senses, as many ways of learning and as many intelligences as possible. You've read Howard Gardner, I hope?"

Like the experiences of the near dead who supposedly see their entire lives in a split second, my life flashed before me. I observed myself making poor choices compounded by previous poor choices about how to spend my minutes, a "woulda, coulda, shoulda" movie of my life. Too much time at work. Too many videos. Too much fretting about nothing. Too much deliberate unawareness. If only I had taken my own advice and seen my minutes as 'poker chips that can only be used once'. I was feeling far less educated than I ought to be. No, I finally managed to admit; I had not read Howard Gardner.

"Oh William, you must! You must! He finally legitimized something that good teachers have known all along. We have many intelligences, many ways to be smart, many ways to learn. He has found eight, and I suspect he will find more. Most important, we now understand that stupidity and failure are often simply cultural predispositions. Our measures of intelligence measure our methods of measurement as much as anything else. Well-designed technology can amplify many of our intelligences that have been dormant for so long. After our educational institutions accept the notion of multiple intelligences, they will tackle something even more important: multiple sensory technology. Think about it—how many senses do we transmit on the Web? Two. This is far from a complete experience. Some day we will transmit all five. As teachers we will need to understand the best way to do that. All of this is inevitable and very exciting, but it is a long way around the barn."

"What do you mean?" I asked.

Edwina Tech became pensive, even a bit subdued. "Some day, centuries from now, after we have taxed our cleverness to the hilt building technology that can capture and send all the sensory information we want to, we will rediscover the most powerful sense of all: imagination. It costs nothing, everyone has one, and upgrades are free. Everyone takes pride in what they imagine because it is theirs. We will find the same thing about ideas that we have discovered about genetics: Diversity helps everyone to survive. The more powerfully technology compels us to transmit single ideas to masses of people, like network television, the more it limits our thinking and endangers our ability to imagine solutions to problems."

"Why don't we just sidestep a few centuries of research and development and cut to the chase?" I asked. "Why not just begin developing our imaginations right now?"

"It's not the path we are on; it is not the process we have embraced. Besides, a few centuries are nothing—literally. Eventually, we will get there. That's all that is important. In any event, regardless of the future, I want you to learn how to stimulate your own imagination before you begin projecting it into the minds of others. Here, let me show you how. Ready?"

I knew there was no such thing as being ready anymore, but I nodded anyway.

"Do you want to know something else that makes me madder than a wet hen?" Edwina asked.

My mind was suddenly overtaken with the image of a hen running around in circles in an open field, cackling fiercely as it tried to escape a downpour. Its feathers were pasted to its squat little body, making it look as if it were wrapped in a skin-tight leisure suit. I could feel the rain splash on my arms as the scent of damp earth engulfed me.

"Do you know what really frosts my mug?" Edwina asked.

I was inside an empty 10-foot frosted beer stein, my nails hissing and screeching as I clawed at the glass trying to get out. As I stood shivering and watching my breath blur the glass, I could suddenly feel the hen pecking at my feet. I danced in place wildly, partly to avoid the angry hen, partly to try to stay warm. The pungent odor of damp bird was so nauseating I started to swoon.

"You know what really gets my knickers in a knot?" Edwina asked.

My underwear lifted into a classic wedgie, the label halfway up my back, the front opening straddling my navel. I could feel the fabric strain as it pulled painfully at my groin. The sound of the hen pecking in the beer stein grew louder and more frantic. The glass was so clouded over from my breath that life on the other side of it appeared hazy, surreal. I was so overwhelmed by the images parading through my mind that Ms. Tech had to snap her fingers repeatedly to get my attention. I shook my head as I refocused and suffered an embarrassment so intense at the thought of Ms. Tech seeing me in my underwear that I started to choke. She touched my shoulder and a calm settled on me like fairy dust.

"See how powerful imagination is?" she asked. "And yours is richly multi-sensory. You are indeed a natural."

I was unable to speak, so she resumed spiritedly. "So, do you know what makes me as mad as a wet hen? How we measure success in school. Honestly! We still use standardized tests that appeal to a few intelligences. Have we learned nothing? Standards are a filter.

They are an overreaction to overpopulation. When you want to separate people for reasons of employment or social status, throw a filter at them—some are bound not to make it through. We are victims of how we measure ourselves."

"Exactly," Credo piped up from an invisible perch somewhere beyond the room. "Like the way you judge me to be a slob because of my clothes."

"But you are a slob," I said, twirling around, trying to catch a glimpse of him. "Fugguduh, Credo. Show yourself!"

"According to who?" Credo asked, appearing at my side in his traditional street garb.

"According to *whom*," Edwina corrected him.

"Who are you to judge me?" Credo continued as he looked directly into my eyes. "My clothes aren't the issue. The real issue is your presumption in using a faulty system of measurement. Besides, living on the street puts a dent in your wardrobe budget."

"Anyone who can stop time can find himself a nice pair of pants," I insisted.

"*A nice pair of pants*?" Credo asked. "I defy you to define that."

"You know freakin' well what I mean," I said. "Like when your teacher tells you to wear a nice pair of pants for the Christmas pageant, or your parents tell you that you are going to a funeral and you need to wear something nice. Nothing extraordinary, nothing expensive, just something that doesn't remind us of the bottom of a compost bin. You know—*nice*."

"None of this is the point," Credo said. "How I dress should have no impact on your life whatsoever. If you felt good about yourself then you wouldn't care what I looked like. It is your insecurity about yourself that makes you judge me. It is the coward's approach to self-improvement: Blame everyone around you for making you feel uncomfortable. Turn your focus inward, my friend, where it belongs."

"I feel fine about who I am!" I insisted. "And if you want to rationalize being a slob by blaming it on my lack of personal development, then go right ahead! Ms. Tech, can I have a new mentor, or could you at least get Credo a fashion consultant?"

Out of the corner of my eye I had been watching Edwina. She was amused, shifting her attention between us like a spectator at a tennis match. Finally she broke into our volley, the skilled teacher trying to get a discussion back on track.

"All the school-reform stuff is a thinly veiled debate about measurement," she began, "which is society's way of deciding what is important. If you want to know what a society values, look at the forms of measurement it uses. On the one hand, everyone complains that schools are not preparing people for the real world. On the other hand, they say let's have standardized testing! One does not address the other, and thus people are confused. Beware—the measurement can become the message. We become the victim rather than the lord of our measurement when it dictates what is important. You only fail as much as your standards tell you that you do."

"So are we supposed to lower our standards?" I asked in a burst of conservatism that I would have a hard time explaining to myself later as anything except part of a purging process.

"No," she replied. "We need to change them."

"May I make a prediction?" Credo interrupted.

"Do we have a choice?" I asked.

"Quickly, Credo," Edwina said. "William is in the middle of a teachable moment." Edwina turned to me and said earnestly, "Teachable moments are those small, magical moments in which you can change the world one person at a time. Learn to recognize them, William."

"Okay," Credo said. "I'll make this quick. Back to projecting more than two senses on the Web. Long term, the predominant sense that will be used to facilitate learning and stimulate recall will be smell. I won't say any more than that."

"You may have something to fear in a world in which the sense of smell predominates," I said.

"Thank you for sharing, Credo," Edwina said.

"And thank you for not saying any more than that," I said.

"You see, William?" Edwina said. "We all have something to be thankful for."

CHAPTER 12 Untangling the World Wide Web
The first step in getting an education is not knowing something you want to learn.

"All right, William," Edwina continued. "Back to the task at hand: explaining the Web to the uninitiated. We have our rules of good teaching, correct?"

"Yes ma'am, we do," I said confidently.

"Good. Then why don't you articulate them for me?"

"Is this a pop quiz?" I asked, a little disappointed.

"You may call it a 'check for knowledge,' if that helps make it more palatable," she replied.

I closed my eyes and began in a monotone. Edwina stopped me.

"I am going to give you some advice passed on to me by a wonderful piano teacher: Practice every scale as though you were playing a beautiful song. Do you understand the meaning of that metaphor?"

"Yes, ma'am."

"Good. And no expounding on the rules of teaching at this point. Just say them with fervor, with a sense of music and with your eyes wide open."

With conviction in my voice, I held forth:

"Rule Number One: Begin at your students' beginning, not yours."

"Most excellent," Edwina said proudly. "Continue."

"Rule Number Two: Know your audience.

"Rule Number Three: Use metaphors that your audience can relate to.

"Rule Number Four: Tell a story.

"Rule Number Five: Involve your students in their own learning.

"Rule Number Six: Honor the media.

"Rule Number Seven: Appeal to as many senses, as many ways of learning and as many intelligences as possible."

"Well done," Edwina said. "In the days to come, you will be able to demonstrate your understanding of them. But for now it is just important that you know what they are. Now, I am going to model the process for you that I use for teaching technology, and then it will be your turn. Do you understand? Now, close your eyes."

"Before we continue, let's remind ourselves of the vision that is driving our learning need: You need to teach your administrators the skills they need to help them understand how to be more positive and productive users of the technology at work."

"That's a very nice way to put it," I conceded.

"Now," Edwina continued, "I am going to model for you the process I use for teaching technology, and then it will be your turn. Do you understand? Now, close your eyes."

I relaxed my body and let my eyelids fall.

"First, who is your representative audience member?" Edwina asked.

"My mother," I said.

"Me too! Okay, splendid," Edwina encouraged. "Task number one is to get your mother to visualize 'the World Wide Web.' We need a metaphor that is going to resonate with her."

"A baby's brain!" I exclaimed. "I was in a chat group the other day where someone was explaining how the Net is a lot like a baby's brain because it is in its primary stages of wiring, creating habits and personality traits that we may have to live with for a long time. But the baby is still free to develop in so many different mutually exclusive ways."

I opened my eyes to see Edwina looking at me a little disappointedly.

"It's a good image," she said. "And an important one. But do you think your mother would relate to that?"

"I'm trying to imagine your mother's bridge club visualizing a gooey gob of tissue and nerve endings," Credo said, once again invisible.

I flared, demanding to know how he knew about my mother's bridge club, warning him once again to stay away from her. Besides, I added, my mother loves babies.

"Enough!" Edwina commanded. "Remember, William, an insecure teacher tries to impress his students with how much he knows. A confident teacher focuses on speaking in images his students can understand. Put your students first. We need an image that your mother, and those she represents, can relate to. Let's try again. How do we visualize the Web? How do we get her to see the big picture? Now, close your eyes."

"Visualize the whole planet," I responded immediately, my arms opening into a circle as if I were holding a big beach ball, while my eyes were clamped shut.

"Yes! There's our metaphor—the Earth. And what image of our planet do you think your mother could relate to?"

"The rotating Earth at the beginning of the soap opera, 'As The World Spins,'" I suggested. "She hasn't missed that show since what's-his-name shot his estranged wife because she was having an affair with the gynecologist who later overdosed on tranquilizers before he could confess to stealing her dog and giving it to that other woman he was having an affair with who needed it for some bizarre religious practice."

"Hmmm," Edwina said, rubbing her chin. "That might work for your mother's bridge club, but it might be a little esoteric for the administrators at your company. How about the picture of the earth taken from the moon that has become so popular?"

"Yes!" I exclaimed, my eyes still closed. "My mother would love that."

"Mine too," said Edwina. "Besides being an image that suits our purpose wonderfully, it is also a rich McLuhanistic reminder that the global village extends as far as our electronic nervous system will take us. So, armed with this metaphor, we turn to our audience and say: imagine you are standing on the moon, looking at the Earth as if you were an astronaut, enjoying the majesty of the blue-and-white sphere floating in space that we all call home. You see it as the single environment that it is, in which everything flows into and connects with everything else—the clouds, the water, even the land, above and below the oceans.

"Now, we put on special glasses that allow us to see all the electronic communication paths that we have created that make up the international telephone system. These glasses let you see with great clarity the big mish-mash of satellites and microwaves, telephone wires, cable, fiber optics and all those things I don't really understand, which wrap the Earth like a blanket. The Earth looks like a big ball of yarn, doesn't it?"

"Uh huh," I said, mesmerized by the images I was painting in my mind.

"Like the clouds and the water," Edwina continued, "the Web is connected throughout the planet. Now, see all those little black dots in the ball of string that look like little knots? The engineers call them nodes; we call them telephones."

"Uh huh," I said, pressing my eyes shut a little harder.

"Now, to understand what the Web is, in your mind's eye reach into the ball of yarn, yank out all the phones and replace them with computers, and voilá! You have the Web! That's all it is. Millions of computers all over the world hooked together using the international phone system. If we see the big ball of yarn as the Web, then each knot—or computer—is a web site."

Edwina waited a minute. "How did I do?"

"Good, good," I said quietly as I opened my eyes. "Are we going to worry about the fact that people can get on the Web using their cable TV systems, little dishes they can attach to your house, and a bunch of other ways, too?"

"Not for now," Edwina said. "One step at a time, and everyone takes their next step."

I blinked a few times. "My mom would love the image of the Earth," I said. "But my boss is now tapping his foot nervously, checking his watch and asking himself why we are telling him this when he could be putting together a leveraged buyout of some unsuspecting Third-World company."

"You're indulging me, remember?" Edwina said. "We'll work on how to put him in a learning mood another time. But for now, remember that he asked you to do this.

"Now that we have the holistic view, William, let's engage in a little reductionism so we can better grasp the whole by comprehending its parts. It's the Western Way. Do you understand what I mean by this?"

"Hmmm."

Edwina looked at me intently.

"Hmmm," I repeated.

"William Tell," Edwina admonished in the stilted meter of Miss Phelps when she was concerned a student was not taking advantage of a learning opportunity. "The first step toward getting an education is being able to admit that you don't know something you want to know. Tension-resolution, remember? If you can't admit when you don't know something you will never learn anything. No tension, no resolution. Make your life a work of art. *At the heart of all art is tension-resolution.*"

I finally admitted that I didn't understand what she had just said.

"Reductionism takes things apart so we can understand them in terms of their elements," she explained. "Physics, chemistry, even art and psychology, 'reduces' things to elementary units of matter or experience so we can understand things on a micro scale, cell by cell, atom by atom, event by event, feeling by feeling. The Easterners think we're crazy to do this sort of thing."

"The Easterners?"

"Hindus, Buddhists, those for whom 'everything is one'. To them the whole can never be separated into parts because the whole has no parts. If it had parts, it wouldn't be whole."

"You have to admit," Credo said, his voice wafting in from nowhere again, "their logic is pretty tight. Hey, do you know what the Zen master said to the hot dog vendor? 'Make me one with everything.' Get it?" He was in hysterics. "God I love that one. I mean, talk about East meeting West!"

"Ignore him," Edwina commanded me. "So, we got the big picture from standing on the moon," she continued. "Now let's look at a few of the parts of the Web. We're going to keep using the phone system metaphor because most people relate to phones. So, what's an image that makes sense to our techno-challenged audience?"

"The old time phone operator—you know, the nice young woman in a chiffon shirt with shoulder pads wearing a bulky headset chatting it up with everyone who calls, saying, 'One moment please,' as she plugs those big black cords with shiny metal plugs into the switchboard. You know, like Sarah on the Andy Griffith show. You never saw her, but you always imagined that was what she looked like."

"Hmmm," Edwina mused. "It might work. It has a nice kinesthetic element to it. And we would be playing the nostalgia card, too. Okay, let's go with it. It's your turn. You take if from here. And remember, your goal is not only to explain what happened to the network, but more importantly, how to help your students become more productive users of the network, understand? And William, as a general rule, remember these four steps in teaching: Step 1. I teach, you observe. Step 2. I teach, you help. Step 3. You teach, I help. Step 4. You teach, I observe. Ready?"

Without a moment's hesitation, I began speaking:

"In the phone system, every phone has a phone number. In the old days when I dialed a phone number, one of the nice phone attendants used to ask whom I was calling and then connect my phone call using a cord plugged into a switchboard. Nowadays, a computer has replaced the switchboard attendant, but they both do the same thing.

"When I go to a web site, the same thing happens," I continued. "Imagine a web attendant appearing on your screen and asking you 'Which site did you want to connect to?' and then connecting your computer to the website using a cord."

"Let's pause there for a moment," Edwina said. "How's he doing?"

"Great image!" Credo exclaimed. "I can see the 'web operator' very clearly."

"Good," Edwina said. "It always helps to check in with your students to make sure they are with you. Continue."

"Now," I resumed, "if I upgrade the system-"

"I would use the word 'improve' rather than 'upgrade,'" Edwina counseled. "It's a little less techie."

"Gotcha," I acknowledged. "If I improve the system by replacing the attendant with a computer, then voilá, you have what is called a Domain Name Server, or DNS for short. I should warn you now that I am about to begin using some TLAs: Three Letter Acronyms. Sometimes it stands for Two Letter Acronyms. But I want to explain a few of them that you have probably heard. It will allow you to hold your own in a conversation with an average 12-year old."

"Nice touch!" Edwina said. "Most adults will be able to relate to that!"

"The first TLA is DNS," I continued, "which stands for Domain Name Server, as I just mentioned. DNSs are computer *switchboard attendants*, directing your *computer phone calls*. They are scattered throughout the Web to make sure you make the right connections when you surf the Net.

"Each web site has the equivalent of a phone number which is called a Universal Resource Locator, or URL for short. For example, the White House's URL is www.whitehouse.gov. When you connect to www.whitehouse.gov, a DNS looks up the URL and connects your computer with its. So, it is imperative that the DNS have an accurate listing of the URLs. Otherwise you could get someone else's phone call. How am I doing?"

"Good, good," Edwina said.

"Behind every URL like www.whitehouse.gov," I continued, "is a long string of numbers called an IP address, which stands for

Internet Protocol address. The IP address and the URL both refer to the same site on the Web. Why the redundancy, you might ask? URLs are created for us 'warm-ware,' or the people who do not relate well to long strings of numbers. On the other hand, an IP address is what computers understand. If we did not have URLs, then instead of remembering the Web address of the White House as www.whitehouse.gov, we would have to remember its IP address: 198.137.240.92. This is not exactly user-friendly.

"Back to the DNS, our computer switchboard attendant," I continued. "The DNS, in fact, does more than just direct your web *phone call.* It translates the URL to an IP address. So when you connect to the White House, you enter the URL, www.whitehouse.gov, then a DNS translates that into the IP address 198.137.240.92, and then your connection is made. This means that putting a computer on the Web is a two-step process. First you give it an IP address, then you give it a URL."

"How is your mother doing at this point, William?" Edwina asked. "Remember—she is the audience."

"I have it on good authority that she is following William's explanation just fine and is very proud of the job he's doing," Credo assured her.

"He does this just to bug me," I whispered to Edwina. "And it works. Could you please tell him to leave my mother alone?"

"Don't let it alarm you," Edwina said. "Pass through it. Besides, your mother can take care of herself. Continue."

I paused. "This is where I get stuck," I admitted.

"Okay, William, then let me help you out. This is where you turn to your VIPs on a conciliatory note as you try to explain to them why the network wasn't working today. Here is one possible way of continuing.

"'What happened was that someone'—notice, William, that I didn't say 'you', because if you accuse a VIP of anything, you lose them—'was that someone gave more than one computer the same IP address. This confused the network. Imagine two people having the same phone number! Also, someone didn't tell the new computer where to find the nearest *computer operator,* or DNS. So, when the new computer tried to connect to the Internet it was told, 'Sorry- I don't know who I am and I don't know how to reach anyone.'

"'I'm trying to help you and the corporation,'" Edwina continued, as though talking to BADI management. "'I'm trying to do the job that is expected of me. If you ever need to add a computer, even if it's on a weekend, call me so I can help you. We'll discuss comp time or overtime, but we won't be discussing lost time if you let me help you.'"

"And one of the VIPs turns to me," I said with conviction, "and says, 'Look, you bionic little twerp, I wear the expensive suit in this joint and if you don't want to find yourself cleaning the toilets in the executive bathroom with your tongue then don't ever talk to me like that again."

Edwina gasped. I was engulfed by total mortification. "I was just repeating what I had heard from my immediate supervisor, Ms. Tech. Forgive me."

"And you say," Credo countered as he appeared in front of us, "'I'm just trying to respect your superior intelligence. You deserve to spend your time doing more than messing around with a bunch of wires. That's my job. You're the big picture people, the visionaries and I would be nothing without you.'"

I opened my eyes wide and nodded. "Now, that just might work."

"Sapes are sapes," Credo continued. "Appeal to their vanity and you can't lose. But you don't have to hate them for being human, William. Just understand that being human has limitations." His voice assumed an apologetic tone. "We would only use it as a last resort, Edwina. Promise."

Edwina shook her head with a kind of mock disappointment and looked intently at me. "Miss Phelps wouldn't give up. Neither will I, and neither will you. You won't need to stoop to cynicism much longer. You'll see. And you'll love the changes you make to your outlook on life! For now, keep your wits about you. Today you will have a wonderful opportunity to test what you have learned."

A smile crept across Edwina's face as she turned to Credo and spoke with great enthusiasm. "I like William very much, Credo. You were right. He will do very well on the Big Day." Edwina winked at me the way Miss Phelps used to when she wanted me to know I had done very well on my arithmetic. She snapped her fingers, and suddenly I was on the subway surrounded by familiarity as I headed for home.

CHAPTER 13 The Problem with Our Gods
Whatever you believe, that's who you are.

The next day after work I ran from my office to Credo's doorway, cursing the rain that threatened to dissolve the chemicals that fixed my hair into the shape of something resembling a Jell-O dessert my grandmother used to make. Then a twinge of revelation poked me in my ribs—Hair? Who cares about my hair? And what am I doing to the Earth?

I cursed my own shortsightedness, as well. Like everyone else enduring the current unexpected heat wave that had engulfed the city, I had *prayed for rain but had not brought an umbrella*, something my grandmother had warned me never to do. As I approached Credo's doorway with a newspaper over my head, I was unable to look at him.

"Well, Edwina was right," I said sheepishly, for the first time moving all the way inside Credo's doorway. I had never been standing this close to him before and got my first strong whiff of his breath. It reeked so badly I considered standing in the rain just to escape it. "I had an opportunity to teach management a few things today, and, well, I did. But I have a confession to make."

"Okay, okay," Credo said. "Hold it right there. I think I know what's coming and this is no place for it. Let's go to church."

"For god's sake, *church?*" I screeched. "That's worse than school!"

Credo snapped his fingers. When my mind cleared, my field of vision was swallowed by the vast, glistening expanse of a cathedral whose stone archways towered over the crowd of people packed into stiff wooden pews. I craned my neck in every direction, gawking like a child at the zoo. Everywhere, the cathedral's stone walls shivered with gold inlay that decorated countless marble statues. Everywhere, the sun tried to squeeze through large stained-glass windows filled with geometric figures and scenes from interstellar space. Everywhere, bronze sculptors had left behind testaments of countless hours of devotional labor in the form of plaques, statues, grillwork and reliefs. There was so much to look at my eyes began to hurt. I diverted my attention to my clothes and was shocked to discover I was dressed in a dark suit, a starched white shirt and a pinstriped tie.

"It was the only thing we could find in your closet," Credo whispered. "Your mother helped me pick it out."

I turned to see Credo sitting next to me. His black topcoat was clean and creased, closed and buttoned. His breath had miraculously become the scent of roses. And he had socks on both feet. I started to object to his harassing my mother, but he motioned me to be quiet and to look up.

I tilted my head back and squinted, trying to discern the artwork adorning the dome that disappeared into the recesses of the vaulted ceiling. As I continued my sweep through the upper regions of the cathedral, I paused to study the stone gargoyles sitting on marble pedestals that hung out over the pews. They looked as though they were ready to pounce on the congregation below. The gargoyle directly overhead seemed to wink at me.

"Whoa!" I could not help saying aloud.

Edwina Tech turned around in the pew in front of me and looked me in the eye. "Shhh," she said softly, placing her index finger over her lips. As she turned back around I felt a familiar youthful embarrassment.

"Please, William," Credo whispered. "Show some respect."

"Fine," I said with a hint of exasperation. "Respect for who?"

"For *whom*," Edwina Tech said as she turned around again "Now, William, please, if you must talk, whisper very quietly. And watch your grammar. You are in a church."

"Sorry, ma'am," I said. "Respect for whom?" I asked as quietly as possible.

"For the patron saint of networkers," Credo said. "From cyberpunks to button-down managers, everyone here is a networker who has come to listen to the master of schematics, virtual gods and data packets."

"Who is this guy?" I yelped as quietly as possible.

"What makes you think it's a guy, cave man?" Credo chided. "*She* sees the big picture. *She* walks the talk. Her name is Billy—The Reverend Willamina Pulpit. And Willamina rules!"

"*Who?*" I asked, looking down at the program in my hands and reading the title of today's sermon: "The Problem with Our Gods." Suddenly a cross between Bach and bebop began pouring from the organ pipes that reached to the ceiling like miniature church spires. Everyone rose to their feet, clapping, swaying and hollering "Will-a-mi-na, Will-a-mi-na!" As I looked up I saw a large woman with bronze skin and a shiny pompadour stride onto the stage. Her long flowing robes trailed behind her like a black waterfall as she took her place at the pulpit and begin to speak with the authority of thunder.

"It was a bad week for children, theologically speaking," Billy Pulpit's voice boomed. Each syllable ricocheted throughout the cathedral before being swallowed by the cold, brittle air. She paced herself, dancing with the listeners' emotions, her voice rising and falling like waves pounding on a breakwater. "In Northern Ireland a carload of children got caught in the ageless crossfire of who's closer to God, the Protestants or the Catholics. Then somewhere in the Middle East a classroom packed with young faces blew into pieces as competing monotheists bashed the holy hell out of each other for the second straight millennium.

"As hard as it was, I knew I was just supposed to get used to this stuff, like taxes and gray hair, but I thought I would have a third cup of coffee before I caved in. It was my ritual. Today, like every day, was a three-cup day. It took that long for me to complete my daily reconciliation with the upside-down world around me. For some reason I remembered a line from an old movie: 'Maybe I can't change the world, but I can keep the world from changing me.' That gave me a little bit of strength, but as usual I needed a metaphor to make life presentable. Then the doorbell rang.

"I opened the door and was greeted by two athletic-looking young men wearing single-color suits and powerfully simple red ties. They smiled brightly, twinkling like souvenirs of over-produced Norman Rockwell Americana. One stood in front of the other, a black book in his left hand. They were itching to start talking, so after we all shook hands and introduced ourselves I asked them what was up.

"They came with a message about the Lord. 'Had I heard of Him?' they asked. I took issue with the word 'the.' I knew for a fact that there were many lords and that where you grew up seemed to determine which one you worshipped. I asked them which lord they were referring to.

"'Which Lord?' they responded aghast. 'Well, *the* Lord, of course, the one and only son of God—Jesus.' Didn't I know that God had given His only son to the world so that we might be redeemed? I took issue with the word 'His.' God, a man? Like them, but unlike me?

"The young men blinked a few times. Well, no, well, yes, well sort of. 'A kind of superman?' I asked. Yes, in a way, they replied, and, they added, 'No disrespect intended, ma'am.' I'm sure it wasn't intended, I told them, but it was definitely received.

"They told me to think of God as much bigger and more powerful than we, as one who shows His face to us as a man lest we be blinded by the brilliance of His light. The athletic young men smiled at their patter. It sounded like some of the few lines they had not been spoon fed by their mentors.

"'But,' I asked, 'I thought God was supposed to be everything, including women and things like rocks, air and water that don't have a sex...right? God should be all of that, don't you think?' The athletes didn't answer. In their minds they were in the Sistine Chapel staring at the ceiling. There was God, white hair flowing, anger in his brow, breathing life into man. The Americana men pushed on.

"'Do you want to be saved?' they asked me, sounding like pitchmen over-anxious for a sale. They seemed to imply, *Hey look, this is a large condominium complex and if we're wasting our time just tell us and we will go peddle the truth somewhere else.* I was impure, they continued, and needed to hop on to the path of salvation—now! They knew the Way—would I like to know how to get there? I told them only if I could be sure. 'Of what?' they asked.

"I told them that I needed to be absolutely certain that their way was the only way, and they assured me they were certain that it was. I asked them that if they were certain, then what did they need faith for? Knowledge and faith were mutually exclusive, were they not? You only needed faith because you couldn't be certain...right?

"After pondering my question for a moment they said they were sorry, they hadn't understood before, that in fact my point was a good one. Their relationship with the Lord was an act of faith, not knowledge. So, I asked, 'If you don't know you are right, it's possible that you're wrong...*right?*' They squinted at me. They assured me that it may take faith to get to Him, but there is only one path and one Lord and theirs was it. Making the Moslems, Hindus, Jews, not to mention the Rosicrucians, Scientologists, et al, wrong? I asked. 'Misled but reformable,' they replied. 'But,' I asked, 'maybe their path was just one of many, the same way all roads used to lead to Rome?' They assured me that God would not confuse His people like that. I assured them that I wouldn't expect any less than a rich diversity of options, just like life itself. They insisted that their scriptures affirmed their point of view. I insisted that in principle God couldn't be less than the whole library. They maintained that one God, *theirs*, was all people could handle. I wanted to know where the souls of the Hindus went when they died. They didn't know. I asked how we could find out. They promised to bring it up at their next staff meeting.

"I asked the Americana men whether they had chosen their religion. They assured me they had. 'What did you choose between?' I asked them. They began to answer confidently and then broke off mid-paragraph, revelation creeping across their faces as they acknowledged to themselves that they had not chosen between anything. I found the silence so painful that I kept the conversation rolling. I asked if they had read, for starters, the Koran, the Gita, the Buddhist sutras or if they had sought an understanding of any of the more than 100 sects of Christianity that were alive in America, all of which claimed some specialty that set them apart, nay, *above*, the rest. 'No,' they answered. I asked the Americana men if they had investigated any of the spiritual ways of indigenous peoples or any of the more personal forms of spirituality that were being practiced. 'No,' they answered quietly. Then surely they had spoken with people who had? No, they hadn't done that either.

"Ladies and Gentleman, networkers and networkees. The problem with our gods was standing right in front of me. I had asked for a metaphor and received one at my door. These men were trying to defend a faith they had never really examined. They had not examined it because it was part of their faith not to examine their faith. This was the tautology upon which religion and intolerance feasted.

"Worse yet, their elders, their scriptures and their peers did not encourage any kind of kinship with those who believed in other Gods. As a matter of fact, by dogmatic necessity, the followers of other gods were the enemy.

"But the most disturbing thing of all was that these eager evangelists had no feeling for God as the notion of perfection independent of our cultures. And they had no sense at all of God as the source of compassion and truth far above the violence, the righteous indignation and the single-mindedness of Religion.

"I was as convinced as ever that the next step in human evolution was for each culture to invent hyper-God, which subsumed, embraced and connected all of religion's little gods. For starters, what our media-conscious world needed was for the Dalai Lama, the Pope and leaders from Judaism, Hinduism, Islam and other religions to appear in public dialogue. Just one photo session plastered all over the Web in which they did no more than share tea at the same table could make the world a much safer place. Then perhaps we could move on to where we ought to be, and include women religious leaders, Native spiritualists and a host of others who are all working for the same Boss. If humankind were really lucky, our religious leaders would create hyper-God live on the 6 o'clock news, resolving to amend their holy books to begin with these words: "The following is an opinion." And if we got ultra lucky, these words would be followed by eight more that could change the world: 'For god's sake, would you please get networked!'"

"Amen!" the congregation hollered.

"Enough was enough. I asked my well-dressed visitors in a conciliatory tone of voice if they would like a cup of coffee. No, they didn't drink coffee and besides, they had some evangelizing to do. So they were off, down on their quota and determined to find someone who needed them much more than I did. Meanwhile, I would work my way through a third cup of coffee, convinced that whatever deity really ran temple Earth was obviously at least as large as all of us, played no favorites and wished no part of creation any harm. God is the network, ladies and gentleman. Amen."

"Amen," the congregation intoned, and everyone bowed their heads. A deep, resonant silence filled the cathedral with the sound of waiting.

Willamina "Billy" Pulpit looked up and eased into the quiet. "I wanted to plug the Americana men into an inter-denominational chat room, like *everyone@god.com*, and see what happened," she said softly, trying not to sound patronizing. "God bless the power of networks."

"God bless the power of networks," the congregation repeated.

There was another silence, this one shorter than the last, during which everyone dropped their heads again, took a deep breath and exhaled more or less in unison.

"Who has a big picture-networking story to tell?" Billy Pulpit suddenly announced, upbeat and resilient. The congregation opened its eyes, looked up, and started to murmur with subdued excitement.

"I do," said a man near the front. The voice-activated microphone homed in on his position and broadcast his voice throughout the cathedral. I looked around and spotted dozens of loud speakers hidden within the folds of the stone archways. "I made friends with three Muslims this week in a virtual clothing store," the man said. "They particularly liked the blue jeans. I introduced them to two Christians, and we all ended up in a private chat room together being real friendly. We might even meet up next summer in Europe together! Praise networking, for it makes the world one."

"Praise networking," chanted the congregation.

"Praise networking, indeed!" bellowed Billy Pulpit. "Who else saw the big picture this week?"

"I did, Reverend Pulpit!" a young woman announced.

"Tell us about it, sister!" Billy Pulpit said.

"I am a school teacher and I just finished a unit with my fourth graders called 'What's Unique, What's Universal.' I use email and video mail to connect my students with students all over the world so they can discuss all sorts of things, such as clothes, gender roles, diet, music. The object of the project..."

"The object of the project!" Billy repeated. "Give that woman two points for rhymin'!"

"Two points!" everyone hollered gleefully.

"Thank you, Rev'rend. Anyway," the teacher continued, "the object is to figure out which customs they think are universal and which are unique to their culture. On one hand, my students are always so surprised to learn that not everyone dresses the way they do, or eats what they do, or thinks the way they do. But on the other hand, they are also always surprised to find out that blue jeans and McDonald's are very popular just about everywhere. It is a blow to ethnocentrism and helps them see the world as one planet capable of sustaining social diversity while embracing commonality."

"You got them livin' in the bosom of irony!" Billy howled. "You got them seeing we are all one, all different and allllllllll right! Praise networking!"

"Praise networking!" hollered the congregation.

"How can I get my children involved in this?" a parishioner asked excitedly.

"I would ask that anyone involved with this project wait around in the back after the service to talk to folks who would like to know more about it," Billy said.

"I will do that," the teacher said. "And praise networking and what it can do!"

"Praise networking!" the congregation said.

A young woman, professionally dressed and fitted with large round glasses, stood up and announced that she had a story that segued nicely with the last one.

"Do tell," said the congregation.

"Indeed," said Billy, smiling broadly. "Media people love a good segue."

"Well," the woman began, "I am an online teacher for a consortium of universities in the United States. Last year I was asked to teach a course to a group of educators using the World Wide Web, and even though I knew I was going to be traveling, I agreed to do it because I knew I could get access to the Web wherever I went."

"You mean you actually got in an airplane and moved your body from one place to another?" a congregation member asked incredulously. Laughter instantly filled the room.

"Yes, I did," she assured them. "And so much for the myth that online communication will make us travel less. I struck up a relationship with some faculty members at a few universities in Germany and, à la Nicolas Negroponte, after sending my data bits there for more than a year, I decided to send my atoms there too.

"Well," she continued, "the last month of my travels took me to Canada, where I used a local Internet provider to reach my students. While I was at a party explaining what I did for a living, a young man politely announced that he was an immigration officer and found what I did very interesting.

"Well, I didn't think anything about it until the next day when I received a call from someone at Immigration who accused me of working illegally in Canada! I told him I was teaching U.S. students and was being paid by a university in the United States. He said the important point was that I was working in Canada and that any job held in Canada had to be offered to Canadians first. He told me that my situation had to be reviewed for possibly displacing Canadian workers, which was in violation of Canadian immigration law. I told him that I couldn't possibly be displacing Canadians because it was a U.S. job, was only available to U.S. citizens and wouldn't be offered to anyone outside the country, unless, of course, it was an international course, which it wasn't.

"Well, then he told me that I was at least in violation of federal tax law for not paying taxes on my income. But it was not a Canadian job I kept arguing; it was a U.S. job and I paid U.S. income taxes and so the issue of Canadian taxes was irrelevant. Well, actually I told him I paid my taxes to Uncle Sam rather than Queen Elizabeth, a statement he found quite offensive. He told me in quite a huff that I was working in Canada and like everyone else in that situation I owed my fair share to the government. I told him that while my butt might be in Canada, my mind was in the United States, that's how cyberspace worked, and that he needed a crash course in the mechanics of the global market as well as proper manners. He told me he would get back to me with a date for my hearing. I told him I couldn't wait, but I never heard from him again.

"Well, the whole experience made me wonder," the woman said. "When I can project my mind one place while sitting in another, which government should I answer to? It made me take a good look at all the governments that controlled my life that were based on where I live. The best of the lot is my neighborhood association. We deal with real issues, like garbage overflow, noisy tourists and curbing our dogs. We deal with real people and someone usually brings a coffee-cake to the monthly meeting. But the larger the government entity, the less responsive it is. The city government's so-so, the state government's nearly intolerable, and the national government is what it is: a reasonable attempt at trying to accomplish the impossible task of satisfying more than a quarter-of-a-billion rabid individualists. Maybe some day we will look at governments as monopolies which no longer serve our best interests and which will have to compete for our citizenship. Maybe some day we will all consider ourselves citizens of Cyberia first and will choose our governments second. Maybe we will choose them the way we choose any professional organization we belong to. Maybe we will commit to them for a certain period of time and then, depending on their track record, either renew our citizenship or go elsewhere."

"Maybe!" said the congregation.

"Excellent questions, sister," Willamina thundered. "And at least part of the answer is obvious—we are all connected and something's gotta' give! It all boils to where's your mind vs. where's your behind!"

"Amen!" the congregation shouted.

Willamina started to stamp out a beat with one foot that cycled through the congregation. Everyone immediately began to clap their hands in unison. In her deepest baritone she began to rap:

> *There's your mind!*
> *And then there's your behind!*
> *And sometimes the two just don't align!*

"And sometimes the two just don't align!" the congregation joined in as they stood up. Billy began to rap another cycle while everyone moved and swayed, clapping their hands with a snap and a funk that was so infectious that no one could resist standing and joining in:

> *There's your mind!*
> *And then there's your behind!*
> *And sometimes the two just don't align!*

"And sometimes the two just don't align!" the congregation yelled back.

On it went, funking down through ultra cycles until Billy put up one hand to stop it, a wide smile on her face. "Amen, brother and sister networkers," she said, pulling a blue-and-gold handkerchief from her pocket and wiping away the sweat that was streaming down her forehead. "Amen. Please be seated."

"AAAAMMMEEENNNN!" returned the congregation, shuffling back into their pews. Almost immediately the congregation was quiet and waiting.

"Another story of the power of networking, I beg you, brothers and sisters," Billy Pulpit implored.

An old man near the rear of the cathedral stood up. "I have a story I would like to share!"

"Tell us!" encouraged the congregation.

"Fellow networkers," he began, "I used to be a divorce lawyer. So I went to a meeting of the local bar association a few weeks ago and pitched networking as a way to get people who don't like each other to communicate and work out their difficulties. I asked these lawyers if any of them had one of those cases where two people are trying to get a divorce but they hate each other so much they can't even talk on the phone without swearing up a storm? Just about everyone said 'yes,' so I made the case for networking as a way for people in that situation to be able to communicate. I suggested that people could come as avatars, or holograms of their favorite movie stars, or just use email, to talk to each other. The idea was to put enough distance between them that they wouldn't power up and get all upset before they even had a chance to say, 'Hello, I hate you.' There was a lot of interest but quite a few lawyers were afraid that if it actually worked then no one would need them in the middle and they wouldn't make any money.

"Then, fellow networkers, an amazing thing happened. Two honest lawyers..."

The entire congregation burst into hysterics, and screeched in unison, "Say what?"

"That's what I said, fellow networkers. Two honest lawyers agreed to try using electronic mail between two people who were trying to get a divorce but who hated each other so much they couldn't even agree on how to split up. And guess what? It worked! We turned off voice and video and made them use just text, and, fellow networkers, an amazing thing happened: It took them so long to type in a swear word that after the first few attempts they just didn't bother. The bottom line is that they worked out a shared-child custody arrangement and a property settlement in a half dozen email messages that they had not been able to work out through their lawyers for months."

"Praise networking!" the congregation said.

"Praise networking indeed," Billy Pulpit thundered, "for it holds the promise of making the world a more peaceful place."

"Reverend Pulpit," a distraught young woman called out in a voice that shook with rage. The people seated next to her put their arms around her.

"Yes, sister," Billy said quietly.

"Bad people do bad things to good people with good networks," she said. "I know for a fact that the KKK, militia groups and God knows who else use networks to help them do mean, vicious things to honest, decent people. My friend—my best friend—died, committed suicide, because the forces of evil—you know, the credit agencies who know all about you and don't hesitate to make a buck by selling what they know to whomever wants it—the forces of evil managed to destroy his good name and his credit so utterly that he felt he had no

choice but to take his own life. And it was all a lie, a big lie! He had
wonderful credit. But he was a doctor who supported abortions, and
his enemies were bound-and-determined to bring him down. So they
sabotaged his information. It's a new kind of warfare, brothers and
sisters. His enemies borrowed his credit information and began to
send information to his house about national cross-dressing conferences. Well, of course, his wife got a hold of it and wanted to know
what else he wasn't telling her about his private life. Then the forces
of evil managed to massage his credit-card purchase information so
that his wife began to suspect he was using her Victoria's Secret
account to buy lingerie. And they did it so subtly and so artfully that
his wife began to suspect that he was buying it for another woman or
worse—a fellow cross-dresser! And if that weren't enough, they
tapped out his credit line with things like nail polish, padded bras,
life-size anatomically correct Barbie dolls and anything else that
would make the lie more complete. He saw his wife and family dying
of shame, so he killed himself. His enemies bought information about
him, *legally*, and then they used it to fabricate a lie that destroyed him.
But it was all a big lie! He was a wonderful friend and father! And he
had wonderful credit, do you hear me? Wonderful!"

The young woman was sobbing uncontrollably. No one moved.
No one uttered a sound. The vast echoing chamber of the cathedral
was deadly silent as everyone waited for her to continue.

"I know technology is an amplifier," she finally said in a voice
barely above a whisper. "And I know it amplifies good and evil. But
surely there is justice in the next world. What happens to these
people, Reverend Pulpit? I need to know what happens to evil
networkers when they die."

"What happens to their souls when they die?" Reverend Willamina Pulpit asked.

"Yaaass," intoned the congregation.

"You want to know what happens to the souls of evil networkers
when they die?" Billy said a little louder.

"YAAAAS," the congregation crooned.

"They go to hell!" she bellowed.

"Amen!" everyone screamed.

"And do you know what hell is?" she asked with fire.

"Tell us, Reverend Pulpit!" the congregation commanded.

"It is whatever you create out of the dark side of your soul. It is the worst of the worst that you have ever known. For a networker, it is a network with only one computer to be shared among an infinite number of people. It is an email server that crashes continually without backup. It is a local-area-network connected to the Internet with a slow, unstable connection that works best on the weekends when no one needs it. It is a group of users who move their computers without telling anyone and yank the cords out of the wall just before lunch so the entire network goes down. It is a phone company whose satellite link is eternally plagued by sunspots. It is a boss who wants every bell and whistle imaginable but doesn't want to pay for them and won't take the time to learn how to use them. Hell! I say, hell!!"

"AMEN!" everyone yelled as they waved their arms and writhed in their seats. "AMEN!"

"You need not worry about the evil networkers of the world, sister," Billy Pulpit assured the young woman. "They will get their due."

"AMEN!"

The congregation buzzed wildly for a moment before the excitement subsided. When calm returned to the cathedral, Billy Pulpit smiled. "Well, let's end on a positive note. Who else saw the big picture this week?"

Credo nudged me. "Go on," he prodded.

"Credo, stop," I said in an angry whisper. "I don't do well in public."

"Go ahead," Credo insisted. "Come on. No one is going laugh."

When I didn't move, Credo grabbed my hand and shoved it into the air. "He did!" Credo announced to the congregation.

"Fugguduh, Credo!" I said, seething and ready to throttle him. As I listened to the speaker system bounce my words throughout the cathedral, the congregation burst into hysterics, applauding and stamping their feet.

"Don't worry, son," Billy Pulpit assured me. "We're all networkers here and we're all allowed to cuss now and again. Tell us your story."

"Umm, well, I'm not exactly sure this counts," I began apologetically. "It's more of a confession."

"Well, son, you're in the right place then," Billy assured me.

"Thank you, sir, uhm, ma'am," I stammered.

"Reverend will do," Billy said with a smile.

"Yes, ma'am, Reverend. I actually used the network this week to get the suits to understand how to treat their employees like human beings. See, the suits—you know, management—they're the people who, well, run the place where I work. Actually I need to stop calling them 'suits.' It's part of my training. They are people too, just a bit misguided. I know the decent thing to do would be to just call them 'sapes.' I am working on that."

"No need for an explanation, son," Billy broke in with a smile. "We all know who the suits are, don't we?"

"Amen!" hollered the congregation.

"But," said Billy, "you are quite right. They are people. And your compassion will serve you well as you try to understand the world. We are here to help, not here to condemn. Please continue, brother networker."

"Well," I said, "then you all know that they don't understand the networking thing, but they act like they do even though they never come to training sessions. And they insist that when they make a mistake it is all someone else's fault."

"Amen!" the congregation hollered again.

"And," I continued, "they make people working for far less than they make do senseless, ridiculous things because of their ignorance. While of course people don't like being paid so much less, it's actually the insult that really hurts. Anyway, so today I got them to actually see what they were doing to people by involving them in a text-only computer conference, in which they thought they were talking just to other suits, but in fact they were talking to me, who was acting like a suit. And because they thought I was one of them, they listened to me. Was that too dishonest to count?"

"Not at all!" thundered Billy Pulpit. "Sounds like an excellent use of technology to me!"

"Praise networking!" the congregation said.

"Praise it indeed!" Billy Pulpit echoed. "And how did you teach these unteachables the basic lessons of humanity?"

"Umm," I began, looking at Ms. Tech, "I chose a metaphor they could relate to: the annual stockholders' convention. I got them to focus on the opening image of everyone in the audience with the company logo up on the screen. I explained in big-picture terms how the convention was more than just a meeting; it was a convocation, a coming together of all the parts of the company that formed one unit that needed to operate like a single entity. I explained that while the convention may consist of many individuals doing many different jobs, it was one group with a common purpose. I got them to understand that the company was no different, that the company was also a single entity and every time all the pieces were in synch and working like a single entity, then everyone was happy and the suits made more money! Then I explained how everyone's job at the convention, from the keynote speakers to the napkin folders, were important parts of the whole, and that if you weren't nice to the napkin folders, well, you got crumpled napkins, and who likes that?"

"Hear, hear," a number of the faithful mumbled as they nodded their heads in approval.

"And I told them that the conference employed keynote speakers and people who folded napkins too, though they had different names, like managers and data-entry clerks, but there was really no difference. And I told them that when everyone is treated like an integral part of the whole, they act like an integral part of the whole, and everyone is happy and the suits make more money!"

"Bravo!" said Edwina Tech, a tear hanging in the corner of one eye. "Well done, William. Well done!"

"Praise networking," Billy Pulpit said. "And praise teachers!"

CHAPTER 14
Learning that the Business of Business is Learning
Plan for change, rather than change your plan.

Following the service, Credo, Edwina and I sat until everyone else had left. After a long silence, during which I bounced echoes throughout the cathedral by scuffing my feet across the tile floor, I asked Credo, "If Billy Pulpit is so enlightened, why all the overkill in the decor? There must be enough gold here to wire a dozen supercomputers. Why not meet outside somewhere in a forest?"

"Because you respond to this environment. It resonates with your Disney chakra."

"My what?" I asked.

"Later," Credo said, dismissing the question with a flip of his hand. "The point is that if you honestly felt more at home with your spirituality outside, then we would be outside. If you honestly felt more at home in a barn, we would be there. But this is what gets your attention. You like the special effects."

I assured him I did not relate to any of it but had to admit it was really well done for what it was. Credo couldn't keep from snickering, implying one more time that he knew more about me than I did myself.

"So," Edwina said, "it sounds as if you have found a way to reach your managers. And it sounds as if they listened."

"Ah yes," I said sarcastically. "That afternoon someone plastered motivational posters all over the place with catchy sayings like, 'All for one and one for all!' and, 'Work isn't work when it's teamwork!' Original, eh? How inspirational! And today we all got little one-line emessages that extol the virtues of sound planning practices like, 'Plan your work and work your plan,' and 'Fail to Plan? Then Plan to Fail!' And get this: Somebody in data entry overheard some of the managers talking about mandatory weekend retreats and required reading. I must admit, when they decide to move, they move fast."

"Sounds like a start," Credo said.

"Sounds like a load of..." I broke off faltering, glancing at Edwina. "It sounds like a load of fertilizer to me. I think I liked it better when they were more obvious about whom they really were. Today they may appear wise, but tomorrow, when wisdom is inconvenient and inconsistent with the bottom line, they will be back to their old unenlightened, venal, hopelessly hierarchical selves. Let's give this some time to see whether it sticks before we claim victory."

I could see that Edwina was truly disappointed and disturbed by my attitude. I wondered if she felt she had miscalculated the depths of my cynicism and had begun to question whether I was worthy of whatever it was she had in mind for me. I felt horrible. 'Snap out it,' I commanded myself. 'This is your life. Paint it.'

"You kids," Credo scoffed. "No sense of delayed gratification. You're not re-configuring a local-area network, for god's sake. You are changing 'the ossified minds of adults with control issues,' remember? And you want to be a teacher? Have some respect for the learning process. It's the way life works."

"You have to have faith, William," Edwina said with a touch of desperation in her voice. "If you lose your faith, you lose everything. Teachers have to believe that in the journey of a million miles it is their job to help students take their first steps. Then we let go with the faith that we made a difference. If we lose that faith, we should not be teachers." Edwina looked at Credo with an earnestness I had not seen before. I could tell something big was about to happen. My coffee hand was starting to twitch.

"William," Edwina said very seriously, "I think it best that you follow a possibility."

"Which possibility?" I asked. "And where am I following it to?"

Credo waited a moment before agreeing with her. "I think you are right," he said to Edwina, again ignoring me, implying, as always, that waiting was part of my learning curve, and that for him to provide answers to questions that I could only understand in hindsight would be a waste of everyone's time. "It's sort of bending the rules, and if it doesn't pan out, Edwina and I will catch hell from The Committee. But we're betting you won't let us down. No pressure, though."

Another wave of exasperation swept through me. "Would it do any good at all to ask a bunch of obvious questions, like, 'Who are you? What do you have in mind for me? What rules? What committee? Why me?' You know, the standard kinds of questions you must hear all the time."

A pause opened wide as we all became aware of the hundreds of tiny noises spinning and reverberating through the empty space of the abandoned church. Credo held up one hand, as if to say he didn't want to be disturbed as both he and Edwina closed their eyes, smiling. "Just thought I'd ask," I said.

I closed my eyes, ready to fall into a familiar void, and was surprised when the sound of the first finger snapping seemed to have no effect. I opened my eyes and was still in church, sitting next to Edwina and Credo who were snapping their fingers repeatedly with restrained passion, like the rhythm section of a tango orchestra. I was the center of a dance, a fact that frightened me as much as excited me. *No sense fighting it,* I thought. I closed my eyes again.

The next moment, I was standing in front of my office door at BADI with very little of the familiar jet lag. My mind was clear, open and focused on the fact that the sign that had hung on my door since my first days at BADI had been replaced. I approached a member of the support staff in the cubicle nearest my door who someone had just called "Josh." He looked unusually happy for a BADI office worker. I asked him what had happened to the sign on my door that read, "Subvert the Dominant Paradigm?" And where did the new one come from that read, "Beware the Paradigm Du Jour?" Josh was laughing as he told me how I had changed signs a long time ago. He told me that I had actually conducted a memorial service for the old sign, and christened the new one with champagne and a short speech about the beginning of a new era. I asked how long ago a "long time ago" was and he guessed a few weeks at least—a long time in silicon years, a short time for most other things. He looked at me with concern and asked if I was all right. "Bad head cold," I told him.

I looked around, making a full sweep of the office and the support staff. Not only was Josh happy, but others around him seemed happy too, or at least they didn't seem unhappy, which was very unusual for one o'clock in the afternoon at BADI. The woman in cubicle number #7 walked up to me, shook my hand and said "congratulations" with such warmth and fervor that I was near tears. When I asked her what for, she said one word before leaving through the double doors at the end of hallway: training.

She was thanking me for training! She was happy; first, because someone cared enough to notice that she was floundering and needed help; second, because the help she received made her more productive; and third, because being productive made her feel happy, which made her more productive, which made her happier. I was witnessing the cascading effects of someone rising to meet the challenge of a personal vision, a skill that was particularly important at BADI where there was no shared corporate vision for employees to turn to for guidance.

I noticed Josh was staring at my right hand. I was flexing it involuntarily, as though squeezing an invisible tennis ball.

"Gotcha," he said, returning a moment later with a cup of coffee. I looked at the coffee suspiciously for a moment, as if I were sizing up a stranger.

"Full strength with a healthy shot of the cow, just how you like," he assured me. "Absolutely guaranteed to rev your rockets."

Before I could ask him a question I had not yet fully formed, he looked at me knowingly, as if we were exchanging a secret handshake, and said, "I understand, sir. Quiet time from 1 to 1:30 PM."

Sir? Quiet time?

I was inside my office at once, absorbed in a desperate scavenger hunt for clues that would tell me what to do during "quiet time," when my computer screen suddenly lit up with the words "Conference 101 is now in session and waiting for you." Moments later I was in the middle of an interactive chat session with BADI management, being addressed by my virtual nom de plum, Mr. Ree. I was interacting with people with catchy names that I did not recognize, but who somehow knew BADI's business intimately.

Suddenly I understood. Now was later, three months later according to the date in the upper right-hand corner of my screen, and the conference I had started for suit talk was still alive. Apparently I had convinced management that BADI needed a free flow of ideas, which could only be accomplished if chatterers honestly believed they could speak their minds without fear of retribution, which could only happen if we were all wrapped in the cloak of anonymity that using a fake online persona provided. In some conferences anyone at BADI, from the heating system mechanics to the Chief Information Officer, could be a chatterer, charitably known in the digital trades simply as a "chatter" so as not to tongue-tie the articulately challenged. However, BADI managers had all agreed that they wanted their own conference, at least for now. They also agreed that chatters needed to use only text, not only to protect themselves, but also because it stimulated more reflective kinds of thought.

They had all bought the idea from me because they thought I was one of them. There was no other way they would hear me. Boldness and innovation rarely translated vertically upward through the ranks and BADI needed desperately to cultivate both if they were going to maintain a competitive edge in their field. Now that everyone was masquerading as an alter ego, I no longer wondered about the ethics of lying about my identity. I was too satisfied with the results. And I couldn't help noticing that because everyone was lying, we were all discovering the truth, just another observation I would have to add to the growing list of things I would think about when I had the time.

I tried to hold back at the beginning of the chat session in order to get my bearings, but it quickly became obvious that I was the group leader. I had actually given homework assignments! Apparently everyone was supposed to research a term from a list I had provided, develop a short explanation of it and describe its connection to BADI's future.

The first chatter to report had the e-name, "Ronald Raygun." The term he researched was "disintermediation," an idea explored by Donald Tapscott in THE DIGITAL ECONOMY. The term referred to the eradication of the middleman and the direct connection of consumer to supplier using the Internet and other means. Disintermediation occurs when customers who once needed you develop the desire and the means to bypass you. By the time you realize it is happening to you, it is too late. Disintermediation was rapidly becoming a way of life. People were buying books, stocks, special-order clothing, food, cars and just about everything else online. In the process they were bypassing not only stores and sales people, but also the cars it took to drive to the stores, as well as the technologies and support services the automobile industry subsumed. The ripple effect was amazing.

"How does this impact BADI?" I asked.

"Not much impact," was generally the reply. BADI was in the big-deal-making business. BADI was more the disintermediator than the disintermediated. "Phew," a number of them typed.

"We can't be disintermediated?" I asked, incredulous.

A lot of hmmming actually appeared on the screen spelled out as "hmmm." The chatters were stalling as embarrassment at their own intellectual laziness took hold.

I was instantly on a roll, reminding them of what Bill Gates had said so many times in so many words. "You can lose it all very quickly simply by assuming you are guaranteed some sort of supremacy in your field. The marketplace isn't a monarchy. It doesn't care what your place in the pecking order was yesterday; it only cares if you are the best today."

More hmmming.

I told everyone I even had evidence of small companies doing medium-size deals almost entirely online, bypassing the need for an organization like BADI altogether. Once they executed enough medium-sized deals on their own then they could begin to do their own big deals without us. They were our competitors and just because they weren't standing right in front of us didn't mean they weren't dangerous. Life moved so quickly in the electronic infosphere that we needed to look beyond the immediate horizon to see who would be at our doorstep tomorrow. "We're next," I warned everyone, "and we need to be vigilant or we will cease to be the hunter, and become the hunted."

I could sense everyone's discomfort. "A good topic for the upcoming retreat," a number of them commented.

Suddenly "sjwwdrrtrrrrttttt" shot across the screen. "Sorry," came some text a moment later. "I am using voice-to-text and just belched. I'm eating burritos. Man, they're tasty but they're gaseous!"

Suzie Q was next, her contribution filling the screen all at once, obviously prepared ahead of time, complete with diagrams and tables. Her term, "adhocracy," was explored by Robert Waterman in his book ADHOCRACY. She explained that an adhocracy was the opposite of hierarchy. In a hierarchy, an organization follows a strict chain of command through the ranks, from top to bottom, forming a pyramid of decision makers. In a hierarchy, maintenance of the organization structure always comes first, despite and oftentimes at the expense of the tasks it has to perform. An adhocracy, on the other hand, re-orders its command structure and information flow to suit the goals of the project at hand, forming a cloud structure that assumes different shapes as conditions change. In an adhocracy, reorganizing the system to facilitate the project at hand always came first, regardless of its impact on traditional structure.

It struck a nerve. People asked for more from Suzie Q.

She explained that in a hierarchy people belonged to departments, while in an adhocracy people belong to resource groups or project teams. In an adhocracy all members of an organization are potential participants in any project, and their selection is based solely on how well their skills and attitudes address the goals of the project. In an adhocracy, not only should managers not seek to maintain a strict sense of order, they should seek to challenge whatever the existing order is, knowing that just behind it lurks an unhealthy complacency and the loss of the peripheral vision needed to stay alive on the savanna of commerce.

"WOW!" I typed, dying to know who was behind the words. I asked how this could help BADI.

The outpouring was as profuse as it was unexpected. A flurry of bullets hit the screen:

- "BADI, for all its innovation, is locked into a strict system of information pass-through, from top to bottom, instead of from critical point to critical point."
- "Why is information restricted at BADI? Wouldn't it be better if all employees had access to information about BADI operations, creating the potential for more perspective of its activities?"
- "We should organize around projects, not around structures. But BADI's structure is too predictable and inflexible for that. Catch 22—the structure won't allow restructuring."

Recalling Edwina's advice to let students personalize their education by becoming involved in their own solutions, I asked for concrete ideas.

"BADI needs an inventory of all the skills that employees have," someone typed. I agreed. The proverbial "employee" was a dead concept, replaced by "knowledge workers" who often had far more to offer in a given project than their job descriptions suggested. Many times workers at BADI were self-taught, and we had no idea what they were capable of. An inventory would allow BADI to build small ad hoc communities of workers, based on the nature of the projects at hand.

"What's the downside?" I asked.

When no one responded, I kept typing, telling them that the adhocracy approach would involve giving up a lot of power. Could they handle that? I also cautioned that support staff members would want more compensation as their value become more recognized. As always in the business world, if you want to say thank you it is best to say it with money.

While no one embraced what I said out of enthusiasm, almost everyone was resigned to its inevitability, survival barely taking precedence over emotional insecurity. "Besides," said one chatter, "theoretically there should be more money available if restructuring meant we would be working more efficiently and effectively." But another chatter, Doc Holiday, wasn't going to give up so easily. He reminded everyone that when a big deal went bad and people's credit cards stopped working, their banks were disconnected, and they went on about their business with no idea that the world was falling apart underneath them, it would be management, not support staff, who would need to undergo facial surgery, change their names and escape to an obscure African country for the rest of their lives.

I wanted to tell Doc Holiday that while that might be true, it was no different for me as head of networking. I lived with the same nightmares of a world run amuck due to my mishandling. I wanted to tell him that many a night had passed in which I lay in bed with the anxiety of an airplane mechanic, wondering if I had done everything just right, knowing that failure to do so could literally destroy the lives of countless people I would never meet. As these thoughts were passing through my mind, I watched a number of people converge on the idea that this was another good topic for the retreat. *Sapes,* I said to myself, fighting off a sense of disappointment. *They can turn avoidance into an art form when they want to.*

Then the chatters started talking about William Tell's new training program. At this point I felt positively voyeuristic and cautiously happy.

"Great job he is doing with that," they said, "though we sure miss having him full time at the helm of networking. And wasn't his attitude changing? He used to have a chip on his shoulder—and it was no microchip," someone joked, "—but now he feels more like one of us."

One of them? I supposed I was. Although I used to see them as extrapolations of what I might morph into if I wasn't careful, I supposed deep down all I really wanted was to be heard, and I knew that would only happen if I joined the club. I "remembered" something Edwina would tell me when I was older: Imagining others to be worse than they really are is just a poor man's way of trying to feel good about himself."

I was beginning to feel very guilty about all the mean things I had said about the "suits" and the "VIPs." That it took a faceless computer conference to be able to appreciate members of management as people with ideas and fears and learning curves to traverse, rather than faceless "suits" on automatic pilot, was "irony in full bloom," to use a Credoism.

Suddenly Credo appeared at my side wearing a referee's uniform. He gave two toots on the large metal whistle attached to the cotton lanyard around his neck and commanded me to raise my hand. When I balked, he grabbed my hand, thrust it into the air ceremoniously, and announced, "Foul on Number 22 for projecting his own insecurities on to someone else. Resume play." And he was gone.

Fair enough, I thought to myself.

Josh tapped lightly on my door, wanting to know if I'd heard a whistle. I smiled without answering, and he retreated into the outer office.

Suddenly my computer beeped and I was focused once again on the conference unfolding on my screen. Apparently I was one of William's champions in the Conference 101! I had supported the training program completely and had agreed to be the one to find one of those pithy, motivational, potentially vacuous sayings that the Board of Directors liked so much; they needed it to describe the training programs in the next quarterly report. I had gone so far as to promise that if I could not find one, I would write one myself.

"Well, what had I come up with?" everyone wanted to know.

On my desktop, in a folder called Conference 101, in a subfolder called Assignments, there was a subfolder called Mine. I reordered the files by most recent date, and a file titled "Learning Poem" popped to the top of the list. I clicked on it and smiled at what I saw. A quick copy-and-paste, and the poem was posted in Conference 101:

> *What you know today, will go away.*
> *What you know tomorrow, you will only borrow.*
> *A love of learning, is your best friend*
> *It changes with you, until the end.*

"Bravo!" resounded the chatters. "Well done!" Someone commented that it reminded him a lot of the banner William Tell had put over the door to the training room.

I wanted to ask, "What training room?" but didn't dare. Instead, I asked about William Tell's banner. "What did it say again?" I claimed it escaped me at the moment.

"Lifelong learning is the lifeblood of any work force. And it's fun too!"

Ah yes, I thought to myself. Now I remembered.

The banter in the chat session began to assume an overly juvenile tone and I couldn't tell whether people were taking the training issue seriously or not, so I asked.

Most said they took it seriously, but only to a certain extent because there was work to be done and training interfered with work. Training was good, as far as it went, but where did it go?

I shook my head. The suits—that is, the management sapes—were doing so well, but in the final analysis they still didn't get it. I lit into them.

"The survival of BADI depends on nothing less than the total reversal of our priorities," I told them as point blank as I could through typed text on a screen. "We shouldn't be trying to make money to educate our staff. We should be educating our staff in order to make money. We should be investing in our staff's education to create the knowledge infrastructure we will need to ensure our profitability in a commercial environment that is constantly changing. Training precedes success, not the other way around. For god's sake, it's all disposable knowledge out there that flows through BADI's corporate nervous system like spikes in the power supply that has an important impact for a very short period of time and then fades quickly into history. The only way to deal with disposable knowledge is through lifelong learning and continual retraining. The corporate loyalty of the '60's and '70's is gone, and in its place is the promise of an education that will help employees when they look for their next job unless management gives them a reason to stick around. Isn't that obvious?"

Uh oh. I worried that my use of a technical metaphor would tip somebody off about my identity. Silence hit the chat room as people digested. I burst into the lull I had inspired.

"Enough for today," I announced. Their homework was to think of a shape that described their vision of what BADI ought to be. "And," I suggested, "focus on vision," adding that while re-training may be the means, vision was the end. A few chatters asked questions that I declined to answer in the name of good sportsmanship, counseling everyone to just have fun. "Play," I told them. "That is when you are most imaginative."

Back in church, Edwina and Credo were smiling proudly at me as Edwina provided a quick critique of my teaching methods. "Great use of interaction," she said. "The idea of having them think in terms of shapes was a wonderful use of their own imagination and metaphor. It gave a number of intelligences a chance to go to work creatively and purposefully." She also told me that in a text-oriented environment role-playing was everything because it provided a lot of implicit information that was non-visual but easy to visualize. The participants in my chat group were turning to me for a leadership role and it was fine for me to step into it.

"More?" Credo asked.

I nodded. If nothing else I at least wanted to see my training room. But I told them I had to ask a question.

"Only one," Credo said.

"How do I know all this stuff?" I asked.

"La vida es corta pero ancha," Credo said.

"You have been studying a lot, dear," Edwina smiled. She snapped her fingers.

I was back my desk. It was the next day—that is, it was three months and a day later. It was 12:52 PM—eight minutes until "quiet time." I raced out of my office into support-staff territory, which looked like it was mid-transformation. The familiar cubicles had been moved to the periphery of the room, giving way to a number of overlapping work areas in which people gathered in small groups. I found Josh and asked him to go with me to the training lab. He was concerned, wanting to know what was up, but I was too fixated on trying to appear as though I knew where I was going to concoct a clever answer. "Nothing," I told him. "I'm just following an inspiration."

As we sped down the hallway I tried not to let on that I was actually following him. Much to my dismay, I could feel extra weight on my belt, my pants pushing out at the thighs, and my movement a bit slower than before. I must have stopped playing racquetball, an all-too-common mistake made by technicians; we lived so much in our heads that our stomachs just took on lives of their own. I felt an unusual attraction to the candy bars staring at me through the glass of the vending machines as we whisked by them in the hall. Bad sign.

We pushed open the door to the training room and flipped on the light. The walls were bare, making the large, windowless room feel cavernous and discouraging. Rows of computers were pointing toward the demonstration workstation at the front of the room, like soldiers awaiting orders from their commanding officer. "Where are all the people?" I wanted to know. Josh shrugged, saying the room still wasn't used all that much, but the people who did use it benefited from it greatly. "Who did the scheduling?" I asked. Josh looked at me inquisitively as he told me he was responsible for booking the room. I told him scheduling wasn't enough. There needed to be encouragement. There needed to be enthusiasm. You can't just build it and wait for people to come. You have to invite them to come. You have to motivate them to come. You have to reward them for coming. He nodded.

I asked him whether he liked it in here. He paused. Then I encouraged him not to worry and to be honest, assuring him that our conversation was just between him and me. He assured me that he was amazed that I had managed to create a training facility at all, and he, umm, didn't want to complain or look a gift-horse in the mouth because actually what they had was so much better, umm, than anything they had before that it was amazing, no, in fact, a miracle that it existed at all-

"Out with it," I ordered, interrupting his run-on.

"It needs more color," he confessed. "And pictures on the wall. And classical music in the background." And Josh told me that he agreed with me about the need to encourage employees to come, rather than simply wait for them to come.

That was all he needed to say. I glanced at my watch—two minutes to quiet time. I ran to my office.

As I sat down in front of my computer, the screen cleared and Conference 101 was just beginning. I wasted no time asking to see their homework, a shape that described their vision of BADI. A blast of one-liners hit the chat room, some serious, others not:

"A funnel."
"A black hole."
"A condom."

"A circle."

"A four dimensional cube."

Then someone with the screen name Ben Dover said, "An eco-system in balance." It wasn't exactly a shape, but I was intrigued. "Tell me more," I encouraged. Ben's words hit the screen with unusual speed. He had probably created them ahead of time and just pasted them into the conversation. He had thought about the issues and was prepared. I liked that.

"Every BADI employee," the words began, "should be seen as an indispensable part of an ecosystem, whose contribution is vital to the integrity of the system, no matter how small it seems. We should not only feel this way about each other, but about ourselves too."

"Go on," I encouraged.

"When all parts of the ecosystem are perfectly in balance, the ecosystem is running at maximum efficiency and stability. That is what BADI should be aiming for," Ben typed.

"Exactly," Jim Nasium typed. "And what's more, within each part of BADI you should be able to see the whole. That is why I used a fractal as my shape."

"Go on," I encouraged.

"It isn't enough to belong," Jim continued. "You need to feel as though you belong. If our shape embodies our vision, then our vision should permeate everything. Any interaction with any BADI em-ployee should reflect the whole of BADI in terms of character and vision, the way a fractal contains the whole in each of its parts."

"Exactly what we have been saying for years," piped up a number of chat room lurkers named Fossil Fool, Kenny Make-it and Betty Dont. "BADI needs a vision statement that employees can relate to. And we ought to start putting together some real PR too, not that crap we hand out to the Board. We need something we can look at that helps us keep our vision in focus."

Back in church, Edwina and Credo were still smiling proudly at me. "More?" Credo asked.

I nodded.

I was at my desk, six months later, 12:52 PM. I sat up at my desk. It was no longer surrounded by walls, but emptied into a large work area filled with people sitting at tables of three or four, work spread out, computers humming, Bach playing off in the distance.

Slogans filled the walls, like, "How you live is what you give," and, "What you learn is what you earn," and "Attitude is Aptitude." My pants were tight and my gut protruded over my belt. I had either not shopped for new clothes because I had failed to face the reality of being overweight, or I was still holding on to the possibility that I would begin playing racquetball again and spare myself the expense of a new wardrobe. However I sized up the situation, the clear fact was that I was fat. But I was also happy.

I smiled at everyone and they smiled back. Then I raced down to the training room, pausing to read the banner over the door before I walked inside. Where once stood rows of computers was now a large open space filled with people working in small groups at makeshift work areas. Everyone looked too young to be working at BADI, a strange thought for me given that I had started working there at 15. The people hovered around laptop computers and made notes on electronic notepads hooked to large screens near their work areas. One outside wall was lined with computers, while the other was lined with specialty workstations for creating video, animation and other kinds of media. Suddenly a young woman jumped up and yelled, "39!" with all the enthusiasm of someone yelling "Bingo!"

Everyone applauded as she made her way to the computer station at the front of the room. As she spoke, she drew on a digital sketch-pad connected to the overhead display screen. She used pictures to explain how she had determined her answer by analyzing the output from a spreadsheet and a few focus-group sessions, all of which helped her determine that 39 would probably satisfy the largest number of customers in the least amount of time. Then she showed a heart-rending video clip of an elderly woman talking about the importance of family and community while overly synthesized music played in the background, evoking my pity despite my best efforts to keep it from doing so. Although I hadn't the faintest idea what was going on, I was impressed. I walked over to one of the tables near the back of the room, caught the attention of a red-haired young man dressed in a shiny black suit and a solid-blue tie, and asked him what was going on.

"Training," he said enthusiastically.

"What kind of training?" I prodded.

"Creative problem-solving," he replied a little impatiently. "A combination of math, communication and sociology applied to the problems of commerce."

"Do they excuse you from school for this?" I asked them.

"This IS school," everyone at the table told me, more or less in unison. They explained that they had been excused from traditional high school to become BADI employees-in-training. They were learning the ways of the real world, not some stuffy old version of reality sandwiched between the covers of a textbook.

"Do you get a diploma?" I asked.

They all smiled, trying not to laugh. Yes, they assured me, they would get a diploma, although that certainly wasn't why they were in the program.

I closed my eyes, feeling the soft rush of sound, expanding and contracting.

"More?" I heard Edwina ask.

"No," I replied as I opened my eyes.

"Phew," she gasped, smiling and pretending to wipe her brow.

"Phew, indeed," Credo said.

They looked genuinely relieved. Before I could ask why, Credo began to talk.

"Many future possibilities of your life exist at the same, for lack of a better word, time. Allowing you to follow a possibility meant that you had to choose one of these. We took the chance that you would choose a path that saw your own future in positive terms, as well as, selfishly speaking, one that kept us in your lives. Thankfully, you did. Once we allowed you to follow a possibility, we had to let you go as far as you wanted to take it. That's how it works. We can't interrupt you when you are painting the future of your choosing."

"I don't remember choosing," I said.

"Exactly," Credo said.

"Exactly *what?*" I said.

"Just, *exactly*," Credo said.

"What he means," Edwina said, "is that you still think in terms of your mind being an omniscient kind of sixth sense which sees and knows everything. The fact is that your mind is simply an overactive filter. Many of the really important decisions you make happen without conscious thought. They flow directly from who you *really* are to a point in the future that defines who you *really* want to be—*morphing*, I believe you would call it. You are on this path with us because you have great intuition. Although you have not spent much time consciously thinking about your future, on other levels your vision for your future is very well-formed. We are in your life because we are very much in touch with your intuition. Does that make sense?"

I had to admit that it did, receptivity overcoming resistance, inch-by-inch.

"We'll talk about filters soon," Credo assured me.

Edwina and Credo studied me with a solemn look of expectation, making me feel there was one more dip in the roller coaster before the ride was over. Before I could ask them what to expect, my mood began to change drastically, the pit of my stomach bunching into a knot as the sour feeling of nausea began to sweep through me.

"I need to go back," I told them, looking around for a place to vomit, just in case.

Edwina and Credo bounced a few glances back and forth and then nodded, concerned but relieved. I didn't bother asking what they knew about me that I was about to find out. I just tried to keep from getting sick.

"All right, but just for a minute," Credo said.

I was back in BADI's training room, same day, same kids laughing at the mention of a diploma and telling me about being part of a real world learning environment rather than an old-fashioned school that tried to make textbook sandwiches out of their brains. I was looking at them when something leapt from me, like a tiger pouncing on prey.

I demanded to know what their vision for the planet was.

"Our what for our what?" they asked.

I demanded to know what their personal philosophies were. As they blinked more or less in unison, I told them that if they didn't have a personal vision, then someone else would supply one for them, and who would that be? Perhaps someone whose motives they had never questioned? And what would *their* vision rest on? Money? Praise? Power? I told them that being smart is like being rich: You have lots of resources, but then what? The test of who you are is what you do with them.

The rest of my questions came at them like UZI spray: "Are you concerned that many of the Superfund toxic-waste sites are a result of computer-chip manufacturing? Would you hire someone who had the gene supposedly linked to alcoholism? If someone gave you an insider stock tip that couldn't be traced, would you use it? What would you tell your kids about a day at the office if it included making an immense profit from wholesaling running shoes made by Third World laborers working at starvation wages? What are your thoughts on the increasing group of disenfranchised people, particularly in inner cities, who can't afford to attend the info party and are being marginalized to the point where they will be forced into extinction or social revolution?"

"Look, buzz wrecker," the kid with red hair told me, rising and pointing his finger in my face. "Me and my classmates have a future. Screw it—we *are* the future. We're going to be well-adjusted, financially secure, lifelong learners and creative problem-solvers. Our contribution to society? We would never need welfare. Our vision for the planet? Keep unemployment low. Our take on helping out the disenfranchised? Quit whining, work hard, look for opportunities and do what you have to in order to succeed. And if that meant toeing the party line, so be it. We're going to be prosperous and happy. End of story."

"THEN WHAT?" I screamed at them.

My head was in a metal bucket, the smell of vomit plugging my nose as the questions I had thrown at them pinged around inside my mind. The questions belonged to a list of things I kept meaning to think about when I found the time. But the time never managed to reveal itself. Steady state had too much velocity.

I pulled my head out of the pail and looked up to see an elderly man leaning on a mop, a look of unperplexed complacency on his face. He was draped in blue overalls that almost completely covered a white flannel shirt with large yellow buttons. A droopy cap covered what I was sure was a shiny bald head.

"Who are you?" I asked.

"I'm the janitor," he said calmly. "And I don't need welfare, either. Here," he said, gently taking the bucket from me, "I can get that for you." As he started to take the bucket, we both realized the tip of my tie had gotten caught in the swivel of the handle. I started to yank at my tie, desperate to be free, when he smiled at me knowingly, calmly. In one fluid, unassuming motion the janitor withdrew a penknife from his pocket, pried loose the handle with it and freed my tie. He smiled effortlessly as he handed me a handkerchief from his back pocket.

The knot in my stomach receded as I wiped my mouth with the janitor's handkerchief. As he looked at me intently without pity or disdain, a gentle burning began to fill the area near my solar plexus.

"I thought I would give you a little taste of your Disney chakra," Credo whispered.

As the janitor walked away, Edwina rubbed the top of my head the way Miss Phelps had after I had downed a pocketful of candy in one gulp the morning after Halloween and then played "dizzy" on the playground, ending up in the teacher's lounge puking my guts out. I asked Edwina whether I had been too enthusiastic with the students. She told me not at all; whatever bumps there may have been in my approach would get worked out over time. The important thing is that they listened.

"Once again, we are glad you took the path you did," Credo said.

"Why?" I asked.

"Free will is the most powerful force in the universe," he said. "We had no idea where you were headed when you returned. We knew you were very agitated and that meant you could have painted a very different painting, one that wouldn't have needed us at all."

"Credo, honestly!" Edwina scolded. "The point is not whether we are included. If William had chosen a path without us, then so be it. Focus, Credo, focus."

"Yes, ma'am," Credo said.

"We would have missed you," Edwina said to me, "but that is hardly the point. What's most important is that you continued to choose a path that saw living in the world in positive terms and as a process with a heart that was based on a sense of vision. Good work, William."

There was still something I didn't understand. What exactly would have happened if I had chosen a different path?

"If you had chosen a path with a lot of negative energy," Credo replied, "then the world would have had to live with the possibility that that is where you probably were headed. The future would have been more or less set at that point and The Committee would have given us hell for asking you to choose a path prematurely. But we gambled and we won."

"I must admit that I was little afraid that your cynicism might triumph over your optimism," Edwina said as she winked at me. "But I was only a little afraid."

I stumbled through a few words before I finally asked them what they meant in concrete terms. Could they lose their license to mentor? They both laughed so long that I didn't wait for them to stop as I gently insisted on an answer. "Something like that," Credo finally said. What if I had chosen a path that hadn't included them?

"We would have gone away," Credo said.

"And where do people like you go exactly?" I asked.

"Well," said Edwina, "I am going home."

Credo turned to me as he got up to leave. "Do you want to walk?" he asked.

I shrugged. "Not particularly."

"Me either. It's a long way to the East Coast." Credo snapped his fingers.

CHAPTER 15 How Life Acts & Smells Like an Onion
So many dimensions, so little time.

Credo and I emerged inside his doorway, escaping the rain that beat down on the pavement with such ferocity that it sounded like an angry machine. He looked at me inquisitively.

"So I decided to change my pants," I said, acknowledging the rather plain khaki trousers I was wearing. "So what? Don't make a big freakin' deal about it. Besides, it's more than I can say for you."

Credo laughed a little, sending a gust of halitosis my way. His breath had reverted to a putrid stench that instantly enveloped me, so I started talking just to distract myself. As I began asking for more details about the mechanics of "following a possibility," he put his hand up to stop me.

"We'll get to that in a minute," he said, as he looked me over. "You don't get the smell thing, do you?"

"Oh, I get it all right," I assured him. "I've probably lost most of my cilia since I met you."

Credo shook his head in disappointment. "You haven't been reading your McLuhan, have you? If you had, you would understand that smell was part of the omnipresent acoustic space that dominated our senses before print. I was trying to make a point."

"If I promise to read McLuhan will you promise to use mouthwash?" I pleaded, as I mulled over the term "omnipresent acoustic space." I had been reading some McLuhan and thought I had at least a vague idea of what it meant. Before Credo could respond I pushed on, telling him I was particularly interested in where all the "unused possibilities" went, whether they were recycled, played out in another universe somewhere or simply chucked into the ether. Credo waved me on, telling me flatly to let my questions sit for a while, and that eventually I would be able to answer them without his help. For now he wanted me to concentrate on what I had learned in church. The frustration at being put off one more time quickly subsided as I rummaged through Billy Pulpit's sermon in mind.

"Take your time," Credo counseled.

"Our gods have not saved us from each other," I finally began. "In fact, they have set us against each other. We must save ourselves, and our best hope of doing so is by connecting with each other. The more connected we become, the less likely we are to damage any part of our own social ecosystem."

"Good work," Credo said.

"Networkers have a unique perspective and a special duty to help because we, more than others, understand that hurting or helping one point in a network hurts or helps the whole network."

"Absolutely," Credo said.

"It would seem that our primary goal should be to see ourselves as extensions of our gods, rather than the other way around."

"Absolutely again. Nice work, William. Wait—did you hear that?" I stopped, listening intently, unable to hear anything. Credo was smiling with immense pleasure.

"It was Mr. Big," Credo said. "He really liked that last statement of yours."

"You'll pardon me," I said, "but as I stand here being suffocated by your halitosis I can't help reflecting on the saying, 'familiarity breeds contempt.' Are you sure that all this connecting is going to help people like each other more, particularly if we are going to begin projecting smell across the network some day?"

"I'm not saying that at all," Credo replied. "We are never going to sit in one big chat group, link virtual hands and declare our unconditional, undying love for each other's avatar. But we can at least evolve for selfish reasons, because we know that hurting others hurts ourselves. We are not talking about altruism here; we are talking about survival and enlightened self-interest."

"So, food, clothing, shelter...and networking?" I asked.

"Not exactly." Credo paused and rubbed his chin for a moment before continuing. "Networking isn't actually about computers. Networking is a metaphor, a medium through which you learn and discover who you are, what you know and what's next in your education. There is no absolute value in having a great network. There are only the lessons we learn in creating a great network. Everything you do is just another path to discover who you are and what you are capable of. The network is a metaphor, your life as William Tell is a metaphor. This dimension is a metaphor—schoolhouse Earth. You know this on a deeper level, and you even sense this on more superficial levels, but you don't quite believe it yet."

As I listened to Credo I tried to escape his breath by backing as far away from him as the confines of the doorway would allow. Doing so only compelled Credo to move closer to me.

"It's time to talk about the nature of multi-dimensional reality," Credo said seriously. "Are you ready?"

"I wasn't falling for that one," I told him. There was no such thing as being ready for anything he was about to tell me, so it didn't make sense to try. Credo smiled approvingly at my comments before clearing his throat and spitting on the sidewalk in preparation for what I sensed was going to be a lengthy oration. Fortunately, he moved through his explanation slowly and deliberately.

"To begin with, there are many dimensions of reality in which we all exist, each of which occupies a different frequency. Each of us exists at each of these different frequencies simultaneously. The dimension with which you are most familiar—the one you call 'here'—has a fairly low frequency. Because of this, it is relatively dense, materially speaking. We observe it with our senses, and to some extent, our thoughts and our feelings. The higher the frequency, the less material or observable we become. Observing anything at higher frequencies requires new senses and new skills."

He paused to allow me to react. I told him that I assumed he was talking about the world of multiple possibilities that existed at the same time, as Edwina and he had explained in church. He shook his head vigorously and told me not at all, that the world of multiple possibilities and the one he was describing were two very different worlds—associated, but different. He asked if I could relate to music, and when I told him a little bit, he explained that life was like an improvised song. The multiple frequencies were the vertical part of the song—the chords and tapestry of notes that occurred at each instant of time—while the multiple possibilities comprised the melody, or the forward motion of the song, which was never entirely sure where it was headed. Our discussion was centered on the chords at the moment, not the melody.

I blinked once too often for Credo to feel comfortable continuing. With an unusual patience he tried another approach, asking me if I understood what the electro-magnetic spectrum was. I told him that as far as I knew it was just a fancy term for light. Did I realize that visible light was just one frequency within a much broader spectrum? "Sort of," I told him; I hadn't stuck around high school long enough to take physics so the idea was a little fuzzy.

"The dimension we call 'here' occupies a position similar to the one occupied by visible light in the electro-magnetic spectrum. Visible light is just one point on a vast continuum of frequencies, which is surrounded by a number of other different frequencies. While we can detect visible light using our eyes, we cannot detect the other frequencies without help in the form of special technology specifically created to detect the other frequencies: radio telescopes, x-ray readers, television sets and so on. Similarly, we—you, me, all of us 'here'—interact in just one frequency in the spectrum of reality while we are surrounded by numerous other frequencies, within which we also interact, but which we can not detect without new tools and new skills."

"I need another metaphor," I told him.

"A metaphor that helps me understand how this works is thinking of myself as being just one idea from a much larger mind. The 'big mind,' so to speak, has invested some of its energy in this dimension as the Credo you know and love, and the rest of its energy at other frequencies. Same with you. Same with everybody. A large part of you, the wisest and least-dense part of you, is always accessible during dreams, time travel, meditation or just walking down the street, if you know how. We met in one of these other dimensions. So did you and Edwina, Mr. Big and Art, whom you will meet soon. That's why we are helping you. All the frequencies come together like the layers of a big onion. The dimension that you call 'here' is just one layer of that very large onion."

"I'll need a translation," I said.

As I repeated Credo's words to myself, "a very large onion," I recalled Edwina Tech's advice to me: "Pay attention to the metaphors people use, William. They reveal a great deal about the people who use them." *He's been eating onions*, I thought to myself; *probably very large ones.* And probably just for the impact it would have on me. The onions were mixed with something else, but I couldn't tell what it was.

"Look at it another way," Credo continued. "Imagine a beam of pure energy speeding through the air. It hits water and slows way, way down, being absorbed, and refracted all over the place." To dramatize his point Credo waved his arms sluggishly through the air, as though he were trying to swim through molasses. It looked to me as if he were doing a dance I had seen on a web site, "The Prehistoric Dances of Your Parents," called the Watusi.

"The real us, the BIG us, is like this energy beam zinging merrily through the air in a dimension beyond time and space, pure and free. Then we decide that part of us should head into the water to explore it and learn from it. That part materializes in this reality, schoolhouse Earth, 4D time-space. The part of us that lives 'here,' in this dimension, assumes a shape, like William Tell. It keeps growing, but at a much slower pace and at a lower frequency because water is a much denser medium than air. Meanwhile, the rest of us, the larger part of us, continues zinging along at multiple frequencies, always connected to the part of ourselves in the water. The many frequencies are never separated." He looked directly at me. "How am I doing?"

"Great," I said sarcastically. "I've been transported to a college dormitory room sometime in the late '60s. A recyclable beeswax candle is burning, the Grateful Dead are playing, and we're sitting around a plastic statue of the Buddha drinking too much really cheap wine talking about how unmaterialistic we want to be when we grow up."

Credo was suddenly indignant, shaking his finger at me and nearly screaming. "How would you know anything about the '60s? Don't you ever defile the '60s! It was the last decade that anyone cared about anything! You have no idea what we went through just so men your age could wear an earring to work. I got kicked out of school for having hair that touched the top of my ears. Women couldn't wear pants and no one could wear blue jeans. The suits didn't like you talking about anything, and if you ever said anything about the government it had better be nice. It was 'yes, sir,' and 'no, sir,' and you were in your seat when the bell rang or you stood in the hallway outside your classroom to be publicly humiliated. We protested our butts off against the Vietnam War, and then the draft ended. Then everyone got real interested in money and voilá—we have the next millennium. Don't you ever tell me about the '60s! Never! Fugguduh!"

Although I knew Credo was harmless, I had to admit that he scared me a little now and again. After I assured him many times that I was sorry, he calmed down enough to spit, wipe his mouth with his sleeve and resume his explanation calmly.

"Even though it is denser in this dimension, we choose to come here because it offers certain benefits and opportunities that can't be found elsewhere. The law of mutual exclusivity rules this frequency and dominates these benefits. Unlike other frequencies, here we can only do one thing at a time. Because we have to choose what we want to do, we have to prioritize and decide what is important. This offers a more focused, deliberate kind of education than you will find at higher frequencies. The learning here is intense and often painful. But the growth is incredible. As you move up the frequency spectrum, life becomes more fluid and multi-tasking until you reach the top, at which there is no time or space; everything happens all at once. There you can do many things. In theory you can do an infinite number of things simultaneously. But 'here' we must do one thing at a time. In the process, we define ourselves as much by what we don't do as by what we do. We are who we aren't."

I told him that while I found what he was saying to be very interesting, it left me feeling as if I weren't in charge of my own life and that I was being subjected to forces I couldn't see or control. When Credo assured me it was exactly the opposite, I asked him to explain further.

"You are solely responsible for projecting who you want to be onto the great canvas of life, painting your life as you see fit. Once you really understand that, you come face to face with just how truly free you are. And then there is no going back. Issues that you used to see in black-and-white terms start to become gray. The grayer they become, the more responsibility you consciously have to assume for your actions in order to live graciously and wisely with the law of mutual exclusivity. Believe me, more than once before your tenure with me is over you will pray for the ignorance that used to limit your freedom. Do you want to know what an up-and-coming field is?"

I smelled a digression in the offing.

"Freedom management," he said before I could respond. "For all of our liberation we still don't understand that if we are truly moving in the direction of greater freedom then we would allow ourselves to want less, to be less competitive, to choose not to be burdened with information we don't want. But that is not how we design our freedom because that doesn't feed the change machine, and we all know what that does to the gross national product. To us, more freedom always means the freedom to include more, to take a step forward into a land of more options, whether we want to go there or not. It cultivates a culture of perpetual dissatisfaction and the feeling that because everything around us is changing, we must change too, whether we really want to or not. Having the wisdom to know when you have enough is a dying art, and freedom managers will begin to assist people in cultivating that wisdom. Anyway, back to the law of mutual exclusivity."

I was waving my hand, erasing an imaginary blackboard, trying to get back to the original thread of what he had been telling me. I told him that if what he said was true, then how was it that neither I, nor any of my friends, seemed to know anything about any of this?

"Would you know math if no one taught you? Besides, you actually do know all of this. Everything I am telling you sits in your brain. You just have to learn how to access it. That's what teachers are for. Being consciously aware of something and knowing it are two very different things. Like I said, we met at other frequencies where your knowledge base is much more developed than it is in this dimension. Now, as for your friends, I don't know. Maybe you need new friends."

I paused just long enough to become aware of Credo's breath again. I pushed forward quickly, trying to avoid focusing on it.

"Let me put this in terms of a metaphor I can understand," I said. "What you are telling me is that I am one stock in a larger portfolio. The portfolio includes investments at various frequencies of existence, and all of our various investments can meet and communicate at the highest frequencies at a huge trading floor in the sky. The stocks in this frequency need to be traded with a lot of effort and deliberation, one at a time. But as we move up the frequency spectrum, stocks become increasingly more fluid and easier to move around, until we get to the mother-of-all stock exchanges at which we can trade as many stocks as we want all at the same time without any effort. The only problem is that I don't know any of this unless an old man with bad breath tells me."

Credo nodded. "Close. I would change the last sentence to read: 'The only problem is that while I intuitively know all this to be true, I cannot become consciously aware of any of it in this dimension unless an old man with bad breath tells me.' Make sense? Again, you are confusing consciously processing something with knowing it. And you might leave out the part about the bad breath if you wanted to practice your compassion. But that's up to you."

"And the intersection between multiple selves and the world of multiple possibilities?" I asked

"I would like to hear what you think," he replied.

"In the world of multiple frequencies, we educate ourselves," I responded. "In the world of possible futures, we act on our education, choosing who we are at each moment, creating our lives as we go. The point at which they intersect is the point at which free will and time intersect, creating 'here and now,' a great rolling present that moves on its own whether we are there or not, but moves under our influence if we are there to guide it."

"Bravo, bravo!" Edwina said. I looked around, but, predictably, saw no one.

Then I heard the voice of Mr. Big. "'Great rolling present,'" he said with gusto. "I love it! I just absolutely love it!"

CHAPTER 16 Where Machines Come From

Catch 33: the illusion of progress. For every two steps forward, there is at least one back, eventually three or more.

"Now, back to this dimension," Credo announced, in the no-nonsense tone of a Zen master teaching me how to sit quietly on a hard wooden floor.

Credo explained that the important thing to remember about the law of mutual exclusivity was that when you got right down to it, people were serial processing machines: While we could consider many responses to a situation, we could only act on one of them. The tension inherent in that situation was the heartbeat of the human condition. And, tangentially, he wanted to put to rest the ridiculous rumor that we, in the modern age, processed more information than our ancestors did. Just because we had more options didn't mean we could handle more information per cubic moment. Credo assured me that the average prehistoric sape living on the savanna was bombarded with the equivalent of the Sunday New York Times every few seconds, just as we are regardless of what we are doing at the time. Throughout the ages we have always been subjected to the same amount of information, just a different kind. The difference was an issue of quality, not quantity.

Much to Credo's amazement, I got up the nerve to interrupt him and asked if the law of mutual exclusivity wasn't at odds with McLuhan's notion that pre-literate and post-literate man experienced an acoustic, simultaneous environment rather than one that was sequential in nature.

Credo stared at me incredulously and asked if I had been reading McLuhan behind his back. I told him that I didn't have time to read books anymore, and that very few of my friends did, but that I had found a web site that listed McLuhan's most important points, which I had studied thoroughly. But, I admitted, I didn't pretend to understand any of what I'd read. I was just regurgitating—an obvious downside to skimming the world in sound bites rather than absorbing it in paragraphs.

"It's just as well you didn't try to read any of his books," Credo said. "It is no coincidence that the man who tried to convince us that print was on its way out was one of this century's most selfishly obtuse and overtly confusing writers. He was a minimalist in the worst sense of the word. He left out every other sentence. However, you raise a good issue that is worth clarifying."

Credo explained that according to McLuhan, history could be viewed as occurring in three phases. Phase One was life before print, which, as I had suggested, was not experienced sequentially. Instead, so-called "tribal man"—McLuhan's term for pre-literate man—lived in acoustic space, a metaphor for space that was dominated by sound, touch, and smell—the senses that came at you from all directions that you couldn't turn off. Tribal man's world was one of simultaneous experience and associative feelings in which all things happened at once. It was a world of involvement in communities, many of which did not even have a word for the concept of "individual."

Phase Two began when print came along and destroyed the acoustic space of tribal man. He became overly dependent on visual stimulation, which came at him from only one direction and which could be turned off by closing his eyelids. Literate man's visual culture was specifically based on phonetic literacy, in which the world was reduced to chunks, one following the other, like letters in a word and words in a sentence, forming a continuous chain of cause-and-effect events that he could see. We literally became our print technology. We adopted habits of mind that made us individuals, reading quietly to ourselves, cultivating private points of view and preferring to live in the interior landscape of our minds rather than being involved within the oral, exterior lives of our communities.

In Phase Three tribal man came home, so to speak. He returned to a world of community involvement and sensory bombardment through electronic networks in which information came at him from all directions and which he couldn't shut off. Our tribe is now the entire world, and through our technology we became re-integrated into a village of global proportions. McLuhan went so far as to say that the primary agent of this re-tribalization—television—was not a visual medium but an audio-tactile one, recreating the sensory environment of tribal man. Despite the fact that our common sense told us that television was visual and lacked touch and smell, we bought it. Foisting flawed pearls of wisdom on the public was the kind of stuff McLuhan got away with all the time. He moved from thought to thought so quickly that no one was fast enough to catch him.

"So," Credo said pointedly as he looked me in the eye, "what's the primary flaw with McLuhan's theory?" I told Credo I thought it probably had something to do with not being able to go home again, just like Jeff Foxworthy said.

It was Thomas Wolf, Credo corrected me, but otherwise I was exactly right.

The idea that we were returning to a global village that was anything like the one we'd left was ludicrous, Credo scoffed. The world prior to print was filled with small, mono-cultural communities. Most information was first-hand—local and verifiable—and supported a consistent mythology. Therefore, there was very little conflict among ideas. It wasn't that tribal man didn't have an interior landscape; it was that he had one in which all the pieces of the world fit together into a coherent rendering of reality.

But today's global citizen is subjected to information in the form of ideas, not pure sensory data. Because the data is filtered data, rather than primary data, it is conflictual by nature. That is, you may think one way about something, then you read a magazine article which challenges your ideas, then you go into a chat group on the Internet and hear a few more viewpoints that are at odds with yours, then you watch a news special which presents even more information that doesn't fit with what you already know, and so on. There's not more information today. Instead there is more filtered, conflictual information that is harder to weave into a single, coherent perception of reality. Because you can only do one thing at a time or think one way about something at any given moment in this dimension, the conflict is intensified. This is why filters are such an important part of life, a subject Credo promised to address later on.

Credo said that McLuhan, the consummate counter-thruster, would probably respond to him with the following argument: Because it takes us time to realize the capabilities of a new medium, we tend to use it to do the work of the old medium while we discover the new medium's unique potential. Therefore, we are trying to take all the conflicting information that we hear through our electronic networks and place it side-by-side, sequentially, trying to fashion a coherent sentence out of it when what we should be doing is integrating it into a unified acoustic space. McLuhan would say that life is no longer either/or, it is both/and.

But, Credo warned, the problem with that reasoning is that in the Information Age we have discovered the limitations of our capabilities to integrate conflictual data. Regardless of what we learn, ultimately we will have to act in a way consistent with whatever our particular belief system is at any given moment, however personal or communal.

Credo looked at me seriously, as if to emphasize his next point.

"We are walking, talking belief systems," he said. "We are belief systems with clothes on. If you want to change yourself, change your belief system, and everything else will follow."

Again, Credo reminded me to focus on the tension between being able to consider many viewpoints but only act on one of them at a time. That was the essence of this dimension. That is where the great rolling present came from. And our belief systems were what allowed us to navigate the great rolling present of infinite possibilities.

I could tell Credo was itching to get on to the next topic, but I couldn't help myself. I told him that I *could* do a lot of things at once. I could start downloading a file from the Internet, begin a web search, run a stockholder report and send a file to an electronic mailing list, all while I was savoring the suds on my morning latte.

Credo smiled. "Catch 33."

"Catch 33?" I asked.

"The illusion of progress. It is something that can be true if you do it, but if you do it, it is no longer completely true. It is just an expensive way to state the law of the conservation of energy."

"One more time, please," I said.

"It is something that must be done to accomplish something else but which, in the process of doing it, undermines what you are trying to accomplish. Two steps forward, at least one back, eventually three or more, but sometimes you have to zoom way, way out to see it. Like using a coupon to buy something you don't really want to save money. Like using the elevator to save time in getting to the gym to work out on a Stair Master. Digital artists are probably the best example. They live a Catch 33, unable to create without technology, but unable to fully create what they want because they have to play nursemaid to a bunch of gadgets. The technology gets them where they want to go but keeps them from getting there entirely. Remind me some day that you need to meet Art. He'll tell you all about it, and he's a little crazy because of it.

"In your case, Catch 33 consists of paying a price for doing a lot of things at once, which actually undermines all the progress you think you are making. Everything you do requires maintenance.

Every gadget you buy, piece of software you install, process you initiate, has a need for attention and a margin of error that feeds the entropy machine.

"On top of direct maintenance there is indirect maintenance—shopping for the best deal, filling out forms, justifying your needs to one of your superiors, training people to use whatever you get, and above all, coordinating your new addition to the technology infrastructure with an existing system that wasn't built to handle it. With every new thing you get and every new activity you become involved with, you become enslaved by its demands. And on top of all of this, every new gadget carries with it the promise—and the threat—of obsolescence and becomes another testimony to the presence of Catch 33 in the world. If you did a direct-cost accounting of the time lost and saved you would find yourself not nearly as far ahead as you think.

"And we haven't even gotten to spiritual or emotional maintenance. You will find that stress is directly proportional to technological dependence and technological failure. If you should happen to wake up one day and decide to simplify your life, you will find that the amount of time and energy it takes to do so is also directly proportional to the amount of technology you have become dependent on. By the way, 'catches' only come in multiples of 11, divisible by itself and 2, 3 or 7. It's a rule."

I stared at him in disbelief. "Whose rule?"

"The Committee's rule."

"What committee?"

"Later. Let me finish this thought. Catch 33 has a corollary that you should know about. It goes something like this: No matter how good a thing you do in one place, you do a bad thing somewhere else. Any action sets up a reaction somewhere else, creating a tug-of-war between two different parts of the world. Let me put it another way: Every connection you make disconnects something somewhere else. This is just a fancy way of stating the law of entropy. Let me show you how it works. Name something good. Anything at all."

"Like what?" I asked.

"Name something that you like that you think is good for the world," Credo replied.

I thought for a moment. "Recycling diapers," I announced.

Credo looked at me inquisitively.

"My sister does it. She has been dead set against disposable diapers since day one. She says it is the ultimate statement of a lazy, wasteful society, and I have to agree. So, she hires a service that comes around once a week to pick up the pile of stink in the white tub on her front porch and drop off a fresh load of clean cotton diapers."

Suddenly it appeared as though Credo had assumed a professorial, pontificatory stance behind a lectern about ten-feet-away. I was conscious of the fact that we had not left his doorway and that whatever was happening was illusory, but I didn't care. Credo adjusted the reading glasses propped on his nose and cleared his throat before he began.

"Assuming the cotton for the diapers was grown in this country, it was probably planted and harvested with the help of underpaid farm workers with no health insurance or legal status, who faced a life of persecution at home and one of near slavery here. What jobs do exist in the cotton trade, that do not require tedious back-breaking labor, are held by the engineers who design the cotton picking equipment, the futures traders who dictate the fortunes of farmers and farm hands from a computer in a high rise on Wall Street, and the government bureaucrats who oversee everything from fertilizer to farm subsidies in an effort to regulate the habits and habitats of the farming life style.

"But why talk about cotton when we can be talking about oil, which has been fashioned into every aspect of the delivery van? The steering wheel, the seat covers, the lubricants, the fuel, the radiator hose, the little Jesus hanging from the rearview mirror—all of it is made of plastic. The plastic is made from oil that is probably extracted from the pristine wilderness of Alaska and gets shipped down south, tempting the law of averages, which says that sooner or later you're going to spill enough of it in a tanker disaster to wipe out an ecosystem.

"But why talk about oil and plastic delivery vans when we could be talking about us? I am no fan of big oil, but to blame them for the Valdez oil disaster was pure avoidance and media pandering. Each one of us should look in the mirror for the cause of that tragedy. Every last one of us is a polluting, resource-bingeing, selfish little sape who just can't seem to help himself. Each one of us drives the wheels of industry unrelentingly to feed our plastic habit. If we all weren't so hell-bent on keeping up with the McCravitz's—"

"Who?" I asked in disbelief...*or was it whom?*

"The McCravitz's," Credo replied nonchalantly. "They lived across the street from me when I was growing up."

"Oh. Right. Gotcha. That universal touchstone of human experience—the McCravitz's. How could I forget?"

"If we weren't so hell-bent on keeping up with the McCravitz's," Credo continued, "the Valdez oil spill might never have happened. But on the other hand, if we weren't rabid about providing our families all the plastic amenities the world had to offer, then some social worker would come along and say we didn't care enough to be responsible parents. There are no awards for walking lightly on the Earth, but there are plenty for raising production and increasing consumption, especially in the name of God, country and family. You either support an ever-increasing gross national product, or you are an anarchist.

"Sorry for getting distracted," Credo continued in his pontificatory voice. "So, where were we? Ah yes, cotton diapers."

"Okay, okay," I said. "Fugguduh, you're cynical! So why bother doing anything at all if it is all so hopeless?"

"Because, as I have been trying to explain to you, you are living out a metaphor," Credo explained. "Nothing here is what it seems. The whole world's a stage, and there is no way to walk lightly on that stage. You can walk more lightly than you used to, or more lightly than others that you compare yourself to, but you can never walk so lightly that the Earth doesn't somehow cringe at your presence.

"Life is a consciousness-building exercise. Your actions can never become perfect, but your ideas and your ideals, your consciousness and what is in your heart, can. The real battlefield of life is on the interior, not the exterior. That is why you were so concerned about those kids in your training lab. They were using only one of their brains. They were only using this one," pointing to his head, "and not this one," pointing to his heart. "Because you know intuitively everything I have taught you so far, and because in your heart you know that life is a metaphor, and a path, and a means to improve consciousness, you were appalled at how two-dimensional their approach to life was. I believe we might say they were operating within a very narrow bandwidth of perception."

Credo stopped and laughed more kindly than usual. Then I realized why—he was laughing at himself, not me. "Distracted by distraction once again. Anyway, where were we? Yes, we were talking about multi-tasking and Catch 33. Do you want to know the real reason you are attracted to doing more than one thing at a time?"

"No," I said, just to test whether Credo was really listening to me. He wasn't. Or perhaps he was and didn't care how I felt, or he knew I was testing him and simply shrugged it off.

"Give me a minute," Credo said. "Some of these things can be a bit hard to explain."

As I waited, my mind became silent, allowing a symphony of sounds to wash over me—cars honking like angry geese at the flotilla of colorful umbrellas that weaved in and out of the traffic; tires hissing through puddles like snakes slithering through tall grass; water gushing down the street next to the curb with such intent that it sounded as if it were speaking to me.

I watched the dancing litter that filled the stream of murky, oil-stained water, focusing so completely on a wad of crumpled paper as it was lifted and floated down the street that I was suddenly experiencing the world from its perspective. Even though the sounds and the smells of the street were overpowering, they moved into the background, elevating the sensation of touch to an unnatural degree. I could feel every pore of the paper as though I were a part of it. I could feel the moisture soaking into its creases, turning the ink into a translucent, illegible blur. I could feel each dip and bounce in the street, as though I were riding an out-of-control roller coaster. Suddenly I felt the paper bump as it hit the pile of debris that had collected on top of one of the metal grates leading to the sewage system. After a struggle, the paper managed to make its way through the debris and disappear beneath the street. I could feel myself falling through darkness, surrounded by the reverberations of street noise pounding from above.

"Whoa!" I yelled. I shook my head as I regained my senses, a little frightened and a little embarrassed that I had gotten so carried away. The episode felt like it had lasted an unexplainably long period of time and left me feeling a bit light-headed, as though I had been meditating too long. As I regained my focus, Credo's breath pounced on me like an anxious cheetah. I was looking for a newspaper to shield my hair, so I could step outside in the rain to escape Credo's breath, when he started talking again. For a split second I was aware of the fact that a newspaper had uses that virtual information carriers did not, like shielding me from the weather.

"You like doing more than one thing at a time," Credo began, "because the more things you can do at once, the more you approach higher frequencies of existence in which you can actually do more than one thing at a time. It is your way of trying to go home, the big home, the source, the multi-dimensional reality that we are all a part of. Slavery was our first attempt. Sapes, jeez! The thinking went something like this: 'We're God's slaves, so wouldn't He want us to have slaves? God wants us to be subservient and to suffer, so shouldn't we dominate others and make them suffer, too? It's all part of The Plan, right?' It's amazing what you can justify to yourself when you are convinced God likes you.

"Every society, from small communities to the so-called great civilizations, has used some form of slavery. The economics are compelling: free labor. But the emotional rationale runs far deeper: Using slaves makes people feel more God-like.

"We never stopped wanting people to do things for us for free, or stopped wanting to aspire toward a multi-dimensional existence. These desires are buried deep within our psyche. They are quite possibly genetic. They are quite possibly linked to the genes for laziness and insecurity. They are a big part of what makes us sapes. Let me put it this way. Everything I needed to know about people on a macro scale I learned in Anthropology 101, and here it is in one sentence: People are inherently insecure; the rest are details.

"But two things happened, and it is hard to tell which came first. We developed a conscience and we developed mass media systems capable of embarrassing ourselves in front of the world. We hate our mass media most when it acts like a mirror, reflecting things we don't like to see. So the question became, 'How do we get someone else to do our work for us while everyone is watching? Simple—don't use people. So we invented machines.

"Machines are our slaves. They allow us to approach other dimensions in which many things happen simultaneously. But, a la Catch 33, in this dimension they dominate us as much as they liberate us. In fact, in the human-machine symbiosis, the humans are the ones with the flexibility so we end up adapting to our machines, rather than the other way around. Why do you think we are chasing the dream of intelligent machines with so much dedication? Because we are tired of being told what to do by our gadgets. We are tired of being slaves of our machines. Do you know what happens when I put a hammer in someone's hand? They look for something to hit. They can't help it. It's as if the hammer were telling the human what to do. The idea that we control our machines is as filled with holes as a piece of Swiss cheese."

That's it! I thought to myself. Swiss cheese was the other odor on Credo's breath. It was a particularly virulent strain, the kind my grandpa used to call "smelly old sock cheese." Onions and smelly old sock Swiss cheese. The combination was nearly lethal.

"Got a breath mint?" Credo asked.

CHAPTER 17 Filters

Choosing your information filter is as important as choosing your neighborhood.

"Be right back!" I said, dashing out the doorway and into the rain. I returned a few minutes later with my hair flat as a doormat and yellow chemicals leaking from my scalp and drizzling down my cheeks.

"Jeeesus, your hair stinks," Credo said.

"Take these," I said, shoving a fistful of mints into his hand.

"Or *you* could take *these*," Credo said, pulling a large onion and a hunk of cheese from his pocket. "Is the point to equalize the environment or to make me conform to you? And even if I took the mints or you ate the onion and the cheese, that would still leave the issue of your hair, which, in my opinion, stinks to high heaven. I suppose I could put some of that slop in my hair to equal things out. Do the women really go for that kind of thing?"

"I don't care what the women go for," I tried to assure him. "I happen to like it. There is nothing wrong with caring about your appearance, which is something that maybe you could learn from me. I do this for me and no one else." As I had been speaking, I checked my zipper and wiped my face, looking for telltale signs of breakfast. All clear.

Credo was in hysterics. "Who are you kidding? If it weren't for the mating dance we wouldn't have much to talk about. So, does Kim go for hair like that?"

In one aggravated motion I grabbed Credo by the collar of his black coat and shoved him against the doorframe, lifting him a few inches off the ground and ripping his coat in the process. A moment hung in the air that filled with the sound of quiet rain and muted traffic. Between us, there developed a buzz like high-voltage electrical power surging across open space. As I let go of Credo's coat, the veins in my forehead began to recede.

"It gets real spooky when you know things about my personal life like that," I said, seething with subdued anger. "I don't like it. I don't like it at all. How do you know about Kim?"

Kim was one of the few corners of my life that I thought I had managed to conceal from the rest of the world. I was afraid to even think about her in Credo's presence. Suddenly I realized how vulnerable I was, not just because I felt my life was completely exposed to a stranger, or even because I felt so pathetically attached to someone I had met briefly on the info-go-round, but because I felt Kim was being taken away from me simply because someone else knew about her. My attachment to her came too naturally, too needfully, and my reaction to Credo had been entirely too reflexive to be considered healthy. I stared over Credo's shoulder at a stain spot on the wall, which opened into a computer screen filled with Kim's painted face. Her voice tranquilized my mind, smoothing out the jagged edges of my inner chatter. My anger brought me back to reality.

"I said, how do you know about her!?" I yelled.

"And, I said, you told me about her!" Credo yelled back.

"Fugguduh, I did not! Is she part of this?"

"Part of what?" Credo asked.

"This. THIS! Dancing lawn chairs, multi-dimensional fugguduhs, fugguduh church services, all your freakin' fugguduhs. Is she real? Is she? Or is she just some image on the Net that doesn't exist? Just tell me that. Am I going to wake up any minute and not remember any of this? Or am I part of some experiment? Is that it? Am I a test subject? Who do you work for?"

"Whom," Credo corrected me.

"WHOM?!" I yelled.

"I don't work for anyone," Credo replied. "I am quite proud of the fact that I haven't had a job in years."

"Everyone works for somebody," I said accusingly. "So, WHOM do you work for? Are you industrial espionage? Are you trying to get me to let you into BADI's network? Or are you CIA? Is BADI doing something illegal? Oh my God, you're INTERPOL, aren't you?"

"No," Credo scoffed.

"FBI?"

"No," Credo replied.

"KGB?"

"No," Credo said patiently.

"UFO? GOP? Defense Department? Microsoft? The Christian Right? Scientology?" I blurted out.

"No, no, no, no, no and no."

"Who are you, then!?" I demanded.

"I'm you," Credo said.

"What the hell does that mean?"

"And I'm your friend," Credo said softly. "I hope that if you learn nothing else from me, you learn that friendship is the greatest gift that can ever be given or received."

I shoved myself out of the doorway and stood in the rain, lifting my face to the sky and opening my mouth as I tried to catch raindrops with my tongue. My eyes were closed and my arms were wide open, as if I were waiting to give someone a bear hug. A few passersby cursed me for monopolizing the sidewalk, but I paid no attention to them.

"Your web page told me about Kim," Credo finally said.

Of course, I thought to myself. *My freaking web page.* I had posted a simple encomium to Kim that I thought no one would ever read, except, perhaps, I hoped, Kim. I said nothing.

"Your web page is a filter," Credo said quietly. "And the next lesson is about filters, particularly media filters and especially the biggest filter of all—schooling. I'm sorry I began the lesson so forcefully."

And I'm sorry I got rough with you, I thought quietly to myself, for some reason determined not to apologize aloud. I stood on tiptoe and started to twirl around slowly as I listened, my eyes closed, my tongue outstretched and reaching for the rain as I retrieved a state of mind from early childhood that helped me escape the responsibility of the moment.

"A media filter," Credo began, "is like that sewer grate in your meditation a moment ago. A whole bunch of garbage comes floating down the street, but only a little bit gets past the grate and into the sewer. You and media work the same way. But instead of random acts of nature determining what gets past the grate, like the vagaries of rain spilling down a dirty old street, you are held hostage by the very deliberate predispositions of media, advertisers and the implicit messages of the technologies you rely on to tell you the truth."

"So am I the piece of paper?" I asked as I twirled faster and faster, like an out-of-control 4th-of-July sparkler.

"No, you are the sewer. You choose the grate, consciously or unconsciously, which determines what kind of garbage gets to you, which determines what kind of sewer you will be. The grate is the gate keeper, or in this case the grate keeper, or perhaps a great gate keeper."

Credo started to laugh. "It's hard sometimes being the only one who knows you're funny."

"I feel your pain."

As I continued to spin around I knocked a man off the sidewalk and into a mud puddle.

"Grow up!" the man yelled.

"Grow down!" I yelled back.

"'Some guessed, but only a few, and down they forgot as up they grew'," Credo recited. "It's e. e. cummings. You need to read him, if you haven't already."

I sat down in a mud puddle facing the doorway and assumed a posture vaguely resembling the lotus position. I held my head in my hands, too dizzy to open my eyes. My hair was flat and stringy, like day-old spaghetti cooked with too little oil. I felt vacant and receptive.

"Filters," I said quietly. "I'm listening."

"If you believe, as you should, that you are a product of your environment, then you will understand that filters are everything. Because we live in a dimension based on the law of mutual exclusivity, we can only watch one TV program, or read one newspaper, or listen to one radio program, at a time, forcing us to concentrate and internalize what we absorb.

"The media filters out a great deal of information, so they are already biased by reasons of selection and omission. They give their little bits of information a particular twist, depending on their advertisers, their board of directors or public expectation. The combination of all those forces turns us into one of its clones, slowly but surely. If you want to do an interesting experiment sometime, look at the same news event as examined by five different magazines. If you want to make it *real* interesting, use magazines from different countries or different social perspectives. You'll swear they were all talking about a different event! So much for objective truth.

"We think that just because we are surrounded by a lot of information that we know a lot. All the information is tainted, however, and we can process very little of it anyway. The ratio of what we know to what we could know about any given subject gets bigger every day. We live with the illusion of being informed without really appreciating how uninformed we are. That's why we have to pay such close attention to schooling."

I didn't disagree with his last point but I didn't follow the rather torturous route he took to get to it. I asked why we had to pay close attention to schooling.

"Because compared to schooling, media is nothing. Schooling is the biggest filter in the world. It is a well-intentioned, all-out assault. A conspiracy! That is another reason you were so concerned about the kids in your training room."

Again, I didn't doubt it for a second, but I wasn't following him entirely. This time, however, I decided not to pursue it, trusting it would become clear later on.

Credo stopped for a moment and became very pensive, staring at the sidewalk, out at the street, and then back at the sidewalk. Finally he looked at me and started talking, a gust of mint-scented halitosis preceding his words.

"Let me put this in terms I know you will be able to appreciate. On one level, people are just like computers. They are made up of hardware and software. The process of living actually determines the circuitry of someone's brain; that is, it determines the hardware they will have for the rest of their lives. For most people, the wiring process is completed by around the age of 7. After that point, any change in how they are 'programmed' needs to be done with software, that is, with culture, in the form of schooling, parenting and socialization. Hardware is who we are; software is who we can be persuaded to become, with some effort. Much of parenting and socialization is brought to bear on schooling. This is where communities focus their efforts on the cultivation of the human mind and define the expectations of its community members.

"This is why the first years of children's lives are so important, not just to them but to everyone around them who has a vested interest in their becoming the kind of people they would like to live next to. That is why there is something particularly horrifying about the filtering we do to children, who are forced, legally and emotionally, to accept what we tell them. Too often we squander the only real chance we have to create people in any kind of image we would actually like. We squander their trust and their openness by giving them a limited—and often twisted—view of life, and then we all live with the consequences. By the way, it is okay to hate people who create children's advertising. I have it on good authority that they are, in fact, evil.

"Later in life, when children grow up and a few of them, we hope, decide to unlearn all the horrendous garbage that's been stuffed into their heads, the only option open to them is to rewrite their own software. It is a difficult process, but anyone can reprogram himself. Those who know how to learn on their own—the true life-long learners—are best prepared to handle it.

"You found the filter of your traditional education frustrating and unappreciative of your talents. So you actively began to rewrite your software at an early age. What was it you yelled as you left school for the last time?"

"See ya later, spirit crushers!" I said.

"So you left the spirit crushers and joined BADI, where your brain and your imagination got the workout they craved. But when you observed the kids in your training room, you were frightened by a different kind of myopia at work, perhaps more powerful than the one you experienced in high school. At school, the bottom line for you was personal development—and avoiding the wrath of the suits. At BADI your bottom line became profit—and also avoiding the wrath of the suits. The biggest picture you could cultivate at BADI was small indeed and as you listened to the trainees talk to you about what was important to them, it was like looking into a high-resolution mirror. You wondered if maybe a traditional education might have helped you—and them—see a slightly larger picture and cultivate the intelligence of your second brain. Perhaps a little bit of history, a smattering of poetry and world literature, and perhaps even a little physics and math beyond algebra—all those things we are fondly rejecting these days as superfluous to the real world—might not have been such a bad idea. It is a thought that continues to haunt you.

"Now, as an adult, you realize that your only hope of becoming who you want to become is to consciously deal with your filters so that you can rewrite your software in a very deliberate and thorough way. But before you can do that, you have something more difficult to contend with—you have to decide who you want to be! You have to get very clear about your ideals and your goals. You have to create a personal vision based on a 'both/and' perspective of the world—one that paradoxically keeps you anchored as you continually evolve, one that is as solid as a rock and flexible as the winds of change, one that says you know who you are but you are not afraid to become someone different. You have to ask yourself who your heroes are, and then not be afraid to see their flaws. And then, after you have done that, you need to consciously decide which filters offer the best chance of shaping you into the person you want to become.

"The sad fact is that most people stall at this point. They don't create a personal vision, largely because they have never been told how to, or even that doing so was important. And because there is no such thing as living without a vision—because we are a vision with flesh and not the other way around—they simply adopt whatever is convenient. No matter what their heart or their intuition tells them, they tend to do what the people around them do, whether those people are at work or on television or in a virtual community. Sapes! They're expeditious to the bitter end. The unfortunate result is that most people live out someone else's vision rather than their own and remain forever separated from a life they could have truly called their own."

"This sounds bleak," I told him.

"It actually gets worse," he assured me. Unfortunately, there was another level of separation, more insidious and more spirit-crushing.

"For most people life is spent in a state of psychic separation as two people living within one mind," Credo continued. "One person is being, doing, acting, living and just generally going about his business, while the other stands about one psychic meter away, mentally off to the side, watching and judging every action. One person just "does," the other judges what it does. At the heart of reclaiming your power and becoming who you want to become is taking control of the second person, using it to consciously monitor growth and direction as you reprogram your life. Most people don't use their second person that way; in fact, most people don't know that it exists. The net result is that the second person simply reinforces limitations that have been present since childhood. The state of separation happens at such an unconscious level that it is hard to detect and even harder to control. People just become more and more themselves, whoever that is, regardless of who they might really want to be if they thought about it.

"Taking back your future is a two-step process. First, you identify your two people and consciously reprogram them. Then you integrate the two people, at which point thought and action combine, and all the chatter in your mind goes away. The moment you do that you have achieved Subdig. This is where you are headed, but it is much further down the road for you. For now, use your separation wisely to monitor your filters and make sure you are becoming who you want to become."

"Subdig?" It was as though he was just going to try to slip the word by me, hoping I wouldn't notice.

Credo nodded matter-of-factly. "Yes, Subdig. It's the true realization of the yearnings of your Walt Disney chakra."

"We need some rules," I said, heaving a sigh of exasperation. "No more than one unexplained term is allowed between us at one time. Now, what is Subdig? It sounds like you have a cold. And please, tell me more about my Walt Disney chakra."

"Talking about cold," Credo said, redirecting the conversation once again, "isn't your butt freezing sitting in that mud puddle?"

"It is, indeed. Cold butt, warm heart. So you're not going to tell me about Subdig, or Walt Disney, are you?"

"Let me finish," Credo said. "So far I have only talked about filters as something you are subjected to. That's because before the Web, we were all victims of our media—we sat and absorbed. But as of the Web, we create and participate. Now, we are all co-conspirators.

"The Web gives everyone the means to filter themselves, to create a public face that might be quite different from their private face. If I didn't know you, I would assume from your web page that you are happier and much more trusting than you really are. I would assume your hair was natural and that you loved your life at BADI. I would assume you are part West Indian."

"The picture was taken after three weeks in Hawaii," I confessed.

"Precisely. All of my assumptions would have been my mistake for relying on that filter. But what else could I do? Since I don't have time to go around personally checking all the information that is on the Web, I am at the mercy of people like you who misrepresent themselves because they use cyberspace to project who they want people to think they are, not who they really are. Yours is a small misrepresentation. But others are quite blatant. Others are outright lies.

"So what?" Credo asked. "Well, I'll tell you what. The Web is becoming the surrogate reality for most people, even more so than television because the Web allows people to interact, have relationships, create communities and become much more emotionally involved than they can with television. Web users are information producers, not just information consumers. As producers they project whatever they want and let the truth be damned. As consumers they accept whatever they see and act on it, further embedding whatever lie they just accepted into the fabric of reality. Before you know it, reality is being regenerated so fast, based on so much misinformation, that truth is a distant dream. As everyone swaps lies with each other, they live in a state of day-old revisionist history.

"The bottom line is this: In an age of conflictual information overload, choosing your filters becomes the most inevitable and important decision you will make in determining who you will become. Choosing your information filters is like choosing where you live. It defines your interior landscape. It sets parameters that control your thinking. It determines who your friends will be and what slant on the world you will have. It decides the mental environment in which you are going to live and what kind of person you want to be when you grow up. When you choose your filters, you are choosing sentinels to watch over your senses, determining who shall get past your conscious mind and into your psyche. Filters surround you. Every friend you have, newspaper you read, web page you peruse and TV advertisement that slips into your unconscious mind is water under the bridge which forms the deep pool of consciousness that nurtures the core of your being. Your filters are your gatekeepers. Gates are everything. It is no coincidence that Bill Gates has the name he does."

"Oh fugguduh, it is too," I said, honestly disgusted. "How else do you explain Steve Wozniak? It is a powerful coincidence and nothing more."

"I have to disagree with you," Credo said. "What's more, Bill Gates, like all of us, chose his name. He had a strong sense of the future, even before he materialized."

"Stop it," I insisted. "Just stop it. We choose our own names?"

"When you get right down to it, we choose everything except our first car."

"Why our first car?" I asked incredulously.

"I don't know," Credo replied thoughtfully. "It's preordained, for some reason. If you grow up somewhere that doesn't use cars, then obviously it's not an issue."

"You mean having that VW Rabbit was preordained?" I asked.

"I'm afraid so," Credo replied.

"But it leaked a ton of oil and the transmission dropped right out of it the first month I had it! Does that mean God hates me?"

"Could be." A split second later Credo was guffawing uproariously. "I was just kidding about the car thing."

"Which part?" I was afraid to ask.

"Now, let's talk about this daily online newspaper you programmed for yourself."

"The Now Times?" I asked. It was just one more thing he mysteriously knew about me.

"Yes. You construct it by sending computer programs you wrote out on to the Web—"

"I call them knowbots," I interrupted. "You probably predicted them."

"I did indeed. Your knowbots go out on to the Web every day to forage for news about advances in networking, and...what else?"

"General computer-industry information," I replied.

"Any world news?" Credo asked.

"No. Well, maybe a little, if it relates to networking."

"Any environmental updates?" Credo inquired.

"Rarely," I replied.

"Any social commentary?" asked Credo.

"Now and again."

"Sports?"

"No," I said emphatically.

"A cartoon or two?" Credo asked hopefully.

"Well, Dilbert, of course. But that's it."

"It is all very dangerous, William. The limitations of your filters keep you from answering the questions you have been storing up over the years, the same questions that you asked the kids in your computer lab. Every morning you get an online newspaper you designed that has searched cyberdom and brought back just the stuff that a very limited part of you wants to know about. I'm not blaming you—trillions of bits of information get posted on the Net each day, and it's inevitable that all of us are going to use increasingly smaller and more focused filters to sort through it. But in the process, we limit our understanding of the world to a very narrow bandwidth of interest.

"While I appreciate that we are in the age of the specialist, when we take it too far then ants become our role models. It is precisely our ability to have a generalist view that allows us to put things in a larger perspective, without which we are no different than the ants. When you limit yourself to just the stuff you want to know, your mind becomes an inbred clone of itself. The information you absorb has no greater social context. At least when you read a regular newspaper you get a bit of that, if only for a brief moment. McLuhan said that reading the newspaper was like stepping into a warm bath. In contrast, reading your online publication is like washing your face with a cold, damp towel.

"In the not-too-distant future, services will emerge that search the Net for information that you have not asked for but which would be good for you to know. You will go to one of these services, admit your myopia and ask for help. The service will produce summaries of world and local events that will help you maintain perspective. Pay particular attention to the local events. They will help you regain control over your life by informing you about things happening in your community that you can actually directly affect. I predict the first service will be called, 'The Big Picture.' I suggest you subscribe."

Credo paused to spit on the sidewalk again before resuming. "But do you know what really burns my britches?" he asked, flinging open his coat.

"No!" I screamed as I covered my eyes.

CHAPTER 18 Agents of Change

In the past, we went to school. In the future, school will come to us.

"Oh stop it," Credo chided. "I just wanted to show you my pants."

I opened my eyes very slowly, telling him how grateful I was that he wasn't naked; seeing him in that condition would have probably ruined everything. After I regained my composure, he asked me again if I wanted to know what really burned his britches. I told him that given their appearance, I assumed it was a three-alarm fire.

I studied the stains on Credo's pants, which indeed looked like scorch marks. There were so many of them that they blurred together, forming the image of a map of a large city in which each borough was represented by a different color. I thought to myself that if I really understood the history of each stain I would probably understand the story of Credo's life, and perhaps unravel the mystery of the universe all at the same time. It occurred to me that I had never questioned the fact that Credo was wearing a full-length coat in the middle of summer. No wonder he was so cranky.

"I'll tell you what burns my britches," Credo said. "It's the fact that we can't even do something *wrong* right. If we are going to take the narrow bandwidth approach to life, then we have the whole gatekeeper thing completely bass ackwards.

"Think about it. You may own your car, but in this country you don't own your own information! While no one would think of taking your car out for a spin without asking—unless they purposely meant to do you some harm—there are people both off and on the Net who steal your information all the time—*perfectly legally!* Every credit card purchase, magazine subscription, fishing license or disagreement with the legal system is a little data dropping that the big information collection companies scoop up without telling us. I call it 'data forensics.' They analyze the droppings, figure out our vulnerabilities and sell the information to companies who can best take advantage of our weakness, all without our knowledge much less our consent. Do you know that some database companies divide your weight by your height and if they figure you are overweight, they send you junk mail for fat people! If they find out you bought a house, look out! Your mailbox begins filling with junk mail about refinancing, garden tools, alarm systems—you name it. And this is some of the nicer stuff they do. Did you know it is legal to get hold of someone's medical records and their driving history? You just have to go about it the right way. If you don't believe me, you need to read PRIVACY FOR SALE. It will give you pause every time you pull out your credit card.

"The database companies say they are helping us by connecting us to people who can sell us what we want, and sometimes that's true. But puleez! If their intent really were to help us, they would reverse the way they do business. We would hire them as agents to represent us in the global data market. We would say to them: 'Here is my résumé, my data, my personal interest information. Keep it in a safe place. Get me off every mailing list except those that have to do with my personal interests. Tell anyone who wants to send me Christmas catalogs to start sending them sometime around the beginning of October and to stop in mid-December. Tell every refinancing business in the world that I am quite happy with my mortgage the way it is. And as the need arises, like Uncle Albert's birthday, send me information about just the things he has listed in his personal interest data bank that he has specified as public information. If his personal interest information isn't listed, then I will provide the information and let my information agent contact mail-order stores.' If we are to live a narrow-bandwidth existence, let's do it right. It could be sweet.

"Sooner or later this is going to happen anyway because access to an overwhelming amount of information is becoming so easy. The Net will become so friendly that even the most technophobic among us will become armchair surfers, searching for and sampling all the information we ever thought we wanted. But what happens when we ask a simple question and get so much information that we can't sort through it, let alone evaluate it, determine its trustworthiness or understand it well enough to figure out how to recast our question in ways that might make the response more manageable? What do we do when we realize that having too much information is no better than having too little since neither allows us to act more responsibly? There are two possible reactions: get nostalgic or hire an information agent.

"Nostalgia is the irrational longing for limitations. It is the desire to be relieved of all the freedom we thought we always wanted until we had it. It is the desire to have someone we think we trust tell us what to do so we can end our confusion, squelch the endless chatter in our minds that weighs and judges everything and just live. The only thing scarier than being overwhelmed by information is putting our minds into the hands of someone we don't really know to do our thinking for us. But in an age of information overload, it happens all the time.

"On the other hand, hiring an information agent to do our information shopping for us is a rational approach to accepting the need for limitations. Agents will depend upon assessment agencies that will evaluate web sites, databases and other information sources, and rate them according to authenticity, accuracy and value. Now there's a growth industry waiting to explode!

"Eventually we will hire our own information agent to help us go to school. Because our agent understands us and works in our best interest, he will craft an individualized approach to learning for us. We will turn to our information agent and say, 'I am this kind of learner interested in this kind of education with these kinds of restrictions on my life.' Our agent will come back and say, 'Then you need to attend this online class, watch this video, listen to this radio program, visit this web site, go to the local school for this particular lecture, become involved in this social gathering, work with this particular mentor, participate in this community project, mentor to this particular business, join this cohort group, and then take this test, complete this project, or submit a portfolio to this professional assessment agency.' School will become a place we go to learn the art of face-to-face interaction. It is where we will go because socializing is as basic a need as eating and dreaming. But it won't be our primary information source anymore. Do you know what the moral of this story is?"

"Be careful what you ask for; you just might get too much of it," I offered.

"Precisely! Nice work, William!"

We both heard a thumping that sounded suspiciously surreal.

"Mr. Big?" I asked.

"Indeed," Credo said. "He is stamping his feet in approval. He thinks you deserve a vacation after all your hard work. So do I. Come on."

I let go of the little bit of anxiety that nagged at me because I had missed my train and relaxed. As I closed my eyes, I could hear Credo's fingers snap.

When I opened my eyes I was staring directly into the austere, pockmarked face of Mr. Dumdown, my high school principal! I immediately checked my fly, then my ears for shaving cream and my teeth for food. And then it hit me—my hair! My pants! Both were soaked and made me look as if I had slept in a mud puddle all night. I was headed for detention for sure.

Dumdown watched me curiously as I patted myself all over.

Amid the flurry of activity I managed to catch a glimpse of myself in Dumdown's glasses; much to my amazement, I looked fine. In fact, I looked older, grayer, more serene and quite dry, if a tad overweight. I was pleased with how I had aged and was, at once, calm. I studied Dumdown for a moment. He was wearing the same bow tie, same suit coat, same wire rim glasses, all of which had survived many cycles of fashion. As usual, he looked as if he were about to explode at any moment. *Now there is man who needs to switch to decaf,* I thought to myself. My coffee hand started to twitch so I put it in my lap, out of sight.

"Good to see you again, William," Dumdown said. "I understand things are going quite well for you at Banter and Associates. I am very happy to hear it."

He wasn't the least bit happy when I left school. He gave me no end of crap for quitting, branding me a failure and telling me that sooner or later I would figure out that only losers left school, and that by the time I figured that out it would be too late.

"And how about you, Mr. Dumdown? All quiet on the high school front?"

"Heh, heh. I suppose so."

"Keeping everyone in line?" I asked.

"Heh, heh, as much as we can," he replied.

"You have to keep those independent thinkers in place, or who knows? They might join the Communist Party, become artists, or worse—they might self-actualize and get a job. Any up-and-coming losers we might be interested in hiring at BADI?"

Dumdown lowered his head and began to play with a pencil as he spoke. "Uh, not that I know of just now. Well, shall we get down to business? You have requested that your son, Credo, be excused from 3rd period math to attend TV school with a group of neighborhood kids. Do you want to explain the situation a little more or shall we let Credo do that for himself?"

I turned to my right—FUGGUDUH! Credo!? I blinked a few times, my mind running in reverse as it strained to morph the Credo I knew backwards through time into the young man sitting beside me.

It was an unnecessary exercise. On some level I knew intuitively that the essence of Credo was sitting next to me in the form of a teenager in black-and-gold clothing, wearing shiny black combat boots and a leather neck collar, and sporting body rings and spiked orange hair. I was ready to have some fun.

I suggested to Dumdown that we let Credo explain the situation to both of us. Credo looked at me with disgust and began to rub one of the nose rings that penetrated his right nostril as he spoke. "I dunno, ya know? It's just that Mr. Loser…"

"That's Mr. *Loeser*," Dumdown corrected him. "L-O-E-S-E-R. It rhymes with dozer."

"I thought it rhymed with boozer," Credo said. "Whatever. He's a geek, ya know? So let me out of prison and stop playing with my head, man."

"Can you be a little bit more specific than that?" I coaxed.

"It's his fault we hate math," Credo said as his voice rose. "I mean, what is it with his German accent that's so bad you can hardly understand him, ya know? And he's really short, so what's that all about?"

"Your English teacher, Ms. Jones, is also short," Dumdown said.

"I know, but she's cool. Short's not bad unless you're a super geek, which Loser-face is. Then it's obviously some big-time issue that he's got that he makes us deal with. I mean, go get a shrink, ya know? I'm busy."

"I will not tolerate such talk, Credo," Mr. Dumdown broke in. "I will tell you right now that you are not following rules and that is not permissible! And you have no manners. No manners at all! And I will tell you right now that a man without manners is no manner of man! And I will tell you right now that without manners you won't get very far in this world!"

"Like me?" I asked.

Dumdown glared as he unconsciously began to tap his pencil on the desk in a brisk staccato.

"Credo," I commanded, "drop the attitude. Just drop it, understand? When you push your attitude out front it gets in the way of us hearing what you're trying to tell us. Your attitude is like a bad interface on a good computer game. I am bumping on it all over the place when all I really want to do is play. Got it?"

"Yeah, yeah, yeah," Credo acquiesced.

"I don't know how much I care about whether or not you follow the rules," I said. "But having manners I do care about. So give it to us one more time from the top, with manners. And focus on what you are trying to say. Here is your moment. We are listening. And stop saying *ya know*."

"Mr. Loeser doesn't get it, ya know?" Credo began. "He's got us reading out of this geometry text book that is not connected to anything, anywhere in the known universe, ya know, and when we tell him to get networked he says, 'Zit down vright now and get to verk.' So we read this dippy little book, puke out some answers and bingo, we're smart? I don't think so.

"So a bunch of us put together this proposal thing, ya know, with an animated computer slide show and everything, about how we could actually build 3-D models of the shapes and things we were studying in class, ya know, and we could walk around inside them and actually measure them like we were right there! Then there is this class in Spain that is doing some of this stuff, too, and we wanted to talk to them about it on the Net and, ya know, sort of combine the math and Spanish things, and get an international web page going and stuff, ya know? Well, do you know what Loser said? 'Zit down vright now and get to verk.' He wouldn't even listen to us! So I told him to shove it up his serial port and you know what he said? 'Zit down vright now and get to verk.' So, screw it, ya know? I tried."

Dumdown was seething with disgust and ready to explode, when I signaled him to let Credo continue.

"So," Credo continued, massaging one of the spikes in his hair, "I want to take math from this lady on TV, Ms. Math, ya know? I saw her last week and she's very cool. She knows how to connect things with numbers in really rad ways, ya know? You get to talk to people all over the world and you use these awesome programs that let you build models and connect them, and draw diagrams for real buildings and bridges and stuff. I don't hate math. I don't hate learning. I don't even hate school, ya know? I mean, cafeteria is most excellent! I just hate being taught by someone who doesn't know his penis from his pencil and keeps telling me to 'Zit down vright now and get to verk,' ya know?"

"You get a B for content and a D for manners, which is better than I thought you would do," I told him.

"What's wrong with my manners, man?" Credo protested.

"They are reprehensible!" Dumdown blurted. "You should be sent to reform school for a semester! Or the Marines. That would smarten you up."

"Shut up, toad-face," I told Dumdown reflexively. It was how my friends and I referred to him when we were in school. It occurred to me that Dumdown actually looked more like a goose with a small beak, but somehow "goose-face" couldn't compete with "toad-face" for impact.

Dumdown started to swoon.

"Sorry, Jerry," I said. "That was way out-of-line. May I call you Jerry?"

Dumdown managed to nod.

"Call him 'toad-face' again, Dad!" Credo shrieked with delight.

"And you shut up," I said. "I was out of line just then, but I admitted it and apologized for it."

"You weren't out-of-line," Credo whispered so quietly neither Dumdown nor I were sure we heard him correctly.

"What did you say?" Dumdown demanded. "Speak up, young man!"

"So what's the hold up?" I asked Dumdown. "If he can learn from the TV teacher, let him do it. I'll pay whatever the extra charge is."

"Well, well, William, it's just not that simple. We have rules and regulations and state standards and a teacher's union to contend with, not to mention the lack of socialization that could result from learning in isolation, and the problems of fitting into a district-wide curriculum."

"Okay," I said, settling into my chair for one of those harshly linear, lopsided conversations Dumdown felt the taxpayers were paying him to have with anyone who challenged the status quo. "Let's take them one by one."

"To begin with," Dumdown started, "the course he wants to take is not even called *mathematics*, it is called *problem solving with numbers*. Most forms we need to fill out about our students' coursework don't have a space for anything called 'problem-solving with numbers.'"

"If you went shopping for a car and the car you really wanted was called a truck instead of a car, would you still buy it?" I asked.

"You always were tricky with a phrase, William," Dumdown countered.

"'Problem solving with numbers' is exactly what math is," I said calmly. "I come from the field; I know. And I will tell you that my math deficiency haunted me for the first few years on the job. I had to spend evenings bringing myself up to speed just on some of the basics."

"You should have stayed in school." Dumdown said as he grinned.

"No. School should have tried to make math make more sense. It should have used math as a bridge to the real world. Then maybe I would have stayed in school."

"So it's all our fault?" Dumdown chided.

"It is at least partly your fault," I replied. "What's next?"

"The TV teacher is from Arizona and is not even licensed to teach in this state, for god's sake," Dumdown said.

"Jerry, that one's simple," I said. "Issue her a temporary teaching certificate. You know it is just a matter of time before we figure out how to handle this kind of stuff. There are plenty of interstate consortium models being tested in this country that allow interstate certification. All of us parents who want to do this will back you up all the way to court. For god's sake, the virtual corporation is a way of life in the real world. How long is it going to take school to catch up? So what's the next problem?"

"The teacher's union is all over me," Dumdown said. "They are worried that people like Ms. Math are going to start replacing local teachers."

"It sounds to me like you have a teacher who maybe ought to be replaced, or who at least ought to be put on notice that they have competition. Look, if you can't retrain him, then fire him or come up with a reasonable alternative. But don't take it out on my kid, understand? What's the next issue?"

"How about the standards?" Dumdown demanded.

"What about them?" I asked. "Let's have a look at them. I have a feeling you are going to find that Ms. Math is covering similar material, just presenting it differently. But if the price Credo pays is that he can't pass a standardized test because he wasn't taught how to take the test, so be it. He'll just have to get a non-standard job, like me. We will cross that bridge when we come to it. What's next?"

"How about the school-wide curriculum?" Dumdown asked. "How will Credo plug what he learns from Ms. Math into the four-year math curriculum that has been carefully crafted through countless hours of after-school meetings by devoted teachers? His eleventh grade teachers are counting on him to know certain material. If he doesn't, he will most certainly fail."

"How pointless is the school-wide curriculum when students are guaranteed not to learn anything by keeping them in a class they all hate? Wouldn't you rather take a chance with a new method that offers some hope? If he is unable to fit in, then I will help him find an alternative to eleventh-grade math, too."

"He will miss his classmates," Dumdown assured me. "Learning is a social activity."

"He will be working with a group of neighborhood kids," I said. "They are free to use my living room. Besides, he will be taking other classes conventionally and is involved in all sorts of extra-curricular activities. And doesn't the TV math program involve actually spending time at a job site?"

"Absolutely tootly," Credo said. "You have to find a real live work place to go to study how people use mathematics on the job, ya know? And I got my place all picked out." Credo leaned toward me and slapped me on the back hard enough to make me cough. "I'm going to work at BADI for a while with you, Dad. Cool, huh?"

I felt the color leave my face. Before I could recover, Dumdown broke in. "While they are in your home will you be there to monitor their activities, William? How do you know they won't spend their time playing that game with their international friends where they stick needles in each other's body parts across the Internet?"

"What!?" I yelled as I turned to Credo.

"It's all virtual and nobody gets hurt," Credo said. "So everyone, ya know, just mother freakin' chill out."

"Your child needs to stay in school and do the work like everyone else!" Dumdown screamed like a drill sergeant. "Cutting him this kind of slack is just going to make him a slacker later in life. Think of the harm you are doing to his moral development!"

"Well, here's my predicament, Jerry," I said calmly. "I know tenth graders often hate their math teachers, and that I am supposed to assume it's the kid's fault. It seems like the natural order of things.

"But I was at a block party the other night and guess what? Every parent with a kid in Loeser's class is saying the same thing about him. Their kids come home and complain that he is a boring, incompetent geek who is completely unresponsive to the students who don't want to be textbook experts. They say he is either completely unable or unwilling to teach mathematics in a more applied way. All the parents tell me that their kids come home from school and say Loser..."

"Loeser!" Dumdown bellowed.

"...that *Loeser* is a geek. So guess what? Maybe that many people aren't wrong. Maybe Loeser *is* a geek!"

"If you take your kid out of Loser's, I mean Loeser's, math class I will go to the board!" Dumdown warned me.

"If you force Credo to stay in a learning situation in which he isn't learning and is guaranteed to fail, then I will go to the board," I countered. "It's that simple. Question: Is he learning math? Answer: No he isn't. Let's try something different; let's make *learning* the number one priority. The bureaucrats will take care of themselves. Think like a parent for a moment instead of a school administrator. If your kid weren't learning math what would you do? You'd try whatever you had to."

"In my day, we would simply buck up and do the work," Dumdown said.

"It's not your day, anymore. It's theirs. It's like all the pundits say: 'Your past is not our kids' future.' You need to wake up, Jerry. Between the Net, 500 channels of TV, video courses, mentor and apprenticeship programs with businesses and community organizations, and the creative imagination of concerned parents, there is enough competition for this school to make your head swim. Because of people like you, sooner or later we're going to be hiring agents to put together customized education programs for our kids that use all the resources available to us. Bottom line: Education is now a buyer's rather than a seller's market. Coming to a place like this is going to be only one option among many. You ought to understand that and work with it, rather than fight it. You have plenty you can offer here to compete in the educational marketplace."

"And just what might that be, in your estimation?" Dumdown asked.

"Just because Credo and his friends cruise the Web they think they are seeing the big picture. They confuse quantity with depth. I am extremely concerned that Credo and his friends have no under-standing of the world that history and literature can provide."

"What did you say?" Dumdown asked incredulously.

"What the fugguduh!" Credo said, even more incredulously. "History? Literature? You're a traitor, ya know, Dad, a traitor!"

"Oh calm down, both of you," I said. "The point isn't to throw away everything we've done in school until now. The point is to keep what works and to change what doesn't. I am very concerned that kids are entering the work force without any real appreciation of how the world works. I am afraid that they have no understanding of the mistakes humankind has made in the past and how to avoid making them in the future. An education isn't supposed to just prepare you for work. It is supposed to prepare you for life. It is supposed to prepare you to contribute to society. It is supposed to help you become an informed voter. Let BADI train him how to integrate math, communication and technology skills into the work place. You can help him develop a sense of his place in the world. If you can't, then I will find some alternative for his humanities courses, too."

"You're a loser!" Dumdown screamed as he stood up and charged toward the door. "You're both losers!"

A moment passed before I said, "That's *Loeser*."

Credo was in hysterics.

"Do you know how far I am going to kick your butt if you screw up with the TV math class?" I warned him.

Credo nodded as he popped his gum.

"As unfair as it seems," I continued, "the whole world is going to be watching people like you, hoping that you fail."

"I know, I know," Credo said.

I got up to leave. "I'll see you tonight at dinner. But in the mean-time I need to 'go to verk.'"

I was suddenly back on the street, standing in Credo's doorway, shaking my head and laughing as I heard Credo "the elder" begin to speak.

"To be fair, school will always offer certain opportunities by virtue of the fact that economies of scale kick in when you bring a lot of people together, like developing a swimming program, offering ballroom dancing, supporting a baseball team or having a chemistry lab. But they will no longer be the main source of information or of learning.

"The important point not to lose sight of here is that while information will be everywhere, wisdom will continue to be in short supply. That's why tomorrow's master teachers will be regarded as much for their wisdom as their knowledge. They will play more of a role in helping students find information than in being responsible for knowing the information themselves. The future teachers of the world are scholars and agents, and above all, students themselves. By the way, I like your idea—let school teach civic responsibility, intercultural appreciation and the other skills we are all going to need if the world is going to be motivated by something other than material success. It could be a good niche for them."

"Thanks," I replied.

"Okay, now where are we? Ah yes—we still have a few more lessons for today."

"Bring 'em on," I said agreeably. "But when do I learn about my Walt Disney chakra?"

"Soon. You know, we ought to go to the circus. Or maybe we'll go to Mitsie's for lunch. That's it—we'll go to Mitsie's. We'll invite some friends. We'll ask Edwina to join us. But first, let's have some wine."

CHAPTER 19 There's No Such Thing as the Technology Itself
With enough practice, we can take back the future.

Credo reached a hand into one of his coat pockets and withdrew a bottle of Merlot. It appeared to be Waterford 1990, a fine year and a fine wine indeed, giving rise to another paradox about a man who I had presumed to lack sophistication despite his magic. From the other pocket he pulled out a common corkscrew, the kind with wings that flipped up as it was twisted into the cork.

"Have I ever told you about the day that I listened to McLuhan explain the history of the Western world by examining the development of the lock and key?" Before I could reply, Credo was off, galloping down memory lane and dragging me with him as I grudgingly admitted to myself that I looked forward to the next chapter of what I was sure was an over-glorified rendition of his past.

"McLuhan's gift was that he never saw a piece of technology as a thing, he saw it as a story," Credo began. "Every tool, machine or scientific breakthrough was a cultural metaphor, a mythological reference point and a means of showing us who we were, if we knew how to see it. One of his favorite images was modern man driving down the highway of life looking into the rear-view mirror at where he had just been. Because modern man was creating change so quickly he could actually see the results of his actions quickly enough to change his behavior and take control of his future. But alas, 'we had the experience but missed the meaning'—you've read T.S. Eliot haven't you? You really should. He was one of McLuhan's favorites.

"To McLuhan, the notion that technology was neutral was laughable. It was like saying an idea was neutral or that change was neutral. Technology was a gatekeeper, always connecting us in one way while disconnecting us in another, encouraging certain things to happen while discouraging others. Technology was always a statement about cultural preference, about who got ahead and who got left out, about our myopia as well as our cleverness. In every piece of technology lurked politics. Have you ever read THE WHALE AND THE REACTOR? Winner tells the story of Robert Moses, "...master builder of roads, parks, bridges and other public works of the 1920s to the 1970s in New York," who designed overpasses too low to allow buses to pass underneath them, making sure that the lower classes couldn't get to certain places in New York. Unfortunately, the hidden story of technology is rarely that obvious.

"But if you really want to understand the very heart of technology, then you need to realize that every technology commodifies some basic longing of the human spirit, as well as an aspect of the human condition, which is deeply embedded in the old part of our brain that we share with our reptilian ancestors. What did the lock and key commodify? On one level, the pleasure and power that comes from safety and privacy, the private point of view of literate man and the empowerment of the individual to isolate himself, all of which was in direct contrast with life until that point, which had been lived more publicly. On a deeper level, it appealed to the primal need to declare territory and feel secure. The fact that a lock could be used to keep a door from opening was merely a byproduct on the way to a metaphor. Does this make sense?"

"I think so," I replied.

"So, the important skill to develop is learning how to read a piece of technology like a book—more like a totem pole. There are a number of questions to ask about a piece of technology that serve as good entry points on that quest: 'How does a technology amplify us? How does it reduce us? What does it replace? How did our parents get along without it? What need does it meet? What basic human longing does it commodify? What behaviors does it encourage and discourage? How does it change our relationship with time and space? How does it change the power structure, our relationships with others, our relationship with ourselves? How does it disconnect us, as well as connect us, from the environment and from each other? Who gets included and who gets left out? And above all...'"

"'Then what?'" I said.

"Precisely. Technology begets technology. It always spawns other technologies to support it, which you will understand when you meet Uncle Henry and Auntie Em."

"Who?" I asked.

"Technology always sows the seeds of other incipient forms of technology just around the corner. We are always on the road to becoming something else. If we learn to read technology the way meteorologists can read cloud patterns, we can become more proactive and less victimized by the march of technology. We can have the experience and *not* miss the meaning. With enough practice, we can take back the future."

Credo spent a few moments playing with the corkscrew, making it perform jumping jacks, ballet and some elementary karate moves. Then he turned to me and asked me what the story behind the corkscrew was.

I was embarrassed to admit that I was drawing a blank and would need his help. Credo began to run through the list of questions. "How does it amplify us? What does it replace? What does it connect us to? What does it disconnect us from?" He told me that all the questions were just different ways of asking the same thing, and once I could answer one of them I could answer them all. "So," he counseled, "choose one and focus on it." But I couldn't even choose a question to focus on, let alone answer.

"No problem," Credo said with unusual calm, suggesting we approach the exercise more concretely. "What is this?" he probed, dangling the corkscrew in front of me.

"Is this a trick question? That's a corkscrew."

"Tell me about it," Credo coaxed.

"Not much to tell. You use it to open wine bottles."

"Would a culture that didn't need to store wine in corked bottles have a cork screw?" he asked.

"No," I said.

"Would a religious culture which abstained from drinking wine have a corkscrew?" Credo inquired.

"Probably not, unless they stored something else in bottles that used corks."

"Would a child or an arthritic person be able to manipulate a cork screw like this?"

"Probably not," I replied. "They'd have to get someone to do it for them."

"Would a culture, which had not yet discovered the properties of the screw, have a cork screw?" he probed.

"No."

"Would a culture which had not yet invented metallurgy have a cork screw?"

"Not like that one," I assured him.

"And what is the likelihood you could make one out of wood or stone?"

"Probably pretty minimal," I conceded.

"Would a culture that had not discovered the basics of chemistry be able to create the wine that went into the bottles?"

"No," I replied after a short hesitation.

"Would a culture that had not yet harnessed the power of fire be able to make the bottle or the metal corkscrew?"

"No."

Credo looked closely at the corkscrew and started to laugh. "See that?" he asked, pointing to a few words hammered into the metal. "It says 'Made in Italy!'"

I wanted to laugh, but wasn't sure why it was funny.

"So," Credo continued, "what story is the corkscrew trying to tell us?"

"I don't know," popped out without hesitation. I just couldn't sort through the myriad of ideas that clogged my mind fast enough to piece a story together. My mind needed more bandwidth.

"William, you are a concrete-sequential kind of guy if I ever met one. Yet you possess great lateral creative abilities. I think the next step is to just let you create a story that allows you to see the corkscrew in whatever context your imagination wants to. Okay. You're on. Your next experience will be totally of your own design."

Credo snapped his fingers and I found myself sitting in a mud puddle somewhere in the jungle, surrounded by the sound of drums pulsating maniacally through the moist night air that pressed against my skin. I rose and peeked through an opening in a row of large bushes in the direction of a shimmering light. A campfire illuminated a ring of dancers in grass skirts who shook as they moved rhythmically around the fire, propelled by the escalating reverberation of the drums, yelling as they lifted their hands toward the night sky in supplication. After the dancers completed a full circle around the fire, they stopped and waited quietly for someone to say "Fugguduh" before they resumed their dance. The ritual mesmerized me until I felt something cold and damp on the back of my head. As I reached up to explore the sensation I realized a large snake was starting to circle my neck.

"Fugguduh!" I screamed.

Before I could consider my next move, two of the dancers had grabbed me, wrenched the snake from my neck and proceeded to lead me toward the fire. The crowd was completely still as I was positioned in front of a large hut with a thatched awning and shields on both sides of the front opening. Out of the shadows of the opening stepped someone who was obviously the chief, his face painted with tiger stripes, his hair filled with feathers, a sash with sparkling stones slung across his chest. Around his neck dangled the same corkscrew Credo had shown to me. One by one, the dancers approached the chief, kissed the corkscrew deferentially and moved back into the circle to wait quietly. The chief walked toward me, the reflection of the fire burning in his eyes as he removed the corkscrew from around his neck. He stopped directly in front of me.

"Fugguduh, Fugguduh, Fugguduh!" he screamed, shaking the corkscrew over my head.

"Fugguduh!" the crowd replied in unison.

The chief moved the wings of the corkscrew up and down making it look like a dancer gyrating in a fertility ritual.

"Fugguduh, Fugguduh, Fugguduh!" he screamed again.

"Fugguduh!" the crowded replied again. Four men grabbed my arms from behind and held me in place.

"Fugguduh," the chief whispered.

"Fugguduh," the crowd whispered in reply.

The chief drew back the arms of the corkscrew, exposing its sharp point that gleamed in the firelight like the eyetooth of an angry tiger. Slowly he brought the corkscrew to within an inch of my right eye. The dancers all put their right hands over their right eyes and bowed their heads. Suddenly I understood what was about to happen. I was a stranger who had seen something I should not have and I was going to be blinded in my right eye because of it. I remember thinking that I was not unlike the head of data processing for BADI's West Coast division who had gotten caught breaking into the database of one of BADI's competitors and had lost high-level network clearance in the financial community for life.

"NO!" I screamed.

I was back on the street listening to the sound of a cork being extracted from a wine bottle. As Credo poured wine into paper cups, he spilled some on his right thigh creating a new borough in the neighborhood map of memories on his pants. After we exchanged salutations and each took a hearty slug of wine, I demanded to know what the last experience was all about. I couldn't help rubbing the back of my neck, looking for the snake.

"That was a hell of a story you created!" Credo announced. "You took the corkscrew completely out its normal social context. You think very metaphorically."

"Is that bad?" I asked.

"Bad? No. It is normally quite good. But the bottom line of this exercise is to determine whether your story increased your ability to see a piece of technology clearly. So, what do we have?"

Possible dysentery, a severe case of the heebie-jeebies and all the makings of a rip-snorting psychosis, I thought to myself. I was feeling just plain stupid and mentally constipated and told Credo so. He said he understood and then asked me to close my eyes, telling me that I already knew everything, and that he was just going to act as a kind of psychic laxative. As I sat immersed in my own inner darkness, he began to lead me through a series of questions.

"Let's ask a few of those questions to get started. What does the corkscrew amplify for us as well as our pre-literate friends?"

When I didn't immediately answer, Credo began to coax. "You're thinking too hard about this. Every technology amplifies some part of the human anatomy. In the case of the corkscrew that would be..."

"Our hands," I ventured.

"Good for openers. Openers—get it? Tell me more."

"It amplified the chief's hands," I said, "by turning it into an instrument to blind me much more effectively than if he had used his fingers, and certainly with a lot more style. It also amplifies our hands by using the power of the screw and the lever to give us a kind of super-hands that allows us to leverage a specific kind of pulling action."

"Excellent," Credo said proudly. "Now, what does the corkscrew replace?"

"For the chief it probably replaced another instrument the chief used to use, maybe a sharp stone."

"In this particular case," Credo said, "it was a spear with a handle inlaid with shiny pebbles collected from a nearby river whose waters were believed to be home of Fugguduh, the local God of Life deity. But there was no way for you to know that. Keep in mind that every technology reduces as well as amplifies us. Both the spear and corkscrew reduced him in the sense that he no longer touched his enemies directly; he used a piece of technology as a medium for harm.

Now, let's bring this a little closer to home: What does the corkscrew replace *for us*?"

Suddenly so much was so clear I couldn't speak fast enough to do my consciousness justice.

"Time!" I exclaimed. My eyes were closed but I could see things vividly, as a series of overlapping connections in high resolution.

"What about time?" Credo prodded.

"The corkscrew doesn't exactly replace time, but it is part of a system that allows us to bottle the future. It means that what we drink is no longer limited to what we fetch or make on a short-term basis. This increases our ability to create communities with a sense of permanence. It is a metaphor for roots, for survival. It allows us to store something we don't immediately need, in case a harvest down the road doesn't turn out too well. It allows us to think in terms of a future."

"Keep going," Credo encouraged.

"And because we can store the wine that the corkscrew facilitates for later use, we can transport it, take it to market, trade it for other things and use it as a kind of currency, all of which increases our mobility and expands our sense of community. And, oh my God, the fire!"

"What fire!?" Credo exclaimed.

"The fire that was used to make the corkscrew, the bottle and to create the wine! It's embedded as energy in all these things. So we are not only transporting the thing, but the power it took to make the things—and the people!"

"What people?!" Credo asked excitedly.

"The people it represents—we are transporting them, too, along with their way of life—a technological culture, a wine-drinking culture, a particular approach to pleasure, a devotion to a world that is not entirely sober and that encourages the use of substances to release inhibitions. All of it changes our relationship with space, time and each other. We can go farther, plan for tomorrow, spread our ideas—and, oh my God, diversity!"

"What about diversity?!" Credo nearly screamed as he hopped to his feet in wild celebration.

"We can increase our access to food and material made by others, as well as to people we ordinarily wouldn't meet, which increases our genetic diversity, our available food supply and our overall chances of survival, leading to an increase in population, which stimulates more trade, more diversity and more growth—and fugguduh—*language!*"

"What about language?!" Credo bellowed like Billy Pulpit in a moment of passion, shaking his hands over his head.

"All of this creates an economic system that eventually gets so unwieldy that we need to develop a common language to facilitate trade and interaction, eventually turning to money, accounting and identification symbols as an international language, which are the first steps in creating a global information system—multiple fugguduhs!—*the Net!*"

"What about the Net!?" Credo asked.

"That's all for now," I said, a little tired. It felt as if my brain ran out of gas.

"Excellent work, William. All roads lead to the Net, sooner or later, don't they? And what basic human need does all this commodify?"

Again I stalled and Credo jumped in to break the silence.

"When you get down to it, there are darn few things that can be commodified. In fact, the entire advertising industry is based on the belief that there are very few things that people respond to, many of which are just different shades of one another and most of which exist in the oldest part of our brain—fear of pain, desire for safety, love of pleasure, the drive for survival. As these percolate to the tip of the iceberg we call conscious thought, they get translated into control, empowerment, youth, sex, fun, community, status, love, the desire to be valued—all those things that help us feel safe and happy. That's why ads don't sell running shoes and cars. They sell the good feelings that come with an involvement with beautiful, skinny, fun-loving people who happen to be wearing a particular brand of running shoe while driving a particular model of car."

I opened my eyes to see Credo suddenly very serious and shaking his finger at me. "Let me tell you something. There are far, far too many people, particularly the self-righteous after-dinner speaking crowd, telling everyone how different things are today than they were 50 years ago. On the surface, change appears to be all around us. But beneath the surface that just isn't so. All technology has done is amplify the fact that we haven't really changed at all. The desires of the average sape have been intact for millennia. If we focused on what hasn't changed, instead of what has, we would have a far better understanding of where we are headed. Understand? Now, what does the corkscrew commodify for the chief and his people?"

"Power," I said bluntly.

"Indeed," Credo said.

"And fear," I added. "Whoever has the corkscrew rules. The rest cringe."

"Good."

"And community," I added. "It was a symbol that everyone recognized."

"Good. And what does it commodify for us?" Credo asked.

"Survival, permanence, a desire for things that last into the future," I said.

"That's what the old brain responds to," Credo said. "How about our new brain?"

"Access to fun? To happiness? To belonging?" I ventured.

"Not bad. And for us, who gets left out and who gets included?"

"When you get right down to it, a corkscrew is fairly egalitarian," I said. "They are cheap, everywhere and easy-to-use."

"Suppose we are talking about the Net," Credo said.

No fair, I thought. He changed gears too quickly, and just when I was getting the hang of the conversation. I deferred, too tired to try to keep up.

"The power of the Net is reserved for those who can afford to log on," he began. "That includes getting a machine, software, training or access. Being left out can make the difference between having a shot at a good job or else working at McDonalds. While I love a Happy Meal as much as the next guy, the upwardly mobile need the tools of mobility, which much of the world still can't afford. Environmentally speaking, don't forget that everything we create exacts an ouch from Mother Nature—Catch 33, remember? How many corkscrews do you think there are in the world?"

I shrugged and told him that I didn't know. Thousands perhaps.

"There are 2,345,789, to be exact," Credo told me. "Each one is made of materials scooped out of the ground. Some are made in far off places where people work in such bad conditions for wages so horrible they can't afford to buy a corkscrew, let alone a bottle of decent wine. Of course there's always Ripple for the masses, which doesn't require a corkscrew. For us, in this day and age, the cork-screw tells the tale of a leisure class with disposable income, time for pleasure, and a penchant for chemically-induced avoidance, all of which rides on top of a wave of technological and scientific invention—don't you agree?"

Credo gave me a nanosecond to respond before he kept rolling. "Yet there is something strangely eternal about all of it, isn't there, William?" He snapped his fingers.

I was at the BADI Christmas party. Everyone was milling around chaotically, unconsciously forming a loose circle around BADI's president. He had just plunged a corkscrew into a large bottle of red wine and extracted the cork ceremoniously. Employees were jockeying for proximity, ingratiating themselves with twitters and smiles. The unspoken rules of the situation dictated when to stand silently in the circle and listen, when to small talk, when to laugh and when to come forward for a glass of holiday wine. Everyone knew that receiving a glass of wine was like being blessed by the chief, while not receiving one was the equivalent of excommunication. I could feel the snake on the back of my neck again like a slimy shadow that wouldn't go away. As my vision cleared I was back on the street looking at Credo.

"And we are just scratching the surface," Credo announced. "Isn't being an anthropologist fun?"

He let the question dangle in mid-air for emphasis.

"I think I peed my pants," I finally said.

"Just tell people you were sitting in a mud puddle."

Credo did not exactly drink his wine. He took a sip, gargled loudly and then swallowed in a boisterous slug. I looked on in amazement. *No wonder he's single,* I thought to myself. That was, I certainly hoped he was single given he was interested in my mother.

"You know," Credo said, "the real lesson of the last exercise—the lesson behind the lesson—is that there is no such thing as the technology itself. It is a lesson you are about to appreciate from another perspective. Have you heard the saying, *'Cars created roads?'*"

I pleaded with Credo to let me rest but he wouldn't hear of it, saying I was just hitting my stride and that now was no time to stop. He told me that the saying was another McLuhanism that went right to the heart of, "Then what?" He asked me if I knew who Uncle Henry and Auntie Em were. I remembered his earlier reference to them but it had caught me too off-guard to respond to at the time. I thought for a moment before asking if he was referring to Dorothy's folks from

"The Wizard of Oz." When he replied that he was, I shook my head in disbelief and told him that I didn't know them personally but that I supposed he did. Of course, he affirmed, assuring me that I was about to get to know them, too. He also told me that he was going to start doubling up on lessons, teaching me more than one thing at a time.

"We are going to use one experience to teach two or three things at once," he explained, "just like multi-tasking with a single computer, with you as the central processing unit. Doing so will give you a more integrated view of things. I would have done it before but you weren't ready. Besides, I thought you would appreciate the approach; it saves time and I know how busy you are."

Because it was the kind of sarcastic comment Credo was prone to make, I couldn't tell whether he was joking or not. A moment later he was in hysterics. Once again, it was all a joke. But it wasn't. But it was. But it wasn't.

"Sorry," Credo said as he blew his nose in his sleeve and flung the residue on to the sidewalk. "By the way, if Uncle Henry and Auntie Em don't make your Disney chakra buzz, then you probably need some sort of professional help. A word of caution: They have nothing to do with the Wizard of Oz. They are simply metaphors that conjure up the appropriate feeling for this particular lesson. We are using them because you relate to them. Understand?"

"I think so."

"Good. Ready?"

"Why do I feel nervous?" I asked.

I braced myself as Credo snapped his fingers.

I was fully conscious but so overwhelmed by the smell of pine and fresh earth swarming the air that I was unable to open my eyes. As I felt the sun wrap me in a soft, warm blanket, I inhaled and exhaled deeply several times, as if taking long slow sips from a fountain. The sounds of summer cicadas buzzed in the distance, massaging me into a state of relaxation.

Finally I opened my eyes. I was standing on a dirt road surrounded by thick, luminescent forest on both sides. In front of me was a store made of rough-hewn beams and large plank siding. A porch wide enough to hold a number of picnic tables and rocking chairs ran the entire length of the building. Over the stairs was a large wooden sign with big white letters that read, *"Uncle Henry and*

Auntie Em's Doohickies, Widgets and Thingamabobs." Beneath it in smaller, italicized print, were the words, *"Where a Second Hand Store is Like Having a Second Set of Hands."*

As I walked into the store, the wooden floors creaked, reminding me of the sound of crickets in the summer night. I could feel my grandpa close by somehow, a presence that filled my heart and brought a glow to my cheeks. I knelt down and pet an old dog, rubbing its head and speaking to it in baby talk. Instantly, I was filled with childhood memories of my own dog, Frequency, whom I called "Freak" for short. As I stood and scanned the store I was struck at once by its simplicity. Everything was made of wood, cloth, or simple metal. Everything smelled as if it came from an honest day's labor. The world felt as if it had a certain unquestionable order that made me feel safe and secure. Credo was right—it all hit me right in my Walt Disney chakra, somewhere in mid-solar plexus. I was comforted to know that I would not need professional help after all.

"Howdy," came the friendly, scratchy voice from behind the counter. "'Name's Auntie Em. What can I do for ya'?"

Her voice pierced my mind and went directly to my heart. I looked up and watched as she approached in a blue-gingham dress that she managed to keep looking pretty, despite an obvious lifetime of hard work. Her face was furrowed but happy. Her eyes were full of simple dreams and devotion to family. I was close to tears. *Disney to the max,* I thought to myself, *and more than a little bit of Oz.*

"Well, I'm not exactly sure, yet," I said, turning away from her and dabbing at my eyes. I wandered over to the shelves. They were filled with all those vaguely familiar, but not entirely recognizable, little doodads that most people could neither identify nor throw away, just in case they needed them someday. They were manifestations of negative entropy that would never come again in quite the same form and were saved precisely for that reason, whether they were still useful or not. There were strange configurations of metal bracketing, screws with left-handed threads, pieces of wood and steel in odd shapes that looked as if they had only one purpose in life, which had long been forgotten.

"Well," I said, "as long as I'm here I think I'll get me a thingama-bob."

"No problem," Auntie Em said as she walked behind the counter and stood next to the large metal cash register. "That whole wall over yonder is full of thingamabobs. Got any idea what yer looking for?"

"There!" I exclaimed, charging over to a cardboard box filled with hundreds of identical objects. Although I hadn't a clue what they were used for, I was oddly attracted to them. I reached into the box and grabbed one of them with conviction. "I'll take one of these."

As I examined the object, three small pieces of metal that looked like a cross between a small mushroom on crutches and a pop rivet fell on the floor.

"Need a case for those little things that just dropped out?" Auntie Em asked as I stooped down to pick them up. "Most people get one just to keep things together. What good's a thingamabob if you can't find all the parts?"

"Sure," I said. "I'll take a case."

"How about a label for that case?" she asked. "Otherwise you'll stick this in your garage and a year later not have the faintest idea what it is."

"I haven't the faintest idea what it is *now*," I confessed.

"Just think how much worse it will be in a year," said Uncle Henry as he emerged from the back room. He was dressed head-to-toe in blue overalls covered with deep pockets. He smiled warmly, continuously, as if he did not know how to do anything else.

"Hmmm. Well, yes, sure, I'll take a label," I said.

"How about a marking pen to write on the label?" asked Auntie Em. "Most people get them. I guess they figure why not, they've come this far."

"Thanks, but I'll use my own marking pen," I replied.

"Won't work," Uncle Henry told me.

"Why not?" I asked.

"The pen was special made to write on that label," he replied. "The label is made of a special material."

"Then I'll use a label I have at home," I said.

"Can't," Auntie Em told me nicely as she shook her head.

"Why not?" I asked patiently.

"Won't stick to the thingamabob case because of the special no-stick surface it's got," she said. "The labels are made special for the thingamabob case; they got a special kind of stick-em material."

"Okay, okay," I relented. "I'll take one thingamabob, a case, a label and a special pen."

"How about a service agreement?" Uncle Henry asked.

"What needs to be serviced?" I asked, trying to hold impatience at bay.

"You never know," Uncle Henry warned me, still smiling.

"No, thanks," I said. "I'm pretty handy. I'll take my chances."

"Suit yourself," Auntie Em told him. "Can you speak Tangalese?"

"Can I speak what?" I asked.

"Tangalese," she said. "This here town is Tangala and this thingamabob was made locally. Tangalese is a local dialect. All the instructions for this thingamabob were written in Tangalese."

"No, I don't speak Tangalese."

"Well," Uncle Henry said, "you'll need our Tangalese-to-English dictionary, then, if you're not going to get a service agreement. We do have the instructions in English on cassette; cassettes are 'bout as high-tech as we get around here."

"I see," I told him. "Well, maybe I could get one of the cassettes, then."

"That's fine," Auntie Em said, "but I gotta' tell ya' something: your cassette player won't work around here."

"Why not?" I asked.

"Because all of the cassette players in Tangala are made to run on 143 volts."

"143 volts?" I nearly screeched. "Why on Earth do you use 143 volts when everyone else in the entire country uses 120?"

"Because that is what is naturally generated by local streams in Tangala," Auntie Em told me. "Folks around here don't like to convert to 120 volts for religious reasons. But we can sell you a converter so you can use any of your electric stuff."

"What religious reasons?" I said, struggling to contain my exasperation.

"Folks in Tangala felt if God had wanted them to use 120 volts, He would have given them a stream that made 120 volts," Auntie Em. "But he give us one that makes 143 volts, so that's what we use."

"That's crazy," I told them

"Shh," Uncle Henry whispered as he put a finger over his lips. "It's sacrilegious to talk about it like that."

"When can we get your mother's signature on this?" Auntie Em asked.

"My mother's signature?" I shrieked. "To buy a thingamabob?"

"It's the Tangalese way," Uncle Henry assured me.

"That's crazy!" I said.

Auntie Em was suddenly very serious. "Is it any crazier," she began, "than pumping billions of dollars of those goldarn advertisements into kids' heads so they can turn around and force their poor parents to buy them stuff they don't need and is bad for 'em, like they do where you come from?"

"Well, no, I guess not," I said.

"In Tangala, parents decide what their children should get," Auntie Em said proudly.

"Don't you trust your mother's judgment?" Uncle Henry asked.

"Yes, I trust my mother, but I'm certainly old enough to make my own decisions."

"She's still your mother, though, isn't she?" asked Auntie Em. "I don't care how old ya get."

"A man who can't trust his mother is a lost soul, in my opinion," said Uncle Henry.

"As I said, I do trust my mother, but…"

"Then trust her to decide whether it's good for you," Auntie Em said. "That's the way we do it, here. It's our custom and it's a good custom. It slows down sales, but it's worth it to us. An' I'll tell ya somethin' else. We don't allow no advertisin' here and we're proud of that, too. No TV, and all the magazines got the ads cut out of 'em. I do it myself, personally."

"Of course, I help," Uncle Henry chimed in.

That's censorship! I wanted to say. I was rubbing my solar plexus while thinking that I could never live in a place like Tangala, when Edwina Tech was suddenly very present in my mind, speaking quietly to me as though she were whispering in my ear.

"William," Edwina began, "did you know that when some countries import our children's television programs they actually have to remove sections of them that exhort children to be the best they can be as individuals, and replace them with instructions telling children to do their best by helping out their communities? It's all a matter of cultural perspective. That is what Auntie Em is trying to tell you."

"Huh?" I said.

"I said," Auntie Em repeated, "you'll either need your mother's signature or you will have to get a permit. A permit can take a while."

"A permit?!" I fumed.

"By the way, are you left-handed?" Auntie Em asked.

"No, I'm not," I said.

"Oh for goodness sake," Uncle Henry said, chuckling and slapping his knee. "Why didn't you say so in the first place? This side of the store is just for left-handed people. You'll want to look in the other half of the store. And as I recall, we just sold the last one of those thingamabobs in a right-handed flavor. You want to order one?"

"No, thank you," I said more forcefully than I had intended. Suddenly I realized that the thingamabobs in my hand belonged to a dismembered corkscrew. Auntie Em suddenly focused on me with an intensity that surprised me. "Young man," she said, "have you been drinkin'?"

"No!"

As I began to focus, I could hear the sound of Credo gargling. "More wine?" he asked.

I didn't bother replying, preferring to sit quietly as I tried to keep my head from exploding.

Credo sat down and sighed. "You know, it's amazing. We keep thinking that all this new technology will change us somehow, that it will force us to become better than we really are. The fact is that while we have become much cleverer, we have become no wiser. Rather than help us in that regard, our technology has just amplified the distance between those two qualities. Before technology can change, people must change. Thank God for entropy, you know?"

I studied Credo inquisitively.

"Thank God that in everything we do we create the seeds of its own demise. In this dimension, entropy is king. The good things don't last, but neither do the bad things. It's a tradeoff. Do you want all the bad things in life to last indefinitely, too? I don't think so.

"If things didn't change, then might would definitely make right. At least we can count on nature chipping away at anything we create and forcing us to constantly think about what we are doing. The need for maintenance forces us to continually ask, 'What is important?' Every time I mow the lawn, I ask myself, 'Would I rather spend my time doing something else rather than taking care of my lawn? Would I rather replace it with a garden? Would I rather just pave it and sell parking-lot space? Would I rather just pay someone else to mow the lawn so I could spend my time doing something that might generate the revenue to pay the person mowing the lawn?' Or do I just say to myself 'Getting the lawn mowed is part of life's maintenance and operation's budget?'"

"What lawn?! I screeched. "You don't have a freakin' lawn!"

"Yes, I do," Credo responded calmly.

"I happen to know about lawns. What kind of fertilizer do you use?"

"You know," Credo said, ignoring my question, "it just occurred to me. You've never been inside! Come on."

The cave of a doorway that had been Credo's home and my oracle swung open. Credo stepped inside and shook himself like a dog trying to shed the rain from its fur.

I followed timidly through a dark corridor and then into a ring of bright light where I refused to believe what was before me. A huge glass dome covered an acre of lush arboretum. The air smelled fresh and sweet. Everywhere was awash with green vegetation punctuated by splashes of plants and flowers of every imaginable color. Credo looked around, calmly at first, and then with great agitation. He ran around the perimeter of the arboretum, popping inside a number of doorways as he made his rounds, desperately searching for something.

When he returned he was panting so loudly that I was worried. He leaned against a palm tree to steady himself as he wiped his forehead with the same sleeve that he used to wipe his nose. "The lawn's gone. There must have been a yard sale." He was instantly in hysterics.

We were back on the street and I was madder then hell.

"Would you please tell me what is going on? And no more fugguduhs! I want the truth!"

"The truth? I thought you already understood that there isn't any truth. Besides, you wouldn't like a world based on truth, anyway."

"Yes I would!" I yelled.

"No you wouldn't!" Credo yelled back.

"Yes I would!"

Credo paused for a moment, put his arm around me and said, "You know, I think it's time you met Art."

Snap.

CHAPTER 20 Art Appreciation
Artists are meteorologists with an attitude.

We emerged on a quiet street in a Norman Rockwell town, walking on a sidewalk lined with ancient maple trees that touched the clouds that floated in a Maxfield Parish sky. All the lawns were tidy, trimmed and taut, as if they had been wrapped in cellophane for centuries. All the gardens were measured, manicured and pleasant in a loud kind of way. Kids giggled as they pulled wagons full of dolls and skateboarded in the street. I could feel a hernia ready to erupt in my Walt Disney chakra as Credo explained that Art was quite an unusual person, and that some would even consider him a weirdo. I asked Credo what Art was doing living in such a conventional neighborhood if he were so strange.

"Art feels he should not be seen as anything special," Credo replied. "He doesn't want to segregate himself from the rest of society. He feels he should be part of the everyday fabric of life, like the plumber and the dogcatcher. He feels that society needs him. Those of us who know him know that the reverse is equally true. He needs an environment like this to live in if his work is going to have any real value—and if he is going to keep from going crazy. God knows what would happen to his mind if he weren't living among the so-called normal people of the world. And despite his rather extreme ways at times, the people around here would actually miss him if he were gone. He's very nice to the children in the neighborhood; it's the adults he has a hard time with."

Credo stopped in front of a simple two-story white house with green trim and an asymmetrical garden. We peered through the windows, past the yellow curtains and the flowerpots, into a darkness that resonated like a living shadow. We walked up the stairs to the front door and stood silently for a few moments before I started to knock.

"Don't knock," Credo warned me. "It will only make him mad. Just walk in. That will probably make him mad too, but he will respect you more."

"Why?" I asked.

"Because if you just walk in you make a statement without caring what he thought about it. Knocking shows weakness, a need to seek permission."

"I thought it was impolite, if not illegal, to just walk into some-one's house," I commented.

"It is," Credo said. "It takes a bit of adjustment to appreciate Art. To him, the difference between knocking and just walking in is the difference between commercial art and fine art. One seeks permission; the other doesn't care what anyone thinks; one follows, while the other leads. And Art hates to follow. Remember—Art, too, is just a metaphor."

As I surveyed the darkness beyond the windows, a feeling of perplexity transformed first into concern and then into fear.

"No need to worry," Credo assured me. "He doesn't bite." Credo abruptly raised his index finger, signaling a correction. "You know, I take that back. He did bite someone once, but that was a long time ago. The guy had it coming—he ruined one of Art's sable-bristle paint brushes."

Credo saw the panic growing in my eyes and smiled.

"Look, don't worry if you don't understand Art. Art is not supposed to be understood. Art is supposed to be appreciated for whatever value he offers you. Art is supposed to mean different things to different people. Above all, Art is a mirror. Rather than focusing on who he is, use the experience to better understand who *you* are. You may find it transformational. Now, just go ahead and walk in."

After hesitating a few moments, during which my stomach did a few somersaults and my pulse hit overdrive, I pushed opened the door and walked into the pitch black entryway. It reminded me uncomfortably of Credo's doorway, a fact I tried not to dwell on. I looked behind me and could see only Credo's outline as a silhouette against the sunlight outside.

"Keep going," Credo prodded.

I inched forward until I heard a loud snap, like the sound of a spring-loaded trap closing. The house suddenly lit up like a disco-theque. Mirrored balls hanging from the ceiling spun in place, twist-ing and spraying images all over the room. The sound of drums reminiscent of my experience in the jungle began to pound out a syncopated, metronomic rap beat, which was accentuated by bass sounds so thick and heavy that the floor vibrated.

I looked up and gasped. I could see myself on stage, surrounded by singers and musicians. I was wearing a blue sequined suit with wide lapels and black dancing shoes. As I moved, my image moved, mirroring my every gesture, except for one surrealistic exception: Each movement of my image appeared perfectly in synch with the drum beat, as if choreographed to be part of the dance. Every attempt I made to purposely move outside the drum beat was futile. My image was in perfect step with the rhythm of the drums as though it were nothing more than a puppet caught in a traction beam.

"Body quantization karaoke," Art hollered from somewhere behind the din, sounding like a pirate enjoying his work. As he spoke, the sound of the drums receded into the background enough to allow conversation, though we still needed to shout.

"It synchronizes body motion based on an established song rhythm," Art continued. "It's triggered by a three-dimensional light beam reader, picked up by a holographically projected body suit and filtered through a stasis equalization generator. It is all controlled by software I wrote; actually, I adapted it from the shaving filter software that Fallacom developed. They didn't intend it to be used for artistic purposes, but that's my job these days, to turn the technology inside out, to take all these tools that are created to conquer the world and turn them into vehicles to travel the terrifying expanses of the interior domain. It's my job to make sure we understand we have no business conquering anything given the rather wretched state of our souls. But all this techno bunk are the tools of our day, and the job of the artist is to use the tools to reflect on the tools because the tools allow us to see who we really are. It's a thankless task if there ever was one! If it were up to me, I could be happy just using a hunk of charcoal and some construction paper."

"Art, I don't think you'd be happy if you were happy," Credo said, giving me a playful nudge.

"Fugguduh upon your soul," Art threw at Credo before fixing his gaze on me. "Have you read McLuhan?"

When I didn't answer him, he screeched, "I said, have you read McLuhan!?"

"Are you talking to me?" I asked.

"Who is this Bozo?" Art asked Credo.

"Don't take it personally," Credo counseled me. "But you are in his house and you should answer the question."

"I want to go now," I said.

"Look, one more time," Art barked. "Yes or no, have you read McLuhan!? "

"Sort of," I ventured.

"I'll take that as a 'no' from 'Mr. Sort Of' over here," Art chided as he turned to Credo. "Where did you find this guy? Haven't you been teaching him anything?"

"What's a mentor to do?" Credo sighed.

"The name's William," I said as forcefully as I could muster. "And thanks for sticking up for me, *mentor!*"

"Listen up, William," Art said. "You might learn something. To McLuhan, all technology is an extension of our body. A car is an extension of our feet, the headlights are an extension of our eyes, the horn is an extension of our mouth, the trunk is an extension of our back, the body an extension of our skin. But to me, everything is an extension of the heart and soul. Technology amplifies our desires, our inadequacies and the wretched state of our inner lives. We can try to hide from each other, but our technology finds us out. That's why it is up to the artist to use the tools of the day to reflect on the tools of the day. Otherwise it's pointless. By the way, thanks for knocking. I ought to have you both arrested. As a matter of fact, I will."

As Credo and I listened to the digital beeps of a phone dialing 911, Credo smiled at me.

"The cops don't bother coming, anymore," Credo assured me quietly. "Hey!" he called out. "Show yourself unless you're too ugly!"

"Not until your friend sings us a song," Art yelled back. "If you come to Art's house, you'd better create some art. How do you like the clothes I picked out for you?"

"Um, well," I said, as I studied the image of myself on the virtual balcony. "It's certainly, well, *interesting.*"

"Well," Art nearly spat, "if that isn't the cop-out phrase of the century...*interesting!*" Art killed the music entirely. It was suddenly so quiet that we could hear the faint sound of the disco ball spinning above us. "Out with it! No dilly-dallying with Art. You either have something to say or you don't, and if you don't, no amount of technology or fancy hair cream is going to help you. Now, do you like the clothes or don't you?"

I inhaled deeply before beginning. "No, I don't—I hate them. I look like something out of the '70s and I hate the '70s. The '70s had no sense of when too much was more than enough."

"Up yours!" Art said. "I grew up during the '70s!"

I apologized for being disrespectful but that just made him madder.

"What's wrong with being disrespectful?" Art demanded. "All great art starts out being disrespectful. It only gains respect when the people it was intended to serve manage to overcome their own lack of respect for the world that the art was designed to reflect in the first place. Make sense? I'm supposed to be disrespectful for a living. It's not easy, but someone's got to do it. So, stop apologizing. Now, what do you want to wear? I can dress you up in anything."

I watched my image on the balcony cycle through styles—upper-polyester business, torn-and-worn grunge, female-impersonation yellow chiffon, lumberjack plaid...

"No, no, no, no," I said. "I want to see..."

"What?" Art called out excitedly. "Talk to me! Make a statement!"

"Ummm..." I said, straining.

"Think body extension. What's the favorite part of your body?"

"I don't know," I said, unconsciously scratching my nose.

"Ah hah, gotcha!" Art announced.

Credo and I stared in disbelief as my image slowly morphed into a large nose.

"Imagine what would have happened if you had scratched your you-know-what," Credo whispered.

"Now, let's dress it up," Art called out. "What does it look like?"

"Two bright blue eyes," I said, excitedly. "I want a Panama hat and a fat, smelly cigar."

"I like it, I like it," Art said, as he flipped some dials and tapped on his keyboard. In one nostril was a fat cigar with a bright red band around its bulging middle. In the other was a set of lips that moved as I spoke. The nose was wearing a hat identical with the one I had worn when I visited Mr. Big.

"Does the nose walk?" Art shouted.

"No!" I commanded. "It has wings."

"And where is it flying off to?" Art asked.

"Out on the Net," I replied, "where no one can smell. And for god's sake, kill the disco ambiance."

"Hold it," Art said. The room was suddenly dark, and then indirect blue lighting began to illuminate sections of the room.

"Much better," I said. "Mix it with soft white in the background. Ah, very good."

"Just one more minute," Art told me. "I'm connected to your web page, but my program isn't done synthesizing it."

"What the freak are you doing with my web page?" I demanded to know.

"What are you so worried about?" Art replied. "It's public, isn't it? I'm using your information to build this song. Where else would the song come from? My program will synthesize what it finds and puke out something that is totally you. Then you will need to sping it—don't sing and don't speak—*sping*. Don't worry; I am using a digital compensator. If you are good, it uses your own voice. If you're not, it will compensate and all you will have to do is move your lips. And you know who decides what good is, don't you? Me. Why? Because I'm the programmer. Because I'm the artist. The rest is magic, but magic that couldn't happen without you. Ready?"

Before I could react, the drums started in a rap cycle, crisp and carnal. The bass joined in, moving through the bottoms of my feet and permeating my entire body.

"Too funky?" Art screamed.

"Not for me!" I yelled back.

A loud whisper began to float throughout the room, riding on top of the rap beat that flew out from nowhere and covered the room in punchy, staccato bursts:

> *Internet...*
> *Whatcha gonna get...*
> *On the Internet...*
> *Whatcha gonna get...*
> *On the Internet...*

Another loud whisper started on the other side of the room in the same rhythm:

> *Information highway,*
> *Goin' my way?*
> *Information highway...*

I glanced at Credo who was dancing with himself, flopping around like an injured bird. His eyes were closed and a goofy smile lit up his face. *He has no sense of rhythm,* I thought to myself. *What kind of mentor has no sense of rhythm?*

The large over-dressed cigar-chomping nose flew up to a microphone perched on a stand and hovered. I was unable to tell whether I had moved or just my image as the nose had moved. As nearly as I could tell, I was standing still as I *spung*. My mouth was opening and closing, somehow connected to the words I heard rapped out in blunt, punctuated meter:

> *Just got back from the Internet,*
> *Can't believe the people I met.*
> *The Page is the rage; I've got one too,*
> *Makes life online a human zoo.*
> *Where everyone wears a cybersuit,*
> *Where some are ugly and some are cute.*
> *Where no one's ever where they are,*
> *Where there's no such thing as near or far.*

The whisper broke in with some casual, non-rhythmic commentary:

> *You see, online you're everywhere at once...*
> *Or nowhere all at the same time...*
> *Does that make sense?*

I was mesmerized as I watched the huge nose move gracefully through its performance. Dancers moved behind it in a spiked, jagged dance step that emphasized each down beat.

"Come on, William. Blow that nose!" Art called out.

Credo handed me a handkerchief. I covered my nose with it, inhaled and blew out with tremendous fury.

The nose shot across the room, laughing, spinning and bouncing off the walls like a pool ball ricocheting off the cushions of a huge billiards table.

"Fugguduh," I whispered. The nose settled behind the microphone as it began to sping again:

> *Just got back from the Internet,*
> *Did a whole lot of surfing and I got real wet.*
> *Rode the waves like there was no end,*

Sent video clips to all my friends.
Fanned the flames in USENET news,
Checked my stocks, bought some shoes.
Emailed someone who I call "Kim,"
I think she's a gal...maybe she's a him...

The casual whisper commentary returned:

Maybe Kim's neither...
Maybe she's a machine...
Does it matter?

I began to sping again:

Just got back from the Internet,
So much happened that I forget.
MUDDs and lists and chat room tease,
A million invisible communities.
I just can't absorb it all!
The Net's so big, my brain's so small.
Yet when I hear that modem tone,
I just thank God I'm goin' home.

Just got back from the Internet,
I don't think that I'm all back yet.
My body's back,
So's my face.
But I left my mind,
In cyberspace.

Suddenly the images vanished, the drums were silent and the disco
ball was dark and motionless. I had a nanosecond to consider the fact
that Kim was in my life again, this time in the form of a song created
by the mere mention of her name on my web page. There truly were
no boundaries in cyberspace, and although I instinctively didn't like
it, I didn't have time to dwell on it. Somehow my web page had
revealed my fear and confusion about Kim and my anxiety about how
healthy it was to have fallen so deeply into the dark, cerebral maw of
technology.

I looked around. The house appeared quite normal, revealing cheap, well-worn furniture, packed bookshelves and mostly bare walls. A high-pitched whistle filled the room. The nose re-appeared high on the wall and seemed to be in a loop as it moved in a circle, bumping into the wall, repeating, "In cyberspace, in cyberspace, in cyberspace..." A short, balding man with thick glasses resting on a large nose emerged from a sound booth in the next room waving his hands and shouting angrily.

"Fugguduh, fugguduh fugguduh, fugguduh, fugguduh, fugguduh!" Art screamed, beyond flustered and well into irate.

"Bravo, bravo," Credo said, clapping enthusiastically.

"Bravo, schmavo!" Art said. "Didn't you see what happened? Fugguduh, fugguduh, fugguduh! God, I hate the technology sometimes. I hate it! See what happened? See? The main computer went down. There was a system crash. See? I didn't save it! And I don't have any back up! So everything you just saw is gone. Gone! All because I didn't back it up, understand? Fugguduh, fugguduh, FUGGUDUH!"

"I thought that was all part of the piece," Credo offered. "I thought it was a commentary on the temporary nature of things."

"Well it was. But it wasn't. And now it has to be, doesn't it? I didn't intend it to happen, but it did. It ruined the art piece, but the art piece became a new art piece, a transient-just-like-life art piece because this is part of the message of technology: The reality we create with technology is so fragile that failures like these are the price we pay. The whole thing is a huge trap, giving us power we don't deserve because we can't deal with it when it doesn't work." He turned to look at me. "How does it feel to see yourself on stage?"

"I didn't exactly see someone I would call myself," I commented.

"You are entirely correct," Art said. "You were perfected in one small way for one short moment. For one short period of time, you could really dance."

"But I *can* already dance," I protested.

"Hah! Not like that!" Art said. "If it weren't for our imperfections we wouldn't even need art. You saw a lie; it was a lie which, to paraphrase Picasso, told us the truth. That's all art really is. Saying this in terms of that so that we might better see how horribly inept we are at being human. Seems almost cruel doesn't it, to have the inspiration to be perfect and not the ability?"

Great, I thought to myself. *Another mentor with an attitude and another thing to think about when I had time.* "And what do you call this art form?" I asked.

"I don't know," Art said. "But I'll tell you this: Cream always floats to the top. I don't care what the art form is, I don't care what your medium is, and I don't care how many gadgets you have to plug in to make it happen, you can't hide behind them. You either have something to say or you don't. Period. Sooner or later, you will reveal who you really are, and the technology just makes it more obvious. It's like Mr. Big told you, 'What happens when you give a bad guitar player a bigger amplifier?' He got that from me by the way, but who cares? The point is that cream floats to the top. Every new art form produces a few masters and a whole lot of followers. All of this will most certainly produce a Picasso or a Beethoven someday."

"You aren't a Picasso or a Beethoven?" I asked.

"SSSHHH!!!" Art warned me. "I can go to hell for eternity just for being in the same room with someone who says something like that! Please. Spare me! No, I'm no Picasso or Beethoven. And neither are you."

"I never said I was," I offered meekly.

"Good. So," he said turning to Credo, "what's today's lesson?"

"I think we just saw it," Credo replied. "Catch 33."

Art began to breathe deeply and rhythmically, swinging both his arms in a circle, one of which nearly struck me in the face.

"Stand back," Credo warned. "He's about to spew."

Credo and I moved well out of Art's way as he let loose in what seemed like one long, uninterrupted, wildly animated exhale.

"Oh, I'll tell you about Catch 33, alright! Mother freakin' technology! When you use it to create art you have to make a deal with the devil. You are granted the power of creation to bring art to life in ways that you would never be able to do otherwise. But you are forced to become part technician, devoting entirely too much of your creative energies to negotiating with a bunch of gadgets, immersed in the left side of your brain while the right side screams for liberation. Contrast this with picking up a violin or a paintbrush and being instantly transported to the home of the muse.

"I spent only a wee little bit of the time involved in creating this body quantization karaoke actually making the art I love: developing the shapes, colors, sounds, dynamics and body movements. I spent entirely too much time in love with, groveling before and infuriated by the technology—voice-activated stasis equalizers, palm-sensitive mice, photovoltaic-triggered holographic body suits, three-dimensional mixers, dozens of software programs tenuously stitched together by my particular needs, etc., etc., etc. It's a huge, complex extended family of things connected by cords and microbeams, a family to which I belong and without whom I would be powerless. God I hate my dependence on all this stuff, but what am I supposed to do? This is the time I grew up in, these are the tools that surround us. As long as there are dreams that can only be reached by way of machine, and as long as the machinery keeps evolving at warp speed, there will be quite a distance to travel to get to one's ideas. And, as with any journey, there is always the possibility—no, *the absolute certainty*—of getting lost.

"There is nothing more frustrating than barreling down the highway of creativity so close to your ideas that you can actually touch them, and blammo, some part of your technological support system shuts down—system errors, gadget incompatibilities, blown fuses...God, I hate it! And it all happens inside a silicon-and-plastic cocoon that is really rather primitive when it comes to *its* ability to understand *me*. By the time I unstick a glitch, it is usually too late. By that time the muse has usually left in despair, dissolving my original inspiration in its wake.

"I will admit that the technology giveth, too. There is nothing more exhilarating than extending my nervous system and emotional schema to include a silicon life form that waltzes with me effortlessly, like a perfectly tuned dance partner across a spacious ballroom floor. At those moments the technology becomes transparent, like the controls of an arcade game. At those moments I feel as if I am merely a conduit through which ideas flow from elsewhere as I whirl in giant, exhilarating strides. At those moments I become pure ether and the technology feels liberating, inevitable, even familiar, like something I didn't know I had been waiting for until it arrived...*until it crashes!*

"So why bother?" Art asked me, never intending for me to respond. Not a problem; I was listening intently and didn't really want to respond. "I'll tell you why," he kept rolling. "Because if we don't use the technology to create art, the technology will control us, rather than the other way around. By making art with technology, we tell technology, 'We are watching you...We still have standards for being human, as irrational as they may seem to a machine, and we don't intend to abandon them.'"

Art stopped to take a long breath, bending over as he exhaled. "Now, go away for a minute," he commanded us as he curled up on the floor, apparently preparing to take a nap.

"Do you want to meet us at Mitsie's for lunch?" Credo asked.

"Sure, sure," Art whispered as he started to doze off. "I'll meet you at Mitsie's."

CHAPTER 21 Appreciating Art Literacy
Our past is no present for the future.

As Credo and I settled into a booth at Mitsie's, Edwina joined us. I was so happy to see her that I clung to her under the auspices of a hug, embracing her as the oasis of emotional stability that she had come to represent to me. When I told her that we were waiting for Art to join us, she and Credo exchanged glances, sharing secret information as they considered the best way to tell me something that I might find disturbing. Finally she smiled at me knowingly.

"It's very good to see you too, William," she said. "But don't wait too long for Art."

"Why not?" I asked.

"Because Art always says he'll join us for lunch right before he takes a nap," Credo said. "But the truth is that Art won't be showing up."

"Oh, then why..." I stopped myself and told them that I understood. I didn't really understand anything, but I didn't want to embarrass anyone or appear stupid.

A waiter was suddenly hovering at their table. "The usual?"

Credo and Edwina nodded.

"Back in a flash," the waiter said before disappearing into the lunch crowd.

My coffee hand was beginning to flex. "And a big cup of coffee for me, please," I added. "There isn't any meat in the special, is there?"

"Why?" Credo asked.

I fidgeted, already sensing that I was about to reveal a commitment to an ideal I hadn't properly considered. "Well," I began hesitantly, "I don't see why I should have to destroy life just to feed myself."

"Isn't it just like a sape to think that the only thing that's alive is something that can run away from you," Credo scoffed. "I suppose you eat fish?"

"Sometimes," I told him.

"And chicken too, on occasion?" Credo asked sarcastically.

I nodded.

"Well, even if you didn't, it wouldn't make any difference," he said. "For your information, there is as much life force in a stalk of celery as there is in a prize hog. The only difference is that a stalk of celery doesn't remind you of something you might have as a pet."

"And it doesn't scream when you kill it," I said defiantly.

"You don't think plants scream just because you can't hear them? No wonder the plants hate us so much. Don't you ever forget something: We need the plants, but they don't need us. Technology's the same way. The plants see us as entirely superfluous houseguests who have no manners and no understanding of when we have worn out our welcome."

"William," Edwina began gently, "it's perhaps better that Art isn't here right now. It will give me a chance to, shall we say, fill in some of the blanks that Arthur didn't address. Arthur has some justifiable concerns about technology, but his perspective lacks balance. If you don't mind, I would like to finish up today's lesson by providing that balance."

After I told her that I was eager to hear her perspective, she began speaking with a quiet conviction that I found captivating.

"As you know, technology amplifies human activity and potential. It can enslave us or it can empower us. The art of living graciously with technology has a great deal to do with making sure that technology amplifies only what we admire about human nature. Let me tell you about an experience that changed my life forever, which will illustrate what I am saying. Not only did it help me understand the true nature of technology, but also the importance of art in education."

The waiter reappeared, setting a large bowl of salad and 5 forks in the center of the table, and then a fork, a small empty bowl and serving spoons in front of Edwina.

"That was fast," I told him.

"Fast is good, just like in your business," the waiter said before scurrying off to another table of customers.

"The fourth and fifth fork are ceremonial," said Credo, "just in case, by some miracle, Art does happen to show up."

I searched his face for a clue.

"Art likes to use two forks," Credo explained.

"Oh, I see," I said, as much as I saw anything anymore.

"And we'd appreciate it," Credo said, "if you would pick one side of the bowl and stick with it. It's more sanitary that way. Edwina gets her own bowl because she's a lady."

"I know your concern with sanitation and will respect it totally," I told him as sarcastically as possible. "Maybe I should get my own bowl, too, just in case you've contracted some interesting disease from your travels through the trash bins of life."

"No way," Credo said, "unless you want to look like a pantywaist. Be a man for god's sake!"

"Credo!" Edwina admonished as she served herself some salad. "You hush up. If William wants his own bowl he should have one and you should encourage him. Eating properly has nothing to do with masculinity. And William, stop criticizing Credo's life style. You need to show more compassion, dear."

I let go of the idea of having my own bowl and once again simply tried to blend in with the madness around me. As Edwina talked, Credo munched so loudly that I leaned further and further forward in order to hear. Edwina caught my attention just in time to let me know that the residue from my hair was about to drip into the salad bowl.

"I was teaching a fifth-grade social studies class," she began, "when one day, after I described the expectations for a project, little freckle-faced Jill Runyon raised her hand and asked, 'May I make a multimedia project instead of writing a report?' Well, do you know those moments in life when you can feel things shift in your soul and nothing is the same, anymore?"

I assured Edwina that I had had quite a few of those moments, especially lately.

"Just before Jill asked that question I was one person," Edwina continued. "Afterward I was someone entirely different. As I considered her question for a few moments, it felt as if a year passed. I could literally hear the sound of old thinking and new thinking chafing against each other like psychic tectonic plates in the innermost depths of my being. I couldn't just dismiss little Jill's request. After all, I was trying to be a good teacher, and just because I didn't understand what she was doing didn't mean she shouldn't do it. I was smart enough to know that in the age of technological change there was no reason for me to assume my past should become her future. So I told her I would be happy to have her make a multimedia project. Secretly, I was very insecure and confused by it all.

"Well, Jill's multimedia project was quite an accomplishment: a web page demonstrating the similarities in dance and music among Native American cultures, complete with video, music, interviews and excellent reporting. She met all the requirements of the assign-ment, demonstrated a great deal of technical expertise and developed other skills that transfer very well to just about any enterprise in life, such as planning a detailed activity, working with a team toward a common goal, finding and using resources within a budget, develop-ing communication skills with a number of media and so on.

"Months passed before I fully realized what a milestone that was in my life. It took me that long to come to grips with the fact that we were living in a new world in which my old companion words, whether on screen or on paper, were no longer our primary form of communication. The more I understood that, the sadder I became. It was like my oldest and dearest friend was dying and leaving me stranded in a world that I did not care for.

"But loss breeds reflection, and I also began to really think about print for the first time in my life. Why? Because for the first time I saw it as *technology*. Do you know what technology is, William?"

"Yes, ma'am. I mean no, ma'am."

"Technology is change made manifest," Edwina said. "Any change at all. But to most people, technology consists of only those changes that happen during their lifetime, not anyone else's. To them, technology is just anything they notice. They notice it because they didn't grow up with it, or because they grew up with it and it aban-doned them, like phonographs and rotary telephones. The technology you grow up with is camouflaged by everyday life. It feels familiar and harmless and there is nothing to compel you to question it. It's only new technology that feels scary and gets all the attention.

"As I felt print leaving me, I began to take a good look at it for the first time and discovered there is nothing inherently friendly about it at all. It has been used to control and enslave peasants, indigenous cultures and anyone who presented a threat to the authorities. It provided children a silent, alternative voice of authority that directly challenged parental rule. And look what it did to community! Like McLuhan said, it *detribalized* us; that is, it reduced communities to their constituent parts, individuals, by providing people with a private point of view. It gave us an eye for an ear. Storytelling in groups was replaced by quietly reading stories by ourselves.

"As you can see, in some ways I quite agree with Arthur that technology has its limitations. But where I disagree with Arthur so strenuously is that his concerns are true for all technologies, old and new. For the first time, I saw print in all its infamy as well as its glory. Indeed, it turned out that my old friend print had a few skeletons in the closet. But while Arthur will sit and stew about his frustrations with technology, I say why bother when there is so much that is so good about it? You can't dwell on the bad things in life or you'll become a cranky old sourpuss like Arthur, and nobody wants that!"

"No, ma'am," I said.

"In retrospect, I see text as a kind of social filter through which only a certain percentage of my students had the ability to pass. The rest of them simply got left behind. Thanks to multimedia, it does not have to be that way. People like Jill Runyon who don't do well with text have so many other options they can use to express themselves. So many of my former students would have flourished with the new multimedia tools! When you get right down to it, do you know what all this multimedia technology really is?"

"No, ma'am."

"It's assistive technology for the artistically challenged," she said. "Technology does for art what word-processing did for writing. The same way that writing has been limited for so long to those who felt at home with the tedious mechanics of penmanship or typing—that is, those who could pass through the writing filter—art had been reserved for those who dedicated their lives to learning how to draw, paint, play musical instruments and manipulate all kinds of media. We became a two-tiered culture consisting of those who created art and those who appreciated what others created.

"Not so, anymore," Edwina continued. "Now, so much is within the grasp of so many. If you have a vision and are willing to take the time to learn how to use multimedia tools, you can do anything from drawing a straight line to writing a symphony. If you gave up trying your hand at creating art because of the work involved, you get a chance to express yourself in ways you only dreamed about. If you are already an artist working with traditional media, you have whole new palettes of tools with which to work. It is so exciting!"

"Yes, ma'am."

"And you know, I'm just not worried we will lose the printed word," said Edwina. "Instead, I think we will rediscover it. Because we are being forced to examine what words do for us, we will better understand when they offer us the best way to communicate, which is the ultimate goal in using any medium. Like the old friends they are, words will come back to us and I hope we will be wise enough to understand their real value. We will find ways to blend our visual and acoustic selves into new ways of understanding the world.

"But in the meantime we have a whole set of new problems. We are on the verge of repeating the mistakes of the past by not insisting that our children become fluent in the literacy of their day. In our case, the new lingua franca is multimedia. Although we now expect kids to combine pictures, music, sound, movies and words in a meaningful, communicative collage, we don't teach them how! Art has become the fourth literacy and it needs to be mainstreamed across every aspect of the curriculum, immediately!"

"Teachers are going to freak out," Credo said. "They are going to feel their control slipping away, and they will go bonkers. Nuts!"

"That's why we need to help them by hiring more art teachers to work across the curriculum," Edwina said. "We did it with reading and writing, and we can do it with art. Sadly, funding for art is always the first thing to go in a school budget. Reversing this is going to be harder than we realize because of the reputation that art has. But we must not give up."

"It's going to be harder than we realize because morons are in charge of the education system," Credo blurted. "Do you remember Career Day in high school? The principal would come on the crappy little intercom you could barely understand—which was your first hint that you were in a text-centric world that had no respect for the audio arts—and tell everyone in the junior and senior class to go to the gymnasium to meet with representatives from various fields of employment to choose a future as insipid and pointless as the principal's. Why? Fear. Cultural inertia. The principal wanted to make sure he would have some company to sit around and talk about nothing with in his sunset years—like a support group for people who are too stupid to know they are alive."

"Credo," Edwina admonished, "we understand your concerns with the education you received, but your negativity is not helpful. Incidentally, William, Credo didn't like schooling either. That is why he was assigned to be your mentor."

"By whom? The Committee?" I implored. "Does The Committee ever take outside input? Perhaps you should get a second opinion when you assign a mentor to someone."

"So down we would all trot to the gymnasium," Credo continued, "like cattle being led to spiritual slaughter. There were a bunch of people sitting at tables with big signs on them, trying to look happy, and the principal would walk up to the microphone and say in so many words, 'Everyone who wants to be a lawyer, consultant or just wants to make a pile of money because you are too shallow to care about anyone or anything, go over here and talk to this guy,' and all the Junior Achievers and Young Republicans would waddle on over to one side of the room. And then the principal would say in so many words, 'Everyone who wants to be a social worker or a teacher or either hasn't woken up to the fact that all they really want out of life is to make a pile of money or isn't smart enough to know they don't have what it takes to make a pile of money, go over here and see this guy,' and all the young Democrats and Socialists would boogie on over to the other side of the room. And then the principal would say in so many words, 'Everyone whose parents come home with dirt on their hands at the end of the day, go see that guy,' and all the guys with greasy hair would stomp over to this table with all the trade-union representatives. And the women just went to a table marked 'Second-Class Citizens,' where they could talk to someone about being an underpaid teacher, mother, stewardess or beautician. You know what I absolutely detest about school? They think it is all about preparing you for work. It isn't; it is supposed to prepare you for life! I mean, if school is supposed to mirror life, isn't one of the things life is supposed to do is prepare you for more life? Fugguduh!"

"Are you quite finished?" Edwina asked him.

"I suppose," Credo replied, as he smushed a package of crackers with his hands.

"Thank you," Edwina said. "You have some very serious issues to work out about your schooling, Credo. I appreciate that you feel shortchanged by your education, but carrying all that negativity around all these years does not do you or anyone else any good. It is not good enough to criticize what you don't like; you must offer solutions for change or else you will end up just feeding the cynicism that you claim to dislike so much. Now, William, Credo's perspective is certainly worth considering. But he, like Art, also lacks balance..."

"But," Credo blurted, "did the principal ever say, 'Anyone who wants to be an artist, go over and see this guy over here?' Noooooo. And why not? Because there were no artists at Career Day. And do you know why? Because what is the first thing that comes to mind when you think of an artist?"

I told him that after meeting Art it was hard to think of just one thing.

"I'll tell you what," Credo continued. "Whenever I tell someone I am an artist…"

"You're an artist?" I asked.

"We're all artists!" Credo replied. "Oh, for god's sake, you haven't been listening to anything I've been telling you?"

"Look," I started, "just because we're here with your friends, don't think you can show off…"

"Never mind," Credo blurted. "Anyway, whenever I tell someone I'm an artist, do you know what they do? First, they look at me with a particular kind of awe mixed with self-loathing. At that moment they respect me totally because I am an artist and they hate themselves completely because they think they're not. Then, a split second later, they look at me with pity as if to say, *You probably haven't eaten in awhile—would you like a sandwich?* Then the last look I get says, *You aren't coming near my daughter, you traitor to the work ethic and the gross national product!*"

During Credo's tirade Edwina had signaled to the waiter who walked up to Credo and threw a glass of water in his face. Edwina handed the waiter a few dollar bills.

"Fugguduh!" Credo hollered.

"Whoa," I said, smiling. "Fugguduh, indeed!"

"And how's everything?" the waiter asked.

"Dandy, you nasty little twerp," Credo scowled.

"Just putting out the fire," the waiter said as he hurried off.

"That is quite enough, Credo," Edwina admonished. "You have some interesting points to make but you are being deliberately rude. It was either cool you off with a bit of water or else I was going to have to report your behavior."

"To who?" I asked eagerly.

"To *whom*," Edwina patiently corrected me. "And for your part young man, stop taking delight in another man's misfortune."

"I'm sorry, Ms. Tech," I said. "To *whom*?"

Edwina Tech ignored me and continued. "Credo, allow me to try to make your point for you with a little less negativity. For a long time educators and concerned citizens have tried to sell the importance of art to the public for a whole host of reasons: because it helps students learn in other content areas (art for math's sake, so to speak); because of the self-discovery it fosters; because of the depth of cultural understanding it promotes; because of the benefits an aesthetic life provides; and so on. We didn't get very far. That is why there was not an artist table on Career Day. We carry a great deal of baggage with us about what art is. I think sometimes that the best thing we could do to promote art in the schools is to change its name.

"But the really exciting part about the era of multimedia is that art is finally coming of age. Presentation, media, entertainment and education are converging, embracing the Arts out of necessity and creating a vast-and-growing world of opportunity and employment. There will be hundreds if not thousands of channels of video, millions of CD ROMs, DVDs and World Wide Web sites and new media we can't even conceive of, all of which will need musicians, videographers, graphic designers, script writers, choreographers and hundreds of other jobs associated with the creative arts. We are headed into an era in which artists are actually going to have work."

To everyone's amazement, Art shuffled over to the table and sat down. Despite Credo and Edwina's obvious desire to welcome him, they said nothing, letting him take his place without fanfare.

"God almighty, who can sleep with Credo here carrying on like a wounded bull moose?" Art grumbled as he grabbed his forks and dove into the salad. "I could hear you 10 blocks away. It looks like you either went for a swim with your clothes on or Edwina is putting you in your place again."

"Nice job explaining Catch 33, Arthur," Edwina told him. "I think William learned a great deal this afternoon. You'll forgive me if I try to restore some balance to your argument."

You were there? I asked silently. Of course she was; she was everywhere. All of them were everywhere all the time, like the Internet.

"I like Catch 77 better," Art said. "So does The Committee."

Credo looked at him sheepishly.

"See!" Art said, pointing a finger accusingly at Credo. "You weren't at The Committee meeting. You should have been there. I'm sure Edwina has scolded you for it."

"I hadn't had a chance to bring that up yet," Edwina said.

"What meeting?" I asked.

"The Committee unanimously passed Catch 77," Art told Credo.

"What Committee?" I asked impatiently.

"No dissent at all?" Credo asked.

"Not a peep," Art replied. "There was a lot of discussion about William's big day that you would have enjoyed, too."

"WHAT BIG DAY?" I screeched. "And why is it suddenly, *my* big day? Why isn't it everyone's big day? This doesn't sound good at all."

"William," Edwina said. "Manners, manners. When you get right down to it, manners are all we have to make people pleasant enough..."

"...that is, *bearable* enough..." Art and Credo broke in, more or less in unison.

"...to make people *pleasant enough* to be around each other," Edwina continued. "It is this pleasantness which allows people to live in close proximity. Manners are just rules of behavior, and it is the existence of such rules that allows a community to remain intact. It is essentially the existence of 'manners' that allows different software programs to talk to each other, though you would call it '*protocol*.'"

Good one, I thought to myself.

"So, please," Edwina continued, "for the sake of those around you, watch your manners."

I apologized as calmly as possible and then begged to know what Catch 77 was and was once again ignored.

"And while we are on the topic of multimedia and what it does for the average Joe," Art cut in, "I'll tell you right up-front that I liked it better when art was misunderstood and fought over, and work was hard to come by. I preferred that it wasn't so mainstream. If we don't reserve weirddom for the artists, who is going to live there?"

"Maybe we can all live there," Edwina suggested.

"Then *there* becomes *here* and no one is living *there* any more," Art protested. "It's dangerous. Without *there* we lose our perspective of *here*. I mean, being an artist is hell, but at least it's hell with a purpose."

"You must take what Art says with a large grain of salt," Edwina assured me. "He loves his work more than he lets on."

As Art continued, Credo was trying to stab a renegade crouton that went shooting across the table.

"I hate it," Art said calmly, trying to stab the same crouton. "I hate it all. I was born in the wrong century. Imagine having a paintbrush that broke down all the time! That's what it's like. Besides, too much of art these days is an exploration of the medium as an end itself, rather than using the medium to actually say something worth listening to. Some like that stuff, but I don't care for it myself. I don't want to bump on the medium; I want to pass through it. The inherent, insidious message in all this multimedia hoopla is what Weizenbaum called the Pig Principal: If something is good, more of it must be better. It's like a big distraction contest—the more successful you are at keeping people from realizing that what they are experiencing actually has no depth, the better you are as an artist. It's blasphemy!

"I'm not saying all this techno-hoopla can't be an art form," Art continued. "The question is, 'What is the art form doing for us?' McLuhan and his one-liners started the whole mess. He'd run around dropping little gems like, 'The medium is the message' and, 'The Global Village,' wherever he went. We'd pick them up, marvel at them for a little while and then, just about the time we'd see their flaws and wanted to ask something obvious like, 'Isn't the message also the message?' or, 'Aren't neighborhoods still important?' he'd drop a bunch more! He just kept littering the landscape with so many of them we could never catch up with him. It was like a trail of breadcrumbs that lead nowhere, except to more bread crumbs."

"It was word-processing that started the whole Catch 77 mess," Credo said. "Everyone started changing things just because they could; they felt they were supposed to because if they could and they didn't then they were being irresponsible and unfair to a machine that had been invented to let them change things whenever they wanted to whether they wanted to or not."

"Heckuva run-on sentence," Art said.

"Big deal," said Credo.

"You do need to work on your run-on sentences," Edwina said with a touch of disapproval in her voice.

"Every generation becomes its tools," Credo continued, "and we have become our word processors. The whole mess began with words, then spread to pictures and sounds."

"Then spread to commitments, values and aesthetics," Art continued for him.

"Everything!" Credo said. "If you could create it with your mind, then you could change it. Thanks to word-processing we now have an editable world."

"Filled with edible words," Art chimed in. "I think I'll eat me a few verbs and a couple of expletives." Art thrust both forks into the bowl of salad with gusto. Credo finally saw the opening he had been waiting for and pursued the crouton with a vengeance.

"Curse you, Credo!" Art yelled, and soon they were chasing the crouton around the table with an enthusiasm I found embarrassing.

"Oh, both of you. You need to look on the brighter side of life," Edwina teased.

"Edwina makes the best of everything, and God bless her for it," Arthur said, turning to me. "She sees all this stuff coming and asks, 'How can I use it to help the children of the world?' I see it coming and ask, 'How can I expose the inherent inhumanity it represents?' We both agree on its inevitability. We just react to it differently."

"Look!" Credo said, pointing out the window.

As Art looked up, Credo speared the crouton and popped it in his mouth. "Gotcha, you old goat," Credo said triumphantly.

"Fugguduh!" Art said. "Well, you win some and you lose some."

"*But you dress for every game!*" Art and Credo said in unison before a short burst of laughter. I was observing Edwina watching them with a boys-will-be-boys patience when Art spoke up.

"Look, Edwina, all I am saying is there's a lot of downside to all of this. First, it's expensive-as-hell. And while it may be getting cheaper all the time, we just keep driving up our expectations. Technology that satisfies yesterday's imagination is always cheap. But we raise our standards daily, and that gets expensive."

Credo belched.

"Just another AGM," Edwina said. "It stands for Attention Getting Mechanism," she explained to me. "It's another sign of your insecurity, Credo."

"But there is something else that really bothers me," Art continued. "All this technology blurs the lines between commercial and fine art more than I would like, and while you can't fool all the people all the time, you can confuse things enough that we lose our aesthetic footing. When we turn to the same kids who are used to being asked to develop an argument using text and tell them to do the same thing with multimedia, it all looks suspiciously like advertising. Eventually the good students will be those who make commercials so convincing that we don't know the lies from the truth—or at least, one lie from another. We call them master storytellers, but they are really advertisers. And it is just going to get worse. Every new medium we harness will just get thrown into the multimedia mix: virtual reality, holography, smellography..."

"Now we're talking," Credo said. "I am going to be a smell artist and make all of you proud of me."

"We're already proud of you," Edwina assured him. "Please continue, Arthur."

"I'm done," Art said dejectedly. "We've got new technologies coming that we can't even dream of right now, and it will just make things worse. That's all I have to say. I'm finished. Thanks to the overachievers of the world, artists have their hands full running around behind them like sanitation engineers, cleaning up after them wherever they go. That's all I am going to say. Besides, if you want to know where art is headed, read business journals. I do. I have to! I would love to just relax and paint. But while we keep inventing machines that amplify our hopelessly egotistical myopia, I don't get to relax and just paint. Nooooo. And that's all I am going to say on the topic. Fini. Caput. The end." He shoved both forks into the bowl of salad enthusiastically but was immediately upset. "Hey, where are the tomatoes? Where's the freakin' waiter? Where are the freakin' tomatoes?"

"You've got a tomato right there on your plate, you old buzzard," Credo said. "So quit your squawkin'."

"I don't like that part of the tomato. It's got some of the stem in it."

"Waste not, want not," Credo chided.

"Now there's a crock if I ever heard one," retorted Art. "I know plenty of folks who don't waste a thing and all it does is make them want more than they have."

"Boys, I think William would like to say something," Edwina interjected.

"Why read business journals when we have a world-renowned predictor in our presence?" I said, trying not to appear as though I was taking sides. "Credo, what's in store for us?"

"All sorts of stuff," he replied matter-of-factly. "And like most technologies, it will be created to serve education and be almost immediately turned into entertainment."

"What's the difference, anymore?" Art grumbled.

"We can use that to our advantage, Arthur," said Edwina.

"You want to know the secret of my success as a predictor?" Credo asked us.

"No," we all said, laughing quietly.

"Well, ha ha, I'm going to tell you, anyway," Credo said. "Most predictors look at where technology is going as if there were an inevitable evolutionary path it were following. Maybe that was true a century ago when things changed pretty slowly and there were relatively few paths technology could take. But today that approach doesn't work. Now that we can create anything we can dream, we shouldn't look at our technology, we should look at our dreams. Developers are hiring psychologists, sociologists, anthropologists and anyone else who can help them understand what people really want. The assumption is that people haven't really changed and aren't going to change. So, if people aren't going to change, and we can do whatever we want, then we are in a great position to create technology that people will buy. The issue is simple: What do we want? Entertainment, safety, freedom from pain, personal empowerment, sexual gratification..."

"How about a sense of purpose?" Edwina cut in, a little annoyed.

"Deep down that is what everyone wants," Credo conceded, "but very few people can face that. They would rather avoid their fear than conquer it. They would rather avoid a desire for meaning than pursue it. The real predictors these days aren't saying everything is going to change. They are saying nothing has. People are the same, and the technology is just an expensive mirror. Not being able to face what you really want is just part of what is not going to change."

I asked for specifics.

"This makes all the genetic stuff a no-brainer," Credo said. "We will design and grow people to specification, live to be 150, grow new arms when we lose them bungee-jumping or whatever. It's already boring.

"Everything will be voice activated—cars, toasters, you name it. It is easier—less effort, less pain. But it is also less-reflective. We will become a knee-jerk culture. The educational establishment will go bonkers. For decades we have used the so-called 'writing process' to get kids to produce words on a page. So, what happens when the writing process becomes the speaking process? We become a bunch of knee-jerk writers. I tried to warn people, but they wouldn't listen."

"What a wonderful tool for the disabled," Edwina said.

"And what a disaster for everyone else," Art grumbled.

"Like all technology, Arthur, we just need to harness it and use it wisely," she said calmly.

"But we're missing the point," Art insisted. "Words don't exist independently of the process it takes to create them. How you bring words to the surface determines the words you create. The deep processing of writing will produce very different words than the spontaneous combustion of speaking."

Edwina continued unfazed. "Then we simply need to make speaking part of a larger process in which we speak first and then use the deep processing that writing offers to refine our thoughts. It could actually improve our communication."

"All I am saying," Art countered, "is that we don't seem to understand that how you do something and what you do are so interwoven that they are inseparable. We become our tools, whether we are producing media or consuming it. The medium is the message and vice versa. I think I hate McLuhan most when he's right."

"Anyway, if you think virtual reality is a big deal," Credo said, "wait until mind-grafting gets here. We are talking about technology that can feed signals from a distance directly to your cortex, bypassing sensory circuitry. Talk about movies on demand! When that happens there will be no way to distinguish a mind graft from reality until you walk into a wall or realize that virtual food doesn't really cut it on an empty stomach. That will lead to 'Beam me up Scotty,' a la Star Trek."

"Credo gave Roddenberry the idea," I whispered to Art with a wink.

"Did he now?" Art chuckled.

"I predicted it and he listened," Credo said defiantly. "For god's sake, it's not that hard to predict. I mean, what's the mandate right now to all innovators? "

"Digitize, meld, shrink," said Art. "Or is it digitize, smell, stink?"

"And once you have made things as small and integrated as possible?" Credo said. "Project it! Beam it! Send as convincing an image as possible as far away as possible. Right now we project sight and sound. At some point we will project taste, touch and smell, too. Then what's the next logical step? Rather than send an image, send the thing itself! When you get right down to it, electronic media and transportation are just opposite ends of the same continuum. They have a similar relationship as matter and energy. By the way, the drive to develop new transportation will be kicked into high gear by the discovery of a new widespread psychological malady called asynchronomia. It's the inability to do anything face-to-face or in real time. It's already starting to show up in kids who spend all day online. It isn't pretty."

We were digesting Credo's ideas and listening to each other munch on salad, when he continued in a mysterious voice.

"Then of course, there's the biggie: subtextometrics."

There was a dead silence at the table as everyone waited for Credo to chew a mouthful of salad and swallow dramatically.

"Well?" Art said. "Out with it. What's subtextometrics? I have the unenviable task of deconstructing all this new technology so that the money mongers know they are being watched. I would appreciate a head start."

"As I understand it," Credo began, "it's the science of measuring what people really mean. The first phase of the technology that is being developed promises to reveal truth in terms of subtext. For example, let's say William here is at a meeting listening to one of his administrators deny his request for more funding for his department. What would go into a subtextometer would be the administrator saying, 'I'm sorry but we don't have the budget for that right now,' and what would come out might be, 'My dad never went to my baseball games when I was a kid because he was too busy working at the office and now I am going to take that out on you.'"

"Interesting idea, but I thought there wasn't any absolute truth," I said.

"There isn't," Credo assured me. "There is only the emotional distance that exists between what you believe to be the truth and what you say you believe to be truth. This has nothing to do with objective truth, which, as you point out, does not exist. Of course, the software developers claim they are standing on a rock-solid foundation of science, and because of that, we will begin accepting what they say as fact, and simply because we believe it, it will become fact, quite independent of what is or isn't real."

"Run-on," Art noted.

"This is all driven," Credo continued, "by our fear of the possibility that truth doesn't exist anywhere and by our overwhelming need to believe in truth, whether it exists or not. This only gets worse as the world gets more confusing. We will come to hate the knowledge we thought we wanted so badly. We will hate all the choices we have to make. Subtextometrics will become the rationalist's religion."

"Whoever owns the subtextometers will rule the world," I said.

"More to the point is whoever programs them will recreate the world in their image," Credo said.

"More to the point is who pays the programmers," Art countered. "Their world view will become our world view simply because they define our choices. A lot like television, just more insidious. It's pretty dangerous stuff. I can see I got my work cut out for me."

"I see marvelous opportunities for teachers," Edwina said. "They might actually be able to understand what is really bothering a child, deal with it and clear the mind for learning."

"Where I see dirt, she sees soil," Art said. "God bless you, Edwina."

"I just see another filter which will help those in charge determine who the jerks are," Credo said. "That is, who the jerks are by *their* standards. All it does is feed the great triangle: resources—population—filters."

After catching a glimpse of concern on my face, Credo explained.

"A lot of the things that bother us today only bother us because they are happening on such a large scale. If a few people drive a few cars or build a few houses, that doesn't pose a resource problem; but a lot of people doing it *does*. War, disease and famine are great filters, but we can't depend on them, anymore. In the future we will begin making decisions about who lives and who doesn't based on more *rational* kinds of considerations, such as who has the best chance of being a productive member of society—that's just a code phrase 'for the friends of those in power.' The thinking will go something like this: As long as there is too little food for too many people and we know someone has to die anyway, then why take the chance we might kill someone we might like? Let's figure out who is going to get the ax in a more deliberate way and try to achieve the greatest good for the greatest number. As it is right now, gene scans, handwriting samples and urine tests can tell an employer, an insurance company, a fiancée or a school district all they need to know to permanently excommunicate anyone they want. Imagine what a subtextometer will do."

"What's wrong, Arthur?" asked Edwina. Art's face had turned ashen as he gaped aimlessly at nothing.

"I am trying to imagine a world in which you can no longer lie," Art moaned quietly. "What a horrible place. No more private fantasies. No more imagination. People will be reduced to thinking and doing only those things that wouldn't embarrass them if they were running for political office. It is the ultimate commercialization of our private lives. We will begin filling the world with so much homogenized information that it will be meaningless and we won't even know it."

"And that is why teachers will become the most important positions in society," Edwina declared. "As the information races past us like shooting stars it will be their job to help students understand life in the broadest sense. Teachers will help them focus on what is important, on being honest with themselves and compassionate with others, on seeing how what they do affects those around them, on their environment, on the quality of their lives and on the state of their community. They will help students understand the right of every citizen to have a private life, physically and mentally, free from government control. At the same time, they will help students understand how much personal liberty they will need to give up to have the kind of community they want. Teachers will help students understand when to use technology and when not to. Teachers will be raised to a new level in society; they will be known for their perspective and wisdom, as much as for their knowledge and skills. The world could become a wonderful place, if we chose to make it that way."

"And where does that fit into the curriculum?" Credo asked sarcastically. "Try getting that past the forces of the moral majority who will say you are intruding on parents' right to make their children extensions of their own ignorance."

A mutual exhaustion settled on us, the kind that comes from traveling in circles for so long that the purpose of the journey is forgotten.

"So," I finally said, "food, clothing, shelter and *art?*"

I watched a silent negotiation take place among the slightest gestures of their bodies.

"Warm," Credo said, speaking for the rest of them. "Very warm."

"Food, clothing, shelter and...*balance*?"

"Colder," Credo said.

"Food, clothing, shelter and *wise teaching*?"

"Bravo!" Edwina said.

"That's it?" I exclaimed. "That's it? You mean, I finally got it!? I don't believe it! Hallelujah!"

"Bravo, but no, you didn't quite get it," Edwina. "First let's talk about Catch 77."

I slumped forward in my chair. "I need a vacation."

"Everything in the whole freakin' tekosystem is just a big Catch 77!" Art howled.

"The tekosystem?" I asked.

"The secondary ecosystem. It's the one we made out of wires, silicon and plastic. Then we glued the whole thing together with mountains of data. It's like the ecosystem because everything is dependent on everything else; you mess with one part of it, and the whole thing starts to unravel. The difference is that ecosystem usually takes decades to show signs of wear and tear. But in the tekosystem, when something breaks, it breaks. Like I said, the whole thing's just a big Catch 77."

"Arthur, would you care to explain yourself?" Edwina asked.

CHAPTER 22 Why Technology Needs People

Catch 77: You have to, just because you can.

"I think we all know where we are headed with this," Arthur said without looking up. "So let's cut to the chase."

Credo nodded. "We all know what needs to happen," he said. "The question is, who is going to do it?"

"Well, it's obvious to me," Art said. "He's your student. You do it."

"Is he ready?" Edwina asked.

"Hah!" Credo exclaimed. "Good question! He tore my coat and hasn't even apologized."

I slapped a hand over my heart and gripped my shirt. A pain in my chest forced me to bend so far forward that my head was in the salad bowl.

"The hurt you are feeling is your Mother Teresa chakra telling you to care more about people and less about yourself," Credo admonished. "It's where you feel the pain of selfishness. You are lucky you feel it. Imagine what it would say about you if you didn't. I know it seems like a small consolation, but when you find yourself surrounded by jerks who are getting the better of you, just remember that it could always be worse—you could be one of them."

My Mother Teresa chakra was burning with mortification. I sat up, ranch dressing dripping from the tip of my nose.

"I'm sorry, Credo," I said weakly. "I know it is a little late, but I really am sorry. I will replace your coat. I should have offered earlier but I was too ashamed of what I had done. I thought you heard me apologize in my mind."

"Of course I did," Credo said. "But the point isn't for me to hear it; it's for you to say it. And I like my coat just fine, thank you, rips and all. To someone like me, the rips are medals of honor for time served heroically on the battlefield of life."

Art leaned forward and wiped the dressing off my nose as he spoke. "Well, if no one else is going to clean up after the kid, I guess I'll do it. You should be doing this, Credo; he's your student."

"It takes a village, don't you think?" Credo offered as he smiled coyly.

"Perhaps," Edwina replied. "But it also takes a mentor who isn't depending on a village to do his job for him. A village full of people like that would not be a very productive place."

"I am not expecting anyone to do my job for me!" Credo burst out angrily. Moments passed during which Credo felt me scrutinize him in the smallest detail, like tiny hands touching him everywhere. He tried explaining that anger was actually a good thing...if used wisely. He explained that it could be used to clean out your pipes and gain a fresh perspective on things...now and then.

"You're stalling," Art said.

"I think Edwina should be the one," Credo said. "William would have more respect for what he learns."

The fear inside me erupted. "What are you talking about!?" I demanded to know. "For god's sake, could you have some respect for me, the student? Credo, you're my teacher. Stick up for my rights, would you?! Mother freakin' fugguduh, somebody help me out here!"

"In other words, you're chicken, Credo," Art said, completely ignoring me.

"Hardly! Edwina, do you agree you should be the one to go into the ring with our friend here?" Credo asked Edwina.

"Yes," Edwina replied.

"See!" Credo said to Art.

"What does that say about you as a mentor?" Art asked accusingly.

"Boys, boys!" Edwina chided.

While they sparred, I began to shake. *In the ring with Edwina?* The part of my torso situated directly below my Walt Disney chakra and to the right of my navel ached so badly I could hear it pounding.

"That's your fear chakra acting up," Credo announced, "and I do want to let everyone know that you have been doing a lot better about letting go of your fear lately. Do you remember the lesson about fear? You'll need it."

I didn't move.

"Fear blocks everything," Credo reminded me. "It deadens the mind and heart. It is a valve that shuts off the flow of energy between who you are and who you want to become. Pure fear is actually fairly acceptable. It is the anxiety that usually comes with fear that mucks things up. Turn fear into razor-sharp awareness. Turn it into awareness without the anxiety. Become aware without being aware that you are aware. It's a form of Subdig."

Edwina looked at Credo inquisitively. "Do you mean "Sibdug?"

"Dang it!" Credo exclaimed. "Yes. Sorry. Sibdug."

"He doesn't even know the right terminology, for god's sake!" I exclaimed. "I want a real mentor!"

"And where did you learn to be so mean!?" Credo barked at me.

Another pause settled upon the table while everyone in the restaurant stopped talking and turned to sneer at me before returning to their conversations. The moment seemed to expand and contract, as though it were breathing. I felt like announcing to everyone in the room that I wasn't mean, just utterly exasperated.

"I'm sorry, Credo," I finally said. "But sometimes you frustrate me."

Art nodded. "Understandable enough." Credo stared out the window.

"Enough, enough," Edwina said to Credo. "He apologized, Credo. Now tell him it's all right."

"It's all right," Credo said quietly, still staring.

"Don't pay any attention to his sympathy play, William. It's just another AGM. Now, into the ring."

Edwina snapped her fingers.

My next thought was that my head felt bloated and unwieldy. I tried to prop up it up with my hands and felt the plastic shawl of a virtual reality suit wrapped around my shoulders. A pair of thick goggles fit tightly over my eyes.

"You are wired up for a VR adventure," Art called out to me from beyond the illusion in my goggles. "Sorry we are using the old stuff, but it was all we had. My real good stuff is on the fritz. Freakin' technology."

Even though what I was seeing was splotchy, digitally groggy and anything but seamless, it was still disorienting enough to make me feel swallowed by the parallel world that filled my head. I was standing on a narrow bridge made of stone. Other than a few castles in the distance, the bridge was the only landmark within a desolate, smoldering, post-holocaust world.

I walked to the edge of the bridge and looked over. The drop was steep and lined with bare, jagged rock, looking like the teeth of a gigantic maw. I tried to focus on the bottom of the cliff that disappeared into the gray rolling mist, but that made me so dizzy that I spread out my arms like an anxious skater in an attempt to keep my balance. That's when I realized I was holding a gun. I tried to drop it, then shake it loose, then throw it, but it was a part of me, feeling like a limb as securely attached as an arm or leg. I was already panicking when I heard the sound of a car approaching. As I watched a black sedan draw up to the far side of the bridge and park, I began to the clutch the gun. A dark figure stepped out of the car and walked up to me.

"Hello, William," Edwina said. She was dressed in a black trench coat and black shoes, looking a bit like me during my dark-clothes phase. Her eyes were shielded from view by the wide brim of her fedora. In her hand was a revolver.

"Edwina! Help me! There is a gun stuck in my hand!" I exclaimed.

"I know," she said. "There's one stuck in my hand too."

"How do I get rid of it?" I cried.

"There is no need to do anything you don't want to do, William," she responded mysteriously.

I reached toward her, as if to point and say there must be a horrible mistake, when I saw the gun in my hand again. Once more I started to shake it from my hand, this time cursing loudly in the process. Edwina lifted her revolver so that it was pointed directly at me.

What happened next I would never be able to fully explain, especially to myself. It was as if wedged in-between my best intentions, my fear of the cliff on either side of the bridge, the insanity of the situation and a strong sense of survival were a jumble of thoughts that pierced my conscience and laid waste to my better judgment. I raised my hand, aimed at Edwina and fired.

"NO!" I screamed.

I was back at Mitsie's, my head in the salad bowl.

"Please, William, sit up and wipe off your face," Credo told me. "You're embarrassing me."

"Because the gun was there you felt compelled to use it," Art said. "You would have done the same thing if you both had water balloons or bazookas."

Even though I was shaking, Edwina smiled at me. "I had my concerns about whether or not you could handle it," she said. "But you did fine."

"Handle it?!" I screeched. "For god's sake, I shot you! I didn't handle it at all!"

"No you didn't. In fact, it was the other way around—it handled you," Art said. "Why? Because it was there. After all, what else is a gun for? There is something about a big bundle of negative entropy like a gun, or a TV, or a left-handed doohicky that just says, 'Use me—why else would I exist?' You get enough people in one room saying the same thing about a particular doohicky, and then the pressure's on for you to use it whether you want to or not. Catch 77: do it because you can, not because you need to or even want to. It's as if you don't have a choice. But you do. But you don't. To paraphrase Maslow: To those with a hammer, the world looks like a nail. Well, I've got so much stuff in my life that to me the world looks like an entire shopping mall. We see the world in terms of our tools, as if they were some magical pair of glasses we all wore. So, the fewer tools you have, the less likely you are to see the world as a big tool shed."

"That's why part of the art of using technology is knowing when not to use it," Credo said. "We consider someone who walks rather than drives to the corner store to get a loaf of bread a good user of technology precisely because he didn't use it when he didn't need to. You have things in your life now that you used to be able to live without just fine. But once they were invented, you were considered socially irresponsible if you didn't use them. Like a cell phone—you have to have one just in case the babysitter calls, know what I mean?"

I remembered thinking I still felt brittle, like a house of cards waiting for a weak wind to take it down, when somewhere in the distance I heard someone snap his fingers. Suddenly I was in a car swerving to miss an oncoming truck as I struggled to regain my vision.

"What the devil are you doing!?" cried the woman sitting next to me in the passenger seat. "You're in the wrong lane! Where do you think you are, England? Were you drinking again? Were you?! God almighty!"

I heard it all like a gnat buzzing in my ear. I turned and looked. The woman was dressed in an evening gown, long silk gloves and a fur shawl. Star-shaped jewels made of silver and emeralds hung from her ears glistening in the glare of the traffic that flooded through the windshield.

"Sorry," I said, taking quick stock of the situation. I was dressed in a tuxedo and my hair was lathered with some kind of goo. I couldn't quite tell what kind of car it was but it was obviously expensive; it was a smooth ride with lots of leather and natural wood paneling and a dashboard that glowed with more options than I had ever remembered wanting. A few moments passed in silence before the woman said with forced softness, "Well, thanks for going to the opera with me. I know you didn't want to."

Her voice was calm and conciliatory, but with an edge that told me certain hell lurked just beneath the surface. I cleared my throat apologetically. "No problem," I said. "It was my pleasure. Ummm, did, ummm..."

"Yes?" she asked impatiently.

"Did I bring my cell phone?" I finally managed to ask.

"Hello? Anybody home? Did William bring his cell phone? Of course you did! Can you remember any time during the past two years when you haven't brought your cell phone? God almighty, you even bring it to bed with you! At least you had the decency to turn it off during the performance."

I was suddenly searching my pockets in a panic. I yanked the cell phone from my overcoat and was about to dial when I stopped.

"What's our number?" I asked.

"What's our phone number?" the woman shrieked. "Is that what you are asking me?"

"WHAT'S OUR FREAKIN' PHONE NUMBER!?" I bellowed.

"555-3434," she answered, shrinking away from me in terror.

I punched a series of buttons and waited. "Hello? Hello? This is William! How are the kids? I mean kid. Yes. Just one kid. Yes, how is she? I mean he. Huh? What? What? Stop! No. He didn't! HE DIDN'T!"

"What? What is it?" the woman next to me barked.

"The boy is in the hospital," I said.

"What boy?" the woman said. "Our boy? Why don't you call him by his name? What happened to Alvin?"

"We named our kid Alvin?" I asked.

"Look, whoever you are, what happened to Alvin?"

"He almost died," I replied. "He was stung by a bee and the sitter didn't know where his medicine was. She said she tried to call but my cell phone was turned off."

"See? SEE?" the woman exclaimed. "You don't even care enough about your own kid not to listen to me when you know you shouldn't. I told you to turn off your cell phone and you should have said no!"

"But the orchestra conductor told everyone to turn off their cell phones during the performance!" I protested.

"And pleasing the conductor is more important to you than your own son's life!?"

"NO!" I yelled.

I was sitting in Mitsie's, feeling dazed and shaken, and unable to focus on my surroundings. As my mind cleared, all I could think of was that I would never name my kid Alvin. Never.

"And yet," Credo said, "if you were living in an era before cell phones, no one would blame you if your kid got killed by a bee sting. Your neighbors would bring over casseroles and offer to help you around the house. However, given the fact that you had a cell phone with you but didn't respond to an emergency because you had turned it off—well, just look at it metaphorically. It's attempted manslaughter, or at least gross negligence, by reason of Catch 77. Your neighbors now sit and snip about your irresponsibility and keep their casseroles to themselves. Get it?"

Oddly enough, I did. It was actually starting to make a lot of sense. The medium wasn't only the message, it was our marching orders. It not only shaped what we did, it determined what we did. We got addicted to it quickly and, like a conquering general, we refused to give up one ounce of newly gained convenience, no matter what it cost us in inconvenience. The burden of information collided with the increased responsibility of knowing what was possible. Because you could do something, you had to. Or so it felt.

"You can't be without email anymore, can you?" Credo asked me. "What happens if your stockbroker needs to contact you? Failing to buy or sell at just the right time could mean the difference between sending your kid to Harvard or a state college. You don't want to do that to your kid, do you? What would the neighbors say? Besides, in the future your kids could you sue you for that sort of thing."

"And you have to have Sterno," Art said, "just in case you can't find any dry wood when you are camping. You don't want your family to freeze, do you? Think of the profound pain, the guilt, the liability!"

"Or a first-aid kit, just in case someone hurts himself," said Credo.

"Or a calculator, just in case someone's got to know the square root of three," Art said.

I sighed. "Now that's going a bit overboard."

Art's nostrils flared as he snapped his fingers. Suddenly my neck hurt. Worse, I was choking. I was being lifted off the ground by a smelly, muscular, overly tattooed young man whose large perspiring hands were around my throat. We were in an alley, surrounded by a group of men with shaved heads and stomp boots, all of whom were dressed in red jackets with identical Greek lettering.

"Tell me the square root of three," the tattooed man said, "or me and my boys will kill you slowly and ship your body parts to your mother."

"NO!" I cried.

I was back at Mitsie's, cringing as Art shook his finger in my face.

"It could happen," Art said. "And no matter how unlikely the possibility, you'd better be prepared for it, don't you think? I mean, what if you aren't? What if you could have done something and you weren't prepared because you didn't have the right technology with you?"

The waiter pulled up next to the table with a wheelbarrow that was loaded with objects fashioned into a miniature replica of Mt. Everest. It contained a calculator, a cell phone, a first aid kit, a laptop computer, a few cans of Sterno, and an assortment of other objects that looked vaguely useful but not entirely necessary. "Because it's there," the waiter said and left quietly.

"There's so much stuff you have to have with you," said Credo, "that you need a frigging wheelbarrow just to cart it all around. There you are, liberated by technology that you are too scared to let go of. Who owns who?"

"Whom," Edwina corrected him, a bit impatiently. She reached into the pile of things in the wheelbarrow and extracted two objects that she handed to me. "Remember this—a gentleman always carries a penknife and a handkerchief." Briefly I remembered vividly the kindness of the janitor who had used his penknife to help free my tie, and then offered me his handkerchief so I could wipe my mouth. He was very present and then vanished from my mind. Edwina leaned toward me and deftly placed a pink embroidered handkerchief and an emerald-green Boy Scout knife on the table in front of me. "If your goal is to be a gentleman, these are all you will need. However, if you have another goal in mind, then life gets more complicated. It is up to you, William."

"So, food, clothing, shelter and appropriate technology?" I asked.

They considered my question carefully, exchanging a volley of glances that implied I had not considered the issue adequately.

"So, food, clothing, shelter and free will?" I asked.

They all smiled approvingly, except Credo.

"Sort of," Credo said, looking at me furtively. "I think you should ask Kim."

CHAPTER 23 Communicating with Kim
What is the meaning of meaning?

I was lying in bed at home, my mind clouding over with sleep as I tried to remember what had just happened. I had been staring at Edwina Tech, transfixed by the light that poured from her eyes, when Credo said something about Kim and then snapped his fingers. I didn't remember coming home or making my way into bed, but those kinds of things neither surprised nor bothered me anymore. I closed my eyes, yielding to the caress of the fresh sheets my mother had put on the bed, thinking about nothing else but Kim, about being a gentleman, and about how to offer a penknife and a handkerchief to someone over the Net. In my mind looped an endless movie of Kim's face filling my computer screen, smiling at me, touching me somehow through the transcendental ether of the Net, and then disappearing. I knew nothing about her except that her voice was so intoxicating that chatting with her had made me truly happy for the first time in many years. I cautiously began to analyze what it meant to be happy and decided a great deal of being happy simply meant forgetting everything that made one unhappy. But I did not probe too deeply. Somewhere within me lurked a voice that wanted to challenge my right to enjoy a few moments of happiness with someone whom I had never really met. Fortunately, I had no desire to listen to it.

I awoke so obsessed with finding Kim on the Net that I did something that had never occurred to me before: I called the office and told the receptionist I was too sick to come to work. But at 6:35 a.m. I received a phone call from a frantic Network Control employee at BADI. Bottlenecks on BADI's information network were everywhere and he needed to know how to run the download accelerator when he was connected to the Hong Kong office. While I was trying to explain how to do this, call-waiting beeped me; it was the network employee in the cubicle across the hall from the first caller, phoning to say that bottlenecks were everywhere. She needed to know which access codes to use to peek into interoffice mail to find redundancies in graphic file transfers that were clogging the network. I was partway through that explanation when someone from London beeped me online and took control of my screen, displaying a map of BADI's international network, with a flashing message at the bottom: 'Bottlenecks are everywhere. What should I do???' In the time it took me to get dressed and leave for work I received six more phone calls, two interactive chat session requests, three faxes and two pager beeps.

"I hate the global village," I muttered as 10 headaches converged on my cranium at once. I ignored my pain and stoically headed for the subway.

At work I tried to feign looking sick until a data-entry clerk giggled as she told me that I didn't need to try. 'Just be your normal stressed-out self and you will do fine,' she said, advice which I found helpful but disturbing, and which I would add to the growing list of important things to think about when I had time.

The day was longer than usual and I missed the 5:12 home. As I was hurrying to the subway to catch the 6:14 I realized that there was no such thing as a day off. Not anymore. Not for me. I was wondering what would happen to BADI if I really got sick and couldn't come in for a week. And I was wondering about the responsibility and power I used to cherish which now felt like weights around my neck and a trap I had walked into so blindly I couldn't fathom my egotistical stupidity. I could not believe I'd actually wanted everything I now had. And I could not believe that I had waited until now to begin wanting some of the things I now craved. Like happiness. A day off. A sense of control over my own life. Less power and more vulnerability. As my mind filled with thoughts I walked past Credo's doorway without even thinking about him.

When I finally arrived home at around 8 o'clock in the evening I was tired and hungry and headed straight for my room despite my mother's protestations and inquiries about my health. She used to say to me, "There is more to life than just computers." Now she said, "There is more to life than just work." The transition between the two felt seamless and, in retrospect, so inevitable as to be embarrassing.

In my room I fired up my computer and began to pace, checking my watch every few seconds. A few keystrokes later I was waiting anxiously for the image on my screen to crystallize.

"Kim, are you there?" I asked. A gauge on my computer screen that looked like a thermometer indicated that my voice was weak. I adjusted the sound level on the camera mounted on the top of my screen.

"Kim?" I asked again, squinting at the blurry outline on my screen.

On the Net, where speed and clarity were always at odds, I usually split the difference, settling for slightly fuzzy pictures that arrived somewhat expeditiously. But tonight I sacrificed everything to clarity. As painful as the waiting was, I wanted to see Kim as clearly as possible.

Her image came in waves, each one adding a bit more detail to the rendering of a woman with blond hair streaked with green swirls, rosy cheeks dashed with silver sparkles, and bright-blue lips and eyebrows. I smiled.

"Kim," I whispered.

"Hello, William," floated mellifluously from the tiny speakers hooked to the sides of my screen. I fought a familiar seduction and pushed forward.

"Are you real?" I asked anxiously.

"William, you didn't even say hello!"

"Sorry. Hello. Well, are you real?" I asked again.

"Can you see me?" she asked.

"Yes..." I ventured, not really sure.

"Then I must be real, don't you think?"

She seemed to be more and more a part of Credo's world in which nothing made sense, but everything made a kind of super-sense, in which everything was a lie through which we saw the truth. I studied the screen for a few moments before continuing.

"How old are you?" I asked.

"William," she said. "A gentleman never asks a lady her age."

"Are you an avatar?"

"No," she replied. "Are you?"

"Are you using filters?"

"Yes, I am," Kim replied calmly. "But isn't everybody? On or off the Net, we'd die without our filters, don't you think? After all, what's makeup, or a fancy haircut, or an inflated sense of self-importance? They're all filters, don't you think?"

I just stared at her, a bit dizzy from what sounded like rehearsed double talk.

"And before you go any further," she continued, "you need to ask yourself whether or not you really want to know more about me. Don't ask questions if you are afraid of the answers. That is another way of saying, 'Before you ask hard questions, make sure that you can handle the difference between fantasy and reality.' Most people can't. In fact, statistically speaking, well more than two-thirds can't."

There was a prolonged pause as I began to tear into the image on my screen as a set of heavily-edited pixels laboriously crafted in someone's cyberlab. Again I had to fight the feeling of lowering my body into a hot tub as Kim's voice massaged an aching spot in my soul. I wanted to believe everything, question nothing. But I shook my head and tensed my body, fighting off the effects of the Kim drug. I was unusually fearless as I charged into the conversation, ignoring the grip of my Disney chakra, which commanded me to believe in miracles, and my fear chakra, which made me too afraid to be honest with myself.

"Maybe we should meet," I offered. "I could drive to wherever you are."

"How do you know that I am some place you can drive to?"

I paused. "Well, are you?"

"William, we barely know each other. Don't you think we should slow down a little?"

"No," I said, a bit panicky. "I need to see you."

"You can see me now," she said, her smile twinkling like distant headlights in the rain.

"But I mean *really* see you," William insisted. "How else can I offer you a penknife and a handkerchief?"

"Excuse me?" she said.

"It's an old saying. Never mind."

"Let me show you something," Kim said.

A report began to take shape in the upper right hand corner of my screen. In large bold letters the title read "Screening Your Screen Dates: The Dangers of Meeting Your Cyber-Acquaintance."

"You should read this before you ask to meet me," she told me. "More than two-thirds of those polled wished they had kept their cyber lives and physical lives separate, due to what many called 'mutual-reality contamination.'"

I read the title and then saw the author's name: Kim Dayly, Ph.D. "Did you write the report?"

"Yes, I did," she replied.

I wanted to think about that for a moment, but couldn't bear the silence.

"Kim, I'm really busy. Seeing as how you wrote it can you just tell me what it says?"

"Just click on the *Summary* button," she insisted, "and you can read the most important points. It will only take you a minute. I'll do something else and pop right back."

"No!" I cried. Kim backed away from the screen as fuzzy worry lines shot across her forehead. I realized I was scaring her and reminded myself that to her I could just be one of those cyberwackos that the government warns people about. I relaxed a notch. "Please, Kim. I want you to tell me. It's been a long day."

"You weren't this serious last time, William. I thought you liked me because I didn't engage your mind too much. We talked about nothing, remember? And I loved it! It was you who said home is where you can put down your sword and shield, drop your guard, and relax after a day of fighting dragons. You told me I felt like home. But now you don't sound as if you want to relax. Now it sounds like the dragons followed you back to the castle tonight."

"Kim, please," I pleaded. "This is important."

"Okay. But we need to make a deal. I thought we were headed for a different kind of relationship. It has to be all right for either one of us to change the rules when one of our needs change, not just you. Do you agree?"

"Yes," I said. "But one question before we continue: Do you have a lot of cyber relationships?"

"Yes," Kim answered matter-of-factly.

"Are they all like ours?" I asked.

"Not at all," she replied. "They are all different. Some are very deep and philosophical, some are very homogenized and friendly, some are mutually antagonistic, and some are just plain fun. Different people for different needs. That's what I love about the Net. Here we don't have to expect one person to be our everything. We can go looking for people who specialize in particular personal attributes. Or we can create a new persona for ourselves to adapt to a situation. Or both."

"And what kind of relationship are we?" I asked.

"Based on our little bit of interaction I would say we're very friendly, but not very deep," she replied.

"Well, I want to get deep."

Kim nodded briskly, the movements of her head appearing somewhat jerky as my net connection waxed and waned. "Okay. Let's do. Back to food, clothing and shelter?"

"Okay," I replied.

"Good. Let's assume neither of us were right the other day and shift perspectives a bit. Let's try considering the question from the perspective of an average sape for a moment."

I was instantly panic-stricken, demanding to know where she heard the term 'sape.' It was a hallmark of Credo's teaching and I was instantly suspicious. Slowly, she explained that it was a term commonly used among anthropologists, that she had received her first degree in anthropology, and that, in fact, it was she who had first formally proposed that the field of anthropology embrace the study of cyberspace as a natural extension of its domain. Her suggestion had fallen upon the deaf ears of those she called 'the bone men' who, in her opinion, spent far too much time wading around in the mud searching for skeleton scraps and not enough time examining the virtual artifacts of the Information Age. Part of me was listening, part was replaying the last few days in my mind, looking for signs of a conspiracy. "You're not in on this with Credo, are you?"

"Talk about non-sequiturs! Who or what is Credo?" Kim asked.

I squinted, pressing my face close to the screen, trying to pierce the technological barrier that separated us in search of clues. But it was impossible to read a face well enough on a computer screen to discern the subtleties of truth. As my eyes began to ache I silently cursed the computer industry for not having produced better screens by now. *Sure, we get faster and faster CPUs,* I ranted to myself silently, *bigger and bigger hard drives, more ergonomic keyboards and video on demand. But can someone please tell me why we are still stuck with screens that haven't improved in 20 years! Don't those industry who-hahs realize they are competing with paper, which has a screen beat by a factor of at least 3-to-1? Don't they realize that paper still rules the world of pictures by such a margin they ought to be embarrassed? Doesn't anyone care that we are all going blind? Doesn't anyone understand that by making it easier to see we could add another 10% to productivity?!*

"Are you all right?" Kim asked. When I didn't answer, she said, "No, I honestly don't know Credo. Who is he? Or she? Or it?"

I leaned back in my chair and exhaled loudly, looking up at the ceiling, sideways at the screen, and then up at the ceiling again as I propped my feet up on the desk. *You can't contain life*, I counseled myself, drawing upon an online chat room conversation from long ago that had stuck with me throughout the years. *Life contains you.*

"William, you need to switch to decaf," Kim said.

The mere mention of caffeine made my coffee hand begin to grope for its cup. I ignored it, as well as her invitation to play, and got down to business. "So, what comes after food, clothing and shelter?" I asked.

"Meaning," she replied.

"I thought it was love," I reminded her.

She giggled. "Sometimes it is. But remember what I just said: let's assume we were both wrong the other day. Assuming we're wrong gives us an excuse to keep learning, 'know what I mean? So let's revisit the question."

Another brief burst of panic. Maybe the answer to the question *"What comes after food, clothing, and shelter?"* was actually situational, changing as life did, as I did, as the weather did. Perhaps I would never be right. Perhaps there was no such thing as being right. Perhaps that was the point. Perhaps Credo, Art and all the rest were just leading me on in some spiritual joyride for their own amusement. Credo and Art might do that to me, but Edwina wouldn't...would she?

"But for now," Kim continued, "it is *meaning* that comes after food, clothing, and shelter."

"Meaning?" I asked

"Right," she assured me.

"No," I flustered. "I mean, what do you mean, *meaning*? Meaning what? I mean, what does it have to do with us?" I could hear how stupid I sounded, which only made me more agitated.

Kim couldn't help laughing a little. "Meaning has everything to do with everything, us included."

"You know what I mean," I said. "Why did you bring it up?"

"Have you ever met anyone in the flesh that you had gotten to know very well via email first?"

Even though she seemed to be evading the issue, I couldn't help being pleasantly distracted by the question. "A few times."

"And what happened?" Kim asked.

Now I was laughing, instantly transported to a memory. "I remember one time in particular. I had been collaborating online with someone in our London office whom I only knew as Pat983@badi.london.com. All along I figured Pat was a guy in his mid-30s. I don't know why. For some reason I thought he was tall and thin, and a little bit '60s—pony-tail, beads, big beard, that sort of thing. Well, I was at a computer convention and someone taps me on the shoulder and says, 'Hi, I'm Pat983.' It could have been my grandmother! She had to be at least 70, about 5-feet-tall and as round as a beach ball. Wow! I will never forget that."

"And when you read her email, did you hear her speak in your mind?" Kim asked.

I had to think about it for a moment, during which I realized that I always heard a tone of voice, no matter whom I was emailing. I supposed everyone did. "Yes," I finally answered.

"And what tone of voice did you hear?"

"Male. Pretty snide. An old-boy-on-the-inside kind of voice. But the real Pat983 sounded more like you with a British accent! Very nice, very sincere. She used to end every message with, 'It all makes so much sense.' In my mind she was being sarcastic as heck, sort of like 'Your check's in the mail.' But when I heard her say it to my face, I realized that she actually meant it! She was being hopeful! Yes, Pat983. That was quite an experience."

"Do you know why you created an image and a tone of voice to represent Pat?" Kim asked.

I paused, recalling some inner chatter. "Actually, I have thought about that quite a bit. It must be some stereotypes I keep in my head about what networkers look like and what gender they belong to. I probably need to change my programming on that one."

"Could be," Kim said. "But the bigger question I am asking is why you created an image—*any image*—in the first place."

"I suppose that's the way we work," I said. "We can't live with a blank screen in our minds. We can't hear someone speak without some sort of tone of voice attached to it. Where there's audio, there's got to be video."

Kim smiled. "Nicely put. I think of it this way: There is what you say and there is what you mean. What you say is what we hear. What you mean is what we really have to listen for—the meta-meaning. Meta-meaning is derived from meta-information: context, inference, implication, voice inflection, body language and anything else that helps you interpret what you hear. We hear on a conscious level, but we listen on an unconscious level. In terms of meaning, what you hear is not nearly as important as what you listen for. In fact, without meaning, there has been no communication at all.

"A string of text on the screen offers no meta-information. We may recognize the words but we don't know how to interpret them. Because human beings crave meaning so badly, they will create it even if there's no meta-information to guide them. Creating meaning, however inaccurate, creates order in an environment in which there would otherwise be emotional chaos.

"This gives email an unusual quality—meaning or meta-information is often supplied by the receiver, not by the sender. What we read, the pictures we make in our minds, the tone of voice we hear—unless it is someone we already know—is usually more a reflection of how we feel about ourselves than how we feel about the person who sent us the message. If you want to conduct an interesting experiment sometime, get a group of people together in the same room and have each one of them inflect the phrase, 'What do you mean?' with a different meaning. I have done it with as many as 20 people without repetition. You can say it so many different ways, and yet each way looks exactly the same on a screen. So, when we unconsciously choose an inflection, where does it come from? *From within us*, where else?"

I couldn't help but be curious. Why, in her opinion, did I create the specific image of Pat that I did?

"I am going to guess because, as you suggested, it was compatible with your preconceptions of a networker. What would have happened if you knew Pat was a grandmother? You would have focused on her persona rather than her words. You didn't want to do that; you wanted to conduct business. So, when your mind was free to create any image it wanted to, it created the one that presented the least impediment to conducting business. I don't know where the beard came from, but you created someone with basically the same attitude that you have, whom you could relate to without a lot of effort. Thus the double-edged sword of the Net. You had a completely inaccurate idea of who Pat983 really was. But it allowed you to take her seriously as a colleague, something you might not have done if you knew she was a 70-year-old woman. Email atones for prejudice quite nicely by allowing you to create a lie that satisfies you. Through a lie, we catch a glimpse of a greater truth."

"Like Art," I said.

"Like art," Kim agreed.

"Shall we take a break?" I asked.

"Let's do," she replied.

"You'll be here when I come back?" I pleaded.

"Yes," she assured me.

"Because there is something I really want to ask you."

"I can't wait," she said.

CHAPTER 24 Email Bonding
What does the phrase "the seasons of man" mean to a woman living at the equator?

I sprinted to the bathroom and locked the door. With my mind racing I relieved myself without focusing, missing the bowl now and again and adding to the discoloration of the tile next to toilet. Once again I was unconsciously setting up a continuation of the battle with my mother about my bathroom habits which had been going on since high school. Without cleaning up, closing the toilet lid, washing my hands, or flushing, I sprinted back to my room. Years later I would realize that had I been truly aware of my actions during that moment I would have had many of the answers I sought from Kim that evening.

I settled in behind my computer, tapped the return key several times, waited impatiently and then started talking before Kim's face was fully formed on my screen.

"Is there a female perspective in all this?" I asked.

She teased me for not saying hello again, and then asked me to define what I meant by "all this."

"You know," I told her, my hands dancing in the air as they tried to circumscribe an anonymous ancient Greek's definition of God I had once heard as *a circle whose center was everywhere and whose circumference was nowhere.* "All *this*—the Net. You know, life in the cyburbs. Do women see it differently from men?"

She asked me if there was anything I knew of in the entire world that women didn't see differently from men. In her opinion, we were lucky that men and women could successfully execute exchanges like "Please pass the salt," and "Do you know where to get the bus?"

But wasn't communication better on the Net? I asked her.

"A number of studies suggest it can be," Kim replied. "Online, people tend to align themselves by reasons of common interest instead of sexual chemistry, as they do in the outersphere, though sometimes common interest can be sexuality. But mind-to-mind communication opens up new frontiers in communication. You would do well, sweet William, to note that much of what liberated us to communicate earlier has now been compromised by your insistence that we use a video connection. We have lost what is best about text and are back to the same old wine in a brand new medium simply because we can see each other. Attachment is the mind killer, William. You must work on letting go."

each other. Attachment is the mind killer, William. You must work on letting go."

Suddenly it seemed like everyone in my life was lecturing me. Then suddenly it seemed like I had it coming because I was infinitely stupid. Then I didn't care. I was enthralled with Kim.

"I belong to a number of online chat groups," Kim continued. "I particularly like Beanie Babies Forever, Cyberchicks, Liars Figure and Figures Lie. My favorite is the one I met you in—Cybersays— because I know the people I am communicating with are interested in what I think. They have to be because they haven't the faintest idea who I really am! The mating dance of meeting someone in a bar and scoping him out physically is replaced by mental intrigue. Interpersonally, there is no more truth to it, but it is a nobler lie. And besides being a lot more interesting, it is always validating because even when someone doesn't like what I say, at least I feel that I have been heard. Do you know what women's number one complaint is about men, at least according to the banter I read in Cyberchicks?"

My mind had drifted a little but her tone of voice snapped me back, my eyes shifting to feign attention as I refocused. I shook my head and asked to know.

"More than 70 percent of the Cyberchicks who responded to my survey said it was that they don't feel listened to. Online, people listen to you, especially when you are using text. The online community procreates, nurtures and unites with words. It stands or falls on the abilities of its members to listen, consider and respond. This is very different from life in the outersphere. That is why some women like it so much online. But online liberation isn't just for women. It's for anyone who finds life in the outersphere oppressive. Studies show that it is most pronounced in education. Do you know why?"

I had other questions to ask but Kim was mid-idea and I enjoyed listening as her voice smoothed over me like the strong hands of a knowing masseuse.

"Why?" I replied.

"What's rule number one about America?" she asked. "Winning is everything," she answered. "In the average American classroom that means being outspoken. And what happens when being outspoken isn't your style? Simple: You lose. That is why life online has became the home of a number of the disenfranchised: midgets, the handi-capped, the unattractive, stutterers, the unconfident, the intimidated, those for whom English is a second language, and basically anyone who has a hard time getting a word in edgewise while people from the dominant strata of society prattle on and on. All these people found acceptance online. You might be interested to know that there are cultures in which students are actually expected to wait a few moments before responding to a question from a teacher as a way of showing respect. I call them 'waiters.' But if you do that in America you're considered to be a dimwit or a troublemaker. Waiters found a home online, too."

She assured me, however, that all of this was just the tip of the iceberg. There is an even greater liberation that the online world offered.

She proceeded to tell me a story about a computer conference community of more than 200 citizens who, according to the report, were given access to more than 100 different conferences for more than two years, and yet chose to spend most of their time in just two. One was called 'Sex, Love and Secret Lives,' in which complete strangers shared the innermost secrets of their sex lives with all the abandon of intimate friends who had consumed way too much wine. The second was called 'Wide Open Forum' in which participants could say anything at all, and often did, routinely bashing the holy heck out of each other. It got so bad that the system operator banished the worst offenders to a special conference called 'Blood Bash.' Otherwise decent, appropriately reticent people were engaging in communication they simply would not have, otherwise. There was a part of them that was encouraged to ignite and burn brightly online that would have been unlit or doused in the outersphere. Net result? *The online medium offers new behavioral opportunities not available in the outersphere, expanding the spectrum of human behavior and exacerbating the complexity of the human condition.* This was all made possible because of the nature of the online medium itself, reinforcing, once again, that communication is not independent of its medium; it is shaped by the medium. Some would even say the medium and message were in such close symbiosis as to be indistinguishable from one another. Grandpa McLuhan was once again smiling at me.

Kim was suddenly sullen. After a gentle prod from me she confessed that she—like everyone else—couldn't wait until the technology became available so that everyone could have good, clear video conferencing through her computer. Like everyone else, she was waiting for the bandwidth that would make this possible.

But another part of her rued the day. As people became enamored of the flicker of moving pictures, they would begin to perceive written words as clunky and unresponsive rather than deliberate and reflective. Video would offer more externalized experiences per cubic moment and take us so many places so quickly that we would yield our individual imaginations to the collective of the lens in a desperate attempt to keep pace. And video was just the beginning. Once we had enough bandwidth to see each other in full motion, we would want enough for virtual reality, and holography, and anything else we would taste and become instantly addicted to.

I felt horrible for having pushed her to use video the last time we communicated and told her so. No matter, she assured me; it was inevitable. While we were some of the few with the technology and the patience to use video over the Net, she knew we were just momentary exceptions in the long march of ever-increasing communication capacity. She could feel herself, and the rest of the world, slowly slipping into the abyss of technological imperative. She figured it was no different than it must have been for our great grandparents when they reluctantly bought their first car. She would do everything she could to keep the written word alive on her screen, but she knew its days were numbered. She asked if I understood the term 'technological imperative.'

I told her I did. In some circles it was known as Catch 77: "Do it because you can, whether you need to or not." If you do it enough times just because you can, sooner or later it unnoticeably mutates into something that needs to happen, slipping into the unconscious embrace of habit.

"Exactly," she said, smiling weakly.

There was a moment during which we both caught our breath. I was numb from her voice, but my mind was alive with a menagerie of new ideas. I apologized for derailing the conversation. We had been talking about Pat983.

"Anyway," she sighed, "all of that discussion certainly was a long way around the barn to get to the point I was trying to make. Where I was headed was this—if you want to get a good idea of who you are, look at the image you created of Pat. We are what we fantasize we want others to be. This is particularly obvious when it comes to email because of all the information that is missing: no body language, no voice inflection, no facial expressions. When you read someone's email you have to supply all that yourself. *When you read your email, you read yourself.*"

"But you and I are not using email," I noted. "I can hear you and see you…so to speak…can't I?"

CHAPTER 25
There Are Two Types of People-
Type A, Type B, and Those Who Can't Count
Anthropology 101 in a sentence: everyone is inherently insecure; the rest are details.

"Finding the truth in any form of communication is an art form," Kim began. "This is more obvious with email than other kinds of communication. Even when you are dealing with someone real-time, full-flesh, it is hard to know what is really being said, where the truth lies, and who really means what, don't you think? I mean everyone lies at least a little, regardless of the medium, don't you think?"

I shook my head in agreement, silently acknowledging the truth of her words and the cynicism implicit in just about everything she was saying. *Don't take it personally,* I whispered to myself. *If you take it personally, you're a goner.*

An honest look of concern filled Kim's face. "William, you look tired."

I broke in before she could continue. "I'm fine. Fine. Just a tad confused. Please keep going."

"Alright then, let's do. But do tell me if you need a break."

"I will, I will," I said, urging her on.

"A lot of our confusion has to do with how we view communication," she continued. "Most people see it as a linear event. You know the old model: *I* say this to *you*; and in between us is some noise that blurs the meaning."

I watched as Kim drew an equation on the screen:

$$\textbf{Sender} \; - > \; \textbf{Noise} \; - > \; \textbf{Receiver}$$

"The assumption here is that what I say is what you hear. It assumes that the sender and receiver share enough of the same life experiences, word definitions, value systems and culture that if it weren't for a little bit of noise, an idea could flow from one person to another, perfectly understood, like copying data from one disk to another. Bad assumption. We have early information theorists to thank for this model, which they based on the behavior of machines. Machines may work that way, but people don't.

"The new model for people is that communication is a shared event, like this:" She drew two circles on the screen that overlapped slightly, like the rings of Olympia, forming a shaded area in the center:

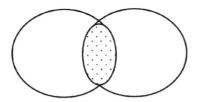

"The old linear model says that one circle fills the other with its contents when they communicate, like copying a file from one disk to another. The new transactional model represented here says that when one person talks to the other they create the shaded area, which is a product of whatever shared meaning they create.

"The linear model is egotistical and immature on a personal level, ethnocentric and bigoted on a larger scale. The transactional model is detached and open on a personal level, multicultural and networked on a larger scale. In McLuhan's terminology, the first model is left hemisphere — visual and sequential. The second is right hemisphere — acoustic and associative. Above all, the second model lets go of the idea that truth exists somewhere independent of our interpretation of events and that it is just a matter of fine-tuning our technology in order to find it. The second model assumes that there is no truth or objective reality. Indeed, it assumes there are only things that happen relative to one another which have no reality other than the meaning we give to them."

"That scares me," I said.

"And when it liberates you, you will be a type-B person."

"Type B?" I asked.

"Let me use an example I know you will be able to relate to. Do you remember what it was like to have the shine wear off a new love? What did you realize when that happened to you?"

My mind froze like un-oiled gears screeching to halt. I stared past the image on the screen, fixating on a few of the dancing pixels that illuminated Kim's chin.

"William, have you ever been in love?"

At 22, I knew I didn't really qualify to have a past, yet my few experiences with love felt like dim memories from long ago. Gradually a few faces came into view, like planets returning from long, elliptical orbits: Roberta, Ramona, Juliene and someone else maybe...Juliene was the only one who'd lasted more than a few months. I remembered because we'd met on Labor Day and hadn't broken up until New Year's Eve. She'd hated the fact that I'd had had other girl friends—a source of constant friction and general unpleasantness. Things got so bad that I was compelled to consider writing my congressman to suggest that the discrimination clause in the constitution be amended to read, "without regard to sex, color, race, creed, national origin, or previous lovers." But I loved her, and when she left I was devastated. Because of Juliene, I had actually talked to a cyber acquaintance in the insurance business about creating love insurance to cover stress, anxiety and maybe even missed workdays caused by staying home to nurse a broken heart.

"Have I ever been in love?" I repeated quietly. "No, not really," I finally answered. "Well, maybe. Sort of. Well, it depends on what you mean by being in love."

Suddenly my mother called out from the other side of the door. "William, dear, who are you talking to?"

I couldn't help wondering, *shouldn't that be "whom" you are talking to?*

CHAPTER 26 Love, Life and Statistical Probabilities

What's love got to do with it? About 33% of everything, give or take a 5% margin of error.

"No one," I tried to assure her.

"Well, you're talking to *someone*," came the demure but insistent voice of my mother. "Are you all right?"

"Yes, Mother," I said just loud enough to penetrate the door. "For god's sake, I'm fine."

"All right then, dear. Night night. I love you."

"I love you too, Mother. Please. Now, good night."

I was too mortified to look at Kim.

"Your mother cares about you, William," Kim admonished.

"I know, I know," I said, half in appreciation, half in pain.

Kim waited for a moment before continuing. "So..."

"Ah yes," I said. "Where were we?"

"I had asked you," Kim began, "what you learn when the shine wears off a new love."

"Right, right..." I said in a subdued voice.

Even through the long stretch of the Net, Kim could obviously sense my pain. She ended the moment by charging ahead.

"Let *me* tell *you* what I realize when the shine wears off a new love," she continued. "I realize that so much of what I considered to be *real* about the other person was just my projection. I realize that I was in love with my projection of what I thought I needed. When the shine wears off, you have two ways of looking at it. Either A: reality rears its ugly head, or, B: reality opens new doors to new possibilities. Most people are either so disappointed by reality that they choose A or get caught between A and B trying to grow new skin without shedding the old. Change doesn't work that way. It is the rare person who chooses B and who can consider the possibility that there exists something better than their idea of reality."

"Are you a type-B person?" I asked.

Kim squeaked with laughter. "Li'l ol' me? Well, I suppose I try to be. But it seems that it is a lesson that I, and most everyone I know, need to re-learn on a continual basis. Did you ever study slugs in high school?"

"Slugs?" I asked.

After she assured me that she was referring to those slimy things that showed up on the sidewalk after a hard rain, I told her that I could honestly say I had not studied them in any detail. After all, I had left school when I was 15 and missed that part of my education. She told me that she would tell me everything I needed to know about them in one sentence: "We're no better than they are." In fact, according to Kim, in some ways they were much more advanced than we were. According to her tenth grade biology teacher, slugs will bump into a wall only three times before turning to head in another direction. She told me that most people she knows will bump into the projection-meets-reality wall far more than three times before figuring out they need to change course. "Oh, to be a slug some days," she said wistfully.

"That's a rather dim forecast for humanity," I suggested.

"Why?" she asked.

"Being less intelligent than a slug doesn't bother you?"

Kim looked at me pensively. "No, it doesn't. How are you at taking advice?"

"All right, I guess," I said, a little taken off guard by the question.

"I suggest you take a look at why you feel a need to be better than a slug," she told me. "It is an insecurity you need to root out and squash like a bug. In the end we're all headed to the same place, anyway."

"And where is that?" I asked.

"To the garden—where else? Death spares no one."

I rose abruptly and began circling my room in an endless loop waiting to abort. The camera followed me, whirring and jerking as I dodged the piles of clothes and stacks of dog-eared magazines. As I turned quickly to look at the screen, I knocked over a cup of cold espresso onto a keyboard that was in several pieces on my desk in the process of being repaired.

"Major fugguduh!" I screeched. I suddenly hated the mess in my room with an intensity that seemed unbearable. It was no longer just the décor of my former self; it was an ancient skin which I had shed many revelations ago. It was all a metaphor, I reminded myself. The half-filled cups of coffee hiding in my room were land mines of the soul I had planted to sabotage my own happiness. The untended dirty clothes were my way of refusing to leave the interior landscape of my mind. The magazines I wouldn't throw out but would never read symbolized an anal retention of old information that, like the pizza boxes in the corner, were a familiar distraction that hindered my evolution.

"You need an interior designer, William," said Kim. My Mother Teresa Chakra erupted with mortification as I realized Kim had just gotten the grand tour of my room because I hadn't the good sense to sit still while I was online.

Before I could respond, my mother called out from the other side of my closed bedroom door. "William, are you alright, dear? What was that sound?"

"Yes, mother, I'm fine, for god's sake!" I hollered. "I'm just, just, making some notes for work!"

"Then why are you cursing?" my mother wanted to know.

"Mother, please! Fugguduh is not cursing!"

"You know how I feel about that word, dear," she insisted gently.

"Mother please, or I will start saying some of those words you are not allowed to say on television!"

"All right, dear," his mother said. "Nighty night again."

I sat down and settled in behind my computer again. "Fugguduh," I muttered as I turned to Kim. "Now, that's embarrassing."

"Don't blame your mother for caring about you," Kim said sternly. "If her concern embarrasses you, then leave home."

"Thanks very much," I said dejectedly.

"By the way, I ran an analysis of your conversation with your mother using some software I helped to develop—Dialogician."

"Great," I said sarcastically.

"The bottom line is this: William, you want your mother to treat you as a child and an adult simultaneously, while she wants to treat you only as a child. On a functional level it will never work."

"Thanks for the family therapy. It *really* helped."

"Maybe we should call it a night," Kim said.

"No!" I said. "I just need to take a break."

"Fine, then," Kim said. "Let's do. I will talk to someone else for a minute."

"No! I don't want you to talk to anyone else right now!" I sat on my bed, exhaling loudly as my hands gripped my calves and my head dropped between my knees. My head felt unbearably heavy. "I'm sorry," I said calmly. "Of course you're right. I should leave home if I don't like it here. And of course you should talk to whomever you like. I'm sorry."

"No problem," Kim assured me. "Besides, I feel honored. I can tell that you are about to take a quantum leap in your personal development and I can say that I helped. What do you say we get back to the reason we started having this conversation in the first place? You wanted to meet me, do you recall?"

Vague memories took shape in my mind. "Yes," I said. "But I don't think you need to explain it to me. I think I understand."

"Let's see, shall we? The best way to find out if you have learned something is to try to explain it to someone else. So, you explain it to me."

I slouched in front of my screen, propping my feet up on the desk and tilting back in the chair. "All right. Here is what I have learned. Even in real-time, full-flesh encounters, your imagination creates a lot of reality that is not really there. It is our ability to romanticize a bad sitatuation that makes life tolerable at times. Much of what you see you project. Technology just amplifies this."

"Good," she encouraged.

"There is a direct relationship between the kind of information a technological medium provides and what you must supply. Email is an obvious case of information deficit. The more sophisticated the technology becomes, the more skill it takes to distinguish fantasy from reality."

"Very good," Kim said proudly.

"Even though I can see you and hear you," I continued, "you exist mostly in my imagination. I would approach an encounter with you expecting to meet my imagination, rather than expecting the unexpected. If I am an A-type person, I would be very disturbed by this; I would probably feel betrayed by you. If I am a B-type person, I would welcome the growth opportunity and view the difference between who you are and what I expected as some measure of who I really am on a fundamental level. I would welcome the opportunity to create a shared reality and learn more about myself. But, as I am not quite a B-type person, you are better left to my imagination, for now, anyway."

"Well done!" Kim said. "You are well on your way to becoming a type-B person."

"You have obviously put a lot of thought into this," I said.

"I'm a researcher," Kim said. "It's my job."

"Am I a research subject?"

Kim smiled. "Not formally. But any honest researcher will tell you that everyone is a potential subject, whether the researcher realizes it at the time or not. I honestly looked forward to chatting with you since our last time. You had a nice energy. I thought you were happy. Now you don't seem so happy."

"I am not so sure that is the goal, anymore," I said.

"If being happy isn't the goal, then what is?"

It was hard to grasp the question in any real way and, after listening to me sputter for a few moments, Kim broke in.

"Imagine you are a teacher talking to your students," she counseled.

"That is very easy to imagine," I said, smiling as pleasant images filled my head.

"Imagine one of them has just asked you, 'Mr. Tell, if happiness isn't the goal, what is?'"

"Love?" I ventured, looking for Kim's approval. "That was how you originally answered the question, 'What comes after food, clothing and shelter...' do you remember? I said 'weapons.' Geez, that's embarrassing, now. I feel like that all happened a dozen lifetimes ago."

"So, William, what is love?" Kim asked.

"You're the researcher," I replied. "You tell me."

Kim smiled at me, a little irked, a little intrigued by my persistence.

"I hope you are aware of the fact that you could tell me anything right now and I would believe it," I confessed.

Now she was laughing. "William, honestly. What do you think would happen to my reputation as a researcher if I started making things up? Fortunately the truth is interesting enough on its own. I can tell give you a fairly detailed percentage breakdown of a response to a related question when it was posed to a number of focus groups last month. Or I can simply tell you what I think it is."

"Where do you get these kinds of figures?" I asked in amazement.

"I'm a researcher, remember? Some would call me 'a pollster.' I can give you the president's rating on a 12-hour basis. That's how often a focus group somewhere in America convenes and is asked questions like, 'Do you like the president? Would you feel comfortable lending him your car? Would you let him go out with your daughter if there were no more than a 10-year age difference?' You know, those kinds of really important questions that affect the future of the world. Or, if you have a more commercial bent, I can quantify the war of the toothpaste advertisements down to a plus-or-minus three-percent margin of error. I can even tell you at the end of each day how many times the words 'good' or 'bad' appeared within six words of the 'Crest' or 'Colgate' in selected chat groups across the country. Of course," she smiled, "you'd have to pay for it and sign a nondisclosure form."

"Of course," I said, returning the smile. "You enjoy your work, don't you?"

"Yes I do," she replied. "But I am also positioning myself for the future. I have a theory that one day, not too far off, the only things that will be allowed to happen are those an insurance company will underwrite. And what do insurance companies thrive on? Statistical probability and fear of the possible. Eventually the only things that will be possible are those that are probable. And I'll be ready for the insurance companies when they take over reality. My algorithms will be fine-tuned, well oiled and ready to crunch all the data they can throw at me. But let's get back to our discussion about love."

"Yes," I agreed, "back to love. So, tell me, what did America say about love last month?"

"Actually, the question given to focus groups consisting of people who had been married more than 20 years was, 'What interpersonal qualities have made your relationship last?' Fully 82 percent of relationships that lasted more than 20 years in which respondents said they were still happy and still loved their partner cited friendship as the number-one factor contributing to their longevity."

"And the other 18 percent?" I queried.

"Ten percent said separate vacations, 2 percent said sharing the same computer platform—the arguments that rage between partners about PC vs. Mac can be very destructive—and 6 percent said they didn't know, it just never it occurred to them not to be happy. Now, this is very different from those who were together after 20 years and who said they were either not happy or didn't know whether they were happy."

"What did they say?"

"Seventy-three percent said 'staying together for the kids' sake, evidently viewing parenting as a quality of interpersonal relatedness. The other 27 percent said they stayed together for a wide variety of reasons, including everything from habit, to sharing the same political party, to not wanting to upset the neighbors, to fears about disappointing God.

"I conducted a detailed meta-analysis of both groups, and here is what I found: the average successful, loving relationship consists half of friendship, and then three other components which share the other half in roughly equal measure: effective intimacy, effective communication and compatibility. Compatibility includes everything from accepting one another's differences to agreeing on who puts new toilet paper in the toilet-paper holders, to making sure you and your partner have complimentary neuroses that you feel comfortable enabling in each other. Friendship has its own category and is also distributed across the rest of the areas as components of the other three categories. That is, many felt that the other three were predicated on friendship." A pie graph illuminated my screen, which consisted of one big slice consuming half the pie marked "friendship," and three smaller slices labeled "intimacy," "effective communication," and "compatibility."

"And what do *you* say love is?" I asked.

"The research is fairly accurate," Kim replied. "But to me there is another dimension that gets lost in a strictly quantitative analysis. Love is a process of becoming whole by eradicating all the insecurities that gnaw at your sense of self-worth. When you complete yourself by exorcising your personal demons and feel good about who you are, then you really have something to offer someone else. So, my intuitive formula consists of five parts, adding 'loving yourself' to the other four. I am still trying to figure out how to accurately measure this aspect of a good relationship. Because it is a personal quality impinging on the shared reality of a relationship, it is a bit difficult. But I can tell you this much: Love has very little to do with Walt Disney." I was suddenly looking at another pie graph that represented her new formula. A moment later a picture of Mickey Mouse appeared on the screen with a slash through it.

"Why do you bring up Walt Disney?" I asked suspiciously. It was another Credoism that generated instant paranoia.

"Why not? You are an odd man sometimes, William."

"Sorry," I said sheepishly. "I guess I am. And how about love in the cyburbs. Is it real?"

"Sure," Kim assured me, "as long as you don't expect too much from it. Remember, much of what you experience in the cyburbs is yourself. As long as you know that, then you will be fine."

I was back at square one with new information. For some reason the image of BADI's training room was foremost in my mind, so real that I felt I could touch it.

"I don't think I can tell my students that love is the most important thing," I said.

"Why not?" Kim asked.

"They wouldn't get it," I despaired. "Maybe I could tell them that love is the most important thing in their personal lives, but they are business students who are much more interested in their professional lives right now. I need to give them something more concrete or they will tune me out just like that." I snapped my fingers for emphasis and my mind went blank.

CHAPTER 27 What's Important
Talk is cheap. Inaction is expensive. Doing pays for itself.

I was back in the BADI training room on the same training day in which 39 had been the magic number. I was facing off with the same red-haired kid with the shiny suit who had been telling me that his contribution to society was his dedication to self-advancement, being a creative problem-solver, staying off welfare and grabbing the opportunities that would make him a productive member of society.

I looked him in the eye. "Then what?" I asked him.

"What do you mean, 'Then what?'" he bristled.

It was a little too much for someone for whom a life of eternal productivity was an end in itself.

"Then what?" he repeated indignantly. "More productivity, more creative problem-solving and more opportunity, that's what!"

He was clearly agitated as the words spewed from his mouth. But I kept rolling. "Does it make you happy?" I asked. "Darn straight," he thundered. "Does it make you feel fulfilled?" I asked. He demanded to know what the difference was. Without waiting for me to reply, he scanned the room nervously to make sure that the people at the other tables weren't watching him. Then he turned to the rest of the people at his table who silently acceded him the right of spokesman. He looked me squarely in the eye and said if the goal of life is not to be responsible, creative, productive and happy, then what was it?

I was staring at him, praying for a spiritual growth spurt, when out something popped. "Kindness," I said confidently.

Everyone at his table stopped what they were doing and looked at me closely. I could tell what they were doing. They were reading me, trying to determine if I was fulfilled, though they would call it "being happy." If I were, then they would seriously consider the value of what I had just told them. If I weren't, they would return to the number 39 with renewed gusto and reinforced myopia. It could set some of them back years, some of them for the rest of their lives.

"Thus the saying in education, 'What you do speaks so loudly I can't hear what you say,'" Edwina seemed to whisper in my ear. "It's an old Chinese proverb."

I fought the urge to try to appear fulfilled, realizing that I had stumbled upon a moment of truth. Either at this point in the future I had achieved some sense of fulfillment, or I hadn't. This was the moment I would found out if I walked the talk, or just talked the talk.

Besides, I counseled myself, *someone might be able to fake happiness, but he can't fake fulfillment.*

While the BADI trainees were silently deliberating, I told them that last month I had gone to the memorial service of a man who had reached the height of his field as a network engineer, entrepreneur and creative genius. This man knew more about how to make money on the Net than anyone in the world. He turned down more high-paying job offers in an average week than most of us would in a life time, and was, above all, responsible, productive, happy and great at taking advantage of opportunities. Yet at his memorial service no one mentioned any of that. Everyone talked about his friendship, his devotion to community and family and, above all, how kind he was.

Kindness. *It was directly opposite meanness on the wheel of life.* Not only was it good for the people around you, it was a way of practicing organic connectivity, empathy and devotion to something beyond oneself without all the messy religious requirements. It honed a special kind of awareness that allowed passage to all the inner senses. And as a bonus, it just happened to be one of the few things people remembered about you after you died. Kindness.

The red-haired kid backed off and actually even smiled a little. "Well, yeah," he said, a bit dazed. "There's that, too."

I was back in my bedroom, my brain a bit rattled. My mother was asking me again if I was okay. I told her I was, sincerely thanked her for her concern, and then stared into my screen at Kim who was looking at me fondly.

"Kindness," she said quoting me, her voice so intoxicating that I was feeling woozy. "How very nice, William."

I asked her whether she saw any of *that.* She wanted to know what I was referring to. I described the kids, the training room, my speech and the events of the last few moments. Again she asked me what I was talking about—she had seen nothing. When I didn't answer, she told me that I was getting a bit too weird and that she was going to sign off.

I begged Kim not to go, to wait just a few moments while I explained that in the last week all that I had become certain of was that I was certain of nothing. I told her that as I remembered my King Lear—the last book I'd read before leaving school—"Nothing will come of nothing," leaving me nowhere indeed. I pleaded with her to understand that I was on a rapid learning curve that was hard to describe, and that I felt I had so many layers of windows and programs open on my psychic desktop at one time that I felt larger than life, pumped so full of ether that the boundary between my skin and the rest of the world was no longer clear. I told her that I had met people who had turned my world upside-down and that if only half of what they said were true, then I had a hard time explaining to myself why people, myself included, were so inherently clueless about the most important things in life; it all seemed like just another disappointing design flaw in reality that I would turn my attention to when I had time. But despite all of that, I felt happy and confident that fulfillment awaited me in the future and that she had played an important role in that.

Kim studied me for a moment and then, with all the gravity of a sinner wrenching a massive confession from deep within her psyche, she told me that she was about to admit to something that she had not planned on telling me because I seemed like a bit of a control freak who would see her as being intrusive. But, she continued cautiously, after listening to me just now she figured she would tell me anyway, and take a chance that I didn't get mad about it.

I was immediately on the defensive, but remained silent and as calm as possible. When I didn't respond, she told me that she had run the contents of my web page and the contents of our previous conversations through a number of analysis programs—content proximity analyzers, forecast interpolators, personality extractors—to name a few. When she synthesized all of the results using a particular kind of meta-analysis she developed, she could predict the degree of fulfillment I would experience relative to a number of possible future paths I could follow. The bottom line was this: She could tell me what do with my life that would make me happy within a plus-or-minus 8 percent margin of error, which she admitted was high but not totally unreasonable. Would I like to know the results?

"How can I say no?" I told her, more scared than excited.

"The reading was very strong, William," she said. "You are a teacher."

As Kim stared at me her face began to melt. I grabbed the monitor with both hands as if I could squeeze the network connection back to life. "Kim—don't go!"

A split second later I realized she was not melting, she was morphing into someone else. My heartbeat picked up speed as I waited to see who she would become. Suddenly I was staring at Credo.

"You ugly bag of dog breath!" I screamed. "Fugguduh! It was you, all along!"

"No, it wasn't," Credo assured me. "I am just butting in, so to speak. Kim is Kim."

"And who, or what, is that?!"

"'Maybe Kim's a him or maybe she's even a machine,'" Art said, paraphrasing my song. "'Does it matter?'"

"Yes, it matters!" I yelled. I could hear my mother get up in the next room. "I'm fine, mother. Go back to bed!" Later I would wonder how close my mother was to dialing 911 that night.

The picture on my screen had widened to include Art and Credo. They were sitting at Mitsie's, an empty salad bowl in front of them.

"Get out of my freakin' life, both of you!" I screamed at them.

"Calm down, William," Credo said. "Give me a moment to explain."

"Out! Out! Out! You are all zits on a wombat's stinky butt and I hate you!" I was reaching for the off button on my monitor when Credo spoke up.

"Edwina, maybe you should talk to the boy," he said.

The scene widened to include Edwina Tech. My mortification chakra was on fire. "I'm sorry, Ms. Tech. I would never have used that kind of language if I had known you were there."

"That's quite all right, William," she assured me. "I don't take it personally."

"Great to see you again!" guffawed Mr. Big. The scene zoomed out again to include Mr. Big, who was sitting where I had sat during lunch. "I got a lawn chair with your name on it whenever you feel the urge to take a look at the biiiiig picture."

"This isn't happening," I said aloud, my initial burst of anger burning out quickly. I realized I wasn't really mad—just intensely confused. I admitted to myself that for some strange reason I trusted all of them. But, by God, they could be annoying!

"Calm down, William," Credo said. "You are missing the point. This was such a teachable moment we couldn't pass it up. You snapped yourself. Don't you see? It was you who snapped yourself to the training room. You don't need us anymore. You have the power, William. Use it wisely, do you understand?"

Beyond my mind chatter there was a tangible stillness that filled me completely. Credo's words were crystal clear.

"I think I understand that," I said. "I think it's another way of saying you only do what you really want to do."

"All right, William, all right!" said Mr. Big. "A toast to William Tell! He's one smart guy who doesn't smell, unlike some people I know." Mr. Big winked at Art, both of whom winked at Credo. Each of them was holding a frosted glass, tall and slender, sporting a tiny parasol with rainbow colors. They touched glasses, hollered, "To William Tell who doesn't smell!" and took a hearty sip.

"Oh, hah hah," Credo drawled, reluctantly joining in.

"Are you The Committee?" I asked.

"We're not the whole Committee, by any means," Mr. Big replied. "But we're regular members. Or some of us are, anyway." Mr. Big was eyeing Credo in mock disapproval and jabbing him in the side.

"Fugguduh," Credo complained. "I miss one meeting and you would think the world is going to end. Do you see how they pick on me, William? Do you see?"

"The Big Day is coming, isn't it?" I asked.

"The Big Day is always coming," Credo said.

"And if you are going to take a big-picture view," said Mr. Big, "it's always here."

While I was, once again, silently bemoaning the fact that I wasn't receiving the straight answer I felt I deserved, Credo morphed back into Kim, who was smiling and telling me that she'd really enjoyed tonight and hoped we would talk again, about anything, everything, or nothing, whatever I preferred. "Kindness," she repeated one more time before we exchanged good nights and blipped out. Moments later, I was in bed fast asleep.

CHAPTER 28 The Big Day
Now has a way of creeping up on you.

The day was beginning with the usual panic of a leveraged buyout coming into its final stages when I was summoned to BADI's inner-sanctum with extreme urgency. *"The network is down!"* a manager in charge of the buy-out exclaimed. It was a favorite inter-office phrase for describing anything that ran on 120 volts that was not working normally. "The network is down!"

For the managers, the escalation of despair in these situations was always exponential. They were just three minutes into the crisis and were already considering leaping from windows or restructuring their vacation debt or even sending their kids to public schools instead of private institutions with names that to me had always sounded suspiciously like secret government projects, like The Billings Academy or The Newberry Institute.

As it turned out, the network was humming along with its usual consistency except for one lone computer somewhere in BADI's global data cloud. I began a routine "ping" around the world, which sent a message through the series of computers comprising BADI's international network that would help me locate the afflicted machine. Seconds later I had enough information to report that although I had identified the rogue computer in the system, the problem was more troublesome than I had feared. I told them that a second, more detailed 'ping' would be required, taking at least a half-hour to execute and analyze. "In a manner of speaking," I reluctantly told BADI administrators, "if the afflicted computer was essential to today's deal and there was no way to work around it, then the network was, for all intents and purposes, down." I recommended that they try to postpone things for about a half-hour.

Instantly, I was feeling the brunt of the suits' disgust with a technology they had not even had a few short years ago, which now was being vilified for not being instantaneous, understanding and perfect. Their questions came at me fast and furious: "Can't you just tweak something and make it behave?" they insisted. "How could you let the network go down this morning when we needed it most? Don't you care about BADI's future?"

They were all familiar questions that suggested the network was acting like a disgruntled employee rather than an emotionally detached machine awaiting a precise stream of data bits. There were the usual vague hints of suspicion and anger directed toward me, as if some-how I were on the network's side, restricting the managers' control and not doing everything in my power to save the day.

Then one of them asked me something that had never occurred to any of them to ask me before: Was there a back door—some spare network they could use to keep their very important, very leveraged buyout moving forward very quickly? She told me she saw some-thing like that on a TV show last night. Did BADI have one?

I had never told the managers about the "extra" network I had developed to monitor operations in emergency situations like this one because I didn't trust their judgment to use it wisely. But now I had no choice. It was, after all, their network. As I described the capabili-ties of the secondary network, I warned them that while they were using it I would not be able to monitor progress of the "ping" I was running on the main network. I also warned them that the secondary network was not nearly as well protected as BADI's main network. It was designed to be fast at the expense of absolute precision simply because it was never intended to be used for anything other than a just-in-case, bare-bones communication system. I told them I would never use the secondary network to transmit important "deal" data. It simply wasn't reliable enough.

Despite my warnings, they insisted it was more dangerous not to stay in the loop with Hamburg, Singapore, Geneva, Taipei and London, making sure the buyout proceeded as planned. They told me that all last month had led up to today. Today was now, and now was the moment. They had to keep moving. Seconds later, BADI manag-ers were on the secondary network system, ignoring me and every-thing I had just told them. I walked back to my office to begin the next test of the main network feeling as if I had just eaten bad meat.

"Ping." Off it went a second time, around the world, an electronic ambassador seeking information, conflict resolution, win-win deals for all machines involved. Now there was nothing for me to do but wait and hope that the managers didn't do anything overly ambitious on the secondary network. I relished a feeling of sweet liberation knowing that anything about to happen would not be my fault. I walked back to my office, slumped in my chair, and suddenly had an amazing thought: For the first time since I started working at BADI I decided to take a walk in the middle of day for no other reason than to get some air—however polluted with noise and exhaust—and just stretch my legs and raise my heartbeat a tad. As I headed down the street, I found myself consciously avoiding Credo's doorway, taking a right just past the pretzel stand and on up to the alley behind BADI's office building.

The back alley was an alien, parallel universe I had never realized existed literally within a few yards of my office. Lurking outside the scrubbed brick and etched glass that enclosed my work world were rats and street scroungers competing for the contents of peeling, dented garbage cans. There were cardboard shacks filled with soiled bedding and wadded clothing, and a fleet of gnarled shopping carts stuffed with everyone else's leftovers that had been foraged from the street. The scene reminded me of the underside of an otherwise shiny immaculate car, pocked with dirt and rust and other signs of entropy in slow motion if I wanted to go out of my way to find them. I eyed some nifty BADI throwaways as potential kitsch décor. In particular was a corroded women's restroom sign that would stand in high relief against the sterile, white walls of my office. The thought embarrassed me as I refocused on the scroungers. They were smoking, talking, even laughing as they passed around a bottle and studied me with immense curiosity. They seemed oddly happy.

I was trying to make sense of the drama playing out in front of me when a stretch limousine pulled up. Out stepped someone who I at first refused to believe was Credo. He was shaven, coifed, suited and sported shiny shoes, cuff links and a red power tie. He waved to the scroungers, calling out hello to them by name. Before I had a chance to react, he began speaking. His voice sounded exactly as it had when we'd first met, smooth and scratchy at the same time—like the old Frank Sinatra records my grandparents used to play for me just to remind me of how things used to be.

"I know I was not the mentor you wanted," he said calmly, without a hint of condescension. "I think you would have preferred anyone other than me. I think you expected someone in a toga who could assume a perfect lotus meditation position and who wouldn't dream of eating a doughnut. I think you wanted someone who smelled a little nicer and who at least wore decent pants. But that was part of The Committee's plan. They wanted to get your attention by giving you the education you wanted in a form you didn't expect. It was the only way to get your attention. The Committee decided that I would be the best one for the job. I hope you weren't too disappointed."

"Who are you?" I asked.

"Like you, I am a lot of people," Credo said.

"For once, could you give me a straight answer?" I pleaded, trying not to sound too desperate.

"I'm a consultant," he said. It was a statement I had heard a zillion times and had grown to distrust. Every who-hah who emailed, called or faxed me these days was some sort of consultant. It was an occupation that meant nothing and which today assumed a meaninglessness of new proportions. Before I could ask for something a bit more substantial, Credo continued.

"I just want you to understand something," he said. "There are some things I can't change. I would if I could, but I can't."

"This sounds bad," I said.

"It isn't really," he said with too little conviction to make me feel any better. "Just remember, the big question is, 'Then what?'"

I nodded. "I understand."

Credo smiled. "I know you do. You've come a long way in a short period of time. Congratulations! We're all very proud of you. Well, I'm off to predict something. I will see you soon. And that's a prediction you can count on!"

Credo started to walk toward the limousine and then turned to face me. "You know, there are some things that happen in life that make no sense at all, at the time. They seem unnecessary, even cruel, and possibly illegal. But in the end, they are great teachers and, in many ways, lifesavers. Like pain."

"God, this sounds bad," I said. "Real bad."

"I guess that all depends on how you define 'bad,'" Credo said.

It was pointless to complain about his circumlocution so I didn't bother. I just waited, listening for the telltale sound of the other shoe falling.

"Oh, wait a minute," Credo said. "How could I forget these?" The other shoe had begun its descent.

He extracted a pair of sunglasses from his suit coat and handed them to me. "They are a gift from Mr. Big."

I thanked him and started to stuff them in my pocket.

"You'll need to put them on, now," Credo warned me.

I asked him why and when he didn't answer, I put them on, feeling the buzz of inevitability from the soles of my shoes to the tips of my fingers. *Yes, indeedy,* I thought to myself. *Something big was definitely going to happen.*

Through the glasses I saw a world that was indecipherable, yet somehow familiar and unthreatening. I was sensing a blur of color and sound in indistinguishable patches. I was feeling a powerful speed, a singularity of purpose and an overwhelming sense of efficiency. It was a world in which there was no such thing as doubt, choice, or hesitancy. There was only source, destination, and as smooth and as straight a line as possible between the two. And then suddenly I realized what was happening. I was riding the "ping" that was testing our main network. I was an international traveler seeing the world through the eyes of a data stream. The glasses did not represent a projection across space, but actually took me across space. It was a technology that, of course, Credo had predicted. Somehow he had arranged for me to get a peek at a beta version of it.

Einstein imagined relativity while riding on a beam of light, and while I wasn't having thoughts nearly that profound, I was having an immense amount of fun as a gymnast of dark space. I was back flipping through satellites, spiraling to Earth, swinging from micro-wave station to microwave station, and vaulting into switching stations where I was stretched, split and sent shooting over coax, fiber, telephone lines, wireless networks and some new media that were unfamiliar to me. What a disappointment phone lines were, particularly compared to fiber optics. Bumpy and hot, like a bad train ride on a humid day; no class at all.

Somewhere in Hamburg, Germany, I began to tingle, feeling what I imagined anticipation might feel like to a bit of data. I saw another bit headed straight for me coming from BADI's secondary network, which I had begged the suits not to use. Both bits were already inside BADI's international network and had gone through all the error-detection routines that were supposed to keep a network sanitized. When I was hit, my bit flipped, and now I was a zero instead of one. And now I was inside BADI's offices in New York and headed out on to BADI's local-area network within my office area as what was referred to in the trades as a "corrupted piece of data."

I watched a series of events cascade with slippery inevitability. The corrupted data caused a YES to become a NO on a disclosure form, immediately triggering a stop payment on an electronic funds transfer. This alerted the company BADI was doing business with in Singapore, who wanted to know why BADI hadn't sent their share of the buyout fee to the holding company in Geneva. BADI managers tried to assure them that that their money was on its way as they spoke, a fact they could verify if they contacted Geneva. Singapore contacted the Geneva holding company and was told that according to their records there was a stop payment on the money transfer from BADI for unexplained reasons. BADI managers schmoozed and spun and joked their way through a few tense minutes, but someone in an office in Singapore got scared enough to back out completely. BADI suits cringed as they watched a multi-million dollar deal go sour because a freak of man-made nature made them seem as though they had withdrawn their share of the buyout money, sending BADI scrambling with too little time to draw from other sources to cover the deal.

One of the middle managers who had been hovering near the edge of instability for too long suddenly frayed. He yanked his laptop computer off his desk, wrenching it from the network and causing a loud pop and a spark to shoot from the plug strip next to his chair. That tripped the main circuit breaker, sending a ripple of panic through everyone else on the fifth floor as they watched their computers blink out in front of them, none of which would have happened if they had installed the backup power supply I had suggested long ago. The man ran to the back of his office and heaved his computer out the window, filling the alley with a scream of anguish I had not heard since the head of BADI's purchasing department had lost an entire year's worth of inventory information because she had failed to make a backup. I took off my glasses and looked up just in time to see the computer hurtling straight for me. My last thought before it struck was, "I'm sure glad he wasn't ticked off at the Xerox machine."

CHAPTER 29 Rebirth
How come you never see the headline, "Psychic Wins Lottery?"

My next conscious moment was brief and crammed with technology: breathing apparatus, puddles of wires, soft lights, things pumping quietly, computer screens scrawled with indecipherable graphs. I felt suspended in a cradle of dull pain as I heard someone I presumed to be a doctor comment that I must be really special because a computer going 40 miles-per-hour would have killed anyone else, just—snapping his fingers—like that.

My mind went blank.

I was sitting at a picnic table surrounded by Mr. Big, Edwina, Credo and a few dozen other people milling around as they enjoyed the sunshine and short-sleeve weather. I felt whole and comfortable as I sipped my lemonade, savoring the sensation of a gentle breeze skipping along my arms.

"How do you feel?" Credo asked. He was dressed in casual clothes that were clean and unassuming. His breath was pleasant, his manner fluid and unpretentious.

I was so bright and alert it scared me. "I feel more like I do now than I did when I met you." I realized that in another dimension my statement would not have made much sense. But *here* it was crystal clear. Credo nodded in approval.

"Is this The Committee?" I asked.

"This is they," Credo answered, smiling and waving so effusively at some people sitting at a table a few yards away that it looked like deliberate overreaction. "Pardon me while I schmooze a little," Credo explained. "I missed the last meeting and now I have to make up for it."

A roundish older woman in a green-and-black flowered dress sauntered over to our table and shook my hand warmly. Then she turned to Credo and told him sternly that "the local" could have used his input on Catch 77. She told him just how disappointed his fellow committee members were that he hadn't been there. Credo exhibited contrition I didn't think he was capable of. The woman gave him a hug and headed back to her table.

"The local?" I asked.

"This is just my chapter of The Committee, Local 421. The main organization is very big." He was suddenly in hysterics. This time I joined him without having to force myself.

Eventually I asked him whether or not I was dead, and he responded by telling me that it depended on what I meant. An old exasperation returned as I told him that if I were dead I would really appreciate knowing it.

While I waited for Credo to respond, a landslide of pure knowledge hit me. It began with the little stuff, like where all my lost keys and checkbooks were, who really shot JFK, the truth behind UFOs, and the identity of who was always stealing my Cheetos at work—those kinds of things. The next level of knowing included understanding how gravity worked and why everything that tasted so good was so unhealthy. In addition, I suddenly knew that Charlene at work had a crush on me and wished I would pay more attention to her, and I understood the mystery behind a few network glitches that had eluded me for years.

Then I was on to the next level and much bigger issues like all the questions I had peppered the kids with at BADI during training day. To these questions I did not receive answers in the usual sense, but was filled with a sense of insight and peace, an unquantifiable knowing that occupied my being like a natural presence. It was a feeling that never entirely left me after that moment.

Then a few strange things happened. I had a conversation with my childhood dog who wanted to thank me for walking him every evening. Then my dead uncle started talking to me, assuring me that the reason my father had left my mother had nothing to do with me. Next I was listening to a stalk of celery scream as I cut it in half, which was followed quickly by getting a hug from Miss Phelps, who was so proud of me she was crying softly. Then suddenly I was aware of all my frequencies and all my possibilities unfolding and folding, washing over me in no time at all, without judgment, without attachment, yet with deep feelings of rootedness and belonging. My awareness returned to the picnic, my lemonade and life in a slight breeze followed by an overwhelming feeling of wholeness.

Credo asked if there was anything else I wanted to know. I asked why we never saw the headline, "Psychic Wins Lottery?"

"Psychics could win lotteries," he said, "but it's an infringement of the worse kind, sort of like spiritual insider trading. Veeeery bad karma, if you know what I mean."

"Food, clothing, shelter and... what?" I asked. Credo smiled as he told me that I had been right when I'd speculated that the next element was situational, but that telling me would have caused a psychic lethargy that would have stunted my growth. He told me that he, Edwina, Art and Mr. Big were sorry for stringing me along and hoped that I understood that it was for my own good. He also told me that while the next element took a number of forms, perhaps the one that embraced them all to some extent—love, religion, meaning, art and education, even weapons—was storytelling. Once we were fed, warm and safe we started dealing with our interior lives by telling each other stories. They contained our passions, ideals, hopes, fears, manners and beliefs. When you got right down to it, for millennia what else was there to do but tell stories? Even now, what are television, the Internet and all the rest of information machines in our lives if not huge story-telling amplifiers?

I told him I'd figured out that "Then what?" was more of a path than a question, and that it was not supposed to have a definitive answer. It was intended to be the constant challenge to improve yourself, however you define it, to keep your heart from hardening, your mind from ossifying and your spirit from decomposing. I told him that it was easy to lose sight of that if you focused on the technology instead of the people it was intended to serve. Mr. Big was hovering in a lawn chair a few feet away squawking his approval. He told me how much he really liked me and that he hoped his next mentee would be just like me. Edwina put her hand on my shoulder tenderly and said, "Bravo, William Tell, bravo."

Then I just had to ask. "Why me?"

"Why not?" Credo replied.

I told him there had to be more to it than that.

"You're right, there is," Credo said. "In the change business you learn early on that if you place any value on enjoying the process yourself, then you are better off dealing with the people who actually enjoy change. There is no sense beating your head against wall. It hurts and it's not nice to the wall. It's best to work with those who are ready to listen. They will, in turn, transform others on a peer-to-peer basis. More organizations and schools have been changed from within than from without. The bottom line is that each one of us only has so much evangelizing energy. Learning how and when to spend it is an art form. You were ready and we all knew we wouldn't be wasting our time working with you."

For a flash I was back in the hospital, conscious enough to sense the machinery, the doctors, my mother and some people watching over me. I studied my mother's face, bunched with worry as she fingered an old pocketbook. *Kindness*, I thought to myself, experiencing a pure form of learning in which I felt remorse without self-condemnation. *I must show her more kindness.*

The red-haired kid I had faced off with at the training session was leaning against the wall near the door, whispering to one of his colleagues: "Hit by a computer," he said with deep admiration. "Now, that's taking it like a pro."

There were a few people standing outside the door whom I could see with the utmost clarity, even though they were blocked from my direct view. And there was a slight woman with brown hair sitting in a plastic chair in the corner of my room as she looked at the floor and cried quietly in between bits of prayer.

It was Charlene! She was the lady from work who had a crush on me. She was the one who wished I would pay more attention to her. Her concern for me flooded the room, mixing with my mother's and forming a network of caring and warmth. In the hazy between-worlds existence in which I found myself, I could hear what sounded vaguely like a drumbeat coming from Charlene, gentle and insistent, calling me. I had to go back. There was so much to do. There was so much to learn, especially from her.

I returned to the picnic and immediately wanted to know when I could go home. Credo assured me that I could go home anytime I wanted to. But he also told me that I didn't have to go back at all. I had the option of staying where I was, permanently changing my sense of *here*.

My response was swift and certain. I was not ready to stay here. There was work to do. I had to go back.

"Even if it means going through an operation, a few weeks of intense pain, some physical therapy and not feeling at the top of your game for awhile?" Credo asked.

"Even if," I replied.

"Even if it means losing your job at BADI because they won't wait for you to get better?" Credo prodded.

"Especially if," I told him.

Yes, there was no question in my mind. I had to go back.

Epilogue   There's No Page Like Home Page
Everything clicks.

Click, click.

I was searching the World Wide Web for information and found nothing. Or, more precisely, I was overloaded to such an extent by what I found that I might as well have found nothing. Searching the Web could be so inclusive and so cumbersome that ignorance began to look pretty good. But I persisted.

As with any kind of shopping, knowing how to look was the key to success. On the Web, that meant knowing how to phrase a search request just right. I decided to narrow my last search by including three "descriptors," or words to search for, that might help limit the response I received. On the Web, less was definitely more.

This time my search looked like this: education AND innovative AND project-based. Rethinking, I changed "education" to just "educat*." The asterisk was a wild card which meant "accept anything you find in this spot." Using "educat*" would find education, educate, educator, and anything at all beginning with "educat." I did the same with innovation, and included the word "alternative" as a possible descriptor. The search became: educat* AND (innovat* OR alternative) AND project-based. I was about to click OKAY when I realized it still wasn't right. How would I get information about "project-oriented" or "project-directed" education? I would need to find the word "project" near the other words I was searching for. Finally I settled on the following search strategy: educat* AND (innovat* OR alternative) AND ((based OR oriented OR directed) NEAR project). It looked good. Click.

Lots of information suddenly crammed my screen. Some of it was pretty good, but it was not what I was looking for. So I tried educat* AND (innovat* OR alternative) AND ((based OR oriented OR directed) NEAR project) AND community.

Now I had way too much. It seemed that everyone used the word community. One hit I got was about "Edna Wheeler and her innovative, educational dancing dog show, a community favorite at local functions."

Next, I tried the following search strategy: Educat* AND (innovat* OR alternative) AND ((based OR oriented OR directed) NEAR project) AND (outreach NEAR community).

Fewer hits. I was getting there. There was some interesting stuff I would get back to—some people I should talk to about forming alliances, some potential organizational models I should study—maybe even a few funding sources I should investigate. It was not exactly what I wanted, but I was getting closer.

Educat* AND (innovat* OR alternative) AND ((based OR oriented or directed) NEAR project) AND (outreach NEAR community) AND heart.

Click. Ahh. There we go. Project REAL—the education project I supposedly had begun and now continued to direct.

There was my picture.

It was a crummy picture of me, leading me to conclude that my students needed more practice putting pictures on the Web. I appreciated their wanting to feature my picture, but I shouldn't even be there. The kids should be on the lead-in page. After all, it was their project, their work and their moment in the sun. I was just coaching them through it. I blinked as I untangled the title on the screen: Project REAL: Re-Education Aligned with Living. Another forced acronym. Just like the wrong approach to technology, it worked backward from what was clever to what was salvageable. Credo must have done this.

"I heard that," Credo said, looking over my shoulder.

I figured the best way to bring myself forward and re-enter the present was to look at my web page; actually, it was the web page of the organization, which, as Credo had explained earlier, I now ran. The quick way to get to it would have been to search simply for "William Tell" or "Project REAL." But no one else out there knew to look for either of these, and I was curious to see how hard we were going to be to find in the overgrown data thicket of the Net. Data foragers followed a path of least persistence. Anyone having to look too hard simply gave up. The average thought process to reach Project REAL was still too convoluted. I wanted anyone interested in new approaches to learning which embedded education in a real world context to be able to find Project REAL before click exhaustion set in. I asked Credo if the kids in my program could figure out a way to fix it. "You bet," he assured me. They were smart kids. It was a good project for Team C.

The counter at the bottom of the web page said there had been more than 100,000 hits in six months. This was good—excellent in fact. A few hundred people had left their email addresses wanting to know more. One was from the Federal Department of Education, a half-dozen were from state governments, another half-dozen were from teachers' organizations, a few were from foundations with lots of money to spend on worthwhile education projects.

"How has my follow-up been with these people?" I asked Credo.

Credo nodded approvingly. "You are adjusting to educational administration very well. You carry yourself with poise and self-assurance. And you know how to say 'gimme' with dignity. You're a suit with a heart and a shrewd sense of business. I think I will call you Millennium Man."

I ignored him as I touched the starched white collar that wrapped around my neck and ran my hand down my red pinstriped tie. It was not my style at all, but that was fine.

"It's called infiltration," Credo said. "The more you look like *one of them*, the more robust a Trojan Horse you can wheel into the fortress."

It was an effective web page all in all, I thought to myself as I continued reading about Project REAL. There was a morphing icon at the bottom, that changed from a heart to a light bulb to a hand lifting upward to a child's face. Nice job. Compact. Not too distracting. The page's overall message was concise and well aligned. The screen wasn't stuffed with overuse. The user interface worked well. It was a map of New York City superimposed on an abstract rendering of the planet. Icons representing projects administered by Project REAL were dispersed throughout the map. The layout could have been tacky but it had a nice aesthetic weave to it. I was anxious to see the kinds of projects I had been involved in. Click.

Credo shook his head, insisting that before I look at any of the project information in detail I needed to review more general information about Project REAL. He warned me that I had to be at work in less than an hour and needed to know what I had been doing for the last 18 months before I got there. I had to admit that he made sense. Click, go back.

"There," Credo said, pointing over my shoulder. "That's all you really need to know. Click on that."

Click.

At the top of the list was a recent article in Business Life Magazine by the same guy who had written about me many years ago. The earlier article had been called, "Teaching Myself to Succeed." This one was an interview with me that he called, "From Boy with a Brain to Man with a Heart: From Teaching Yourself to Succeed to Teaching Others to Do the Same." It was the lead story. The cover of the magazine featured a picture of me surrounded by teenagers, technology, and walls filled with murals, computer art and project time lines. Before I could ask anything, Credo started talking.

"Nice title for the article, eh?" he joked, a little slyly, a little proudly. "So, maybe I called Business Life and gave him a few ideas. Is that so bad? I had to get permission from The Committee to do it."

"Who did you call him as?" I asked.

"As me," Credo said, a little indignant.

"And who is that?" I insisted on knowing.

"President of Tricor Consultants and an associate member of the School Administrators Council on Improving Education."

I pushed back from the screen and scoured Credo from head to foot. He was looking starched, rectangular and entirely believable in the dull-gray suit of an administrator. "I don't want to know," I confessed, though more pleased than upset by what I was looking at. "I just plain do not want to know anything, anymore."

"Read the first paragraph," he prodded. "It's a doozy."

Click.

Business Life: Fortunately for Newton, so the story goes, an apple fell on his head. And fortunately for us, William Tell was struck by a flying computer heaved from a second-story window. Newton discovered gravity. Tell discovered a new path out of the doldrums of schooling and into the real world of education for an otherwise disenfranchised group of young people. While it is neither my style nor the style of my readers to delight in another man's misfortune, everyone agrees—William Tell included—that it was a most propitious knock on the head. Despite weeks in a hospital and an excruciating journey back to health, Tell's accident turned out to be the beginning of a journey that would benefit some of the most needy and deserving people in our city. According to Tell, "I woke up and I was different. I saw life as short but infinite and full of possibility. Suddenly I was reacquainted with what was important and I was anxious to translate my revelation into action.

I admitted to Credo that I liked how it sounded. It wasn't every day I was compared to Newton. My hand started to flex looking for something to grab on to.

"Coffee?" Credo asked.

"I don't think so," I said. "I don't think I drink coffee anymore... do I?"

Credo smiled. "No, you don't."

"So, what do I drink?" I asked.

"Tea sometimes, to be sociable. But mostly water. Would you like some?"

"Sure," I said.

Credo walked to a small refrigerator in the corner of the room and returned with a plastic bottle of spring water. He handed it to me and then tapped his watch anxiously, prodding me to hurry. I took a few long drinks and resumed reading.

Business Life: I had the pleasure of writing an article about Tell nearly nine years ago when he went to work at age 15 as Banter and Associates Diversified Investor's networking wunderkind. In that position he clearly developed the skills and insider's view of the modern world needed to create a program for kids that could help them find a real and lasting place in society. Last year he left BADI and followed his heart to do just that. I called him up and asked if I could spend a day at Project REAL to learn what it was all about. He was only too happy to have me come by. But he warned me that a group of students working on copy for a newspaper story might ask for my help. I welcomed the opportunity.

I asked Credo if the BADI suits were mad when I didn't come back. I paused for a moment. "Did I call them suits? I should have called them management."

Credo smiled. "You may now call them whatever you like, but only to your inner circle. Outside that circle, they are management. As to whether they were mad or not, they didn't give themselves the chance. They replaced you and just kept on rolling. However, you will be happy to know that your training lab is doing great. BADI employees are happier and better trained than ever. And management has smartened up quite a bit, especially after you broached the idea of not suing them for getting hit by a flying computer."

"I threatened to sue them?" I asked.

"No, you threatened not to," Credo said. "You told them if they would give you the bottom floor of the abandoned building they owned across the street there would be no need for litigation. It didn't hurt that BADI could write it off as a charitable donation. Very clever, William."

In the stainless-steel lamp that hung over the desk I caught a glimpse of the scar above my ear that looked like a skid mark, the telltale reminder of a head-on collision with a flying computer. Credo leaned over my shoulder, grabbed the mouse and clicked to expose more of the article. "We're back in real time and need to hurry. Read."

Business Life: So, William, tell us what you do.

Tell: Consider it a translation from the ideal to the real. Project REAL—which stands for Re-Education Aligned for Life—is an experientially based high school with a high degree of community outreach, technological skill development, team-based communication and applied academics. The school is built on community action. The community comes to us with potential projects for the students. We evaluate each one on the basis of its vision, impact and the degree to which it allows REAL students to develop marketable skills, further their education and increase their understanding of the world.

BL: What are you looking for in each of those elements?

Tell: The vision must include a concise statement about why the project is important to the community. We don't really care whether it is proposed by a non-profit organization, the public sector, or private enterprise. I just want to know how many people it would serve and employ, what kind of product or service it would deliver and what the overall long-term impacts would be.

BL: Define impacts.

Tell: Impacts cover economic, social and environmental impacts. Every new enterprise sends a ripple throughout society and there are always winners and losers. We want to see the potential upside and downside of a project spelled out very clearly. Don't bother telling us everything is going to be great because it never is. We are looking for honest proposals that are thoughtful, which seek to minimize impacts rather than eliminate them, and which try to achieve a balance between the competing forces of progress and tradition. You know the cliché: Think globally, act locally. And finally, a proposal needs to spell out the learning opportunities for the students. A project needs to offer significant learning potential or we can't consider it.

BL: As we toured the REAL facility, I was impressed with how Tell and his crew of high school students had resurrected the abandoned warehouse across the street from Banter and Associates Diversified Investors (BADI), Tell's old haunt. Life inside REAL was a bit frantic, distracted and untidy, but in a constructive sort of way. Students were crowded around computers, video cameras, drafting boards and meeting tables. On the wall were timelines for projects with target dates for checkpoints, rough drafts, trial presentations to the class for peer feedback, and final presentations to the client.

In a room in the back, I observed a group of students using an interesting approach to watching a program about the history of the Civil Rights Movement. They would watch, stop the tape, discuss what they had seen, write down questions, and then start the tape again. I asked them later what they did with the questions and they told me they discussed them with a local teacher who showed up every Thursday morning. They said they were also part of an international discussion and mentoring group that was comparing how the Civil War was portrayed in high school history classes in other countries.

In another room, one student was drawing a diagram on a blackboard while three other students asked questions. I later learned that they were finalizing a draft of a project plan that they were going to present to the rest of the class for feedback.

A few students walked by me and said hello as they headed toward the door with clipboards and bag lunches. One of them stopped and asked whether I was the journalist who could help with the newspaper article. When I told them I was, they asked if they could make an appointment with me. The kids didn't know it, but that constituted a moment of truth for me. If I told them I was too busy, then I officially became part of the problem and had no right to complain about the status of education in this country. I agreed to help and we set up an appointment in my office. I wanted them to see a real publication environment in action.

Always rising above the din at REAL was the sound of ideas, of what Tell called *the great rolling present*. If, like me, you are used to a conventional school you might have had a hard time figuring out what was going on. So I asked Tell the obvious: What are the students learning? He suggested he respond as though I were a potential client wanting to know how Project REAL defined "significant learning potential."

BL: Tell me what academic areas are covered at Project REAL. I guess you call them 'learning areas?'

Tell: That's right. There are five learning areas that we address. The first is communication. This is a critical literacy that is infused throughout everything the students do. Students need opportunities to not only practice effective written and spoken language — usually in English and Spanish, but not always — but also to practice presenting complex ideas to others, particularly in a client-provider relationship. They also need experience leading and participating in team-based projects. This includes the art of interpersonal dynamics, particularly the ability to let go of your ego and to honor good ideas, no matter where they come from. Communication also includes the ability to create or manage images, video, sound and other artistic elements within the context of an overall presentation. We do a lot of what most people would call art training. To me, it is all 'art,' the fourth 'R' of education, along with reading, 'riting and 'rithmetic. So, any project that gives students a chance to flex these communication muscles is going to be viewed very highly.

Thinking and creative problem solving is the second important area. One aspect of this area is creating a detailed, order-dependent plan of action for every project. Students are taught effective brainstorming and idea generation, and then are required to synthesize the ideas in the form of a concrete plan. We like our students to practice examining ideas critically in order to root out hidden inconsistencies and bias, as well as to discover hidden connections and potential. So, projects that allow students to generate ideas, dissect them and put them back together from a fresh perspective are highly regarded. We have quiet rooms in the back where one or two people will go just to think, to re-balance and to tune us out so they can tune themselves in. Given all this, we tend to shy away from manual labor-based projects and go more for projects with a high level of cognitive detail.

Credo told me the AFL-CIO sent me an angry letter about that last statement, saying that it denigrated the value of honest labor by suggesting that workers didn't know how to think. But, Credo continued, I had handled it beautifully, inviting labor representatives to the project and treating them like royalty. In a video clip that made local television I had stressed the multi-faceted nature of the labor market, as well as the need for more interaction among youth programs to make sure that each student got the placement he or she deserved and needed. I was very convincing, Credo told me, because I really meant it. Project REAL now had some strong ties with labor groups that lead to some interesting projects. Credo told me to keep reading.

BL: So far you have covered communication and creative problem solving. What are the other learning areas?

Tell: Community engagement is the third important area. The more a project requires students to interact with people from the community, the better. We want students to see the people and organizations in their community as resources and part of a living school. We want students to be able to carry themselves as adults; to sit at a table with business leaders, politicians, parents and community members; and be taken seriously. This is largely a matter of developing self-esteem, the ability to actively listen to others and the sensitivity needed to interact with people who see the world differently than they do. The goal at Project REAL is not just for all students to reach their fullest potential as individuals. It is also for all students to be the best community members they can be. This begins with a more holistic appreciation of the social environment in which they live and work. And it includes giving back to the communities that nurture them, as well.

Applied academics is the fourth important area. This can come in a variety of ways, from researching local history, to understanding the math needed to develop a business plan, to grasping scientific principles that are key to a project's success. If the faculty team at REAL is deficient in an area, we find someone in the community to help. We have an arrangement with community colleges to allow our students to attend lectures and use laboratories on an as-needed basis. We also make good use of TV educators, video series, web information servers and other resources. Most academic studies at REAL are pursued in small groups. Very few students learn alone. I spend a great deal of my time helping teams develop a project-specific academic plan and then helping them find the best resources to carry it out.

The last area is what I call 'the big picture.' We not only want whatever our students do to be connected to their immediate community, we also want it to be connected to humanity. So, we offer a course called "Great Ideas."

BL: I would like to hear more about that, but first explain how *classes* work here because I don't think most people would recognize Project Real as a school.

Tell: There is a great deal of parent, relative and volunteer involvement—aunts, uncles, friends and members of the community who volunteer their time. These people are critical to the success of the program. If it weren't unrealistic and unfair we would demand that every student find adult volunteers, preferably parents or relatives, to be involved with REAL.

BL: And where are the teachers?

Tell: You don't see many teachers today because it is a teacher-project day during which teachers spend time working in their fields, updating their skills and supplementing their income. We encourage them to do this and we make every effort to accommodate opportunities they get in this area.

BL: Are there classes here in the conventional sense?

Tell: Sure. We aren't anti-classes. The 'class' as we have all experienced it can still be an effective and efficient way to learn. So, we offer classes in the areas of applied math, communication, research techniques, great ideas and the appropriate use of technology. Applied math is just as it sounds: problem-solving using numbers. There is no shortage of problems in the real world that require these skills. The class is surprisingly popular. Communication class covers everything from writing, to public speaking, to interpersonal dynamics, to assembling an effective presentation using a number of media. Topics are covered on an as-needed basis.

Research techniques involve two skill sets: gathering data and analyzing data. The first is fairly straightforward. Students learn how to find resources on the Web, in the community, at the library, from satellite TV—wherever. It also involves how to conduct interviews to gather information from individuals. Maybe you should employ a few of our students to conduct background research for one of your articles sometime and let me know how they do.

BL: I'll do it.

Tell: The second skill set involved in research is showing students how to use various kinds of quantitative and qualitative analysis to extract meaning from the data they collect. We firmly believe that there is a lot of unnecessary and misguided disagreement in the research community about qualitative vs. quantitative research. At Project REAL we believe every project needs to use both. Anthropologists and statisticians should work together.

BL: There was no question that Tell was an enthusiastic and dedicated educator who was committed to all aspects of Project REAL. But when he talked about the great ideas class, his eyes really lit up. This was a mandatory, twice-a-week seminar he facilitated, which explored the great ideas of science, history, literature and the overall evolution of culture and ideas. It was the students' chance to step back from the present, see the triumphs and mistakes of the past and begin to think about the kind of future they wanted to help create. *It was their chance to see the big picture.*

BL: Tell me more about the great ideas class.

Tell: The class actually has a very practical goal: to help students become more informed citizens and voters. Education is not just about learning how to work; it is also about learning how to live. I say to educators, policy makers and parents, 'Don't just think about what kind of workers you want; also think about what kind of neighbors you want.' School should help create the kind of people you want to live next to—virtually or geographically. In the great ideas class, we study ideas and develop skills that will help with that. We study philosophy, political science, religion, sociology—whatever seems to fit what is going on at the time. The students understand that the world is run not by money or technology, but by belief systems. They understand that *whatever you believe is who you are,* and that they need to make choices about what they believe if they are going to direct their growth.

BL: Can your students do well on, for example, a math SAT exam?

Tell: Parts of it, yes. Overall, no. That begs another discussion, however, about just how important those scores are.

BL: How about on standardized biology or chemistry exams?

Tell: On ideas, yes. On details, no.

BL: How about history or literature?

Tell: On concepts yes, facts and dates, no. Again, you need to look at what is important. Assumptions made in the past about what is important should not drive future education needs. Look at it this way: Do you think the average high school graduate could do what our students could do?

BL: Probably not.

Tell: And whom would you hire, someone with impressive SAT scores or someone with an impressive work record and portfolio?

BL: You have a point.

Tell: Believe it or not, I am not criticizing a liberal-arts education. In many ways it provides a valuable service to society by helping students develop a sense of perspective about the world that I sometimes wish I had. A BA or BS program is a wonderful place to park for four years while you are figuring out what's next. This is why I consider the great ideas class the most important activity in the REAL program, although it appears from the outside to be the least practical.

But, on the other hand, liberal-arts students could benefit from the kinds of activities at REAL. Imagine a liberal-arts degree with mandatory community-service components, project-based learning, portfolio development and applied-learning instruction. Now *there's* a potent idea. Even if such a magical program existed, my students are not headed in the direction of a liberal-arts degree when they enter Project REAL. My students need to see more connectivity with the immediate environment and more immediate possibilities of employment and personal fulfillment than a four-year degree offers, or else I will lose them. Consider this: It used to be that if you actually knew how to do something at the end of your four-year degree, that was a bonus. That has reversed. Now, what you really need is to be competent; if you happen to have a degree, *that* is a bonus.

BL: We were talking about the actual classes you offer. We have covered math, communication, research and great ideas...

Tell: Sorry. I get sidetracked easily. Appropriate use of technology is the last area. The best projects from a technological standpoint are those in which the technology is used as a means rather than an end, in which technology is used strategically, creatively and even sparingly.

BL: Sparingly? I am surprised to hear you say that. One of the complaints I hear most often from taxpayers is that we spend too much money on technology that just sits there and doesn't get used.

Tell: Let me put it this way. If someone dries his clothes on a clothes line rather than using an electric dryer we don't criticize him for not using his 'dryer technology' often enough. We credit him with being a discriminating user of technology who has a balanced perspective of life. The art of using technology is knowing when to use it and when not to. The best way to cultivate that perspective at Project REAL is to develop clear goals about a project first, and then ask ourselves what tools are needed to succeed. While a consideration of the tools on-hand may influence the goals of the project, the tools should serve rather than drive the human need that the project is intended to fulfill. This is difficult because technology has inherent biases and so often seems to tell us what to do, rather than the other way around. But we do the best we can.

BL: Are you worried about the growing split in society between the info haves and the have-nots—the so-called digital divide?

Tell: The most pronounced digital divide I see is between parents and their children! Sure I'm concerned, particularly in the short term, but less so in the long term when technology becomes ubiquitous and cheap.

However, there is no lack of things to worry about in the future. Sometime in the years ahead we will have computers and other instruments of the information trades that cost no more than a television or a telephone and Internet access that will be cheap and abundant. At that point, access will no longer be the issue, and we will turn our focus, once again, to inequities in the educational resources necessary to be able to take advantage of opportunities that become available. We will rediscover that on-going education, whether formal or informal, is no longer an activity. Instead, it is a lifestyle that you can't escape. The most serious divide will be between those who have good mentors and those who don't. In the meantime, what is important to Project REAL is that our clients be able to replicate whatever we help them do. A major consideration of any project is restricting our use of technology to the technology the client will have after we leave.

BL: What worries you when it comes to technology?

Tell: People's growing feeling of powerlessness, and of feeling victimized by the future—*victimyopia* I call it. There was a time when cars came in basically one style: big, dumb, unsafe, loud, polluting and resource-guzzling. It took an oil embargo in the 1970s to wake us up. Then we began demanding cars that were smaller, less resource-intensive, safer, less harmful to the environment and more intelligent. And we got them.

There is no reason we can't do that with information technology. Right now all we are telling computer manufacturers is to make machines that are faster and cheaper, while ignoring everything else. If we demanded computers that were made of chips that were more friendly to the Earth, screens that didn't make us go blind, and software more in touch with human needs, we would get them. A more demanding public wouldn't produce less technology; it would produce better technology which was more aligned with our values and less driven by our fears of personal obsolescence. It would make us more proactive and less reactive. People need to understand that they are in charge and that they have the power to take back the future.

BL: Do some consider you a Luddite for your views?

Tell (laughing): I have been accused of being everything from a techno-lover to techno-leveler to a supply-side Bolshevik. In my opinion, my accusers are only pointing out the weakness in their own worldview.

To the Luddites I say this: Where would you want us to stop the clock when we turn back time? At black-and-white television?

At the radio? At the printing press? At the plow? Before we get too nostalgic for the good old days of 'Leave it to Beaver,' let's remember that it was during that time that Martin Luther King had to lead a march just to argue for African American people's right to vote—a right which they supposedly already had. It was a time when women made less-than-half of what a man made for the same work. It was a time when the world was poised for nuclear war and when there was absolutely no understanding of the environmental or social damage caused by the progress we all cherished so much. The good old days? Sure, if all you want to remember is the good old stuff. But otherwise, I don't think so.

The technophiles on the other side are no better. They are the ones who fail to see that while we are getting no wiser, our machines are getting more powerful, and that the imbalance between these two conditions is potentially devastating, physically, socially and spiritually. They are the ones who feel that whoever dies with the most toys wins. Well, from where I sit, whoever dies with the most toys still dies. But whoever learns to use the toys wisely and imparts their sense of wisdom to others lives on.

In a word, what we are after, and what we so desperately lack, is *balance*. There is no need to glorify or deceive ourselves about either the past or the future. We should seek balance in the present. Imparting a sense of balance to students is the single most important thing teachers can do, regardless of the content area in which they teach.

BL: I am impressed with the kinds of training and moral coaching your students are receiving. But I would like to know whether they emerge from Project REAL with a degree, diploma or certificate of any kind.

Tell: They do not receive a degree in the conventional sense.

BL: How about a GED (General Education Degree), the test administered by the state based on a set of basic academic standards. Surely your students emerge with at least one of those.

Tell: To gear Project REAL to a test would kill Project REAL. But the basic coursework REAL offers manages to cover much of what is included in a GED. There are many avenues for students to get help with basic academics, and I encourage my students to take advantage of them. Rather than a degree, my students leave the program with a portfolio much like portfolios created by a designer or an architect. The portfolio includes project descriptions, student products and an assessment by faculty, businesses and community groups with whom they have worked—and by themselves—of their skills, abilities and future potential. It also includes a personal vision statement that addresses not only what they want to be but also who they want to be, as well as how they plan to use their skills to help their communities.

BL: So what should we do with the GED—get rid of it?

Tell: Every time the pendulum swings in education reform I feel as if I need to duck. In the short time I've been involved in education I have watched the back-to-basics crowd duke it out with the constructivists, both of whom were trying to distance themselves from the religious right and sidestep the secular humanists while seeking funding from mainstream America. As Shalvey says, 'Beware the paradigm du jour.' What we are after is balance and clarity. Don't begin with a philosophy; begin with a goal. Don't throw out the GED just because of some emotional reaction to what it has represented in the past. Treat it as if you would a piece of technology you want to redesign: Keep what works and either fix or discard the rest.

The GED provides a useful cultural reference point that simply needs to be updated. The real problem with the GED is that it occurs out of context. Businesses should offer a value-added GED with an applied component: a GAED: General Applied Education Degree. The GED needs components that reflect applied knowledge, portfolio development and workplace communication skills. Being able to pursue a GAED should be part of an employment package, like health benefits and access to childcare. Completing a GAED should be treated more as a rite of passage rather than obtaining a degree. The locus of celebration for that passage should be the community in which GAED students pursue their learning.

Getting a GED to please the state is a soulless exercise. Getting a GAED to become part of a learning community or work team invites the emotional involvement of the participants. Any teacher will tell you that when it comes to student success there is no substitute for intrinsic motivation.

BL: A big question remains for me that I know will be on everyone's mind who reads my article: How does someone of your minimal years seem to understand so much?

Tell: *La vida es corta pero ancha.*
BL: Sorry, but once again I am embarrassed by my own lack of bilingualism.
Tell: It means, '*Life is short but it's wide.*'

It was all beginning to feel very familiar and I was honestly impressed with myself. I asked Credo when I had done all of this. He told me I had written the grant proposals when I was in the hospital, had received funding shortly thereafter and had been running REAL for more than a year—all with Charlene's help, of course. It turns out I was a good grant writer and I had hit the granting cycle just right. I'd managed to use every buzzword in a grant reader's dictionary and by the time I was done with the philanthropists of the world it had been a one-two punch to the Disney chakra and I was funded. I'd even managed to give myself a decent salary.

I wanted to know what else I had been doing. A short trip to India, Credo told me, where I'd met a guru with some interesting things to say about life, death and the true nature of existence. It was fun for a while, but I was glad to be back home. And then there was Charlene from data processing at BADI, now my partner in crime at Project REAL. Things were pretty serious with her. And a lot of fun.

But not at the beginning. She sat by my bed for three days waiting for me to come out of a coma, worried sick. And not just about my health. She was just as worried that I'd wake up and wonder what she was doing there.

"You never gave her the time of day," Credo scolded me. "What on Earth were you thinking by ignoring her?"

"Simple," I told him. "I *wasn't* thinking. But now I am."

And I was getting along much better with my mother, particularly since I was trying hard not to take out my embarrassment at living at home at age 24 on her. Charlene and I had placed a security deposit on a nice place not too far from Project REAL by subway and were moving in next month.

"And then there are the two of us," Credo said with a phony kind of enthusiasm that made me very suspicious.

"The two of who?" I asked.

"Whom," Credo corrected me.

"The two of whom?"

"Your mother and I," Credo replied.

"I, who—you? You and my mother?!" I nearly screeched.

"Yes," Credo said.

"What about you and my mother?"

"You know," Credo said as he winked.

Tilt. Too much data and too little bandwidth.

"Would you mind so terribly," Credo wanted to know, "if we were related? What would you think about calling me Dad?"

Further tilt. Way too much. Over the edge. My emotional network was crashing. Denial set in, closing like a steel trap around the area of my brain incapable of dealing with what I was hearing. Every chakra was lit up like the Fourth of July. In total denial, I turned my attention to my mouse and started clicking.

Click back to the main page, to the city map with icons leading to Project REAL projects. Click. REAL project descriptions. Click. The first project that was featured was "Project Energizer."

Project Energizer. Two years ago the renters of the Willsby Apartments managed to buy their own apartment building to keep from losing their homes to a construction firm that wanted to develop the land their building sat on. Now the new owners are struggling to pay for building maintenance. REAL students are helping them perform a detailed analysis of energy-use habits and maintenance techniques. Then, using spreadsheet and financial-projection software, they will help them determine lifestyle and maintenance changes that could save money and improve living standards. Savings are projected to be used for a rotating capital maintenance fund. Anything left over will be used to create a rooftop garden. Barton Engineering and Anderson Architects are helping REAL students with the project.

Click. Another project called, "Seniors and Seniors."

Seniors and Seniors. Senior high school students at Project REAL are helping senior citizens get on to the Net and dispense the wisdom of the ages to help troubled teens. The project also helps arrange face-to-face counseling with troubled youth. Seniors citizens are using the Net to form friendships with each other, to find jobs and volunteer work, to locate health and recreation information, and to seek financial-assistance programs. Compton

Computer and Genesis Telephone are helping with the project. The high school students help them with some of the footwork for these projects.

Click. "Water Is Us."

Water Is Us. Less than 25 percent of neighborhood ground water was being monitored before local chemical companies teamed up with Project REAL students to conduct an ongoing assessment of water quality in a few locations. The results have been shocking, revealing levels of contamination that city officials are taking very seriously. Phase Two of the project will involve using the Internet and a network of civic-minded chemical companies and health organizations to work with students at other schools—in the city, throughout the country and beyond—to establish a water monitoring system run by high school students. Some Project REAL students have already begun to consider careers in environmental engineering.

Click. "Adopt-a-Business."

Adopt-a-Business. REAL students are helping local businesses build a web presence, increasing electronic sales and helping them overcome the tyranny of 'location, location, location.' The Chamber of Commerce, as well as Grant's Department Store management, are helping out.

I remembered this one very clearly. I had thought of it when I went to my very favorite clothes store in a funky part of town only to find it destroyed by vandalism and boarded up.

"This is a good one, William," Credo said, pointing to Adopt-a-Business on my screen. "A few businesses have gone from near closure to profit because of this. You are proving that you can live in an out-of-the-way neighborhood and still do a brisk business online."

"Did you predict it?" I asked.

"Of course!" Credo assured me. "But who cares? I can literally hear the walls of the school crumbling down around you and transforming into something vibrant and connected. By the way, I tried to talk you out of the project name because you couldn't squeeze a decent acronym out of it, but you were too bullheaded. Anyway, are you ready to go to work? You've got a busy schedule today: The head of the Chamber of Commerce is coming by at 11 and the president of the Downtown Business Association is going to swing by around two. And the Mayor's office called and wanted to talk to you. By the way, it is time to let go and allow Charlene handle some of that stuff. I know your name is on the grant and all the legal work, but she's every bit as good as you are. Better even."

"Fine by me," I said.

"Hah," Credo scoffed. "That's what you think. Change is hard, even when you want to. Anyway, just work on it."

There were a number of video clips I wanted to see. Apparently I had addressed the BADI stockholder meeting and some of my students had won an award from the city school board.

"No," Credo, insisted, shaking his head. "Don't play any of the video right now. It's still too slow over the Net and we need to get going."

I stood and looked around: soft lighting, polished steel, frosted glass, a dark Oriental rug with armchairs to match, a view of the financial district, an unnaturally neat computer station with no wires showing, almost no printed material anywhere. Nothing computed.

"This is my office," Credo explained.

"So I see," I whispered, mesmerized.

"Come on," Credo said as he headed for the door. "I'll give you a ride. We really do need to get going. It's getting late. You are back in real time."

I looked at my watch. The metal flex band that dug into my skin was gone, replaced by one made of smooth leather inlaid with a scene of Alaska.

"Charlene gave it to you," Credo told me. "You two had a great cruise up the Inside Passage last year."

A sudden head-on collision with a vivid memory made me feel I had finally landed in my body for the first time since my return. Charlene and I had sailed from Vancouver up the northwest coast to Juneau, Alaska. Along the way we had been subdued by the slow passage of trees, the intoxicating smell of salt and the feeling of spray dancing on our arms. It had been a timeless stretch with no phones, no data bits; nothing but now, floating in natal waters, whales, dark-orange skies at night, and the lovely, disorienting sound all around us of a ferry moving through the ocean. Charlene. My body tingled as my brain began to fire.

As we rode to work in the back of Credo's limousine, the present drew nearer and nearer, anticipation picking up momentum like a destination I could see coming into view from an airplane window during landing. I was looking forward to seeing Charlene, my mother and my students. I grabbed above my belt—little bit of a spare tire, but nothing too bad. Phew.

Suddenly, I was overwhelmed by it all. A mild case of shock set in as I closed my eyes and shook my head, hoping it would help make things fall into place a little better. Credo saw my bewilderment and told me not to worry. He explained that return time was proportional to time elapsed. And if I ever found myself minus a detail, I could just blame it on the guy who hit me with the flying computer. Above all, Credo counseled, this was my new reality and I should relax and enjoy my success.

At Project REAL I stood in the doorway greeting each student who walked into the room by name, something I remembered enjoying every day. With very few exceptions, they all looked me in the eye with enough spirit to let me know they were alive and well and ready for something to happen. It was a look that suggested they ordinarily didn't give adults the time of day, but in my case they would make an exception. I watched as the room filled and everyone went about their business. I knew that it was my place to wait, to command quietly, to watch for a teachable moment, to continue the never-ending hunt for the right resources to help with their quest to learn. Above all, my job was to be a cultural insider, bridging their world with the world outside.

Although my sense of presence was building rapidly and much of what I saw was now completely familiar, I couldn't quite remember what the people at the table in the corner were doing. They looked upset, apparently with me.

"Those students are working on the graphics for the 'Adopt-a-Business' program," Credo pointed out. "You pushed them. Boy, did you push them!"

"I did?" I asked, a little afraid.

"Yes!" Credo thundered. "You have no patience with superfluous graphics. You forced them to tighten up their message, throw out all the spinning icons, reduce the number of graphics by half and rethink how to align all the elements of the page. You outlawed the word 'cool.' You told them they had to use words that were more descriptive, like 'effective,' or 'enjoyable,' when they discussed the project among themselves or with anyone else. You were a little ticked off at them for losing sight of the project's primary purpose, which, you reminded them, was to provide the clients with a product that communicated their needs effectively, and NOT to show off how much they knew about putting animation on the Web."

"Do they still like me?" I asked.

"They don't always like you,' Credo responded. "But they always love you."

There was a long pause as we both watched the contained pandemonium in at Project REAL. Then I looked at Credo. "I don't suppose it would help to ask who you really are?" I asked solemnly.

"Let me put it this way," Credo replied. "There is no more important position in society than that of teacher, especially in this culture, especially now. The future is rushing up to meet us with unbelievable force and our survival, as well as the quality of our survival, depends on the quality of our teachers. I have been asked to assist in the screening and recruitment process. That's all."

A student called out my name from within wanting to know why he couldn't download economic statistics from the state's web page. He was trying to correlate education and economic opportunity based on geographic location within the city. Apparently I had talked someone from an actuarial firm into letting one of our students spend a few days working in a real number-crunching environment to see how it was really done, and he wanted to show up with an actual project to work on. He asked if I could help him for a minute. I looked at Credo and told him I had to go.

"Watch this," Credo said, as he snapped his fingers. I braced myself and then—nothing. Nothing at all. That was the point, he told me.

"When you pass through that door," Credo said, "you will know everything you need to know. And at that point, you will be on your own. We will leave you but we will never be far away."

I told him that as oxymoronic as that sounded, I understood.

"Good," Credo said. "Now, before you go in there would you snap us somewhere? I can't do it for you anymore, so you have to do it for both of us."

"Where are we going?" I asked.

"Trust me," Credo said. "It won't take any time at all."

I snapped my fingers and was instantly returned to the picnic table I had visited when I lay nearly comatose in the hospital. This time, however, the table was much longer and filled with dozens of people who had gathered more formally than last time. Apparently, they were in the middle of a meeting when they stopped, welcomed me, and asked me to sit down. I felt immediately at home in my short-sleeved shirt as the warm sun and the gentle breeze washed over my bare arms.

A kindly looking woman at the head of the picnic table introduced herself as this year's president of Division III, which was comprised of 15 local units of The Committee. She told me that I had been summoned so that I could ask them any one question I wanted to. It was sort of a bonus for a job well done. She cautioned me to choose my one question wisely. After thinking for a moment I asked, "So, what's the plan?"

Everyone erupted in applause. In a scoring system reminiscent of the Olympics, they withdrew placards with large black numbers on them from their laps and held them over their heads: 9.4, 9.6, 9.5, 9.6, 9.7 and so on. Nothing was below a 9.4.

"How do you get a 10?" I asked. I would wonder later how they already knew what their vote was going to be.

"Sorry," said the woman. "Just one question. Now let's see if I can answer it for you."

"The plan," she continued, "is to cultivate as many of you as possible, franchise Project REAL and spread the idea as far as it will go. The real issue here is teacher training. Teachers are the network. They are the conduits through which the ideas flow. Without them, any plan is hopeless. We would appreciate it if you would keep an eye out for anyone you think might do as well with the training as you have. Also, you might think of a snappier name than Project REAL. But, it will do for now," she said, winking at me.

Credo jumped up from his seat and burst out, "How about the Credo Reconstructionist Elevated Education Domain? We could refer to it by its acronym: C-R-E-E-D. Get it? It would become more of a belief system than an institution!"

A burst of good-natured disgust erupted from Edwina as the rest of The Committee members winced audibly. "Send him back to the minor leagues!" someone yelled. "To the showers!" howled another.

"Honestly, Credo," Edwina said. "This has nothing to do with you. This is William's moment."

"I know that," Credo said. "I really do. I just thought the name had a nice ring to it. I'm just trying to help."

"You will be part of The Committee someday, William," the president continued as she smiled at me. "And we are all looking forward to it. Now, why don't you send yourself back to work so you can get on with your day and we can get on with ours?"

Everyone set their placards on the picnic table, stood up facing me and started clapping again. I scanned the table—Mr. Big, Art, Edwina, Credo and many others—all looking at me with a sense of affection and admiration I had never experienced before. At that moment I knew I had passed Credo's final exam. Whenever I died, however I died, I would die without regret. I thanked them all and then snapped my fingers.

I was back at Project REAL, still standing in the doorway while the same student asked for help downloading economic statistics from the state's web page. I smiled and told him I would be right there.

After a long pause, Credo asked, "What are you thinking?"

"I am thinking I'll walk in there and never go to work again," I told him. I snapped my fingers and headed inside.